Tightrope

LEAH FRIED

Translated by Chani Goldwasser

Tightrope

a novel

FELDHEIM PUBLISHERS
JERUSALEM • NEW YORK

First published 2002
ISBN 0-9707572-5-5

Copyright © 2002 by Leah Fried

All rights reserved.

No part of this publication may be
translated, reproduced, stored in a retrieval
system, adapted or transmitted in any form or by any
means, electronic, mechanical, photocopying,
recording, or otherwise, without permission
in writing from the copyright holder.

Feldheim Publishers
202 Airport Executive Park,
Nanuet, NY 10954

10 9 8 7 6 5 4 3 2 1

Printed in Israel

Dedicated with deep love to

— my beloved mother, a never-ending wellspring of self-sacrifice and giving from which I drew riches more precious than gold: understanding and acceptance, insight and love.

— my esteemed mother-in-law, a spiritual heroine who encourages my writing, is an enthusiastic fan of my books, and whose life experience enriches me.

— my wonderful daughters-in-law who, like my daughters, placed their full trust in me. Thanks to their advice, support and encouragement, the writing of this book was made possible.

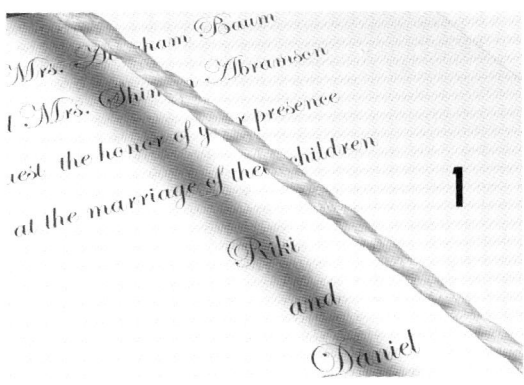

1

IT WAS A MOONLESS NIGHT. Total darkness reigned, and even the stars were barely visible. The only illumination came from streetlights and the flickering neon signs above stores.

The car turned off the main road down a side street. Without the neon signs, the darkness seemed that much more threatening. In the back seat, Sima felt the unease that had been building within her all evening intensify and threaten to take over.

She was afraid to talk, afraid to so much as shift position. One hand cradled her sleeping daughter's head; with the other, she smoothed the girl's hair. Only when she was sure the child was fast asleep did she dare voice her thoughts.

"Shimon," she began quietly. "Shimon…"

"Hmmm?"

"Shimon, aren't you afraid?"

"Afraid of what?"

"Of what we've done."

Unconsciously, Shimon pressed his foot down harder on the

gas pedal. The car surged forward into the blackness.

"What are you doing?" his wife screamed in fright.

The little girl opened her eyes and blinked. Sima patted her face gently and lightly stroked the soft lashes until her eyes closed once more. "Shhh. Everything's okay. Go back to sleep, *mama'le*," she whispered. "Go to sleep."

The car resumed its regular speed, and the darkened side street was soon far behind them.

"What do you mean?" Shimon casually picked up the conversation.

Sima made no reply. She caressed the child on her lap again, making sure she was deeply asleep before speaking.

"We didn't discuss tonight's affair yet." Her remark was seemingly out of context. "How do you feel about tonight? About everything?"

By now, they were on the winding highway, making their descent through the hills.

"How do I feel?" Shimon shrugged. His hands gripped the steering wheel steadily. "What do you mean, 'how do I feel'? I'm trying to be happy, to thank *Hakadosh baruch Hu*. What am I supposed to feel? Why are you asking?" His tone was suddenly sharp.

"Because I have this awful feeling," Sima whispered. "I...I don't know what to think. I can't get back to myself. She was so different when we met her...so refined and reserved, so suitable for our Daniel. Anyway, that's what everyone said...and suddenly..." Her voice trailed off. "It was awful, Shimon, the way she looked tonight!"

Her husband shrugged again and muttered something unintelligible.

"She was so heavily made up — eye shadow, mascara, the works. Our *kalla*...our Daniel's *kalla* ...our tzaddik! Who would have believed it? And the way she wore her hair! I don't even want to talk about it. I'm afraid to say what I'm thinking aloud."

By now, Sima's voice was tinged with hysteria. "Someone tricked us!" she sobbed. "Everything there was too loud. The whole affair was somehow — I don't know — not in good taste, not refined enough. I'm scared, Shimon. This is not for our Daniel. I tell you, Shimon, it's not for him."

The mountainous route had smoothed out into rolling farmland. An industrial area came into view. The dark chimneys rising upward looked to Sima like the threatening watchtowers of a huge prison.

"Can't we back out of it? Can we break it off?" she asked plaintively, like a child who has changed her mind.

Shimon shrugged his shoulders once again.

She couldn't see his face. "*Nu*, say something," she insisted. "What do you think?"

"I have no idea what you're talking about." His deep voice was calm and even. "I think you're just panicking at the thought of having taken such a meaningful step. It happens sometimes."

"It didn't happen after Ariel's engagement," she argued heatedly, "and not after Mali's either! This is the first time I feel this way."

"It's too late, Sima. The *vort* is over," her husband said, trying to place things in their proper perspective. "The engagement announcement is already printed on the front page of tomorrow's newspaper."

The car suddenly jerked forward with a screech, then skidded in a dizzying zigzag on the smooth, empty road. Panic-stricken, Sima gripped the headrest of the seat in front of her and choked back a scream.

Shimon, lips clamped together, turned the wheel sharply to the right and hit the brakes hard. The car came to a halt on the shoulder. "I hope we're not stuck," he muttered as he opened the door to the cold night.

■ ■ ■

Inside a building of Jerusalem stone, on a side street leading down from David Yellin Street, the lights were still on. Half-empty cake platters and soda bottles were scattered on the tables in the dining room. In the children's room, two folding beds were stacked on top of each other. The state of disarray bore witness to the fact that a joyous occasion had just been celebrated there.

"It was a lovely affair, *baruch Hashem*," said the mother of the family, struggling to dislodge one bed from the other. "Now we have to prepare for the engagement party."

"You look so tired, Chaya," replied her sister Leah, who had arrived only toward the very end of the evening. "You'll have time to start thinking about the engagement party tomorrow. Let me help you clean up this mess so that you can all get to bed and get a decent night's sleep."

"How can I sleep on a night like this?" Chaya Baum asked with a smile that was immediately followed by a long yawn. "We're all exhausted, but at the same time very grateful we've been blessed with this *simcha*. And Riki is so happy."

Riki's younger sister and little brothers were already fast asleep on the bed in her room. The glowing *kalla* leaned back in the armchair that had been brought in from the dining room. In a daze of wonderment, she tried to replay some of the magical moments of what was, so far, the most meaningful event in her life.

■ ■ ■

Back on the Jerusalem-Tel Aviv highway, Sima Abramson exited the car, leaving a sleeping Tehilla inside. Her husband was crouching at the back of the car, trying to figure out the problem.

"It's only a flat," he finally announced, the relief evident on his face. "It will take a while to change, but I should be able to get us out of this mess without any help."

While her husband was busy changing the flat tire, Sima

walked to the guardrail at the side of the road and stared into the distance. Traffic was sparse. Here and there, the blinking lights of an approaching car dissipated the inky blackness somewhat, but as soon as the car moved on, the darkness closed in on her again.

Her Daniel. He was a quiet boy, true, and something of a loner. But he was such a good boy, so honest and fine. Everyone agreed he deserved a great girl. Had she been too hasty? Had she made the decision too quickly, because she was feeling pressured?

Shimon, predictably, had been calm and unruffled. "Don't worry," he had told her. "Daniel will find his *bashert*, just like Mali and Ariel did."

She hadn't believed him. Her mother's heart had been beset with anxiety. Daniel was so unlike Ariel, his older brother, or Naftali, the one just after him. Those two and their sister Mali were lively, talkative, self-assured — all leaders in their social circles. Daniel had always been so shy and withdrawn, his lack of self-confidence obvious in everything he did.

Her other children's talents were readily apparent, while Daniel's hadn't shown up so well. Not that he was any less intelligent than the others. If anything, he was perhaps an even deeper thinker. But he lacked their personality and wit. She had been troubled about him, and her fears were realized when the time came to find a *shidduch* for him. Time passed, and Daniel got older, but they couldn't seem to find the right girl for him. Sima's concern and anxiety grew with each passing week — his older brother had been a father at his age, and here he wasn't even engaged yet!

Then this *shidduch* had come along. They said the girl was wonderful, on the quiet side, and only slightly older than the average age at which most girls get engaged, which meant she was one of the last girls in her class still single.

The obvious question was, "Why isn't she engaged yet?" Sima had asked that question repeatedly as she made inquiries. Mrs. Cohen, who had suggested the *shidduch*, told her it was because of the family. Riki Baum needed a true *ben Torah*, a boy who sat and learned, but most serious boys didn't want the daughter of a man who worked as the cook in a yeshiva.

While Riki's father was an honest, hardworking man — respectable in every sense of the word — he was far from what you could call a Torah scholar. In addition, he couldn't even afford half an apartment in one of the new development projects sprouting up all over Israel, let alone provide an entire apartment in Jerusalem or Bnei Brak, which was what many of the top boys expected. (Wasn't Daniel a top boy?) So, that was the story. At least, that's what Mrs. Cohen said, and Sima had believed her.

Her Daniel was a sincere *yeshiva bachur* who really knew how to learn. Although he wasn't the top boy in his yeshiva, he was certainly a *masmid* who hoped to stay in learning all his life, and he needed a quality girl. If Riki Baum was all she was said to be, money didn't matter that much. They could afford to buy an apartment for the young couple. The nursing home they owned and ran brought in good money.

Now, in the dark of night, after they had signed an agreement with the *kalla's* parents and celebrated a *vort*, she felt faint with fear. Now she was sure of it — she had been too rash. She had fallen for the matchmaker's glib talk and had neglected to ask enough questions. Otherwise, how could she have made such a mistake? Almost nothing remained of the description of Riki Baum as a quiet, refined girl.

Tonight, Riki had sailed around her house, boisterously exuberant, conversing loudly with the group of friends surrounding her. (Who had ever heard of inviting so many friends to a *vort*?) She had paid almost no attention to her future mother-in-law and the rest of the family. When Sima had introduced the *kalla* to Aunt Olga from England, who was scheduled to fly home the next day and had therefore been especially invited to tonight's affair, Riki merely smiled and then moved on to another friend who had just appeared in the doorway.

Sima clearly recalled the disappointed, somewhat shocked expression on her dear aunt's face. The memory did nothing to ease the doubts nagging at her heart.

When she met the *kalla* for the first time, Riki's hair was tied back in a simple, pleasing ponytail. Tonight, it had been gathered in an elaborate updo, with curling tendrils falling from her forehead into her eyes. Sima had always detested this hairstyle when she had seen it on other girls. She wasn't sure exactly why it bothered her so much. Maybe it just didn't seem modest or refined enough. Who would have dreamed that her *kalla* would look like that?

Alongside his overly stylish *kalla*, Daniel had seemed even more wan and remote than usual. And the family! She had been told they were simple people, but why hadn't she made more of an effort to find out what that meant? The mother was a pleasant woman, true, but she obviously didn't know how to guide her daughter to behave more appropriately. She had appeared quite pleased with her daughter's ostentatious look.

Later, when Sima had been introduced to the grandmother, Mrs. Baum's mother, someone had whispered in her ear, "Here's the grandmother. She's a pillar of strength. Did you know she raised her children on her own? She was divorced when they were only babies."

Just like that! She hadn't known! What a way to find out, at the *vort*. Sima was terrified to think what other bombshells she might discover as time went on.

"Shimon." She turned to her husband, who was crouching near the wheel of the car. "The father of Mr. Baum, the *mechutan* — who is he anyway?"

"The father is not alive anymore," Shimon grunted from under the car. "Neither is the mother. You know that Mr. Baum has no parents."

"But who were they?" she asked urgently. "They aren't people without a past or a family background. He once had parents. I want to know who they were and where they came from."

"They were from Romania," Shimon replied. "Why are you shouting?"

"I'm afraid. We were too pressured. We let them lead us like fools into reaching an agreement with a family we really know nothing about, and now — now it's too late to turn back. The engagement announcement will appear in tomorrow's paper. We're letting our son bind his future to someone who is not at all suitable for him…or for us."

2

RIKI WOKE TO A BRIGHT NEW DAY. The room was bathed in sunshine, and her mother stood in the doorway with a smile on her face.

"Good morning, *kalla*! Did you sleep well?"

"I don't even remember falling asleep. I could sleep more." Riki yawned as if to emphasize the justice of her claim. "I still feel so tired."

"Too bad, Riki," her mother said playfully. "This isn't exactly the best time to sleep. You've had only five phone calls so far, and each caller can't wait to talk to you. Only one of them gave her name — Atara. She asked you to call her the minute you wake up. By the way, the paper printed your engagement announcement at the top of the list."

Riki quickly sat up in bed and rubbed the last traces of sleep from her eyes. She looked around for the *netilas yadayim* cup and basin.

"I'll get it," her mother said. "You were so tired yesterday that you went to bed without preparing it. I'll bring you the paper at the same time. Wait till you see it!" she laughed.

What a super mother she is, Riki thought. If she hadn't been stuck with unwashed hands, she'd have jumped up and planted a warm kiss on her cheek.

In no time at all, her mother was back, holding a blue plastic basin and matching *netilas yadayim* cup filled with water. She dropped the paper on the bedspread.

Riki washed her hands and dried them. After reciting one of the most fervent Modeh Anis in her life, she picked up the paper to confirm what still seemed like a dream. There it was! *Daniel Abramson and Rivka Baum — engaged.*

The names — her *chassan's* and her own — leaped out at her. The letters danced merrily before her eyes, and try as she might to make them stand still, they would not pay her any heed. Rivka Baum — yes, Rivka Baum — in an engagement announcement right alongside Daniel Abramson!

What would Mrs. Gutfarb at the grocery store down the block think when she saw the announcement? Or Tzippy Arieli, the girl she had worked with on the program for the weeklong camp sponsored by her high school? They had shared a seat on the bus all the way home from camp, but she hadn't breathed a word to her about the impending event.

The phone rang. Riki swung her feet over the side of the bed and picked it up. It was Atara, sounding breathless with excitement. "Hi, *kalla*! *Mazel tov*!" she exclaimed. "So, you finally woke up. I was getting worried you'd sleep all day and miss out on something really important."

"What's going on?" Riki asked. Atara was her best friend, and she'd been at the Baums' all last night.

"The girls in your Bnos group said they can't wait until Shabbos, so they're making a party for you in school today — at eleven."

"Don't tell me — you're the one who arranged it, didn't you?" Riki laughed. "Just wait — I'll get you for this."

"It wasn't me, Riki, honest," Atara protested. "They insisted. They said you can't be a *kalla* without everyone dancing to celebrate, and that it's not their fault you graduated a year ago."

"They're the greatest."

"Well, it's not every day their Bnos leader gets engaged, is it? So you'll be ready at ten-thirty? I'll come by with Rachel to pick you up. We'll all go together."

Before Riki could digest the news, the phone rang again. It was Aunt Tzippora, her mother's oldest sister, from Beersheba. She allowed her aunt's hearty laugh to sweep over her. Aunt Tzippora had a booming laugh that surfaced whenever she was happy or excited. It was a sincere, heartfelt laugh filled with warmth. Strangely, it always sounded suspiciously like she was trying to hide the fact that she was crying at the same time.

"So you really did it," Aunt Tzippora said. "How happy and excited we were to hear the good news — and you never even dropped a single hint when you spoke to Tzvi two days ago, did you? All right, young lady, when our time comes we'll still show you that we know how to keep secrets, too! Your mother didn't breathe a word of it either."

"She wasn't sure until the last minute," Riki said, finally managing to get a word in edgewise.

"Oh, so that's why. Well, you got a real *ben Torah*, just like you wanted, didn't you? You sure were determined about it. Your Uncle Shloima told me, 'I think that girl ought to get off her high horse and stop insisting on a *ben Taira* who will sit and learn all day long. Only the daughters of wealthy men get real *yeshiva bachrim*.' But I said to him, 'Shloima, you're wrong! You don't know our Riki. She's sincere about what she says she wants. She really and truly wants a Torah home, and Hashem will help her — you'll see.

"So *mazel tov*, Riki," concluded her aunt, and Riki thought she could hear muffled sobs at the other end of the line as she thanked her aunt for her warm wishes and hung up.

After dressing and davening, she went straight to the kitchen, although she was sure she couldn't possibly eat a thing knowing the Bnos group was waiting for her at school. Her mother, caught up in her daughter's excitement, didn't press her to eat. All she asked was that she drink something before going.

"You can't go out on an empty stomach, Riki," she said emphatically. "You need your strength, today more than any other day." She tucked a bag of cookies and fruit into Riki's handbag, and then stood back to watch her get ready to leave the house.

"Atara and Rachel will be here soon," Riki told her mother as she stood in front of the mirror. "I don't think I'll need the cookies. If I know my Bnos group and my friends, they've prepared plenty of nosh."

Her mother laughed, mentally blessing her daughter's two closest friends. Atara and Rachel were both already engaged, and had been for some time. They had been very concerned for Riki. Chaya was sure they had both given great information on Riki, and that they were truly sharing her joy now. They had both been let in on the secret, along with the closest family members.

It had been Rachel who, at the very last minute, suggested Riki change her hairstyle to give her a more glamorous look.

She thought back to the phone call she had received from her sister Leah at five in the afternoon the day before.

"Listen, Chaya," she had said, "I have a neighbor who says she knows the Abramsons well. She says they're very stylish, sophisticated people. They live, as I'm sure you know, in a luxurious home in that exclusive neighborhood between Bnei Brak and Ramat Gan. I've heard she's even got live-in help.

"My neighbor," Leah had continued eagerly, "says Sima Abramson is a woman with very good taste. The whole family dresses well. You can't let Riki go to her *vort* looking like a little girl with her ponytail and her gray Shabbos suit. You've got to do something to make her look more sophisticated, a little more glamorous. Remember, the grandmothers will probably be there, too. I'm sure the *machtenista* is anxious to show her mother and mother-in-law a *kalla* who looks as though she fits in with the family. Make sure she wears more makeup than usual — give her some color. It's okay. As a *kalla*, she's allowed to look more mature. You can tell her I said so."

Leah's phone call had thrown her into a panic. She had been calm and cool as a cucumber until that phone call, secure in the knowledge that her Riki was getting a modest, refined *chassan*. She was grateful the boy's family was not asking them for money they didn't have. They obviously valued her daughter's fine qualities more than a big dowry.

It hadn't occurred to her that taking a boy from a wealthy family would present any special difficulties. Leah's advice had unleashed a flurry of doubts that threatened to overwhelm her. The tables weren't set, the Waldorf salad wasn't ready, one cake was still in the oven, and here Leah was talking about drastic changes in her daughter's outfit and the general tone of the engagement party.

"What's wrong with her gray Shabbos suit?" she had asked.

"Oh, come on, Chaya," her younger sister, considered the fashion maven in the family, had said dismissively. "It's too dull. I mean, you've got to take the other side's standards into consideration. You can't embarrass them by presenting a pale, colorless *kalla* to all the members of their family."

"She's not pale," Chaya had protested. "She's got a great tan. She just got home from camp."

"You know that's not what I meant. Just try to give her some sparkle, that's all."

Then Rachel had come to help, heard about the dilemma and suggested that Riki wear her hair piled on top of her head. "It's really spectacular," she had said. "My cousin wore her hair like that at her engagement, and I think Riki's hair is the perfect length for it." She wasted no time and called her sister's friend, a popular hair stylist, to ask if she would accept Riki immediately, without an appointment.

Atara, who showed up a short while later, helped them

reach a decision about the dress. After Aunt Leah had taken all the wind out of Chaya's sails, she was ready to grab at any alternative to the gray suit. It was already too late to go shopping for something new, and Riki's wardrobe contained nothing more elegant than the gray suit, which was the newest thing she owned.

Atara saved the day by running home and returning with a black chiffon dress with a sheer gold overcoat. The dress had been sent to her from America for her own engagement, but it was too small. Riki tried it on, and it fit her beautifully.

Her friends stayed on to help her complete the new look. They listened to Riki's muted complaints that she felt strange and not at all like herself, and encouraged her to take Aunt Leah's advice.

Her friends are really special, Chaya thought to herself as she waited for them to come pick up Riki.

Taste is a very personal thing, and if they had asked her, she'd have said that she thought Riki looked better and more radiant in her gray suit and ponytail — her natural look — than in the sophisticated outfit she ended up wearing. She knew that deep inside, Riki hadn't been comfortable with the change either. Still, they had done what they felt had to be done. With the help of her two loyal friends, Riki had represented both herself and her family with distinction, and that was what counted.

In any case, Chaya hoped that her *machtenista* had seen beyond Riki's stylish appearance and noticed the outpouring of love Riki's friends had shown her. She couldn't believe how many girls had come to take part in her daughter's *simcha*. Perhaps it was the timing — camp had ended just one day earlier — that had caused the special feeling of unity and made the counselors and other staff members feel they had to come.

Did the *machtenista* appreciate what it meant that Riki had been asked to come to camp and help out, even though she had graduated more than a year ago, because of her experience in past years? Were they aware of what a successful, dynamic counselor she had been?

They ought to be told. In any case, the *mechutanim* had certainly received a wonderful, quality girl in every sense of the word. If until now they only heard about her, then they had certainly seen for themselves last night that every word was true.

Some ten minutes later, three girls left the Baum household, chattering happily as they walked out the front door. Rachel and Atara flanked a radiant Riki, sparkling with all the feelings of gratitude and excitement only a newly engaged girl can feel.

Ahead of her was a special day waiting to unfold its mysteries before her.

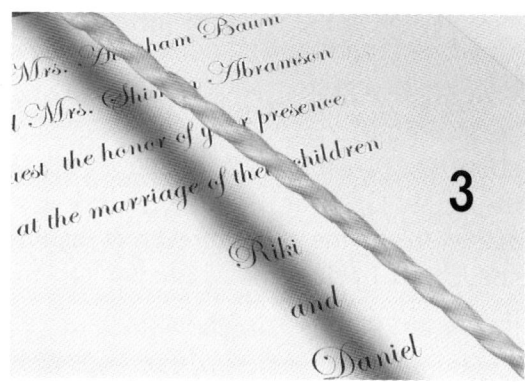

3

SHIMON ABRAMSON SAT AT HIS DESK in the office of Nachalas Avos, the nursing home he owned and ran.

The nursing home was designed so that its main entrance opened onto what was actually the third floor. The first two floors housed the geriatric ward, while the very infirm had rooms on the fourth floor. Elderly people who were still in possession of their faculties and were healthy enough to maintain their independence shared the third floor with his office. These people represented the healthier, brighter side of life in the home. They enjoyed socializing with other residents and with their families, and participated in lectures and *shiurim*.

Shimon usually allowed himself the luxury of coming to work late. The staff — from the doctors and nurses all the way down to the janitors — could be trusted to do their jobs properly, under the close supervision of the Abramsons.

This morning, though, Shimon knew he had to be in the office at a relatively early hour. He was exhausted after a sleepless night of mixed emotions and a sense of confusion he couldn't seem to shake, but he had an important appointment scheduled, one he had noted in his diary long before Daniel's *shidduch* had gotten under way.

Mr. and Mrs. Stone, a middle-aged couple, wanted to inquire about the possibility of having Mrs. Stone's father admitted to the home. This was the sort of meeting Mr. Abramson never delegated to anyone else, not even to his wife, Sima, who played no small part in the efficient management of the institution they had founded.

He sat in his office, feeling somewhat grumpy about the bad timing of the meeting. He would have loved to stay home and recuperate today. Although he had made a supreme effort to appear calm and unperturbed to his wife, his heart was in a state of turmoil. Her agitated manner had affected him as well. Had they really made a mistake?

In shul after davening, his neighbors and friends had surrounded him and warmly shaken his hand. Sometimes, people's participation in one's *simcha* is uplifting and enjoyable, but his friends' hearty *mazel tovs* this morning had only increased his discomfort. It seemed clear to him that the reason they were being so effusive was that they knew of his hard time in finding a *shidduch* for Daniel.

His relationship with Daniel had never been a bed of roses. His son's lack of self-confidence had been obvious even when he was very young, and it had proven to be a particularly difficult problem during his teenage years.

Maybe they really had been too hasty, as his wife had suggested. Maybe they hadn't made enough inquiries about the family because they were so happy someone was interested in their son at last.

Deep inside, Shimon knew that he had always been worried about this son of his. His relationship with Daniel had had its ups and downs. There were periods of anger, tension and disappointment. Had he perhaps failed to properly weigh the pros and cons of the *shidduch* they had finalized yesterday because he didn't value his son enough?

The *kalla's* father was not what one would call a *talmid chacham*, to put it mildly. That's what he had been told. But so what? Wasn't he a G-d-fearing Jew? That was surely the most important thing! He had raised his children to be good Jews in the tradition sense of the word, sent them to the right schools. What was important was that his Daniel was a boy who studied, not brilliant but diligent. He would help his son stay in learning, *be'ezras Hashem*, but he knew that his son's future hinged upon his *kalla's* character.

Sima had frightened him with her gloomy predictions. Never mind the father — or the brother who learned in a trade school that combined Torah study with vocational training. (Another point he had discovered only last night. How could Sima have missed this vital piece of information?) The *kalla* was supposed to be a wonderful girl, only now it seemed she was not so exceptional after all. What a mess. He didn't think his son was of such inferior quality that he had to settle for a second-rate girl. In the final analysis, Daniel was actually more modest and sensitive than the other children.

Shimon hadn't said anything to his wife. He had begged her to calm down and told her that she was surely mistaken. She must have been confused because of her emotional state. He had even suggested that she call the matchmaker again and discreetly make some more inquiries just to calm herself. There wasn't much they could do.

He told her that the *kalla* would slowly become a part of their family, and she would see how things stood in their home. That was what he really thought. There really was nothing else they could do.

He grew calmer as he slowly came to terms with the situation. By the time Mr. and Mrs. Stone knocked at his office door, he felt ready to receive them.

■ ■ ■

In the kitchen of her Jerusalem home, Chaya Baum wiped the table clean of the morning's leftovers. Little Shuki had finally woken up and gone to cheder, equipped with a note to his rebbe announcing the sensational news of his sister's engagement. Devora was davening in her room before leaving for day camp. The telephone had finally stopped ringing.

Enjoying the rare moment of silence, Chaya began to consider the possibility of eating a light breakfast before getting on with her work. As she opened the refrigerator to look for some sandwich spread, she suddenly realized she was humming an old song from her childhood. It was a song her mother used to sing about a young boy, exhorting him to become a Torah scholar. Chaya had been raised with this song.

On the wings of the pleasant melody, Chaya's thoughts drifted far from her kitchen. When her mother sang this song, her children knew their mother's heart was filled with peace and happiness, and they too would feel secure and happy.

Chaya and her sisters, Tzippora and Leah, used to love this song, because it symbolized a sense of serenity and calm in the daily hustle and bustle of their lives.

When she matured and understood more about life, she realized that their lifestyle was unconventional. Her home was not like everyone else's. In her friends' houses, there was a father and a mother. She was the only one with a mother who worked almost all day long and a father who lived in some distant *moshav* and came to see them at Aunt Rivka's house once a year.

In time, as she observed what went on in her friends' homes, she pieced together the puzzle. She saw fathers coming home in the evening and learning with their children. Occasionally, she would visit a friend's house at dinnertime and watch the father helping to feed the little ones. She saw mothers who were more relaxed than her own, and homes that ran more smoothly than theirs.

Eventually, she grew smart enough to realize that not every home was harmonious and that the presence of a father in the home did not necessarily represent a miracle solution to every problem. Her intuition told her, though, that it was a necessary condition for a good home.

She used to daydream about the home she would build. It would be a good home, a beautiful home full of warmth and laughter, with enough room for everyone. There would be a father who came home at night and put the children to bed, and a mother who cooked in the kitchen and didn't go out to work.

When she reached marriageable age, she was more certain than ever of the kind of husband she wanted. Her seminary education, along with her own life experience, had taught her that the child in the song her mother always sang — the one who grew up to become a great Torah scholar — was the ideal image of the person with which to build a Jewish home. That was the kind of husband she wanted — someone refined and spiritual, a devout Jew who immersed himself in the sea of Torah.

Then reality hit her like a slap in the face.

Sometimes, during the years after her marriage, it occurred to Chaya that perhaps she had accepted her lot too quickly. When she had become of age, there was no father at her side to look for a good boy for her. As for the matchmakers, they didn't really know her. All they knew was that she was the daughter of Bella who worked at the packaging plant. No one knew her innermost thoughts, her ambitions, the level of her intellect or her spiritual standards.

Bella's daughter was just right for the son of Schumacher, the cobbler who worked with his father in the store. One *shadchan* was not even embarrassed to suggest Yehuda Karp, who had joined a Mizrachi kibbutz.

She hadn't allowed herself to become bitter. Her mother had slowly convinced her to accept her fate.

"Don't wait for a prince on a white horse, Chayale," she would say. "The *bachur* you're dreaming about wants someone from a family with no problems. We're a family with a problem, and we don't have enough money to cover it up, either. I don't want a sick boy for you, Chayale. It's important you get someone healthy in mind and body, a decent man who will be a good father to your children. That's what you need to think about."

Then Avraham Baum had come into the picture. Her mother's uncle had suggested him — he was the grandson of a friend of his. The uncle, so devoted to his niece and her family, had vouched that he knew this boy from the day he was born.

True, he was not the star of the yeshiva; in fact, he found it difficult to sit and learn. For the past two years, he'd been working in the diamond trade as a polisher and earning a decent living.

"He's a serious boy who sets aside time to study, and he'll build a Torah home with you, you'll see," her uncle had urged.

That had been then. Now Chaya sighed as she sat down at the table in the quiet kitchen and allowed her mind to wander.

A Torah home? That was stretching it. Yes, Avraham was a G-d-fearing Jew, a workingman who cared for his family's needs — but he was not what you could call a spiritual man from whom one could draw strength or aspire to more. He was certainly no example of lofty spiritual yearning. But they had built a home, baruch Hashem.

A tear slid down Chaya's cheek. A large part of her dreams had come true. They laughed a lot, and her children's friends loved to visit. There was always a hot meal waiting, and she was always available for her family. She had never found it necessary to go out to work, and Avraham often helped her put the children to bed.

Her mother, who visited occasionally, drew such *nachas*. Once, in a moment of candor, she had told her, "You know, Chayale, I sometimes used to wonder if children always have to pay a price for their parents' mistakes, whether the lot of one generation need necessarily influence the fate of the next.

"I was afraid, Chayale, that my own lot in life would pursue my children, that you would not succeed in building good homes of your own. But Hashem helped us, and you all built such good homes."

Chaya had only been married a short time when she heard her mother's revelations, and she was still trying to come to terms with her shattered dreams. She'd clamped her lips shut and bitten back the retort that stood on the tip of her tongue.

She did not say that she felt she *was* paying a price. That night, though, as she tossed and turned in bed, mulling things over, she told herself that her mother was right, and that she, Chaya, would do everything in her power to prevent her fate from casting a shadow over her own children's lives.

She rose from the table. Feeling nervous, she turned to the window that looked out onto the street. It was empty at that hour of the morning. There was only an Arab woman walking on the opposite side of the street, balancing a straw basket on her shoulder.

She had indeed done everything in her power, Chaya thought, but some things seemed to be beyond her control. Her Ephraim, for example, had not wanted to carry on learning in a yeshiva, although they would have gladly allowed him to.

"I don't have the staying power to sit in front of a Gemara all day," he told them. "I want to go out and get a job, maybe metalworking or carpentry, and be a good Jew like Dad."

A vocational institution where he would learn electrical engineering seemed to be their best option. Did they have a choice?

Then Riki's *shidduchim* had begun to come unstuck. Good suggestions that had been proposed suddenly disappeared without a trace. Riki had adamantly refused to consider any of the other, less impressive *shidduchim*, and Chaya had staunchly supported her decision.

This time, I refuse to compromise! she had told herself. Her Riki was a diamond, a quality girl with a head on her shoulders. No, she would not allow her daughter to suffer for something she had no part in.

Sometimes, Chaya wondered whether the trouble they had encountered doing a *shidduch* was really because of her own family background. She felt as if life was dealing her mother a mocking slap in the face. *Ha, ha, ha, lady! Problems do extend from one generation to another, and how! Children have to suffer because of their parents' mistakes.*

Or maybe not. The large pine tree facing her window swayed gently, and a calming breeze blew across her forehead.

Enough of these depressing thoughts. Last night, Riki had gotten engaged to the kind of boy she had always wanted: a real *ben Torah*. He had a refined look. He might be a little shy and withdrawn, but he was supposed to be a true *masmid*. Riki, who had had her fill of disappointments, knew how to differentiate between what really mattered and what didn't (or perhaps his shyness didn't bother her at all?), and she had arrived at the right decision.

She had been so happy today. Chaya had seen the sparkle of joy in her eyes. There was nothing phony about Riki; if she said she was happy, she really was.

The telephone rang, pulling Chaya away from the window. It was probably another "*mazel tov*" call.

"Hello?" she said, expecting a warm, genial reply.

Instead, she heard a dull, lifeless voice say, "Hello. This is Sima Abramson, your new *machtenista*."

4

SIMA ABRAMSON, *MACHTENISTA* — the words had a lovely ring to them. They evoked happy feelings of anticipation. Yes, her *machtenista*.

"Good morning, Mrs. Abramson," Chaya responded, somewhat surprised by Mrs. Abramson's tone of voice. "How was your ride home? How was your night?"

"It passed, somehow," the voice on the other end of the line replied, sounding tired. "I didn't sleep very well."

"Of course not," Chaya was quick to say. "Who could sleep on such a night? We were so…pleased with the *chassan* yesterday. The truth is," she continued, "it was the first time I got a chance to meet him. He's so *eidel*. My husband told me that the *devar Torah* he said over was special. You know, some *chassanim* wouldn't talk in front of such a crowd."

"Yes, he really is a very special boy," Mrs. Abramson said, her voice taking on a trace of animation for the first time since the beginning of their conversation. "He demands a lot of himself. He's a real *masmid*, always learning. But surely you've heard all this," she gave an apologetic laugh. "I don't need to tell you."

"Of course not. We know," Chaya tried to say, but Sima didn't seem to hear her. She went right on talking.

"I always knew he needed a top girl."

Well, he got one, baruch Hashem, Chaya Baum reflected.

"A girl who will appreciate his learning," Mrs. Abramson went on, "his depth, his gentleness. Ever since he was a child, he's been very sensitive. He wouldn't hurt a fly, do you know that?

"I remember once some boys on the block were teasing a wounded bird — Danny was five at the time — and he began to cry, I mean really cry and make a scene. He ran home to call me.

"The children got scared and ran away. He asked me to take the poor bird home and care for it. That's the kind of child he was. Even now, whenever something needs to be done at home, he can be counted on to help out."

A small bird perched on the window ledge of Chaya Baum's kitchen and snatched up a piece of stale bread lying there. Her eyes followed the bird's movements as it hopped around, and the phone began to feel heavy on her shoulder.

"There's an old man who lives on the street here," the words flowed unchecked through the receiver. "Danny goes to visit him every Friday. What exactly he does there, I don't know. Danny doesn't tell me everything. He's very deep. The more you get to know him, the more you come to realize what a diamond he is."

Something nagged at Chaya, disturbing her ability to concentrate on what Sima was saying, as though the little bird was pecking away inside her head. *What does this pesky bird want?* She rubbed her temples, trying to rid herself of whatever was cluttering up her head.

A diamond — of course. *Well, Riki was a diamond too. Sima would have to be reminded of that. She would surely be happy to hear more about the lovely kalla her son was engaged to.*

"Well, of course he's special," she managed to say at last.

"Riki's in seventh heaven. She went to her old high school today with two of her friends for a party her Bnos group arranged in her honor. I felt so moved just watching her. I was so happy for her.

"You know, Riki is also a person who never demanded anything for herself. Imagine! Last night she said to me, 'Mommy, believe me, I really don't think I have to get something new to wear to the engagement party.'"

"Oh! That reminds me. What about the engagement party?" asked Sima. "I really called about that too. Where and when are you thinking of having it?"

The sudden turn in the conversation was too abrupt for Chaya, and a small sigh escaped her as she looked around for a chair to sit down in.

"Uh…we haven't really thought about it yet," she said. "Actually, I'm still walking around in a daze. Doing a *shidduch* with a first daughter is not so easy," she said, trying to share her feelings. "Surely you know that, Mrs. Abramson. I'm still too excited and overwhelmed to be practical."

"Oh, of course! I didn't intend to pressure you." Something in the *machtenista's* voice softened, and she sounded slightly less demanding. Chaya heard the hesitation in her voice as she said, "By the way, speaking of clothes, I think soft, pastel shades would suit her very well."

"What shades?" Chaya wasn't sure she had heard right.

"Pastels. I know a little about fashion. Gentler colors."

Is she serious? Chaya wondered. *Why is she saying this? Is she voicing her opinion or thinking out loud? Is she trying to interfere with the kalla's choice of clothing? Is this what's done? What in the world is going on?*

"My extended family will be present at the engagement party," Sima continued, now sounding slightly apologetic. "The dress she wore yesterday — I mean the colors — made her look a little pale. It's only a suggestion."

So, she didn't make a good impression on you yesterday. And here I thought you were so pleased with her, that she was charming and radiant.

Chaya realized she was clutching the receiver tightly. She made a conscious effort to relax her grip. Sima's voice sounded farther away now.

"I thought I'd meet the *kalla* this afternoon to choose a watch."

Chaya collected herself and clenched the receiver closer to her ear again. Her new *machtenista* kept catching her off guard.

"A watch? Today?"

"Well, why put it off?" asked the *machtenista*. "Today happens to be a very convenient day for me to get out. If it's not convenient for Riki, though, we can postpone it for a different day."

Chaya suddenly felt a surge of relief. There was something about the way Sima used her daughter's name so naturally that made her feel better. She suddenly realized that this was the first time since the beginning of the conversation she had called her daughter "Riki" and not "the *kalla*." Also, she said she wanted to buy her a watch.

Chaya stood up, and the two ended the conversation by finalizing arrangements for Sima to meet Riki that afternoon.

It was only when she put the phone down that she realized how stiff her fingers were. She flexed them to restore the circulation, surprised at herself.

"I never realized that a phone conversation with a *machtenista* could be so exhausting," she muttered to herself.

A glance at the clock on the wall told her that time hadn't stood still. She gave up on the idea of having breakfast and decided to have another cup of coffee instead.

A flood of questions and doubts plagued her. Hard as she tried to reconstruct the conversation, she couldn't put her finger on what was bothering her.

Instead of a carton of milk, she took a bottle of water out of the refrigerator. She noticed her mistake and poured herself a glass of water — any drink would do, she told herself.

Everything was fine, after all. Her Riki was going to buy a watch with the *machtenista* today. It was sure to be a beautiful piece of jewelry.

So why wasn't she happy? Why was she feeling overwhelmed by an uncomfortable mood that left no room for the joy she had felt before? There would be a watch, there would be an engagement party, *be'ezras Hashem* — so what was the problem? Nothing had changed: her mood swings were just getting the better of her. Was she a little child, then? Or were such feelings normal for someone whose oldest daughter had just gotten engaged? Who could she ask?

Chaya spent another two hours of confusion and doubt in the kitchen of her small apartment. A flood of phone calls helped pass the time. The heartfelt *mazel tov* wishes of good friends and the warm feeling that people were sharing in her *simcha* helped her feel better.

Yet the sense of unease was still there, niggling away at her joy. When her daughter came home for lunch, looking like a glowing, golden ray of sun and bursting with the details of her party at school, Chaya make a very courageous and very maternal decision. No matter what she felt, she would never share her feelings with her daughter.

■ ■ ■

"I just spoke to the *machtenista*," Sima reported to her husband over the phone.

Shimon was seated in his office in the nursing home, while Sima was still at home, settled comfortably in the white leather sofa in the corner of their living room. She was still bleary-eyed from the sleepless night she had spent and utterly drained from the strain of the conversation she had just conducted with Mrs. Baum.

"I tried to steer the conversation toward the issues that are bothering us," she continued, "but I wasn't very successful. When I tried to hint to her what a serious boy Daniel is, and how important it is to us that he marries a quality girl, she hurried to regale me with stories about the *kalla*, her school and her friends again.

"I did manage to say something about the dress. I wanted her to understand that we just don't go for such things, but I'm not sure she caught on. I quickly changed the subject, because I think most mothers don't see their daughters objectively.

"I don't think there's any choice, then," she concluded, "but to speak directly to the *kalla*."

"Never!" Shimon exclaimed sharply. A furrow of frustration appeared on his forehead. "Please, I beg you, don't say anything to her."

Sima leaned forward on the sofa. "Why not? I can't leave things like this." The tremor in her voice belied the tension she felt. "We must talk about these issues face-to-face *before* the engagement! She has to know what we expect of her. Shimon, I must be certain just what the girl we took for our son is like.

"I already made up with her mother that I'd meet with the *kalla* today to go buy a watch. I purposely asked that we go today. While we shop, I'll have the opportunity for a quiet chat with her — without anyone else listening in.

"I'll be careful," Sima reassured both her husband and herself. "I'll be very careful. I just think," she added resolutely, "that in our case, better sooner than later. Don't you agree?"

Was she right? Shimon couldn't decide. He knew that despite his wife's adamant stance, she was waiting desperately for his approval. All of a sudden, he felt his opposition to the idea waver. He was still reluctant, but, on the other hand, what if his wife was right? They were, after all, talking about laying firm foundations for the next generation — and such a thing merited serious attention.

"All right," he sighed into the receiver, "have it your way. You're Danny's mother. And may Hashem be with you."

5

THE NUMBER 402 BUS FROM JERUSALEM to Tel Aviv sped along the highway. It was late in the afternoon, and traffic was light. Riki Baum sat near the open window, her hair flying in the wind. A wayward curl tumbled onto her forehead, and she reached out to brush it aside. *My hair is so stubborn*, she thought with a smile. *How hard I worked to pull it straight before I left the house! But it refuses to stay put, always bouncing back to its natural curliness.*

The hairdresser did a good job last night, mused Riki, *perhaps too good a job*. Everyone had complimented her on her hair, but she had felt awkward and uncomfortable, as though she were dressed up as someone else.

Her friends had been pretty generous with compliments this morning, too. Atara said she had never seen such a glowing, graceful *kalla*. "The way you greeted everyone so graciously and knew just what to say was really special," she said. "You gave everyone the attention they deserved. Sometimes, *kallas* act shy and formal when they meet their friends at the engagement, but you smiled and radiated joy, like a real *kalla* is meant to do."

Was she really so happy? Everyone thought so — her mother, her father, her friends, the girls in the Bnos group she led. But was she really?

Riki leaned back in her seat, allowing her thoughts to wander unrestrained. *It's okay. You're alone now*, she told herself. The high-backed seats on the bus concealed her from the other passengers. The seat next to hers was empty, too. She liked it that way. Now she was under no pressure to smile, talk or put on an act for other people.

Oh no, was she putting on an act? No! Surely she wasn't. Chas veshalom! She was happy, happy with her *shidduch*, happy to be a *kalla* and happy with her *chassan*.

Then why wasn't she feeling it?

The smooth motion of the bus, as it sped along the highway, helped her think clearly. She continued her conversation with herself.

What was wrong? Nothing, really. It was just that in the morning, when Ayali Zuckerman met her in the street, she'd casually mentioned that her brother knew the *chassan*. Her expression and tone of voice had been somewhat noncommittal, and she hadn't said anything other than the fact that her brother knew him. Later, Gitty Bruk tactlessly told her that Daniel had once been suggested for her sister's friend, who wasn't interested. Maybe then or maybe not, she couldn't say exactly when, Riki had begun feeling a lump in her throat that made it very difficult for her to breathe.

The lump in her throat scared her. Was a new *kalla* supposed to feel that way? She didn't know who she could ask. She felt tears stinging her eyelids.

Atara and Rachel had walked her to school that morning looking for all the world like two bridesmaids, and they had been waiting for her to act accordingly. She had indeed played her part by chattering on and on, the classic sign of internal happiness.

At home, she found her mother waiting for her with a smile

on her face, anxious to hear about her morning. *Today was a big day in Mommy's life,* Riki had thought. *Her oldest daughter has finally gotten engaged to a ben Torah from a distinguished family.* She hadn't had the heart to cast a cloud on her mother's joy, and she had continued chattering ceaselessly in an effort to hide her confusion and fear.

When her mother told her that her future mother-in-law wanted to take her shopping for a watch, she felt a sense of relief, and the choking feeling eased up a little.

Now, as she sat looking out the bus window, Riki still felt the same sense of relief. She was eager to spend some time with her future mother-in-law. She hoped that spending time with her would somehow restore her sense of calm and dispel any lingering doubts.

She tried to mentally reconstruct the events leading up to her engagement and organize her thoughts somewhat. Daniel was the kind of *bachur* she wanted; she couldn't have prayed for anyone better. From her father's inquiries, she knew that he was a *masmid*, a *ba'al middos*, and well accepted by his friends. In his conversations with her, he had displayed a broad range of knowledge on almost every topic under the sun. She could tell he had "*tochen,*" in the words of the matchmaker. There was, therefore, no objective reason to say no, and she had, indeed, quickly agreed to the *shidduch* after just one date. *Oh! There it was again, that lump in her throat!*

Riki's breath caught. What was happening to her? Had she been too hasty? Had she been too quick to sign the deal of her life without considering all angles carefully enough? She leaned forward in her seat in an effort to overcome that annoying feeling in the pit of her stomach.

Alone at the very end of the bus, she tried to reconstruct the conversation she'd had with her *chassan* just before the *vort*. Perhaps she hadn't noticed it at the time — or perhaps she had chosen to ignore it, but Riki was somewhat disappointed by that last meeting. Something indefinable bothered her now.

Everything had been the same as before. Her *chassan* had sat in his seat with the same slightly withdrawn look she had come to know. He had responded to her comments and brought up some of his own observations on the subject of building a Jewish home. Everything had been just fine, really, but…maybe it was his monotonous tone of voice, as though he was reciting something he had learned earlier in the day? Or the few long moments of quiet that sprung up between them every now and then, when he had stumbled for words and they had been a long time coming? Yes, that was what bothered her.

He was too quiet. She needed a livelier *bachur*, someone less shy and hesitant. Why had she been in such a hurry to decide, to give the matchmaker a positive response? Why had she ignored what had obviously bothered her?

The view outside did nothing to improve Riki's mood. The poplar trees swayed from side to side, as if shaking their heads at her. At that very moment, just as a wave of self-pity swept over her and her tears burst freely forth, Riki suddenly had a flash of understanding. *No, she hadn't ignored it. She had been perfectly honest with herself. She had duly deliberated the issue and concluded that she wanted the shidduch despite this shortcoming.*

The truth was that she had always known that when the time came, she would have to give up on something in order to get everything else she wanted. She had her priorities straight. Most of all, she wanted a *ben Torah*, a *masmid*, a good family, and, of course, good *middos*.

When she met her *chassan*, she realized he had all the qualities she was looking for. As far as everything else, well, she had understood her father's not-so-subtle references to the consequences of Ephraim's having chosen to learn in a vocational school. She had also taken into account her mother's gloomy predictions about the quality of *shidduch* they might expect. Yes, she had taken it all into account and done the arithmetic.

It was only today, when Gitty Bruk had told her that her sister's friend hadn't wanted him, that she felt something cracking within her, threatening to destroy her happiness. *No! She wouldn't allow it!* She knew she had to get back to herself and wipe away her tears before she met her future mother-in-law.

She had *not* been rash. She had *not* been reckless. She had made her choice. And it was the right choice! Quietness is not necessarily a shortcoming. Even if it was, so what? She had her own set of priorities, that was all. There was something positive about a reserved nature, too. Shy, hesitant behavior often hints at modesty and gentleness, and she could certainly be happy about that.

■ ■ ■

She spotted her future mother-in-law walking toward their prearranged meeting spot. She looked tense and worried. When she saw Riki, she smiled in relief.

"I'm late," she apologized.

"Not at all." Riki smiled, brimming with goodwill. "I just got here."

"I'm so glad." Sima looked Riki up and down as she spoke. "The phone rang just as I was about to leave. I thought it would be a short conversation, but that wasn't quite the case." She chuckled. "I'm sure you're familiar with this type of situation. It was someone very distinguished, with all the time in the world, and I couldn't think of a way to cut the conversation short."

Riki laughed too, feeling the last bit of tension slowly drain away. They began walking slowly along Rabbi Akiva Street.

"Is it far from here?" Riki asked.

"Not very," Sima replied. "We'll take a taxi. I'm going to take you to a woman who sells jewelry in her house. She has lovely things. We bought Dassi's watch there, too. You remember Dassi, don't you? Ariel's wife? You met her last night."

Riki nodded. She thought she remembered someone tall and thin introducing herself as Dassi. She hoped she was right. Everything had been so confusing. She had tried to behave appropriately, to keep her wits about her, as Atara had put it. Deep inside, though, she had felt overwhelmed and confused.

"You look so sweet in a ponytail," Sima mentioned as they took their seats in the taxi.

"Thanks. I always wear my hair like this." Riki smiled.

"I know," her future mother-in-law said, smiling again. "That's why I mentioned it. It suits you perfectly. I don't think you need to do anything more elaborate than that for the engagement party."

"For what?" Riki wasn't sure she'd heard right. The whoosh of a passing bus had made it hard to hear.

"The engagement party," repeated Sima. "The way you wore your hair last night was…mmm…very nice and fashionable, but I think it was too much for your face. If you ask me, you'll look lovely without it. I think a ponytail is such a natural, pretty hairstyle. Who needs all those tendrils? What for?"

"I guess you're right," Riki murmured, trying to stick the wayward curl back behind her ear. She *was* right, her *chassan's* mother. She too had asked herself the same question last night: what for?

"In our family," Sima continued, "we don't like showy, ostentatious things. Even though we are well-off, *baruch Hashem*, we're basically simple, conservative people. We don't get swept up with the latest fads. Mali, too, has a very clear-cut sense of what she'll wear and what she won't, and so does Dassi. I'm only telling you this because you are, after all, about to become part of our family."

Riki wanted to say that she was like that, too, and so were her parents. She wanted to explain that her hairstyle the night before at the *vort* was one big mistake, and that she had worn her hair that way because Aunt Leah had told her mother that the Abramsons were "stylish and sophisticated" people.

But no sound came out of her throat. She just mumbled something unintelligible and nodded her head, which Sima took as a signal that it was okay to continue.

"The truth is, when you get to know Daniel better, you'll see that he's like that, too. He's got a lot to offer, but he is so modest. He runs away from loud, conspicuous people. He's very refined, and always has been. One's inner self, he always says, doesn't need any public relations. It always rises to the surface."

"How true," replied Riki, appreciative of her *chassan*'s wise remark. She was glad to hear about the different facets of his personality.

Still, the feeling of uneasiness she had felt when her mother-in-law first began speaking grew steadily stronger, to the point where she felt downright uncomfortable.

"That's why I'm telling you that I don't think you need to wear that hairstyle at the engagement party," Sima said, taking her courage to forge ahead from her *kalla*'s seeming willingness to listen and accept. "I, for one, would be thrilled if you'd wear your hair just as it is now, in a simple ponytail. Our whole family will be at the engagement party — my mother-in-law, who is a very highly respected woman, my mother, my grandmother and all the aunts. They're all quite prominent, and they're all eager to meet Daniel's *kalla*. In our family, as I told you, even in the extended family, we go for a solid, conservative look. We don't like ostentation. Someone who's real quality doesn't need it. Believe me, simplicity is the most beautiful style of all."

"Of course. I agree," Riki finally managed to say. "I never thought otherwise. I myself was not all that excited about the way I wore my hair last night. The truth is, a friend talked me into it."

"Friends," sniffed Sima Abramson, waving a hand in dismissal. "One has to put friends in the proper perspective as well, especially after marriage. After all, when a woman is married, she follows her husband. Friends become very secondary in her life."

"True," whispered Riki. She felt defeated and misunderstood. "In any case, as far as my hair is concerned, don't worry about it. My family also likes to keep things simple. There's nothing to worry about."

"I'm not worried in the slightest," Sima protested, sensing she had overdone it and wanting to tone down the impact of what she had said. "I never was worried, and I'm not worried now. I know you're okay, and that's why I allowed myself to be so open with you. I knew you would understand. I never for a moment thought you wore your hair that way on principle. That's why I said to myself, 'Why not make things clear, right now, in a friendly conversation?' Don't you agree?"

"Yes. Of course." Riki's voice was still a whisper. "You're right."

■ ■ ■

On the bus back to Jerusalem, Riki once again took the back seat. She sat in the darkness, trying to think about the watch she had chosen. For a fleeting moment, she could see it clearly — the sparkling band, the two rows of diamonds circling the face, the golden hands. Then the image vanished, and all she could concentrate on was the sound of the bus's motor, which seemed to be working to a threatening, terrifying rhythm: *In our family, in our family, in our family... In our family we don't like, in our family we don't do, in our family we don't go for...*

She put her hands over her ears and squeezed her eyes shut, trying to block out the words, but they pursued her relentlessly.

You're not good enough for us, they taunted. *We did you a favor by letting you into our family*, they hissed.

"But I'm the one who compromised!" she silently screamed. "I weighed the options, considered my priorities and decided to overlook something — so how is it that *I'm* not good enough? She should be happy with me, she should…"

In our family, it's different, the voices responded, pushing her into a corner. *In our family, everyone's respectable and distinguished, don't you see? We're very reserved.*

"In our family, too!" Riki wanted to shout.

Only the thought of the golden watch sent a few sparks of light into the darkness.

■ ■ ■

At the same time, Sima was walking home, feeling pleased with herself. A huge weight had been lifted from her heart. She had done the right thing by talking to the *kalla*. She really was a sweet girl. She had accepted what Sima had to say in a gracious manner, making no fuss at all. She would have to tell Shimon about it.

"See, you were worried for nothing," she would tell him. "Everything went just fine. I'm glad I spoke openly to her."

Was it really such a good thing you spoke your mind, Mrs. Abramson?

Did everything really go just fine?

Only time would tell.

6

Two years later...

SIMA ABRAMSON COMPLETED HER INSPECTION of the floor where the frailer residents of the Nachalas Avos nursing home lived, and made her way up the stairs to the entrance level. There, she crossed the lobby and exited to the shady patio that extended into the lush garden. She had a special fondness for this enchanted corner that she personally tended to.

The sight of "her" (as she liked to think of them) elderly residents seated amidst flowering plants and greenery, breathing in the early morning air, always gave her a sense of great satisfaction. She had taken pains with this garden, as she had with all details of the nursing home's design, and the finished product was a credit to both her caring and her determination.

Mrs. Weiss, who had spied the director from the wheelchair she was sitting in under a palm, waved a time-wrinkled hand and called out, "Mrs. Abramson, come over here. We haven't seen you yet today."

The other elderly residents on the patio turned in Sima's direction and murmured greetings.

Sima moved between them, smiling and exchanging

snatches of small talk, until she reached Mrs. Weiss, who did nothing to hide her impatience at the to her unnecessary delays.

"How are you today, Mrs. Weiss?" asked the director, putting an arm round the older woman's shoulders.

"Not so good. No, not good at all, if I must say so," the old woman grumbled at the figure above her. "Like always."

Without giving the director a chance to comment, Mrs. Weiss stated the source of her discontent. "Do you see that?" She pointed to one of the old women nearby. "Her daughter's already here."

Sima turned in the direction indicated and saw that Mrs. Blau's devoted daughter, Shoshana, was already seated at her mother's side. It was a sight that evoked open envy in almost all the residents at Nachalas Avos.

Shoshana Coleman, in her early fifties, arrived punctually at the same time every morning to spend a few hours in the company of her elderly mother. Right then, she was solicitously reading aloud the latest news from the daily paper, oblivious to the jealousy her presence evoked in the other residents.

"I could sure do with a daughter to visit me every morning," Mrs. Weiss complained in Sima's ear. "But what can I do if my daughter lives across the ocean? There's no getting around it — a a son is a son until he takes a wife, but a daughter is a daughter for the rest of her life."

The director of Nachalas Avos was used to Mrs. Weiss's constant dissatisfaction. The elderly woman's face seemed set in a permanent frown, and her verbal expressions ranged from annoyance to anger. Sima saw beyond the external shell, though, and admired Mrs. Weiss for her many good qualities.

"Now, now," Sima said, patting her lightly on the shoulder, "you know you have wonderful sons."

"Yes, wonderful," Mrs. Weiss said cynically. "If they're so wonderful, then why don't they visit more often? When was the last time they came? Was it Sunday or Monday? I don't know about you, but I've already forgotten. Today is Wednesday."

"Well, perhaps they were here Monday and plan to come today. Then only a day will have gone by."

"Oh, Mrs. Abramson, you're so very naive," Mrs. Weiss smiled. "My sons work, or didn't you know? They're busy making money. But for their mother, they have no time."

"What do your daughters-in-law do?" Sima searched her memory in an effort to remember whether Mrs. Weiss had ever told her anything about her daughters-in-law.

"I haven't the faintest idea," the elderly woman said. "Does anyone bother telling me anything? If only their wives allowed them, Mrs. Abramson, you can be sure my sons would come visit me more often. Everything — everything, I tell you! — depends on the wife. That's the way it goes. Daughters-in-law are a matter of *mazel*, and *mazel* is one thing I never had."

"Come now, Mrs. Weiss," Sima said, taking the old woman's hand gently in her own, "you shouldn't grumble so much. Look at the beautiful flowers growing here for you and the lovely sun smiling at you. And you got up today, *baruch Hashem*, to a new morning, alive and well. I'm sure everyone loves you and thinks highly of you."

"Don't I wish it were true!" Mrs. Weiss removed her hand from Sima's. "What difference does it make to me what they think of me, if I'm sitting here alone?" Her tone was still bitter.

The sound of Shoshana Coleman's voice drifted over to them. "A Tel Aviv teenager was killed diving in Eilat," she read from the newspaper.

"They're all crazy," Mrs. Weiss summed up the situation. "That's all they can think of to do in life — die. But I'm telling you, Mrs. Abramson, things are a lot different with a daughter. If my daughter were around, she wouldn't leave me here to rot."

"Mrs. Abramson, please," the secretary softly but effectively paged the director over speakers strategically placed throughout the nursing home.

Sima broke off her conversation and hurried to the office,

wondering why she had been unexpectedly paged.

"You have a phone call, Mrs. Abramson," her secretary said. "Will you take it here or in your office?"

"Who is it?"

"I think it's your son."

"That's okay, then. I'll take it here." She took the phone and spoke into the receiver. "Hello?"

"Hi, it's Danny."

"Oh, Danny. What's new?" She wondered why he was calling her at work.

"Ma, I apologize for calling so late in the week, but can we come for Shabbos?"

Sima glanced at the clock on the wall opposite her. Its hands pointed to half-past eleven. It was Wednesday, early enough to prepare for guests — if they hadn't planned on spending Shabbos with Mali and her family. The plans weren't final, but she had already told her daughter that she would bring the fish and a few salads.

"Ma," she heard Danny ask, "is it a problem?"

"No, not at all. Just let me think a moment." She decided to explain, for clarity's sake. "We were thinking of maybe going to Mali's for Shabbos. We haven't been there for a long time."

"Oh! Then forget I said anything."

Sima thought she heard disappointment in her son's voice and quickly said, "But it's not final. We haven't seen you in a long time, either. Look, nothing's definite yet, but let me ask you this: Are you asking because you have a special reason for wanting to come this Shabbos or did you just feel like coming?"

"No, there's no special reason. We haven't come for a long time, but if it's not convenient we can push it off for another Shabbos."

"Now wait a second. First let me talk it over with your father. Stay on the line while I call him."

Intuitively, she knew it was better not to refuse the young couple. How had Mrs. Weiss put it? Things were different with a daughter. Mali would understand a refusal, but Riki might misinterpret it. She quickly punched in the numbers of her husband's cell phone.

Mr. Abramson was in the middle of lengthy negotiations with a building contractor. He and his wife had decided to add a new wing to Nachalas Avos, one that would provide both emergency medical care and long-term convalescent care.

"Sorry, but I'm really tied up right now." Sima could hear the tension in his voice and was sorry she was disturbing him. "Whatever you decide is fine with me."

She went back to her son. "Come for Shabbos, Danny. It's fine," she said decisively. "I'll fix it with Mali. She hasn't started preparing for Shabbos anyway. Please come. We're expecting you."

It was only after she clicked off that she felt an ominous premonition that something would go wrong.

■ ■ ■

"It's all settled. We're going for Shabbos," Daniel Abramson announced to his young wife after he hung up with his mother.

"She agreed?" Riki asked.

"Yes, quite happily," Daniel answered somewhat jubilantly.

"Good," Riki murmured, turning to her baby. Little Yossi had cried nonstop almost all night and was still cranky. Was it his stomach bothering him or could he be starting to teethe? She had no idea, but it didn't matter. Whatever the cause, she felt drained and exhausted. That was why, when her husband had suggested going to his parents for Shabbos, she had impulsively agreed. Just knowing she wouldn't have to prepare Shabbos that week was a huge relief.

When Daniel had actually picked up the phone to call his mother, though, Riki felt a familiar reluctance. She regretted her impulsive decision, but it was already too late to say anything.

Daniel failed to see the look of tension on his wife's face when he made his announcement because she had turned her head away, trying to hide her disappointment.

"So, sweetie," she whispered almost soundlessly to the four-month-old baby cradled in her arms, "your grandmother agreed to have us. I was sort of hoping she wouldn't. I don't exactly love spending Shabbos at her house. But," she sighed, "she's your Daddy's mommy, so we're going and that's that. I hope everything works out for the best."

7

RIKI AWOKE ON SHABBOS MORNING to a beautiful day. A soft breeze gently ruffled the lilac-colored curtains, and a golden sunbeam illuminated the wall opposite her.

All's well. She smiled with satisfaction, trying to shake the last vestiges of sleep from her eyes. The baby was fast asleep in the white crib at her side, and the house was steeped in silence.

She glanced at her watch. It was only eight-thirty. She could afford to doze off again for a short while. The men wouldn't be home from davening until ten-thirty. That meant she had plenty of time to get up and get ready, even daven Shacharis. She yawned and turned over, following the sunbeams as they played on the wall and enjoying their warmth on her face.

The truth was that there was nothing better than staying at the Abramsons'. The big, pleasant house was much more comfortable than her parents' small apartment. There, for example, she didn't have the same privacy she enjoyed over here. She liked the spacious room that was set aside for the married children's use.

It wasn't like that at her mother's. There, they slept in the children's room instead of Devora and Shuki, her younger sister and brother, who thought nothing of walking in without knocking whenever they wanted something, be it a sock, a notebook or just a doll's shoe.

Here, everything was different. They even had a private bathroom and a separate entrance. Her mother-in-law was a terrific cook, too. All in all, she really made an effort to be a gracious hostess and make them feel comfortable. Then why did she always have such a sinking feeling about coming? There was no good reason, she told herself. She would just have to change her attitude.

Just that night, for instance, Yossi had cried almost nonstop. It was probably his teeth, but she was upset at the thought that he was disturbing everyone in the house. Her mother-in-law had knocked gently on the door and asked if there was anything she could do to help. She had even offered to take the baby and try to calm him down.

How she enjoyed this wonderful peace and quiet. At her parents', Devora and Shuki would be busy playing or singing at the top of their lungs, neglecting to take their married sister's sleepless night into consideration. Here, Tehilla, her husband's youngest sister, had surely been warned to walk on tiptoe so as not to disturb.

It was good here. She must remember that. The scent of freshly cut grass wafted into the room. She must remember all this the next time Danny suggested they visit his parents.

■ ■ ■

The meal was well under way. The first course was over, and they had sung "Dror Yikra," when Gila's voice took center stage. She was talking to her mother, unaware of the interest she was arousing.

"Are you listening, Mommy? She met me in the hall on the way to the teacher's room, and she smiled in a nice sort of way. I didn't even think she remembered me."

"'Hi, Gila!' she said. 'How are you? I haven't seen you in a while.' And then she said, 'We might be working together in the near future.'

"At first I didn't understand what she was talking about," Gila told her mother. "I must have given her a funny look, because she said, 'I think you're going to be in twelfth grade this year. Aren't you planning on being a group leader?'

"I thought I was going to faint on the spot. 'I-I haven't given it any thought,' I stammered. 'I don't know, really.'"

Gila turned to the rest of the family. "I didn't know a thing about it!"

"Who is this? Who's she talking about?" her father interrupted.

"Shoshi Gross, the head of our Bnos group," Gila explained. "She was my teacher when I was in sixth grade. She's the one in charge of choosing the leaders." Gila spoke quickly, obviously excited.

"You don't realize what this means," she said, trying to make the importance of the event clear to her listeners. "I couldn't believe it. It's just about the only thing everyone's been talking about for the past six months. They say this year's class has a lot of good girls to choose from, so there's a lot of guessing going on. Just wait — you'll be proud of your daughter yet." She grinned impishly. "Here she went to school not suspecting a thing, and the Bnos coordinator herself invites her to be a group leader! Just like that." Gila's eyes shone. "What do you say, Mommy?"

"That's great, Gila!" The words escaped Riki's lips before her mother-in-law could answer. She hadn't realized how closely she identified with her young sister-in-law. "It's wonderful when it happens that way."

What she really meant to say was that this proved what a top girl Gila was and how happy they should all be that her talents were appreciated. She felt very proud to hear that her sister-in-law was so well thought of.

Mr. Abramson looked pleased, too. He was smiling, and his

eyes shone with *nachas*. Danny and Tehilla both looked at their sister with undisguised admiration.

Only her mother remained reserved as she said, "It sounds nice, Gila, but I'm not sure I want you to be a group leader."

"Well, it's still not final," Gila said. "Nothing's been decided yet. I just wanted you to know what happened. It's enough for me to know that I passed the test, that's all. I know what they're thinking, and now the decision is up to me."

"That may be true," her mother said, still unwilling to be carried away by her daughter's enthusiasm. "But *I'm* telling you that I don't see being a Bnos leader as the ultimate goal a girl should aim for. Being a leader is not always synonymous with perfection. We all know very successful leaders, Gila, who managed to attract a lot of attention but didn't prove themselves in their everyday lives."

No one in the family noticed Riki's face go white.

"What's that supposed to mean?" Gila was confused. "What do you mean by everyday lives?"

"Just what I said," her mother answered pointedly. "They may be fantastic leaders, counselors who are stars in camp, but they don't know how to prepare a meal. They don't know how to run a home because they didn't keep things in perspective," she finished derisively.

"Being chosen means the girl is wonderful on the outside, impressing others, coming up with all kinds of sophisticated ideas until there's no place left for learning how to run a home."

Is she trying to tell me something? Riki thought in astonishment.

Gila opened her mouth to say something, but her mother continued before she could get a word out.

"But that's *not* what life is all about!" Mrs. Abramson continued, her enthusiasm for the subject apparent. "The basic question is: what is meant when we say someone is a 'good girl'? Do we mean she's a charming girl who is easily swayed by what others think, or do we define a 'good girl' as the girl who is self-contained, quiet, with good *middos*, the girl who puts emphasis on values?"

Both are right! Riki wanted to say. *A top girl can also have values. It's not a contradiction.* She felt as though her vocal chords were paralyzed, and a slight shiver ran down her spine.

"My leader happens to be a real hit — and she's very well organized," Gila said in a choked voice. "I don't think it's a contradiction. But I'm not sure I want to do it. They say it's a big responsibility to prepare all the activities week after week."

"Well, now it's Shabbos," her father broke in, "and here we are talking about weekday matters."

He began to sing *zemiros* and stopped to say, "The entrance exam to becoming a leader, Gila," he smiled, "will be a pot of delicious cholent, like your mother makes. That way we'll have all bases covered!"

Sima smiled with satisfaction at his words and everyone laughed — everyone except Riki. *Zemiros* were resumed where they had left off.

Riki's expression remained stony and her complexion pale. *How can she do this to me*? she silently fumed. *How can she talk like that about leaders in front of me*?

"Riki, can you please pass the salad?"

There was no response.

"Riki?" Gila tried again.

Daniel passed her the bowl.

"Riki, are you listening?" Tehilla asked. "This morning I showed Yossi my teddy bear, and he laughed out loud. Every time I held it up in front of him, he laughed. You should have seen him. He loved it!"

Riki glanced at her. "Great." She gave a halfhearted smile.

Daniel turned to his wife questioningly and noticed how pale she was. "Are you feeling okay, Riki?" he asked quietly.

TIGHTROPE | 55

"Yes, everything's fine." She stared intently at the glass in front of her.

Daniel shrugged and continued singing with his father.

Just before the meal ended, Sima realized that something was amiss. Riki had been unhappy throughout almost the entire meal, she noted.

Gila also thought her sister-in-law was too quiet. When she had asked Riki if she would be able to help her with a school project on the topic of *simcha*, Riki had dispiritedly replied that she wasn't sure she could be of help. "We'll see," was all she said. Usually, Riki met Gila's requests of this nature with enthusiasm, offering her the use of her own notes on the subject. But now…

When Riki took a *bentcher* before *Shir Hamaalos*, bentched on her own and got up from the table, Sima's suspicions were confirmed. She watched her daughter-in-law's short exchange with Daniel and saw her go to her room.

"Did anything happen?" she asked her son.

"No, nothing special," he muttered in reply. "She's still tired from being up at night, that's all."

A few moments later, when he came into their room, Daniel was shocked to see his wife's red eyes. He glanced automatically in the direction of the baby's crib and saw that little Yossi's eyes were following the mobile hanging over his head. He was gurgling and smiling.

"Should I ask Tehilla to watch him while you rest?" he asked in concern.

"No, there's no need," Riki answered, her voice quivering and her lips trembling suspiciously. "He's not my problem."

"Then what is? What's happening to you? Are you crying?"

She didn't answer. A strangled sob escaped her.

Daniel stood there, helpless and astonished at what was going on.

"Why do you think I rushed away from the table?" she

finally asked, dabbing her eyes with a tissue.

"I thought you must be tired," he answered.

"Tired? Why would I be tired? I managed to make up my lost sleep this morning. I thought you understood. Your mother insulted me in front of everyone at the table. I don't know how I survived until the end of the meal."

"How did she insult you?" Daniel asked, dismayed.

"I can't believe you didn't notice. Didn't you hear how she talked about being a group leader? She doesn't 'see it as a goal,'" Riki said, mimicking her mother-in-law's tone of voice. "'A leader only cares about impressing people, and in the end she doesn't know how to run a house properly.'" There was a tremor in Riki's voice as she blew her nose. "A leader is a girl without values, don't you get it? That's a leader, in her opinion."

"But Riki," Daniel tried to reason with her, "what on earth has all this got to do with you? She was just giving her opinion in general. I can't see what was so insulting."

"Why can't you see the connection, Daniel? She was giving her opinion on leaders, and I, for your information, was a leader. And not just a leader, but a real hit! A fantastic counselor — exactly the way she described it. Someone who has no values and all she wants is to make waves and be a hit, until there's no place left for learning to run a home."

"Riki, I can't believe my ears." Now Daniel was upset. "She didn't mean you at all!"

"So she managed to run me down without meaning to. That's even worse. How could she be so tactless as to speak about this topic when she knows, all too well, that I myself was a leader?"

Daniel almost gave up. "Riki, I beg you, you're hurting yourself. Who even remembers that you were a leader?"

"You may not remember," she answered in a withering tone, "but she remembers perfectly well."

"I know my mother. I promise you, she didn't mean anything. She's just very open, and she prefers to say things straight out. She wanted to put Gila's enthusiasm in perspective, that's all."

"And you want to protect your mother too much. You try too hard to understand her, instead of me! You'd be better off investing your energies in understanding me a little more rather than justifying her behavior." Her voice was choked.

An invisible wall of tension split the room in two.

"I'm only trying to help," he exclaimed virtuously.

Riki bent over the crib and scooped Yossi into her arms. She turned to the window and then faced her husband, unable to check her tears.

"I want to tell you something. I know she meant it. I can't tell you how or why I know it, but she meant every word she said! From the very first, she didn't approve of me being a leader and having lots of friends. She's always thought of me as the type of girl who wants to impress people, the type who cares what others think of her, just like she said at the table. She's scared I won't be a *balebusta*. She always manages to dig it in somehow. It's not the first time."

"I think you're imagining it," Daniel interrupted. "I never heard her say any such thing about you. What makes you think she's not happy about your friends? Where do you get these ideas from?"

"Where from?" She gave a bitter smile and turned to the window. "Nowhere!"

She would never tell him about that conversation when her mother-in-law had been so open with her. She didn't know why, but she just couldn't bring herself to tell him. Those voices on the bus still rang in her ears. "*You're not good enough. We don't like ostentation. We're very conservative...*"

No, she couldn't tell him about it. He would never understand.

Yossi began to cry, and Riki picked him up. Something in his mother's serious expression, the tension in the way she was holding him, made him cry harder. She looked lovingly at him and took herself in hand.

"No, darling. Don't cry, sweetheart." She rocked him in her arms, trying with all her might to conjure up a smile.

8

O**N SUNDAY MORNING, SIMA LEFT** for work with a heavy heart. The black mood that had been pursuing her since the previous night had not disappeared.

It had begun from the time her son and daughter-in-law had boarded the bus and waved good-bye — or more precisely, since the time Danny had waved and Riki had not.

That night, Sima could find no peace. This was not the way she had envisaged the conclusion of the young couple's visit. She sighed as she stopped at the light at the corner of Rabbi Akiva and Chazon Ish streets, then checked in both directions to make sure no one had seen the taut, unsmiling expression on her face.

No, no one was standing in her vicinity. She stood alone on the curb as the light changed to green, indicating that it was safe to cross the street.

What had happened? What had she done yesterday to offend her daughter-in-law?

A woman walking toward her nodded a greeting, but Sima

didn't even notice. Her thoughts carried her back to the previous day.

By the time Riki had emerged from her room after the Shabbos *seuda* to join them, it was time for *seuda shelishis*. Gila had gone to a friend's house, and Sima was seated at the table waiting for her daughter-in-law. From the time of Riki's hasty departure from the table at lunchtime, Sima had neither seen nor heard her.

Tehilla sat down next to her, regaling her with tales about her friends and her teacher, enjoying the undivided attention she rarely got. Then Riki had come in with a sullen expression on her face.

For some reason, her expression had infuriated Sima. All the same, she beckoned her warmly to join them at the table.

Riki mumbled something in reply.

"Why don't you wash? It's almost *shkia*," said her mother-in-law. "The men probably won't be coming home for the meal. They're davening with the Rebbe."

Riki didn't reply. Like an automaton, she turned and went into the kitchen, washed, and then sat down to the meal. She took a piece of her *challa* and sat staring into space, not saying a word.

"Where's Yossi? Is he sleeping?" Tehilla broke the silence.

Sometimes a chatterbox like Tehilla is a blessing, Sima thought.

"I think so," Riki mumbled.

"Can I hold him?" Tehilla wheedled.

"Not now," Riki replied.

"Why?" Tehilla begged.

"Because!" Riki answered curtly. Then, more softly, she added, "It's a shame to disturb him when he's happy. He'll only start screaming again."

Again, silence.

TIGHTROPE ∎ 61

Sima wanted to say something, anything that would lighten the heavy atmosphere. What could she say that would put a smile on her daughter-in-law's face and please her?

Something hardened inside her, though, and her lips pressed together in a thin line.

No. She wouldn't do anything to mollify Riki. She didn't deserve this treatment from her daughter-in-law. Her sudden departure from the Shabbos table had been impolite, rude and even insulting — but Sima had paid scant attention, thinking it was something between the couple. Then Riki had closeted herself in her room for hours. That could also be for a personal reason — perhaps she was tired or in need of quiet or privacy. She could certainly understand that. But what was wrong now? The hurt expression on her face, the unexplained silence — it was just too much.

For some mysterious reason, Riki was directing her displeasure at her. Why? She had no idea, but she was outraged at the unfairness of the situation.

It was infuriating. She had not asked them to come. Danny was the one who had called to ask if they could come. She had made other arrangements for Shabbos, better ones. She had planned to go to Mali's and had only changed her plans because they wanted to come.

She had taken the trouble to prepare apple kugel for Danny and bake the chocolate cake Riki especially liked. At night, she had tried to help with Yossi, and in the morning, she had asked Tehilla to be as quiet as possible.

And now this? She wasn't asking for any acknowledgment. She didn't want anything in return. All she wanted was that her daughter-in-law be polite and civil and refrain from spoiling the pleasant atmosphere in their home. Was that too much to ask?

She took some more potato salad and carried on eating in silence. If Riki wanted to keep up this depressing silence, let her go ahead. She would take no steps to defuse the situation.

The same thing had happened the last time the young couple came for Shabbos. It was on Shabbos afternoon when for some odd reason, when they went to visit her sister-in-law, Riki had worn the same offended expression on her face and had not exchanged a word with her mother-in-law all the way there. That Shabbos, Sima had tried to ignore the uncomfortable atmosphere her daughter-in-law's behavior was creating. She had tried to make small talk to soften Riki's offensive, annoying expression.

But not this time. Her daughter-in-law would take full responsibility for what she was doing. Without giving it a second thought, Sima picked up a *bentcher* and quietly recited Birkas Hamazon.

"I'm going out to the garden to read," she murmured. She went out on the patio, sat down in the chaise lounge and was soon deeply absorbed in the pages of a thick book that had never particularly interested her before.

On *motzaei Shabbos*, when Danny came into the kitchen, she had asked him, "Danny, what happened to Riki today?"

He shrugged and mumbled, "Nothing."

"But she was so —" she searched for the right words "— serious or worried. Did anything happen?"

"No, nothing. She was just in a bad mood," he answered, hurrying away. This infuriated her more than anything else.

Now, when she stepped up onto the crowded sidewalk, Sima knew all too well what had particularly irked her. The orchestrated silence of the two of them, Danny's attempt to hide it. He'd always been so open, sharing his problems with her.

If she had said something wrong, if there was something Riki didn't like about her house, why hadn't he told her?

Later, she had accompanied them to the bus stop, a sense of foreboding in her heart. This was not the way she had expected

TIGHTROPE | 63

Shabbos to end. She had tried so hard to please them, and yet, here was Riki, walking alongside her in thunderous, accusing silence. Danny had tried to defuse the situation, speaking to her, telling her what he was learning. But she was already too hurt to go along with his pretense that everything was just fine.

When the bus pulled up, she kissed her adorable grandson, and Danny smiled broadly and thanked her. Riki thanked her as well, and tried to smile, but the smile held no meaning for her mother-in-law.

■ ■ ■

In the lobby of Nachalas Avos, Shoshana Coleman scanned the newspaper for an article that would interest her mother.

The elderly Mrs. Blau sat in her wheelchair, her eyes closed as she dozed, waiting patiently for her daughter to find whatever it was she was looking for. She didn't mind waiting. It made no difference to her whether her daughter read aloud or turned the pages, so long as she was sitting next to her, thinking about her, doing things for her. Shoshana was looking for a good story. *Nu*, any story was good for her, as long as Shoshana read it aloud in her pleasant voice. She felt secure, knowing her daughter was right beside her.

Shoshana thumbed through the paper, past the tiresome political debates, to the women's pages, where the articles were lighter and better suited to her mother's short concentration span.

At the top of the last page, she found it. It was in the education column, written by a teacher with many years of experience.

The first line was simple and appealing: The teacher handed every student her own special flower, made of brightly colored oak tag. Every flower was a different color and shape.

Shoshana cleared her throat and went on reading.

"*Each child has her own special flower,*" the teacher told the students. "*Each of you is blessed with her very own unique personality* that Hashem has given you, and you alone. Our personalities are special gifts Hashem gives us so that we may grow and blossom."

The girls were asked to bring home the flowers and ask their mothers to write, in the center of the flower, what they felt was the most special character trait Hashem had given their daughters.

The girls were all eager to receive their flowers. Only Rina, an unruly little girl with a stormy temper, was subdued. Then, with an expression of rage, she took the flower, crumpled it and said, "I don't need the flower."

Cries of horror rose from all sides.

"Look what she did!"

"She's really going to get it!"

Rina seemed surprised by the reaction. Suddenly realizing the import of what she had just done, she looked fearfully at the teacher, who came over to her and asked quietly, "Why did you do that? Why don't you want the flower?"

"Because I don't need it," she repeated, shifting uncomfortably. '"My mother won't have anything to write about me, anyway. There's nothing nice she can write."

Shoshana's voice trailed off. Little Rina, the girl in the story, broke her heart. In her mind's eye, she saw herself as a child, standing shamefaced in front of her mother after she'd been told off for getting into trouble at school. "You've messed up again! Look at you! Instead of helping, you act just like a baby. Why didn't you clean up your room like I told you to? I can't get this kid to do anything!"

Shoshana didn't realize that she had stopped reading aloud. Her thoughts were with the child at home. The child was so familiar, and the voices that seemed to echo inside her were familiar too.

I can't get this kid to do anything! When will we have some nachas from her?

She came back to earth, realizing that she had stopped reading. She had allowed her thoughts to get the better of her.

She glanced at her mother, who was sitting in her wheelchair in the same position she had been before, except that her head was drooping and her eyes were closed. Her mother was asleep.

She didn't even hear me, Shoshana realized. *These kinds of things don't interest her. They never did.*

She was surprised at the feeling of bitterness toward her mother that rose up within her.

The Rina in the article and she were one and the same, and the voice echoing inside her belonged to her mother. The pain she had buried for so many years now threatened to engulf her. The newspaper slipped from between her fingers and fell to the floor.

Yehudis, her sister, had always been her mother's favorite. Yehudis was the good girl, the one who was always neat and clean and well behaved. Shmuel Chaim, her brother, was the brightest, cleverest child a parent could want. She, on the other hand, had been a perpetually disheveled troublemaker no one ever expected to amount to anything. Funny how now — she glanced at her frail, helpless mother — now her mother wanted only her, not Yehudis who lived up north, nor Shmuel Chaim, the glib salesman, who did her a favor by coming to visit once a month. No, now she wanted only Shoshana.

The emotional pain grew until it became a thick vise of steel gripping her heart. She visited her mother every day, sat beside her for hours, trying to help her and make her life easier. Yet while she smiled and chatted, her heart felt like stone. Today, more than ever, she felt she had to break through the impenetrable wall. But how? Who could help her do it?

She suddenly spotted Sima Abramson entering the lobby. The owner flashed a smile of goodwill to everyone and greeted the residents with a cheery "good morning."

Sima Abramson! An idea occurred to Shoshana. *There's a woman with a lot of experience. It might do me some good to have a talk with her.*

All the residents seated in the lobby smiled warmly at Sima.

"Good morning, Mrs. Abramson. How are you?"

"How was Shabbos? I waited for you."

Shoshana threw her sleeping mother a glance and turned to call for a nurse to take her mother back to bed. Sima smiled to her in greeting as she left the nursing home. Another chore on her list could now be crossed off.

The elderly Mrs. Weiss waved to Sima. "Hello, Mrs. Abramson." She winked and indicated Mrs. Blau's chair. "See? Didn't I tell you?" she said with undisguised envy. "Her daughter was here again! My daughter-in-law never comes. That's how it is with daughters-in-law."

Sima, fighting back the depressing thoughts that threatened to emerge, called all her resources into play to smile at Mrs. Weiss.

"Don't worry, Mrs. Weiss. I'm sure your daughter-in-law will come soon."

In the face of the open pleasure that greeted her upon her arrival and the sense of trust she felt from all the residents, Sima could not avoid the question that insisted on popping up in her mind.

How is it that you get along with everyone, find all the right answers, face life with confidence, yet can't get along with your own daughter-in-law?

9

NAOMI STONE WAS WAITING FOR SIMA in her office. Sima knew her well. She was Mr. Schiller's daughter.

How interesting, the thought flashed through her mind. *Mr. Schiller entered the nursing home on the day of Daniel's engagement.* Naomi, his daughter, visited him regularly. A compulsive worrier, she inundated Sima with questions and requests on her father's behalf, down to the smallest detail.

This time was no different. After a friendly nod in Sima's direction, her expression turned anxious. "Hello, Mrs. Abramson. I wanted to make sure the doctor will be here today."

"Yes, he will. He always comes on Sundays."

"Wonderful," Naomi said. "I just wanted to be sure, and to let you know that my father doesn't look well this morning. He's got no color in his cheeks, and he seems weaker than usual. I won't be here when the doctor comes, so please tell him what I said and ask him to check if there's any reason for the weakness. I'm worried his heart condition might be taking a turn for the worse."

"I'm writing this all down." Sima sounded confident and

authoritative. "You have nothing to worry about. I will convey your concerns to the doctor, and we will also keep your father under close observation."

Naomi's strained expression relaxed. "Thank you very much," she murmured. "I want to ask you something else. As you know, I come twice a week to take my father out for an afternoon walk, but I won't be able to make it this afternoon. Is it possible…I mean, would it be too much to ask that a staff member or a nurse take him out today?"

Sima stopped writing, her hand poised in mid-sentence. This was certainly an unexpected and wholly irregular request.

"We have a rather small staff." She raised her eyes from the page and continued in gentle tones. "I'm sorry, but I don't think it is possible for us to oblige. However," her voice became authoritative again and overflowing with goodwill, "is there no one in the family who could come instead?"

"No," Naomi replied. "That's the whole problem, or I wouldn't have asked. I can't come today. We have a family *simcha*, and we're taking the children, too."

"But what about the rest of the family? I was under the impression there's another son living here."

Naomi's face changed colors. "Forget it, Mrs. Abramson. That's a sore spot. I don't want to ask my brother and his wife for their help. I don't need any favors from them."

"What kind of favors? You're not asking for a favor for yourself," Sima said. "We're talking about your brother's duty to honor his father."

Naomi waved her hand in dismissal. "This is a very sensitive issue in our family, and I don't really like to talk about it. For some reason, everyone — my brother and another sister, as well — seems to think that I'm responsible for everything that goes on here in the nursing home. Everyone is busy with his or her own life, and everyone has excuses.

"While we're on the subject, I have to let you know that I'm going to have to travel abroad soon for a rather extended period of time, and I'm really worried about my father. If we were a more caring, involved family, I would be much calmer. We've discussed the topic endlessly and argued about it as well. There's no point in asking them."

Sima refused to give up so easily. She felt it was a shame — a shame that Mr. Schiller would not go for his afternoon walk and a shame that there was tension in the family over him. An idea suddenly occurred to her.

"If you would like," she suggested, " I can, as the director of the nursing home, call your brother and ask him whether he or anyone in his family might be able to come. This needn't have anything to do with you. I'll explain that we heard that you wouldn't be able to make it today, and that we think it would be a shame for his father to miss his daily walk. I think if the question is put directly, without the emotional involvement, there will be no problem."

"Do you really think it will work?" the woman's eyes lit up.

"I have no doubt about it," Sima answered confidently.

"Well then, go ahead." She hesitated for a moment, still not entirely convinced. "But please make it clear that the request did not come from me."

"Of course. I'll call right after you leave, so you won't feel uncomfortable. As far as your trip is concerned, I think the right solution might be to hire a private caregiver to help fill some of your father's empty hours. Perhaps the cost could be split among the three families. Many families do that. Trust me — I can tell you from experience that a caregiver can be an excellent companion and a good solution when family members are unable—" she deliberately avoided saying unwilling "—to come."

"Thank you so much," Naomi said gratefully. "That sounds like a wonderful idea, one that didn't cross my mind at all. Thanks."

She left Mrs. Abramson's office feeling tremendous relief and only then realized how much the issue of her trip abroad had been weighing on her mind. Now she could relax, feeling fully confident the matter would be handled in the best possible way. Clearly, her father was in capable hands at this nursing home.

Sima also felt certain the matter would be quickly and easily resolved. She dialed Mr. Schiller's son certain he would agree to come. After all, why shouldn't he? Was it so hard to find an hour or two a week for an elderly father? She was sure the problems Naomi mentioned stemmed from tension and petty disagreements between the family members. This kind of situation was not new to her. If the call came from the administrator of the nursing home, it was different, much more simple and to the point. That was why she had offered to intervene.

Naomi's sister-in-law answered the phone. Sima's conversation with her went more or less as she had expected it to. The woman sounded, at first, as though she was caught off guard by the request. She quickly regained her composure, though, and asked if there were any other viable options, deliberated aloud about her own plans for the afternoon and then, of course, acquiesced to the director's request.

"He is our father and who more than we wants the best for him? We will definitely make every effort. You can tell him we'll be there."

■ ■ ■

How easy that was. How simple. Sima replaced the receiver with a familiar sense of satisfaction. She felt this way every time she brought things to a successful conclusion — and there were many such incidents to her credit. Sima attributed her success to the practical, direct approach she took in most cases. Instead of beating around the bush, she said what had to be said in a clear, pleasant manner.

At home, she dealt with things in pretty much the same way, and had solved many of her children's problems without them even knowing it. *There was that time with Danny's study partner*, she suddenly remembered. Danny had been about twelve years old when he suddenly decided he didn't want to go to the daily *masmidim* program. Both she and her husband found his attitude strange, because he had always loved the *mashgiach* and the learning, and the added incentive of winning prizes.

She had tried to talk to her son about the situation, but he hadn't been very forthcoming. She spoke to some of his friends, and she found out that the problem was his *chavrusa*. The boy he learned with was a difficult child who had trouble with his learning, and he often vented his frustration by bullying Danny. Her husband had urged Danny to go to the *mashgiach*, but the child had refused. He felt uncomfortable, and perhaps he had also been afraid of how his friend would react.

"In that case, you're welcome to stay home," his father had told him sternly. Sima had not agreed with her husband's tough stance, and she had told him so outright, though not in front of the children, of course.

"Why involve the child," she had asked, "when it can be settled quietly, in one frank conversation with the *mashgiach*?"

Her husband did not reply and allowed her to do as she thought best. She made some phone calls that very evening, clarified the situation, and asked that Danny's *chavrusa* be changed. The situation was resolved with Danny none the wiser.

Danny. Her thoughts turned to her son. Danny. That wasn't the only time she had solved his problems or smoothed things over for him like that. Only now…only now things were careening out of her control.

The sense of satisfaction she had been enjoying evaporated. She felt as though she was walking a narrow tightrope, where she had to be super vigilant with her every move. The black mood she had experienced in the morning threatened to take over once again.

She could not understand how things had reached such a state. Everything had gone so smoothly in the beginning. The engagement party was beautiful and so filled with joy. True,

Riki had been reserved, but Sima had been so relieved to find that her fears after the *vort* were completely unfounded. At the engagement party, Riki had greeted everyone in the family so nicely. She'd made a wonderful impression on Sima's mother, her mother-in-law and the rest of the family. Most important, she had been dressed appropriately, and she had worn her hair in a modest fashion. Yes, she was glad she had spoken to her so openly the day after the *vort*.

The rest of the engagement period passed smoothly and pleasantly, as did the wedding and the *sheva brachos*. Throughout the *simcha*, Riki and her family had reflected quality and good taste. Many of her guests had pointed that out.

Riki had always behaved very respectfully toward her, too, if a little distant. She had been perturbed by Riki's reserve, but she had shrugged it off. Now that she thought of it, Riki had never actually demonstrated any natural, spontaneous warmth toward her, the way Dassi did for example. But then, daughters-in-law need not be alike.

The telephone was right there on her desk. What could be simpler than to call Daniel and ask him straight out, "Look here, Danny, I'm feeling hurt by what happened yesterday. I have no idea how things stand between you and your wife, and maybe even between you and me, but I made a great effort to be a good hostess, and instead of thanks, I get a slap in the face in the form of a sour expression and deafening silence. What on earth did I do? Why do I deserve this?"

Yes, what would be wrong with such a candid conversation? She could even add that this kind of behavior was unpleasant for her and that her feelings should be taken into consideration. Maybe she would say that if there was a problem, could they please tell her about it. Anything was better than that accusing gaze, as though she had done something wrong.

How could it be that she, who helped and supported everyone else, wanted to hurt her son and daughter-in-law?

Sima felt humiliated and betrayed as she sat at her desk.

No, she could not hold such a conversation. The rules were different here. They were new rules, confusing and strange to her. She was still unclear as to how things had gotten this far. Everything had been fine in the beginning.

She, for her part, had tried to be a devoted mother-in-law to both her daughters-in-law. As soon as she had the opportunity, she had bought Riki the same fancy towels she had bought for her own daughter, Mali, and for Ariel's wife, Dassi. She had even given her an extra set of bed linen. Riki had thanked her for the gifts, albeit not very warmly. Still, there was nothing specific about her behavior that indicated she bore her mother-in-law a grudge of any sort.

As far as she could see, there was no reason for Riki to be upset with her. Sometimes, when the couple came for Shabbos, she noticed that Riki was withdrawn and never really participated in the conversation at the table. This annoyed her somewhat, especially in light of the fact that Riki was known to be a popular and sociable girl. But she pretended not to notice it and made no comment about it. *Maybe I should have said something,* the thought occurred to her. *Who knows?*

It was only recently, since Yossi was born, that matters had taken a turn for the worse. She had no idea why. She had expected the birth of her grandchild to bring them closer, but the opposite was true. Yossi had been so like Daniel as a newborn. She had immediately felt herself bonding with him, as if Yossi was her own child. They had covered most of the expenses of the birth. She had bought one of the best cribs available.

She sighed. She had heard so much about Riki's good *middos* before the wedding, but, much to her chagrin, there was no sign of such sterling character traits when Riki thanked her for the gift. A halfhearted "thank you" was all she got for a top quality crib, one of the newest on the market. Everything had been so unexpected, so different from what she had anticipated. *You do your best,* she thought bitterly, *invest so much effort, and in the end it looks as if you've been trying to hurt rather than help.*

Someone knocked on the door of her office. Her secretary came in and told her that Dr. Geller had arrived. The doctor wanted to know whether the laboratory tests had been arranged.

Sima stood up, suddenly recalling that Mr. Schiller's daughter had asked her to speak to the doctor about her father.

"Yes, the laboratory tests have been taken care of," she replied. "But I want to speak to Dr. Geller about Mr. Schiller, room 4."

Sima decided to go directly to the elderly gentleman's room. She wanted to assess his situation for herself.

Responsible, authoritative and confident as ever, Sima went about her work, leaving her doubts and insecurities in their private drawer, concealed in the secret compartment of her desk.

DANIEL ABRAMSON SPENT that same Sunday morning feeling worried too. He tried unsuccessfully to concentrate on the *sugya* in front of him and to pay attention to what his *chavrusa* was saying.

Nothing helped. The words would not arrange themselves into sentences and refused to penetrate his consciousness.

In the morning, when he left, his wife had been asleep — or had pretended to be asleep. He had not exchanged a single word with her. It had seemed to him that the very walls of his house were shouting at him in her stead, pointing an accusing finger and filling the rooms with depression and gloom.

On the way home from his parents' house the night before, Daniel had sat in withdrawn silence next to the bus window. The expression on his mother's face when she had seen them off weighed heavily on his heart.

He loved and respected his mother. She had always been so devoted and caring, investing her whole self into her children. He wanted to repay her in kind, to give her *nachas* and make her proud of him and his family, but the opposite was taking place.

His recent visits seemed to cause her only heartache. The expression on her face was one he knew well. It was an expression of dejection, disappointment and pain. *Why? Why does it have to be this way?*

"You're not saying anything. How come?" he had heard his wife, sitting next to him on the bus, whisper.

He had mumbled something unintelligible in reply. He found it difficult to share his feelings with her.

"Are you angry about something?"

"Angry? Why on earth should I be angry?" Then the words he had fought to keep back escaped him. "It's just that it's hard for me to see my mother like that. She tries so hard to be a good hostess and in the end, instead of thanking her, you say goodbye so coldly, leaving her with a feeling of heartache. She stood there at the bus stop with such an expression of…she looked so pitiful. I mean, it's hard. That's all."

His voice had trailed off as he turned back to the window, unaware of what was happening next to him. He hadn't seen the shocked look on his wife's face or the fact that her lips were trembling as she fought for control, trying to choke back her sobs. It was only when she finally found her voice that he realized what he had done.

"*She* looked pitiful?" Riki was whispering so that none of the other passengers would hear their conversation, but her words came out in a hiss. "Is that all you have to say?" She was furious. "You're upset that she has heartache? What about my heartache? Why doesn't that bother you?"

"Of course it does. What makes you think it doesn't bother me?" he had answered defensively. "I'm sorry all this is happening. It's really a shame."

"All *what* is happening?" Riki's voice had risen a little and he hushed her, but she was too carried away to pay attention. "Am I in any way responsible for what's 'happening'? Did I ask to be insulted at the Shabbos table?"

"She did not intentionally insult you!" he retorted, immediately regretting his outburst but at a loss for words to soften its impact.

The words poured out of Riki in a torrent. "She didn't? Then why did she leave me all by myself with Yossi the whole afternoon? I didn't even tell you about it. She hardly spoke to me during *seuda shelishis*. Then she got up from the table and went out onto the patio with a book, completely ignoring me, as though I were part of the woodwork. She didn't say a single word to me." Tears spilled from Riki's eyes.

"Gila wasn't home, so my company was Tehilla, a kid of six. Me and Tehilla — what a great team! — while my mother-in-law sat by herself, reading, as if I didn't exist. If that wasn't intentional, then there is a major misunderstanding here. But what's the difference anyway."

He hadn't answered, fearful of provoking her still further. The people behind them were probably straining their ears to pick up the conversation. He was under no obligation to provide them with free entertainment.

"She would never do this to your sister Mali," he heard his wife say.

How true! he had noted silently, feeling a tug at his heart. *My mother would never do this to Mali, that's for sure.*

"So you're not saying anything," Riki had commented, without giving him a chance to reply. "Okay, I'll keep quiet if that's what you want. It's better that way. I thought you would understand. I never dreamed that after everything I went through this Shabbos, you'd focus all your sympathy on your mother, and I would end up the guilty one."

The baby woke up and began crying. Riki had wordlessly bent down to get the bottle of water from the bag at her feet. "Here you are," she had murmured in the baby's ears. "Mommy's giving Yossi a drink right away. Don't cry, sweetie." She had focused on his intent drinking, absorbing herself completely in the baby, as though no one else in the world existed except the two of them.

■ ■ ■

Now he was sitting in *kollel*, worried and confused. He had hoped he would be able to calm down, that the learning would take his mind off his problem for a few hours — but he found he couldn't concentrate on the material in front of him. His thoughts kept flashing back to the events of *motzaei Shabbos*.

When they had arrived home, neither one of them said a word about the matter. This morning, he had left the house before they'd had a chance to talk. Worst of all, he had a sinking feeling that his wife was planning to keep up this infuriating state of silence.

How could he explain to her that she was punishing herself? What could he say to convince her that he cared about her feelings, but had no way of helping her? After all, it was his mother they were talking about.

Maybe there is a way, the thought occurred to him. *Yes, that was it!* Maybe he ought to get more involved in the situation and ask his mother to treat Riki with extra warmth and consideration, as if she were Mali. He could tell her that Riki was a sensitive soul who needed closeness and warmth.

His *chavrusa's* explanations suddenly made sense. He began to absorb what was being said. The *sugya* slowly became clearer in his mind.

■ ■ ■

Chaya Baum had just finished straightening up the bedrooms. She was heading to the laundry room to tackle the pile of laundry waiting there, when her thoughts turned to her daughter Riki.

What was wrong with her? She hadn't heard a thing from her since Thursday. She had been positive Riki would call her to tell how Shabbos had gone and how Yossi was doing. She wondered what his other grandmother thought of him. Did she notice the intelligent look in his eyes?

Chaya was definitely curious and even a little puzzled. She checked her watch. The hands pointed to five past ten. She knew Riki didn't work on Sundays, and it was not like her to stay out of touch for so long. Perhaps Yossi was sick? She decided to ignore the wash for the moment and went into the kitchen to dial her daughter's number.

■ ■ ■

Riki's baby wasn't acting himself that morning — but his fretfulness had nothing to do with an ailment of any sort. He sensed his mother's black mood; he felt that her heart was not entirely with him. His behavior reflected his insecurity, and the result was that his young mother felt increasingly helpless.

When she woke up and found that her husband had already left, she searched the house for a note of some sort, something that expressed his concern for her. When she found nothing, she sank into a state of gloomy despair.

Yossi had woken up a short while later, demanding to be fed. She fed him distractedly, neglecting to smile at him. Yossi had stared at her with large, puzzled eyes. He'd begun eating nicely but had suddenly stopped and broken out into loud cries.

"What's the matter? Why are you crying?" She tried burping him and rocking him, but she felt her impatience mounting. His cries had interrupted her brooding.

She hadn't told Daniel anything about the way things stood between her and his mother. She hadn't wanted to spoil his happiness, and besides, it was *lashon hara*. Aside from subtle hints on a few occasions, she had exercised admirable self-control and never let anything slip.

After their last visit, though, something had snapped. She felt she couldn't keep it all in any longer, so she had told him what was bothering her. His reaction left her feeling confused. Why hadn't he shown more sensitivity? She suddenly felt lost and very alone.

"What's wrong with you? Why are you crying?" She was

almost in tears as she held the wailing baby in her arms. If things weren't bad enough with the way her mother-in-law had insulted her, her husband was now doing the same by telling her she had misconstrued the events and was imagining things.

His mother was right. *She*, his wife, was not! He had gotten up in the morning and gone off to *kollel* without even saying good-bye.

She wandered aimlessly around the house with the baby in her arms, her tears dripping on his head.

Then the phone rang.

11

"**Hello, Riki?**" The voice Riki heard when she picked up the phone sounded tense. She hoped nothing was wrong, but hid her concern with a casual greeting.

"Hi, Mommy. How are you?"

"What's doing, Riki?"

"Everything's fine." There was something in the way she replied that made it sound as if everything was far from fine.

"You haven't called since Thursday, and I was worried. Is everything okay?"

"Sure." She paused and then added, "More or less."

"It sounds more like 'less' than 'more.'"

A moment of silence followed. Then, "What makes you think so?"

"The way you sound. I know something's wrong. Is Yossi okay?"

Yossi chose that particular moment to burst out crying, much to the dismay of his grandmother on the other end of the line.

"What's the matter with him?" she shouted into the receiver.

"Nothing, Mommy. He's just uncomfortable. I'll switch the receiver to my other hand. One second."

"Riki."

"Yes?"

"I don't like the sound of your voice. Are you sick? Why are you hiding things from me?"

"I'm not sick." The words came out in a sob. She hadn't meant to cry, but once she got started, she couldn't stop. It was her mother she was talking to, her mother who loved her. She would surely understand.

"It's something else, Mommy." Her sobs grew stronger. "Something else entirely. I'm not sick, *chas veshalom*, but everything is so hard."

"What happened? What are you talking about?"

Chaya felt as though she had been dealt a blow to the head. Her temples pounded, and the walls of the kitchen swam dizzyingly in front of her eyes.

"I was there for Shabbos." Riki's voice sounded tortured. "I can't take it anymore. She humiliates me!" She broke out in a fresh flood of tears.

"Who does, Riki?"

"My mother-in-law. It couldn't be worse."

"Riki, please try to calm down. You're frightening Yossi. Go wash your face and take a drink. I'll wait on the line. We'll have a calm conversation. I can spare the time."

Riki mechanically carried out her mother's instructions. Her mother's warm, caring voice was like a balm to her turbulent emotions. She felt like a little girl again, secure in the knowledge that her mother was at her side. That alone was enough to help her calm down.

She gently laid the baby in his carriage, went to wash her face, then poured herself a glass of apple juice. She lifted the receiver and rocked the carriage with her free hand.

"Mommy?"

"Yes, darling. I'm still here."

Riki began to tell her about the turn things had taken at the Shabbos table, when Sima Abramson had made detrimental comments about group leaders, and how Riki had felt it was an indirect put down of her.

"But Riki," Chaya Baum said when the torrent of words slowed to a halt, "I'm not at all sure that this had anything to do with you. I don't think she meant you at all."

"You too! Just like Danny. He said the same thing. No one wants to see my side of it." Her voice trembled. "She did it deliberately, Mommy, and I can prove it. It's not the first time she's criticized me. It was the same on our last visit. You've got to hear what happened."

Riki launched into the story. "On Shabbos afternoon, we were about to go to visit Danny's aunt, Yocheved, when my mother-in-law suddenly stopped in the doorway and said, 'Riki, are you sure that wave of hair in your eyes doesn't disturb you? Half your face is hidden.'

"I didn't answer, or maybe I did. I can't remember anymore. Then she continued. 'Try to brush it back,' she suggested. 'I think that's the way it's meant to be. I think that *sheitel* just wasn't cut right.'"

"Well, maybe it wasn't." Again, Chaya tried to side with her *machtenista*. "Maybe she thought the wave really bothered you, and she was only trying to help. What's wrong with that?"

"Mommy," Riki's voice took on a plaintive tone as she enunciated each word slowly and deliberately, "she thought of it right at the last minute when we were on our way out the door. She looked me up and down to make sure I was dressed appropriately, according to her family's exacting standards." Her voice was cynical. "She doesn't trust me to dress right. And it's not the first time."

"What makes you say that?" Chaya Baum was shocked.

"You always look lovely. You have good taste. Why wouldn't she trust you?"

"Mommy, I never told you this." Riki's voice broke. She was close to tears. "I didn't want to upset you. I knew it would hurt you. It all began after the *vort*, when I went with her to choose a watch. I came home very upset, remember?"

Of course her mother remembered.

"You asked me what was the matter, why I wasn't happy. You wanted to hear about the watch, but I didn't want to talk. Do you remember?"

Chaya nodded. She remembered only too well. "Go on."

"On the way to the store, she had a conversation with me. She asked me to change my hairstyle for the engagement party. She hinted that the dress I wore to the *vort* didn't fit in with her family's conservative tastes. She thought I wouldn't fit in with her family. Since then, I've been on trial. That's what happened when we were on our way to visit the aunt. Do you see what I mean? She just checked me out before we left. She doesn't trust me, Mommy."

Chaya was shocked. How could her *machtenista* have done a thing like that? How could it be that her daughter was so wronged and she, Chaya, had known nothing about it?

Yes, she believed her Riki. She could imagine how she felt. She had received a similar message the morning after the *vort*, when she'd had that awful conversation with her new *machtenista*. She still remembered every word of that conversation. The *machtenista* had innocently said something about Riki wearing a color that would suit her better.

A heavy sigh escaped her.

"Mommy?"

"Yes, Riki."

"Why are you so quiet?"

"I'm just thinking about what you said," she answered softly.

She hadn't said anything about it to Riki at the time. In fact,

TIGHTROPE | 85

she had decided she would never tell her. She hadn't wanted to spoil her daughter's happiness. She hadn't wanted Riki's relationship with her mother-in-law to be doomed from the start. Despite her good intentions, it seemed the relationship had deteriorated all the same.

Was now the time to tell her? Should she confirm her daughter's feelings by telling her that she, too, had heard similar words on that fateful day? Would that strengthen Riki's self-confidence and make her feel better? Or would it have just the opposite effect?

"So what do you think, Mommy?" Riki's voice sounded hopeful as she waited for the empathy and encouragement she was sure were forthcoming.

"I'm thinking about what you said. I never knew. It really hurts me to think that you were suffering and I didn't even know. How come you didn't tell me? It's a shame. You would have felt better if you had shared it with me."

"I already told you why." Riki sounded calmer and more cheerful now. "I knew you'd be very upset. I just tried to forget about it. I had lots of happy things to think about. I thought she'd get to know me and things would change. But they didn't. She's never trusted me.

"Take the story of Yossi's crib. She's the only one who knows where to buy it. She can't trust me to pick out a crib because she doesn't trust my taste. In her family, they buy only the best. And in ours? We probably buy only the cheapest.

"The towels you bought me, Mommy, were obviously not good enough. There's a special line they buy, the kind that doesn't get worn out quickly. Do you get the picture? Naturally, Dassi and Mali have that kind too. Remember the fancy coffee set Danny and I got as a wedding present, the one I put away at the top of a closet? She suggested I keep it on hand, because, to quote her, 'We do a lot of entertaining.' She always keeps a set on hand. It's very important, she says. Let's face it. We're too plain and ordinary for her, and she can't accept that."

Chaya found herself irritated by the picture Riki presented.

"Why isn't she happy with us? What's wrong with our family?" She immediately regretted her words.

"Let's not kid ourselves about our family, Mommy. We have a wonderful, warm family, maybe even better than theirs, but let's not forget that we have our weak spots, like our lack of style. We all knew right from the start that the Abramsons would never have agreed to the match if Danny hadn't had a hard time making a *shidduch*. We never talked about it, but it was obvious. But who cares? Danny is a great guy. So what if he's shy and quiet? It's not the end of the world.

"The problem is the way my mother-in-law feels about me. I tried really hard not to pay attention to it, to smooth things over, but her comment about my *sheitel* brought that first conversation flooding back to my mind.

"And then this Shabbos! Mommy, I can't take it anymore."

12

THE CONVERSATION HAD ENDED, but Chaya was still sitting near the phone, trying to take in what she had just heard from Riki.

Her Riki was suffering, really suffering, and she hadn't even told her. Now that she thought about it, she realized that her daughter had never shown any warm feelings for her mother-in-law. Sima, too, was very reserved when it came to talking about Riki, and that was something that both perplexed and disturbed Chaya. She hadn't expected things to be this way. After all, Riki was a truly special girl, and she thought it would be only natural for her mother-in-law to notice that and mention it to her from time to time.

Until now, she'd attributed this to her *machtenista*'s reserved personality. After all, not everyone is aware of how important it is for one side to hear the other side speak well of their children, she'd reasoned. She herself always tried to note Daniel's strong points — why begrudge someone their *nachas*? It had never occurred to her that Sima's reticence on the subject of her daughter-in-law stemmed from the fact that she was displeased with her. She found the very idea unthinkable!

Could it be? Her Riki? How could anyone fail to be charmed by her? Her precious daughter was always so good, so well mannered, so...so wonderful. Her kindergarten teacher had called her "the cream of the crop." She still remembered those words. The first grade teacher, and then the second, and all the teachers all the way on through high school had sung Riki's praises. Her friends loved her, and so did her brothers and sisters. She was so sensitive and understanding, so eager to help. Chaya knew that the way a person acts at home with his family is the real test of his character, and Riki had passed with flying colors. It was hard to believe that instead of jumping for joy over the spectacular treasure they had acquired, her *machtenista* was looking for things to criticize!

Chaya felt the anger rising up within her. If only she could speak her mind to Mrs. Abramson!

Do you think your Daniel is perfect? she would say. *If I were to don the same faultfinding pair of glasses you use, wouldn't I be able to find fault with him? His long silences at the Shabbos table, especially when we have company, are so embarrassing! Do you think that gives us pleasure? True, when he does finally open his mouth, his every word is a gem, but still. I can almost hear our guests thinking,* So where's the talented boy you took as a husband for your daughter?

When he comes to us for Shabbos, he's so quiet in shul, so bashful — how do you think my husband feels about that? The poor man was so proud to go to shul with his new son-in-law, a ben yeshiva who he thought would surely interact with his friends, say the right things and bring honor to our family. Yet the moment he enters the shul, Daniel disappears into a corner and doesn't say a word to anyone unless directly addressed. It's not that I need everyone to know how intelligent he is. After all, we know that he's a real ben Torah, in the fullest sense of the word. But still...

And our Ephraim! A deep sigh escaped Chaya's lips. *I had so hoped, dear Mrs. Abramson,* her imaginary conversation went on, *that your son's entry into our family would do my Ephraim some good. I thought Daniel would talk to him, sort of take him under his wing. Unfortunately, Daniel doesn't seem to be very willing to help out, even after repeated hints. Here I was already spinning my dreams, imagining they might have a nightly study session together — but my dreams have not come true.*

Yes, Mrs. Abramson, that's the way the situation stands, if you want to know the truth. If I wanted to look, I could find plenty to fault with your son — it's just that I don't want to look. I try to find the good in him so that I can bring him closer to us and to make my daughter happy and help the two of them build a home in which peace and harmony reign.

Chaya leaned back in her chair, looking defeated. Yes, she knew exactly what she would tell Mrs. Abramson to her face, if only that were possible. She knew she could never do something like that, but her thoughts rushed on.

Wasn't Daniel — well, mediocre — for a girl of Riki's caliber? She had thought so when the *shidduch* was still in its initial stages, but she hadn't said a word, of course. She knew that when it came to *shidduchim*, logic was sometimes irrelevant. If Riki hadn't noticed what she had noticed, and the boy found favor in her eyes, she wasn't one to try to obstruct Heaven's design and ruin her daughter's chances for happiness.

Chaya absentmindedly rose from her chair, propelled by a distinct sense of unease. She walked out of the kitchen and stood beside the large window in the living room.

A young woman was wheeling a twin carriage in the street below. *She could almost be Riki,* mused Chaya. Her eyes followed the young woman as she walked down the block, but her mind was far away in Riki's house.

Was Riki happy? What did she know about Riki's life, now that she was married? Obviously, Riki was fairly adept at keeping secrets. Aside from all the other revelations Riki had made today, she had learned, for the first time, that Riki had picked up on Danny's shortcomings when she had met him, just as she had. She had decided to overlook them.

Chaya felt the pain spread through her until it reached her heart and squeezed it so hard she thought it would burst.

So, she had not succeeded in bestowing happiness on her daughter after all. Riki, like her, had been forced to compromise. Her joy on the evening of her engagement had almost certainly been incomplete. She, too, had probably watched her dreams shatter in the face of reality.

What was it her daughter had told her earlier in the morning in a very wise tone of voice? Chaya had been surprised to discover that it was this comment that had hurt her more than anything else:

"Let's not kid ourselves about our family. We can't deny the fact that we have a few weak spots," Riki had said.

What had she been referring to? Did she mean her father, who was considered a simple workingman? Was she talking about their not being able to buy her an apartment or even half an apartment? Was she thinking of Ephraim, who had left yeshiva? Could she mean her grandmother, who had raised her children all on her own? Or might Riki have been referring to other things, things that hadn't even occurred to her?

Chaya left the window and walked through her house, wondering what else Riki might have meant. She found a small apple in the vegetable bin. Slowly and deliberately, she washed it off and then peeled it. She concentrated intently on what she was doing, hoping the simple actions would help her get rid of the tension building up within her, if only for a few moments.

Could it be that she was accusing me of something? the horrible thought struck her. She sensed that the few words Riki had uttered represented just the tip of a very large iceberg.

Her discovery of Riki's latent feelings and emotions, and the thought that she had been completely unaware of their existence, began to undermine her self-confidence. *Who knows?* the thought plagued her. *What if Riki has been harboring a store of bitterness against her father and me for years now?*

Had Riki secretly been comparing, all those years, the quality of her own home and the social standing of her family to those of her friends, some of whom had grown up in higher class homes?

Chaya Baum feared that might be the case. Might her daughter have been jealous of them? Might she have been angry with her parents, considering them responsible for her unfortunate situation? Could it be that she had agreed to marry Daniel out of a sense of coming to terms with reality, just as she had?

Chaya's pain was unbearable. All these years, she'd thought she was doing what was best for her daughter. She'd been proud of the fact that she'd provided her with a warm, happy home, although doing so demanded a great deal of dedication, even self-sacrifice, on her part. She'd helped her daughter achieve her maximum potential and made sure she lacked for nothing.

And yet, in the end, all she received was a slap in the face. Riki perceived all this in an entirely different light. Her parents were not good enough for her, it seemed. No, there were "weak spots."

Scenes from her own childhood rushed forward, distracting her from her chores.

She saw her own mother, gritting her teeth and working so hard to support the family that there was hardly any time left for her to spend with her daughter. She remembered the terribly difficult years of growing up without a father. Her home had been so different from everyone else's. How much effort it had taken to rid herself of the "poor little girl" image! With her own two hands, she'd built herself up and managed to grow up normal and healthy, just like her friends.

She had built her own home. True, it wasn't fancy or especially elegant, but it was warm and loving, not at all like the home she'd grown up in. Her children hadn't known the wretchedness of her childhood. Now here came reality, laughing in her face. *Ha-ha*, it spat. *History repeats itself, my dear woman, or didn't you know?*

Chaya was too intelligent to wallow in self-pity. Something inside told her to quit dwelling on what was less than perfect and get on with life. After all, she was familiar with the situation of a bitter daughter complaining that her parents were responsible for her lot in life. Hadn't she herself felt that way?

Her thoughts drifted back to those sleepless nights she'd spent tossing and turning in bed, wrestling with troublesome thoughts and questions she hardly dared raise. *Did you really have to get divorced and break up our home?* she would mentally ask her mother. *Was there no other way? Couldn't you have provided me with a normal, secure home? Don't you think you acted too rashly, even irresponsibly, failing to take into consideration your daughter's future?*

At first, these questions occurred to her only occasionally, on particularly bad days, but as time went on, she grew gradually more convinced that the answer to all of her questions was a resounding "yes." Her mother had most certainly wronged her.

Her mother, of course, hadn't noticed a thing. She had never given her any reason to, never breathed a word of what she felt. Deep inside, though, her anger and resentment toward her mother festered and grew.

And now? A frightening thought suddenly occurred to her: *Ribbono shel Olam, are You punishing me for having felt that way toward my mother? Are You punishing me for the questions I tormented myself with at night in bed? Or…or are You trying to teach me the hard way how foolish I was for harboring such feelings, how greatly I erred in my judgment of her?*

Who can judge the level of a mother's self-sacrifice? Perhaps her mother, too, had done what she thought was best for her children at the time.

Chaya felt the band of tension slowly ease. Yes, now she understood. It was clear as day to her that her mother had done the best she could for her children, just as she had done the best she could for her own children. The sense of injustice she had felt upon hearing her daughter's comment, the knowledge that her daughter faulted her for things that were beyond her power to control was not a trial unique to her. Her mother would have felt that way too had she known her daughter's true feelings about her.

She was grateful to *Hakadosh baruch Hu* for having granted her the wisdom to understand that. "Thank you, Hashem," she whispered.

How was her mother feeling this morning? She hadn't spoken to her in a while. She would give her a call. Perhaps she needed her.

13

LIFE WAS TOO BUSY FOR RIKI to spend time feeling sorry for herself. In fact, she felt guilty that she had allowed herself to get carried away with self-pity when there was so much to be happy about. Just watching Yossi rocking vigorously on all fours was enough to fill her heart with satisfaction and gratitude. Besides, she had her new job to think about.

The principal of the school where she had a substitute teaching job had called her into her office that morning and told her about the collective bas mitzva party to be celebrated by the entire sixth grade.

"We like to combine the bas mitzva with the preparations for Shavuos, so it is usually held on Rosh Chodesh Sivan or a day or two later. It would be appropriate, of course, to include something from *Megillas Rus* in the program and a focus on *kabbalas haTorah*. Do you think you could organize the event?"

The question and the way it was asked left Riki with little choice. After all, when she had accepted the substituting job a month before, the principal had hinted something about a future bas mitzva party. Riki was pretty sure one of the reasons she had landed the job was her talent for organizing events and performances. The principal knew Riki from her days as a Bnos counselor at her school.

Now, Riki sat in her living room trying to put pen to paper to come up with a basic theme for a performance. Yossi was babbling happily in the stroller beside her, and two of her neighbor's children sat on the floor, busy with the paper and stickers she had given them. Fraidy, her neighbor, had asked if they could stay at her house until her younger sister came to baby-sit. Her baby was running a fever, and she was anxious to get to the doctor during office hours.

At first, Riki had been taken aback by the request. She had finally found the time to begin her project, and baby-sitting would disrupt her plans. On second thought, though, she knew she was perfectly capable of handling the situation, so why not help a neighbor in need?

She had some toys, paper and stickers tucked away at the back of Yossi's closet. So what if Yossi was still a baby? A home ought to be open to children of all ages. Sometimes Mali's or Dassi's children came over, and sometimes, like now, she looked after a neighbor's children for a while. Riki didn't want her house to be the kind where children climbed the walls in boredom.

The heartwarming sights and sounds of the three adorable children sitting in the living room and playing contentedly distracted her from the work she was meant to be doing.

The day would come, *be'ezras Hashem*, when her home would be filled with children. They would have their friends over to play, and there would always be room for everyone. She wouldn't spend her money on fancy carpets or furniture — no, not her. She would stock up on games, just as her mother had done, and she'd always have a jar of cookies handy to add to the fun.

When Fraidy had brought the children over, Moishy hadn't wanted to come in or even let go of his mother's hand. Riki had managed to lure him in with a shiny gold-foil-covered chocolate coin that she had taken out of a jar just like the one her mother kept treats in.

Thinking about her mother caused a warm feeling to spread through her. Would she ever manage to recreate the unique atmosphere that had reigned in her childhood home? Would she be able to radiate the same unconditional love and warmth? The girls on her block had always loved to come to her house. They always felt welcome. In Riki's house, everyone knew, you could play hide-and-seek under the beds or build a tent out of blankets in the children's room.

Riki caught sight of the white sheet of paper on which she had begun to jot down her ideas for the bas mitzva performance. Her mother had never had to deal with responsibilities outside the home, such as the organization of complicated projects. She had never had any sort of career. Her mother considered her home her whole world, and she had invested her heart and soul into making it a wonderful, comfortable place to be. Baby-sitting other people's children was never a problem for her. There was never any conflict of interest between her activities at home and anything outside the home. Her home was her castle.

No, she could never be exactly like her mother, Riki mused, at least not at this stage in her life. Her father had worked to support the family, whereas her husband was in *kollel*. Everything had its price. She was working outside her home, while her mother had not.

Still, she could certainly try to follow her mother's example. She decided that she would try to create that same warm, homey atmosphere.

Yossi was squirming around in his stroller, gurgling to no one in particular. She scooped him up and swung him high up toward the ceiling. Moishy and Shmulik, the neighbor's children, stopped playing to enjoy the show, and they all laughed happily together.

The doorbell rang. Riki opened the door to find the children's young aunt, who asked whether her nephews were there.

"Moishy and Shmulik? Here they are. Come on in."

The children ran to their aunt, waving their creations proudly.

"Look what I made," the younger one said, pointing to his paper.

"I stuck stickers, too," his older brother announced.

"You can take everything with you and finish up at home, okay?" Riki smiled. "If you need anything, feel free to knock on my door," she said to the girl at the door.

Esty, all of eleven years old, flashed a knowing grin. "I would have come to you anyway," she said. "We all know that 'When Fraidy isn't home you can ask our neighbor Riki.'"

After they left, Riki put Yossi back in his stroller and sat down at the table again, trying to take up where she left off before they came. She spent a few minutes staring blankly into space and shook her head in frustration. She couldn't seem to come up with a single original idea. She would have to ask someone more experienced, or someone with a rich imagination who could help fuel her own.

Yehudis Weiss! Yehudis was her downstairs neighbor. Why hadn't she thought of her before? Yehudis was a sixth-grade homeroom teacher in a different school. What could be better? Maybe she would even have a ready script that Riki could just adapt.

She glanced at the clock. It was only six, a good time to drop in for a chat. Yehudis's baby didn't have a fixed bedtime and her husband, like Riki's, would still be in *kollel* at this hour. Scooping Yossi into her arms, it occurred to her that it might be nice to bring her neighbor a few slices of the cheesecake she'd baked the day before. She was rather proud of it, as it tasted delicious even if it wasn't as light and airy as the cookbook illustration. After a moment's deliberation, she slid the cake back into the refrigerator.

Yehudis Weiss opened the door with a smile. She was on the phone, but she motioned to Riki to come right in.

"Just a minute," she whispered, pointing to the couch.

"Yes, it's a friend of mine who lives upstairs from me," Riki heard her report to whoever was on the other end of the line. "It's okay. She probably came to take a break," she winked conspiratorially at Riki. "I'm sure she'll let me talk to you for another few minutes, won't you?" she asked, directing the question to Riki. "It's my mother-in-law," she added. "I'll be only another few minutes."

"Go ahead, it's okay," replied Riki. She sat down on the couch and placed Yossi on the floor beside her. One side of the phone call washed over her whether she wanted to hear it or not.

"Yes, what I called about before," she heard her neighbor say, "was to ask for your baked fish recipe. Yes, the one you sometimes serve on Friday night."

"What? You gave it to me already? Well, mine just doesn't come out like yours. I must be doing something wrong. Menachem is crazy over that dish. He always tells me that no one makes fish like his mother, and I'd like to get it right this week."

Riki couldn't believe her ears. Was Yehudis really talking to her mother-in-law? Why, she was openly admitting that her mother-in-law's culinary skills were better than her own! Not only that, but she was calmly declaring that her husband liked the fish his mother prepared better than anything else! What generosity of spirit. Never in a million years would she be able to talk to her mother-in-law that way.

"Yes, I have a pen." She heard her friend's voice from the kitchen. "You can start. I'm writing it down."

No. She would never be able to grant her mother-in-law so generous a compliment. Her mother-in-law's opinion of her was not the greatest as it was. She certainly didn't need to add to her list all the things she didn't do as well as her.

Riki remembered the fallen cheesecake she had left in the refrigerator. She had gotten the recipe from a friend, but it had come without any instructions. She had considered calling her mother-in-law the other night to ask for her advice. Her mother-in-law was, after all, a pro in the kitchen, and her cakes always came out picture perfect. She hadn't dared do such a thing, though, and she didn't think she'd ever be able to.

She was struck by a sudden pang of jealousy. She would have loved to speak to her mother-in-law the way Yehudis did, so naturally and with so much warmth. It seemed wonderful.

Why couldn't she? Why was Yehudis able to have such conversations with her mother-in-law while she couldn't? Was she any different from Yehudis? Maybe her mother-in-law was different from Yehudis's mother-in-law. Who was building the wall between them? Was it her?

No! It couldn't be! She was no different from Yehudis. She just wished things could be different between her and her mother-in-law. After all, she got along so well with everyone else — neighbors, acquaintances and friends. She had never had any social problems.

"That's it. I hung up." Yehudis sat down next to her. "I'm sorry. I called her the minute before you walked in, so I couldn't get off the phone that fast."

"That's okay. After all, I didn't tell you I was coming, so why should you interrupt your conversation because of me? By the way, I'm really impressed with the way you talk to your mother-in-law. I couldn't help but overhear," she apologized. "You're so generous to her. I am absolutely jealous."

"What's the big deal?" Yehudis replied, puzzled. "My mother-in-law is a wonderful woman. She helps us in every way she can and never begrudges me anything. Now that I think of it, it's a good thing you came down because you saved me a trip up to your house. I was just going up to ask your advice. We're planning a surprise birthday party in my mother-in-law's honor. I asked her for her fish recipe because that's what I'm planning to bring. The whole story about my husband insisting her fish is the best he's ever had was just an excuse to get the recipe out of her without her suspecting anything," Yehudis chuckled.

"What I wanted to ask you about," she continued, "was what to buy her as a gift. My sister-in-law and I want to buy a gift together, but we haven't come up with anything. Do you have any ideas?"

Riki's mind was a blank. She couldn't think of a single reasonable suggestion. "A sweater, maybe?" she finally ventured.

"A sweater?" Yehudis repeated, surprised. "A sweater, for a mother-in-law? A sweater is something you buy for yourself. I mean, everyone has her own personal taste in clothes. I was thinking more along the lines of a pretty serving dish, or maybe a silver picture frame. But I couldn't think of anything special enough."

Riki couldn't either. The whole conversation seemed absurd to her. Yossi was getting restless, and Riki realized that this wasn't the right time to ask for help regarding the bas mitzva party. She said good-bye to her neighbor and left, closing the door behind her.

A sweater! she said to herself as she climbed the stairs. *How did such an absurd suggestion pop into my mind? A sweater, of all things.* Since when does one buy a sweater for a mother-in-law?

She imagined the cozy feel of soft wool. Maybe that was just what she needed in her relationship with her mother-in-law — something natural and warm to melt the ice between them. No, in her relationship with her mother-in-law, she wouldn't have opted for a decorative gift like the ones Yehudis suggested. She would have chosen something soft and cozy that you felt like hugging close.

Riki continued slowly climbing the stairs, still basking in the pleasant atmosphere of the phone call she had overheard at her neighbor's house. *What's come over you, Riki? Haven't you always longed to build a happy home? How did your young, smiling self turn into such an oppressive, grumbling wretch? Don't you know you're disturbing your husband's studies? He is undoubtedly suffering from the situation. You wanted a husband who would sit and learn. Nu, where are you in this venture?*

By the time she reached the second-floor landing, her frustration was complete. What about all the fancy speeches she used to give about respecting others, respecting one's parents, judging people favorably and loving your fellow Jew as yourself? Why couldn't the bitterness inside her melt? Where was her inner strength, those spiritual reservoirs she used to speak to her groups about?

She remembered snatches of those talks. "Only one who serves Hashem is truly free," she heard herself declaim. After all, she had explained to the group of girls, everyone is responsible for his own situation in life. Each of us can choose whether to get angry or remain calm, whether to wallow in other people's insults or ignore them.

She had spoken with such confidence then. Her ideas had been so strong, her vision so unclouded by the obstacles she faced today.

Why couldn't she find it in her heart to be generous to others? Was she no longer capable of behaving with an *ayin tova*?

Perhaps her mother-in-law could indeed use a "sweater" to help repair the relationship between them. *And what do I need?* she mused. *I think I could use a vacuum cleaner to get the dust out of my eyes.*

How ironic! She used to enjoy metaphors like that way back when she was a Bnos leader, but could they be of any real help to her now?

She wondered.

14

"WHAT'S WITH THIS NOTICE? Can I take it down?" Morah Dina, the first-grade teacher, stood facing the bulletin board in the teachers' lounge, trying to find an empty space to tack up the invitation she held in her hand.

"What notice?" asked another teacher coming up behind her.

"That yellow one." Dina pointed to a creased, faded piece of paper occupying a central spot on the bulletin board. "I want to hang up my son's bar mitzva invitation, but there's no free space. I think this notice has been hanging here for at least two weeks. Do you think we still need it?"

At ten past ten, it was recess time at Ohr Rivka. Dozens of teachers crowded into the cramped teachers' lounge, sitting around a long table that occupied almost the entire room. Dina was about to remove the yellow notice from the bulletin board when a voice from the corner of the room suddenly called out, "No! Don't take it off!"

The noisy clatter of spoons stirring steaming cups of coffee and tea stopped for a moment. Curious pairs of eyes turned in the direction of the voice. Rachel, the vivacious arts and crafts teacher, stood in the corner. Cheeks flushed, she explained heatedly, "It's a very important notice. Someone needs help, and so far, no one's responded. The Caring Heart organization asked me to hang it up here. Can we let it stay up a little longer? Maybe some teachers will still pay attention to the notice. Maybe someone knows someone else who can help."

A murmur of curiosity rippled through the room. Heads turned in the direction of the bulletin board; others swiveled toward Rachel.

"What's it all about?"

"What kind of help are they looking for?"

"What notice is she talking about?"

Rachel, pleased at the attention the notice had inadvertently earned, made the most of the opportunity. "Dina," she asked the teacher still standing next to the bulletin board, "would you mind reading the notice aloud, now that we have everyone's attention?"

Hesitating for just a moment, Dina cleared her throat and began to read:

"Wanted: Warm, loving care for a sweet one-and-a-half-year-old baby girl with Down syndrome two afternoons a week."

Once again, murmurs filled the room, louder this time.

"I read that notice plenty of times, but what can I do?"

"What can I tell you, I just about manage with my own."

"My heart aches when I hear such things. If they're asking for help, the situation must be desperate. But it's hard to respond to such a request. Not everyone can do it."

"You're right — and that's why no one *has* responded yet. You heard what Rachel said."

Esther Schwartz, another substitute teacher, turned to Riki. "It's not just any baby. We're not only talking about finding time. I think you'd have to know something about Down syndrome. I, for one, would be afraid of the responsibility."

"I don't know if that's true," Riki disagreed. "I mean, children with Down syndrome function on different levels. It's really very individual.

"I was a counselor in Ezer Mizion's day camp for children with special needs two years running, and taking care of a Down syndrome child doesn't faze me. I would imagine that if this notice is put up for anyone to answer, the job doesn't take special training."

"Maybe you should think about it, then," Esther suggested.

"Me?" Riki turned to her in surprise. "I have a baby at home. Believe me, it's hard enough balancing home and work as it is. How can I take on anything else?"

"Why do they need help? Is the mother sick, or what?" a young teacher asked.

"What makes you think she's sick?" a voice said. "She probably just gave birth or something like that. There doesn't have to be a special reason for the mother of a special needs child to feel she needs extra help twice a week."

"You're right," Rachel said. "The mother isn't sick, but she's near collapse. She has ten children, with the oldest fifteen. He's in yeshiva. Then comes a bunch of boys, with, I think, a ten-year-old girl in the middle. The youngest is two months old. The father's in *kollel*. After the baby was born, neighbors helped with the little girl. Some of the older girls in the neighborhood took her out after school, but it didn't last long." Rachel summed up the situation with a sad shrug.

"Three weeks ago," she continued, "Mrs. Perlstein, the coordinator of the Caring Heart organization, approached me and asked if I could put a notice in the teachers' lounge. She's surprised at the lack of response. She says it's never happened to her before."

No response at all! I wonder if my mother would be interested, Riki thought. In her mind's eye, she could already see the little girl playing happily on her mother's kitchen floor. The warm image was completed by her sister and brother lovingly handing toys to the child, who smiled gratefully in return.

"Children with Down syndrome are so warm and affectionate. The poor kid. No response for a whole month! With a new baby, the mother is probably not getting a good night's sleep, either."

Riki recalled what a difficult time she'd had at first with her Yossi. How could anyone ignore such a heartfelt appeal? She felt she had to do something to help. Maybe she'd call her mother that very day. She remembered how when she was in first grade, her mother had cared for a baby with Down syndrome for a few months until a permanent arrangement could be found.

The memory became clearer in her mind. How could she have forgotten? When they had come to take the child, she'd sobbed into her pillow — she'd grown so close to him. What had his name been?

The shrill ringing of the bell startled her, cutting off her thoughts in midstream. Chairs scraped back as teachers stood up and began moving toward the door. Morah Dina finally managed to find a spot for her invitation on the upper right-hand side of the large corkboard.

"You're all invited to my son's bar mitzva," she called out after the departing teachers. "Please take a look at the card hanging here and consider it a personal invitation."

The small room, so full and crowded just a few minutes ago, was almost empty. Only a few teachers and half-empty cups remained. Rachel was already at the door when Riki tapped her on the shoulder.

"Rachel," she said quietly, "I think I might be able to help."

"Really?" Rachel's eyes lit up. "Are you thinking of taking the little girl?"

"No, not me," Riki hurried to make things clear. "It's my mother — I think she might be able to."

She was suddenly overcome by a wave of misgivings.

Whatever made her suggest such a thing without asking her mother first? Her mother was no youngster, and the workload had grown considerably since the time when she was a little girl.

"It's a possibility. I'm not sure," she concluded hesitantly.

"Where does she live?" asked Rachel, practical as ever.

"In the center of town, just off Strauss," Riki responded reluctantly, afraid she'd gotten into a mess and annoyed at herself. "On second thought—"

"It won't work," Rachel cut her off. "The girl's in Ramot. It's too far to bring her. Wait a minute, though. *You* live in Ramot, don't you?" There was a new gleam in Rachel's eye. "What about you?"

"Me?"

"Yes, you. Why not?" The gleam turned to a blaze. "You're perfect for it. Besides, you're the generous, volunteering type."

"Me? What makes you think so?"

"Riki volunteered at a day camp for children with Down syndrome," offered Esther Schwartz, who had somehow suddenly appeared to provide that bit of information.

"You see?" Rachel announced gleefully. "We heard so much about you. You're the type who doesn't scare easily. Challenges don't faze you. This is a *chessed* of unlimited proportions, believe me. Mrs. Perlstein, the coordinator, will do anything to make the job easier. She'll provide guidance and support. You won't be on your own. It's a tremendous *chessed*."

A tremendous chessed. The words struck a hidden chord, one of eagerness to help others, a wish long hidden deep within Riki's heart waiting to be realized.

"I'll have to think about it," she finally said. The words were out before she had a chance to think them through. "I must run to class. I'll be in touch."

On the way home from school during the late afternoon, Riki spotted the by-now familiar yellow notice on a lamppost. The paper blew in the wind, barely clinging to the thin piece of Scotch tape. It was only a matter of time before it would float away and get trampled under the feet of passersby. Somewhere out there a sweet little girl needed some care while right now, her little Yossi was probably smiling up at his father, who had surely picked him up from the baby-sitter.

She entered the corner store to buy bread and milk. There, at the entrance, she spotted the same notice. Was it a Heaven-sent message of some sort? Why hadn't she noticed it before?

"Wanted: Warm home..." Was her home warm? She certainly wanted it to be, with small children playing on the rug and lots of warmth and love and laughter. Did warmth create itself, or did it require someone to painstakingly gather logs, pile them up in a heap, and light them, one by one, until a warm fire rose in the fireplace and spread its pleasant warmth throughout the entire house?

Perhaps *Hakadosh baruch Hu* was indeed sending her a message. Maybe He wanted her to do something, to grow and improve. She would talk to Daniel about it.

At home, her husband and little boy were waiting for her. Yossi was sitting in Daniel's lap, a contented look on his face. He smiled at his mother when he saw her.

"Someone named Rachel called twice," her husband told her as she dropped her briefcase on the floor. "It sounded urgent. She asked that you call the moment you come in."

"I don't understand," murmured Riki by way of an answer. "I spoke to her at ten o'clock this morning about a baby who needs care," she said and then quickly filled Daniel in on the details of that morning's discussion in the teacher's lounge. "I thought we might try it for a day or two. It would be a chance to do a real *chessed*. And I think Yossi would enjoy the company. What do you think?" She waited eagerly to hear her husband's opinion.

Daniel listened quietly, as was his habit. He thought the matter over for a moment before responding, with a quick smile,

"Why not? Doesn't it say *'Mila dibeita'*? It's up to the woman of the house, no? As it is you collect all the neighbors' children and bring them over here! Just today, I scraped a few stickers off the kitchen chairs and fished a crayon out of the bathtub drain. Why not? It really is a mitzva."

Riki picked up the phone to call Rachel.

15

THE AFTERNOON'S EVENTS took a wholly unexpected turn. Barely an hour had passed since Riki had spoken on the phone with Rachel about caring for the little girl two afternoons a week, when she heard a timid knock on the door.

Riki hesitated, debating whether or not to answer it. It was probably one of the neighbors' children wanting to borrow something or perhaps to play with Yossi, who had finally dropped off to sleep moments earlier. Daniel had just left for his afternoon study session, so Riki now had a golden opportunity to snuggle under the covers and catch a few moments of rest from her busy day.

She briefly considered ignoring the knock, hoping the caller would soon give up and go away, but it seemed that whoever was standing at the door had no intention of giving up so fast. On the contrary, it seemed to Riki that the knocks were growing steadily more insistent with each passing moment. Soon the caller gave up knocking and began buzzing the bell, which echoed loudly through the quiet apartment. Now Riki ran hurriedly to answer the door before the bell woke Yossi. When she did, she encountered a totally unexpected sight.

In the doorway stood a blue-eyed, curly-haired girl who looked to be about ten. In one arm, she struggled to hold a toddler; in the other, she clutched a bottle of milk and a disposable diaper. Clearly uncomfortable, the girl blurted out, "My mother said to bring her here."

Before Riki could make sense out of what was going on, the girl held out the baby for Riki to take.

"Your mother what?" Riki asked, still not understanding what was going on. Her arms remained limply at her sides, as if unsure of what was expected of them at this moment.

"My mother said you're going to take care of my sister," the girl tried again, tightening her hold on the child once more. For the first time since she'd opened the door, Riki looked at the toddler's chubby face. That's when it all clicked.

"Oh, so this is her!" she exclaimed, finally grasping who her visitors were.

Reaching out, Riki took the child from her big sister. "No one told me she'd be coming today," she said, explaining her behavior. She was surprised and confused — and just the tiniest bit annoyed. "We didn't speak about when I would begin. I thought I'd start next week. Are you sure you were told to bring her here today?"

"Uh-huh," the girl said with a shrug. She handed Riki the disposable diaper. "My mother told me she found a baby-sitter and said I should bring you my sister." She turned around and skipped down the steps, clearly glad to be done with the uncomfortable job her mother had assigned her.

"Wait a minute!" Riki called after her, still in a state of shock. "When are you coming back to pick her up?"

The answer she received was the same annoying shrug. "I don't know," the girl called up the stairwell. "I'll ask my mother."

"Please do," said Riki. "And tell her that this is my first time, so I still don't know...." She wanted to explain that she had not yet received any instructions, that she had no idea what to do, that she was confused. "We haven't spoken at all," she finally said, "so I think it would be a good idea if you came to pick her up in two hours, okay?" She glanced at her watch. "Come back at five."

"Okay," the girl sang out, skipping down two more stairs.

"Wait!" Riki out again. "When is she supposed to eat?"

Another shrug. Riki could see the desperate look in the girl's blue eyes as she struggled to come up with an answer.

"Uh, maybe in, um, another hour? She usually cries when she's hungry."

"All right," Riki said, finally letting her go. She wasn't going to get much more than shrugs in reply anyway. "Run on home, and don't forget to come pick her up at five, okay?"

The sound of the retreating footsteps almost drowned out the faint "okay" echoing through the hallway.

"Good for you, Riki," she muttered to herself. "You've gotten yourself into big trouble this time. What are you going to do now? What came over Rachel? I distinctly heard her say I'd be given guidance and a chance to meet with the mother. She made it clear that she wasn't talking about today!"

The toddler squirmed in her arms. Riki looked at her, and she returned the stare, reflecting Riki's terror in her own eyes.

"Oh, I'm sorry, sweetie." Riki snapped back to reality and hugged the child close. "I must look really scary to you. Don't be scared of me, honey. What's your name? Rachel? Tami? Rivki? No one even told me!"

She put the bottle of milk and the disposable diaper on the table.

"Anyway, my annoyance has nothing to do with you," she assured the child. "I'm just confused, and I think it's unfair to be treated this way, but that's not your problem. You didn't do anything wrong. Come on, let's think of something to do, okay?

Should I call you Chani or maybe Shifra? Then we'll call Rachel and, boy, will she get it!"

The baby suddenly smiled.

"You're cute!" Riki exclaimed, pleased to note that she really was a sweet little girl. "At least it won't be hard to love you," she rambled on.

She looked around for a place to set the child down so that she'd have a few minutes to get organized and plan the rest of the two-hour period. She was too big for a baby carriage, and Yossi was in the crib, still fast asleep. Instinctively, Riki bent down and sat the little girl on the floor. Worried it might be too cold for her on the marble floor, Riki hurried to get a blanket to spread under her. She had taken no more than a few steps when she heard a soft thud behind her followed by a wail of pain and protest.

Riki spun around. Oh no! The baby had toppled over and banged her head. Her sobs grew stronger.

I should have thought of that, Riki chided herself. *She looks big enough to sit by herself, but I know nothing about her development. Yossi's so much younger, but he's been able to sit alone for some time now. It didn't occur to me that a child this age might not be able to manage.*

Filled with concern and self-reproach, Riki scooped up the child and carried her into the room to look for a blanket.

The baby was still whimpering softly, and Riki found herself stroking the soft, curly hair over and over in an effort to comfort her. Noticing that her chin was wet, Riki reached for a tissue and gently wiped the baby's face.

Looking around for something to distract her with, Riki suddenly spotted the tape recorder on a shelf in her dining room. She hit the Play button, and a bouncy melody filled the room. The baby immediately stopped crying and smiled at Riki, who smiled back in relief.

■ ■ ■

The coordinator of the Caring Heart organization turned various shades of scarlet and purple as she listened to Rachel's account of what had transpired over the telephone.

"Do you mean to tell me the child is already there?" Mrs. Perlstein asked in disbelief.

"That's what Riki Abramson told me just now," Rachel replied. "An hour after I told you Riki was willing to volunteer, Faigy showed up at her door with the baby. I thought maybe we'd misunderstood each other," she explained. "I thought I'd made it clear that Riki was willing to begin next week. I feel really uncomfortable, because I promised her she'd receive training and support, and now everything just fell on her all at once."

"I understood you perfectly," sighed Mrs. Perlstein, "and I passed on the message that way too. The mother probably misunderstood. Or else she didn't hear me right, which just proves how badly she needs the help. Anyway, I'm dropping everything right now to run over to the volunteer's house to give her some tips. I wouldn't want her to give up before she even tries."

■ ■ ■

Mrs. Perlstein paused for a moment before ringing the Abramsons' bell. Breathing heavily with exertion, she took a few deep breaths and waited for the wild pounding of her heart to subside. She'd run the entire distance from her house to Riki's. She used the time to compose an apology in her mind and braced herself to meet an irate — or frantically helpless — young woman.

The scene that greeted her when Riki opened the door was not at all what she'd expected. The young woman who invited her inside seemed calm and in control. Pleasant music filled the house, and Mrs. Perlstein soon spotted little Brachi lying contentedly on the floor in the guest room.

"I see you're managing beautifully," she said, forgetting all about the speech she'd prepared. "Rachel told me you were absolutely frantic, so I rushed over immediately."

"Well, it did come as a surprise," Riki admitted. "I wasn't expecting the baby today. I phoned Rachel as soon as I could to tell her what had happened. Then I started thinking about what I ought to do."

"Well, it looks like you did exactly the right thing." Mrs. Perlstein was obviously impressed. "The music, for example — that's just the right thing for her. How did you know that putting on a tape was a good idea? Did Rachel tell you?"

"No, it wasn't Rachel. I just remembered that children with Down syndrome usually love music. At least that's what I heard when I volunteered in a day camp for special children."

"And the rest?" Mrs. Perlstein swept her arm to indicate the brightly colored toys strewn on the blanket around the baby, who was playing with a cuddly fur teddy bear. "We teach all our volunteers to use tactile toys — like that teddy bear, for instance. Where did you get that idea from? Was that also from the day camp?"

"No, not at all," Riki replied. "It just occurred to me. Maybe I heard about it when I took my baby for a checkup. The nurse did say that stimulation was very important for children's sensory and motor development, so I looked around the house to see what I could give her."

The bell rang for the third time that afternoon. This time, though, the door opened even before Riki could answer it. A hearty "Hello!" sounded from the doorway.

"Mommy?" Riki asked, recognizing the voice immediately. "What a surprise! I'm so glad you came!"

Chaya Baum appeared in the doorway of the dining room, holding her handbag and two shopping bags. Her eyes widened in astonishment as she took in the scene before her. "Riki, what's going on here?"

Before Riki could reply, her mother, noticing Mrs. Perlstein for the first time, said a polite hello.

"Are you her mother?" Mrs. Perlstein asked warmly.

"Yes, I guess I am." Chaya gave a tentative smile.

"In that case," declared Mrs. Perlstein emphatically, "I want you to know that you have an absolutely wonderful daughter!"

16

MR. BAUM WAS JUST ABOUT TO LOCK the kitchen doors in the *yeshiva ketana* where he worked, when he suddenly noticed a lonely looking boy pacing the narrow hallway that led to the kitchen.

There was nothing unusual about the boy's being there, given that the pay phone was located at the far end of the passage. Still, something about his manner caught Mr. Baum's attention.

"Looking for something?" he asked, inserting his key in the lock.

"No," the boy said, shrugging his shoulders.

To Avraham Baum, his voice sounded a little choked up. He even thought there might be tears in the boy's eyes, but he couldn't be sure.

Another first-year student, he mused. *He probably couldn't get through to his parents tonight, and he's feeling homesick.* He felt a sudden rush of fatherly warmth toward the lonely boy, but what could he do?

As he turned to leave, an idea suddenly occurred to him.

"Hey, listen," he called after the boy, who stopped in his tracks and turned around. "Come here a minute, okay?"

The boy approached him slowly, wondering what the cook wanted.

"How about a snack?" Avraham asked, putting an arm around the boy's thin shoulders.

"Me? What for?" the boy wondered aloud.

"Yes, you. Who else?" Avraham said jovially. "There's a chunk of cold watermelon left over from today's lunch. How about it? There's nothing like a delicious piece of watermelon to make you forget your troubles."

"I haven't got any troubles," the boy said with a smile.

"Best news I've heard all day," Avraham gave him a friendly slap on the back. "Come on, make a *bracha* and enjoy," he said warmly, opening the kitchen doors and leading the boy inside.

■ ■ ■

When Avraham got home, Shuki came running to greet him.

"Daddy," he cried, "I won a prize at *masmidim*! I haven't missed even one day the whole month."

"Hey, that's great." Avraham gathered up Shuki in his arms for a hug.

If not me or Ephraim, he thought to himself, *maybe at least Shuki will amount to something.*

He was in a good mood. The image of the boy at yeshiva still lingered in his mind. By the time he had left the yeshiva, the boy had been smiling as he munched on the juicy red watermelon with obvious pleasure.

Devora was already in bed, and his wife was in the kitchen putting the finishing touches on his meal. She had gotten home just under an hour ago.

"Regards from Riki," she said, sitting down at the table.

"Riki?" He was mildly surprised. "When did you see her? Was she here today?"

Before his wife could answer, Shuki came into the kitchen and sat down at the table with them.

"Shuki, you've already eaten supper," his mother reminded him. "If you're still hungry, take a couple of cookies and a glass of milk, and don't forget to brush your teeth when you're finished. Then it's bedtime for you."

Shuki made a face.

"Shuki! Get moving!" she demanded more sharply than usual. She was impatient to share her thoughts with her husband.

The two waited until Shuki left the kitchen. Chaya then took up where she'd left off.

"No, she didn't come by today. This time, I visited her for a change."

"What made you decide to do that?" Riki was a fairly frequent visitor. Their central location made it easy for her to pop over for a brief visit whenever she was in the center of town on an errand. Besides, she and Daniel often came for Shabbos. There was really no reason for his wife to travel all the way out to Ramot to see Riki.

"I was out shopping this afternoon," she explained, "and I saw a sweet little outfit for Yossi, nothing too expensive. It had this little green shirt that I thought would match his eyes beautifully, and matching pants and suspenders. And then… I don't know…I just suddenly felt the urge to see her, in her house. I wanted to feel the pulse of that house, or maybe feel closer to her. I've been a bundle of nerves ever since that telephone conversation I had with her. Do I know the whole truth about her life? Who knows what else she might be hiding? What if something's wrong?"

Avraham shook his head. "You're imaging things."

"You may be right," Chaya conceded. "Anyway, I surprised

her, and you'll never guess what happened. I walked in to find a little baby girl with Down syndrome playing on a blanket! Riki volunteered to watch her two afternoons a week. I was shocked," she told her husband, who seemed no less surprised. "The coordinator of the volunteer organization was there, too. After she left, I told Riki exactly what I thought of the whole thing.

"'Why did you agree to take such a thing on yourself?' I asked her. 'You have so much on your head as it is — your own baby plus teaching. How can you handle a special child, too? What made you think you could manage it?'"

"Well, what did she say?" her husband asked, wondering himself if it wasn't too much for Riki.

"She looked me in the eye," Chaya related with undisguised satisfaction, "and she said, 'It was you, Mommy! I knew that you would have done it. I've always dreamed of building the kind of home I grew up in, a home where everyone gives and gives.'"

Chaya's voice cracked. "She says she pictured me and our home. Can you imagine? That's what she said! She pictured a baby crawling on the dining-room floor, with Shuki and Devora around her while I stood in the kitchen, calm, cool and collected. That's when she decided that she could do it too."

She fell silent, waiting to hear her husband's reaction. Although Avraham Baum was not by nature an expressive man, it was clear he was listening to his wife's words with great interest. He kept his eyes on his plate, but he wasn't really eating. His wife's description had moved him deeply.

"Ever since that phone call," Chaya whispered, "I thought our home hadn't been a good enough example for her. I was falling apart over it. I felt as though all my efforts over the years had been for nothing. But now I see I was wrong. The opposite is true. She wants nothing more than to have a home just like ours!"

A tear glistened in the corner of her eye. "I've been eating myself up all this time for nothing."

"That's exactly what I told you," her husband said. "I told you you were imagining things, but you didn't want to listen. People tend to get carried away when they're hurt and blow things out of proportion."

"You're right," Chaya agreed. "*Baruch Hashem*, the two hours I spent in Riki's house tonight more than made up for the anguish of the past few days. Everything was so calm and organized." Her eyes lit up. "The coordinator was so impressed. Do you know what she told me? She said, 'You have a wonderful daughter.' Those were her very words!"

"Listen, Riki *is* special. You should have seen how she thanked me for the outfit I bought Yossi. I mean, I know it was a present, but it didn't cost that much. She made such a big deal out of it, though, as if I'd bought him the most expensive outfit in the store. She always knows what to say to make a person feel good. She's really something. It's just a shame," she concluded with a sigh, "her mother-in-law doesn't seem to appreciate what a wonderful daughter-in-law she has."

"Well, that shouldn't bother you."

"That shouldn't bother me?" echoed Chaya. "Why not?" She was tense, her happy, expansive mood gone. "It could have a serious impact on Riki's future happiness. I've been debating whether to call the *machtenista* and talk to her. I could tell her about my visit to Riki's house today, what I saw there and what the coordinator said. Maybe then I could throw in that Riki feels her mother-in-law doesn't appreciate her. The more I think of it, the more I'm convinced I should say something to her. I'll explain to her how important it is for a mother-in-law to give her daughter-in-law the feeling that she likes her and admires her. I have so much to say to her!"

"Think it over very carefully before you do anything," Avraham finally managed to interject into his wife's impassioned speech. "You're assuming a conversation like that might help, but it just might make things worse."

Ever the practical one, his rational approach took the wind out of her sails. "If you think you can handle a conversation like that without getting all worked up and angry, if you think you can stay calm and pleasant, then go ahead and try. Hashem will surely help. Personally, I think it would be better if you just stuck a couple of nice stories and anecdotes about Riki and Daniel into your conversations with her every now and then."

"I'm not going to say a single kind word about Daniel from now on!" Chaya was adamant. Then, feeling she'd been too harsh, she added, "I know, I know. We're not playing a kids' game here. But still, it hurts. I've praised Daniel so much. Isn't Riki worth a compliment once in a while, too?"

"Riki's worth plenty of compliments, not just one," her husband said emphatically. "But if you really want to help her, what you ought to do is give her some encouragement. I don't know how helpful it is for you to get carried away every time she tells you about her mother-in-law."

"What do you mean?" Chaya was indignant. "My daughter's suffering and I shouldn't even hear her out?"

"I didn't say that. Listen, empathize and understand that she's going through a difficult time, just like you've been doing until now. But if you both get all worked up about it, it's not going to help. What's your goal — to give Riki the feeling that you don't like her mother-in-law either? Then what? Do you want her to show her dislike openly? Then her mother-in-law will certainly have good reason to find fault with her. What for?

"Look at it this way," he continued. "If Riki doesn't think well of her mother-in-law, maybe she's been acting according to the way she feels, cold and distant. That's going to produce a similar reaction on her mother-in-law's part. That's how it works — the way we treat others is the way they treat us back. But if you tell Riki that you're certain her mother-in-law means no harm and you try to give her the benefit of the doubt, I think it will be the best help you can give her."

It was a whole new way of looking at it. "Do you think Riki might be acting like what you said just now? I'll have to find out. If she is, then it's up to us to give her guidance. That's what parents are for."

Avraham looked at his watch and rose to get a *bentcher*. "My *Daf Yomi shiur* starts soon," he commented. "I've got to go now. But think about what I said, okay?"

■ ■ ■

Think she did. She stayed in the kitchen a long time after he left, musing over what he had said. His simple, wise words, although somewhat difficult to accept, had a surprisingly calming effect on her. A flexible person by nature, Chaya possessed the ability to accept a way of thinking different from her own. She was grateful to her husband for his sound advice, delivered with such a sense of stability and calm.

He's right, she thought. *It's always so distressing and hurtful when a person allows himself to get caught up in a fit of revenge, his only concern to prove the other person wrong. Many a disaster could be avoided with a positive approach, like my husband suggested, with humility and patience.*

Avraham, my "simple workingman husband," she mused. But then, what does *simple* mean?

When she was first married, Chaya had lived with the feeling that she'd compromised on her *shidduch* because of her background. Over the years, though, she'd come to realize she'd been mistaken. Avraham, with his two feet on the ground, saw things with more clarity than she did with all her philosophizing and education. Avraham was the one who had taught them all to take pleasure in the little things in life, to find the good in every event. He was also the one who had helped her make their home what it was — a home in which, as Riki put it, everyone was happy and loving, warm and helpful. Avraham's even temper and solid approach to life balanced her own tendency to get worked up and jump to conclusions.

She was lucky, Chaya realized, that she hadn't acted on her original plan. In her years of marriage to Avraham, she'd learned to see beyond the label others had tagged him with. She'd come to appreciate his finer qualities.

Eventually, she came to the conclusion that her feelings of having compromised stemmed from a warped outlook on life. External factors in no way force people to agree to an unsuitable *shidduch*.

The details of each person's life are orchestrated by G-d Himself, so that when the time comes, he marries the one destined for him from before the time of his birth. Who knows better than the *Ribbono shel Olam* which partner best suits us?

Yes, she must speak to Riki about all this. If she was looking for a way to offer her daughter *chizuk* and encouragement, this was one area in which Riki needed help. She knew it in her heart.

Daniel — she felt a rush of warmth and admiration just thinking of him. The negative thoughts she'd harbored about him when she was distressed now seemed silly. The supposed faults she ticked off on her mental checklist suddenly didn't seem that important. How many other men his age would let their wives volunteer for such a job and give them so much support and encouragement along the way?

She also liked his fine, quiet personality. True, his unassuming nature did not always serve to make a favorable first impression on others, but it really was an advantage for the people he came into daily contact with. He was a superb listener, too, always attentive and understanding.

This, then, was how she would help her daughter.

Riki's words drifted through her thoughts once again. "Mommy, let's not pretend we're not aware that the Abramson family would never have considered us for a *shidduch* if Danny hadn't been having such a hard time." The words no longer hurt her. To Chaya, it was clear that her daughter, like so many others, was entertaining a mistaken outlook on life that made things difficult for her. What she said, the way she put it, proved as much. Riki must be brought to realize that Daniel was the ideal partner for her, the one designated for from Above.

Chaya was determined her daughter would never utter such a sentence again.

17

MALKA WEISS PADDED TO THE KITCHEN in slippered feet, passing the dining room on her way. On the table were the remains of last night's party. The day before, her children had organized a surprise birthday party for her. She'd been delighted with her beloved — and clearly loving — family and had enjoyed herself immensely.

Her daughters had promised to clean up right after school. They'd been too tired last night, and she hadn't wanted to spoil the lovely atmosphere by insisting on them doing it at once, especially after they'd worked so hard arranging the whole thing.

The credit for the idea of throwing a surprise party really went to her daughters-in-law, Yehudis and Chani. They had called the children at home, suggested the idea and overseen all the details — at least, that was what her daughters had told her last night. Her heart swelled with *nachas* and love.

The water boiled, and Malka poured herself a cup of coffee. Through the arched kitchen window, she could see the clear blue sky, more full of promise than ever.

No, she wasn't a little girl who needed such elaborate birthday parties. Had her children asked her if she wanted a party, she would have told them to forget it and allow the day to pass the same way as every other one. She would have been content to celebrate the day by offering a heartfelt prayer of thanks to the Creator for having granted her another year of life and for giving her the *nachas* of such wonderful children and grandchildren.

What really moved her was the depth of her family's emotions. Their desire to make her happy was evident in all the thought and effort they had invested in getting every detail right.

Her married children had given her a beautiful leather-bound siddur. Her old siddur, the one she'd received for her engagement, was falling apart from years of use. When she'd bought Chani, her second daughter-in-law, a siddur, she'd debated for a moment whether to buy herself one as well, but felt it wasn't necessary. *You've got married children already,* she'd chided herself. *Why do you want to pretend you're a young kalla?* She'd continued pouring out her *tefillos* from the yellowed pages of her aging siddur.

Now she had a new one, bound in rich, soft leather. Malka walked over to the bookcase to look at it once again. It wasn't the style *kallos* received; it was something altogether different, as if it was made especially for her. Someone very sensitive and loving had picked this particular *siddur* for her.

Her son Menachem had whispered that it had been Yehudis's idea. Chani had written a moving dedication inside the cover. Her two sons, Menachem and Shmuel, had purchased the gift together.

Fingering the gold embossed letters on the cover, Malka knew that her best gifts by far were her daughters-in-law themselves. They were so devoted to her, they might have been her own daughters. She had no doubt the very first *tefilla* she'd offer up to Hashem from the new siddur would be one of thanks for the wonderful family He'd given her.

Malka gathered a number of empty soda bottles and Chani's cake tray (what a delicious cake she'd baked in honor of the occasion!) and headed back to the kitchen. *After all, not every mother-in-law has such a good relationship with her daughters-in-law.*

Her glance fell on the tray of fish Yehudis had brought, and she laughed out loud, recalling the telephone conversation with her daughter-in-law the week before. She hadn't suspected a thing when Yehudis asked for the recipe. She'd fallen for Yehudis's story hook, line and sinker when she'd said Menachem loved her fish and wouldn't touch anything else. As a professional social worker, Malka was used to analyzing feelings and relationships, and she knew enough to genuinely appreciate Yehudis's gesture.

Yehudis and Chani are both so much more mature than I was at their age, she mused, making her way to the dining room once more. She'd noticed that Yehudis often praised Menachem in her presence, and she was aware that she did it to give her pleasure. In doing so, she'd allowed the natural bond that Yehudis was well aware existed between mother and child to continue after her son's marriage as well. "Why shouldn't you enjoy hearing good things about your son?" she'd once said to Malka. Unlike many other young wives, she wasn't afraid the closeness would interfere in her life.

"I remember when my mother married off my eldest brother," she'd told Malka during one of their heart-to-heart Friday night talks. "She was so pleased to hear from her daughter-in-law what a considerate, helpful husband he was and how well he was learning. After all, a mother is still a mother even after her children are married, isn't she? A daughter-in-law ought to respect that."

She herself had never talked that openly with her own mother-in-law, although she was no less caring or sensitive than Yehudis. She had never seen the point in discussions that only served to stress how close her husband and his mother were. She'd have been indignant if her husband had even said that he liked his mother's fish better than hers. And she certainly wouldn't have said anything remotely like what Chani told her yesterday. She'd phoned her son Shmuel and chatted with Chani for about fifteen minutes, then asked how Shmuel was doing.

"Oh, he's just walking in from *kollel* now," Chani reported.

"Okay, then, send him best regards," she'd replied, intending to hang up immediately so as not to disturb.

"Wait a minute! Don't you want to talk to him?" Chani had asked in genuine puzzlement.

"Oh, of course I do, but I'll call later," Malka answered with a chuckle.

"Oh, come on!" Chani laughed. "The minute he hears it's his mother on the phone, his whole face lights up. Hold on a sec — here he is."

No, Malka thought, gazing at the beautiful view from the window, *I wasn't exactly what you'd call generous with my mother-in-law. Was I less caring than they are?*

Malka puttered around the kitchen, straightening it up before she left for work. *What a mess. This is the only thing that bothers me about them.* The mess they left behind whenever they came to visit was really inexcusable. Sure, she understood them. She understood them all too well. She remembered herself as a young wife. The tremendous responsibility of building a new home can seem overwhelming, and a visit to one's parents or in-laws comes as a welcome opportunity to relax. *I've got to take a break*, the thinking went. *Let someone else serve, clear off the table and keep an eye on the kids for a change.*

Malka wanted to give her married children a chance to rest and recuperate — but there was a limit to what she could do. She had a full-time job, and the girls still at home had a hard time managing the kitchen without her help.

If only we had a maid to wait on us, she mused, removing a tray full of half-empty paper cups and the compote glassware, *I'd be more than willing to host the kids whenever they felt like coming for a visit.* The fruit compote they had eaten the night before was the same kind her mother-in-law had once brought her when she'd come for a visit. "I brought some compote, the kind Yisrael likes," she had proudly announced, placing the jar in Malka's hands.

On another occasion, she'd baked a poppy seed cake especially for Yisrael. Malka recalled how hurt she had been both times, although now she couldn't understand what had so upset her then. Had she truly been so inconsiderate of her mother-in-law's feelings?

In all fairness to herself, she'd never really had the opportunity to make room for the special bond between mother and son because her mother-in-law had seen to that herself.

Looking back, Malka realized that she should not have felt so hurt. Her mother-in-law had come to Eretz Yisrael just a short while before the Holocaust broke out. Although she was fortunate to pass through those terrible years in safety, she lost her entire family. She was alone until she met Malka's father-in-law, also the sole survivor of a large family. Then she'd had two sons and a daughter — the *"yahrtzeit lecht"* for her family.

Her husband had found work as a contractor. He had worked long hours to support his family, while she dedicated herself to the task of raising her three children, who represented all her hopes and dreams, her entire world. When her oldest, the girl, got married and moved abroad, her mother-in-law's world grew dark. She couldn't cope with separation yet again.

Then the two boys, Yisrael and Aryeh, got married, one after the other, and she'd found herself with an empty nest at a relatively young age. Outwardly, she appeared to be a most fortunate woman. She had a good husband who made a comfortable living, and she'd married off her children in good health. In truth, though, she felt empty and unfulfilled. She had no satisfying or worthwhile occupation with which to fill her time.

The separation from her children had been difficult for her, Malka later understood. She had drawn her fulfillment and satisfaction from caring for them, and she'd had trouble accepting that they'd built their own homes and were now independent. As a result, she sometimes interfered in their lives, or would call and, as soon as Malka picked up the phone, demand to speak with her son without so much as a "How are you?" She'd obviously had no idea how much this behavior hurt her daughter-in-law.

Maybe that's why I'm supersensitive when it comes to telephone conversations with my sons, she thought. She made a point of never asking to speak with her son without first chatting pleasantly with her daughter-in-law, unless, of course, it was her son who answered her call. If she had something important to tell him, she tried to fill in her daughter-in-law so she wouldn't feel left out. In general, since her first son had gotten married, she'd made it a habit to address all her comments and questions to the couple, rather than to her son alone.

It hadn't been hard for her to act this way. Yes, she was close with her sons, but wasn't it only natural to extend that love to a new daughter-in-law joining the family?

I'm positive my sensitivity to the situation — because of my mother-in-law's unfortunate treatment of me — allows my daughters-in-law to feel good about our relationship. What was it she herself once told me in a rare moment of candor? "I never had a mother-in-law to learn from."

How much truth lay in that statement! Now, for the first time, Malka fully appreciated those wise words. Her mother-in-law had described the situation in a nutshell. She had never been given the tools to welcome a new daughter-in-law into the family. She had gone into the battle unprepared, without ever having been a daughter-in-law herself. The poor thing. She hadn't even had a chance to learn from someone else's mistakes.

In the bright kitchen, where the multicolored balloons still lent an air of festivity to the room, Malka suddenly felt a surge of pity for her elderly mother-in-law. In her mind's eye, she pictured her sitting in the lobby of the nursing home, bitter and full of complaints. She was still so dependent on her sons, and spent her every waking moment waiting for their visits. What a lonely existence.

Years ago, Malka hadn't understood her mother-in-law. She was young and inexperienced when it came to people's emotions. Now, as a professional social worker, she understood.

Why shouldn't she make up for lost time? Who said it was too late? Why couldn't she let bygones be bygones and begin showering her mother-in-law with love? Why shouldn't she visit her more often than once a week? She would help her out as the wife of her beloved son, without expecting too much in return. If she couldn't expect her mother-in-law to accept her as a daughter or even to give her a compliment now and then, so be it.

Also, she would make a conscious decision to allow the warm, natural bond between her husband and her mother-in-law to flourish unchecked.

With a start, Malka realized it was late. How time flew when she was in a hurry! She still had three clients to call on that day.

She eagerly reached for the new siddur, more anxious than ever to thank Hashem for His kindness.

She had another idea of how to thank Him, too. She would become a better daughter-in-law, taking her cue from her sons' wives. That very morning, she would go visit her elderly mother-in-law at the Nachalas Avos nursing home.

18

Silver-haired Gavriel Vidal leaned forward in his seat behind the driver of the number 66 bus to peer into the rearview mirror. The eyes staring back at him looked too tired, and the puffy bags beneath them irritated him. He reached up to smooth his hair, then he suddenly sat up with a start. Slipping his hand into his pocket, he withdrew a medium-sized black kippa and quickly placed it on his head.

He glanced impatiently at his watch and reached up to press the bell. He'd have to hurry. Old Mr. Schiller was probably waiting for him.

When the bus pulled up at the stop, Gavriel rose to his full height, just short of six feet, and got off. Walking briskly, he soon found himself on the small side street leading to the nursing home. He stopped at a kiosk for the morning paper and, after a moment's deliberation, a chocolate bar. With the paper tucked under his arm, he turned down the path to the nursing home.

Mr. Schiller was waiting impatiently in his private room, his siddur open before him and his tefillin bag at his side.

"Good morning, Mr. Schiller," Gavriel's voice rang out cheerfully. He patted the old man lightly on the back. "How was your night? Did you have a good breakfast?"

Mr. Schiller responded with nods and gestures, pointing to his tefillin as if to say, *Stop talking and let's get started.*

"Of course," Gavriel murmured. "I'm here to help you with your prayers, not to talk, isn't that so? I know, I'm a little late today. I had to take care of something at the bank, and there was a long line."

He began helping Mr. Schiller with his tefillin, taking the *batim* out of the boxes, unwinding the straps and then winding them around the old man's arm.

Sima Abramson entered the lobby with a purposeful stride and a somewhat troubled expression. She was clutching Tehilla's small hand in her own. The child seemed to be following her mother reluctantly.

"Good morning," she announced in the general direction of the small groups of residents and visitors gathered in the lobby.

"Good morning," Nadia replied from behind the snack bar. "What's wrong?" she asked, pointing at Tehilla. "Is she sick today?"

"No, she's not sick," Sima responded curtly. From the corner of her eye, she spotted Shoshana Coleman sitting next to her mother, looking in her direction. She nodded a greeting.

"Then why isn't she in school?"

"Nothing special." Sima smoothed Tehilla's hair. "I don't know myself whether or not to give in to her. This morning, she said her stomach hurt and insisted she couldn't go to school. Strangely enough, as soon as I told her she could stay home, the pain disappeared."

"No, it didn't," Tehilla objected. "It's not gone. My stomach still hurts a lot!"

"Her stomach was bothering her yesterday too," Sima told

Nadia, "and the day before as well. As far as she's concerned, the whole school might as well close down. Maybe we'll just send her back to kindergarten. How would that be, Tehilla? In kindergarten you'll have dolls and toys, and you won't have any homework to do."

"Maybe you ought to take her to the doctor," suggested Rina, one of the nurses, who had overheard the conversation. "She might have really caught something."

"I plan on doing just that," Sima said. "We have an appointment for eleven. In the meantime, Rina, can you take her with you to the supply room? You can let her help you organize the shelves."

Someone entered the lobby and greeted everyone with a cheerful "good morning." Sima turned around and recognized Malka Weiss, Ayala Weiss's daughter-in-law.

Sima wondered at the visit. It wasn't Malka Weiss's usual time to come.

"Your mother-in-law will be pleasantly surprised," she told the unexpected visitor. "I haven't seen her yet this morning. I think she's in the garden out back."

Malka nodded. Sima noticed she was carrying a foil-covered tray.

"I know she'll be surprised," Malka commented. "I just popped over for a few minutes to celebrate with her. It was my birthday yesterday, and my family prepared a surprise party in my honor. Can you imagine, at my age? I brought her some cake."

Sima walked with her to the back garden, curious to see how Mrs. Weiss senior would react.

In the corner of the patio, the elderly Mrs. Weiss sat up and rubbed her eyes in disbelief. "What's this? What have you brought me?" she asked, pointing to the tray as Malka hurried to remove the silver foil. "Oh. Cake. What happened? Did someone have a baby? No? What? Your birthday? Who made you a birthday party? Pull up a chair. Sit a while.

TIGHTROPE | 135

"You see? Someone remembered me, too," she called to Sima, spotting her at the doorway. "Come have a piece of cake."

"That's the director," she explained to her daughter-in-law. "Do you know her?"

"Yes, of course I do," Malka said as she sat down. "Please, have a piece." She offered a slice to Sima, who had walked over to join them. "You must taste this. It's delicious. My daughter-in-law baked it herself. Since my daughters-in-law were kind enough to surprise me with a birthday party, I decided to surprise *my* mother-in-law too." She turned to address her mother-in-law. "Shall I make you a cup of tea to go with the cake?"

"Okay. Why not?" the elder Mrs. Weiss agreed. She was still overwhelmed by her daughter-in-law's gesture.

Malka rose to prepare the tea, but Sima waved her back to her seat. "It's all right. I'll ask one of the aides to bring you a pot of tea. You sit here with your mother-in-law. You can't imagine how eagerly she awaits these visits. She usually sits here all alone. Now that she has company for a change, it's a shame for her to miss even a minute of it."

Malka caught the thinly veiled criticism, but chose to ignore it, telling herself, *She probably feels it's her duty to comment.*

The elder Mrs. Weiss turned and spotted her friend Mrs. Blau, who was sitting with her daughter, Shoshana Coleman. Today she had no reason to envy Mrs. Blau. Today she too had visitors; she too had someone who remembered her. *See*, she mentally informed Mrs. Blau, *here's my daughter-in-law, spending some time with me, just like that, on an ordinary morning. And look what delicious cake she brought with her!*

As she watched them, she saw the daughter stand up and ask her mother, "Would you like a cup of tea, too?" *That's funny*, Mrs. Weiss thought. *I hope Mrs. Blau won't start being jealous of me.*

On her way to the kitchen to get the tea for her mother, Shoshana spotted the director busy writing on her notepad.

"Uh, excuse me, Mrs. Abramson," she murmured. "Sorry to interrupt."

Sima looked up with a question in her eyes.

Shoshana took that as permission to continue. "It's about your little girl. I heard you talking about her stomachache. I don't want to interfere, but you can't be too careful. A child is only a child, and stomachaches can be serious."

Oblivious to the look on the director's face, she continued. "Of course, you may be right. It may very well be that she's faking. However, that in itself indicates a problem. She might be having trouble with a teacher or with the girls in her class. Maybe there's too much pressure. Whatever the reason, though, it's not her fault. Teasing her about going back to kindergarten is not going to solve the problem."

Sima's first reaction was to defend herself. "What gave you the impression that I wasn't taking it seriously?" The last thing she'd expected from Shoshana Coleman was a lecture on parenting. "We have a doctor's appointment scheduled."

"Look," Shoshana said quietly, "I didn't mean to sound like I was attacking you. I'm sure you're taking it seriously. It's just that I'm supersensitive to this kind of thing. You see, when I was a child, I suffered a lot from the way my problems were dismissed. I may be fifty years old now, but inside I sometimes still feel like I'm only seven. You wouldn't believe the scars I bear.

"I'll give you just one example. When I was in the fourth grade, I became scared stiff of taking out the garbage. I must have had an overactive imagination. That's the only way I can explain this irrational fear I had then. I was positive there was a huge monster lurking near the garbage cans just waiting to grab me and carry me off to its den. Naturally, I didn't dare tell this to anyone, least of all my mother. I knew she'd just laugh. She always called me a dreamer.

"What happened was that every time I said I was afraid to take out the garbage, she'd say I was just lazy and making up excuses and that I never did anything around the house.

"That left a scar, Mrs. Abramson. To this very day, I can't understand why she never once stopped to think what might be causing me to be so stubborn about the garbage. Why didn't she ever take the time to find out? Maybe she could have helped me learn to overcome my fears. Do you understand what I'm trying to say? People think that because children are small they can say what they want about them. We adults think we know them better than they know themselves. But scars like that last, Mrs. Abramson. Believe me, they last."

Tehilla suddenly came running in from the supply room. "Mommy!" she called out, interrupting the conversation. "Nadia said to tell you the curtain store called. She told them to call again in five minutes."

"Tell her I'm coming," Sima instructed her daughter. To Shoshana Coleman, she said, "You're right. We really do need to be more considerate when talking to children. But I know my daughter. She's not my first. I'm sure you understand that as the youngest child at home, she senses that I don't always have the determination to stick to my guns. Which, unfortunately, is the truth. I used to be much firmer with my children. Nowadays I have so much on my mind that I let her get away with far too much. She senses this and takes advantage of the situation."

"Did you ever consider that she might be acting that way precisely because you're so busy?" Shoshana refused to concede that her theory might be wrong. "If, as you say, she senses you're not focused on her, she might be trying to spend more time with you. You might want to think about it from that point of view."

"Could be." Sima felt the entire conversation was out of place. Why was this woman interfering with the way she was bringing up her daughter? She ought to just go back and take care of her mother and leave everyone else to take care of his own business. She didn't need any advice when it came to parenting, and she had to catch that phone call.

"I hope you'll excuse me now," she said to the woman. "I've got to run. Thanks anyway."

Shoshana remained standing in place, surprised at the abrupt manner in which the director had ended their conversation. Had she said something inappropriate, or was she just imagining that Mrs. Abramson seemed offended?

Sima took the stairs instead of the elevator. In the hall, she passed Mr. Schiller, who was being wheeled out to the porch. *Mr. Schiller seems better now that the new caregiver comes every day. Thank G-d it occurred to me to suggest to his daughter that she hire a private caregiver for the morning hours and that I caught her before she traveled abroad.* She made a mental note to tell Mrs. Stone about her father's improvement the next time she called.

What could the curtain store want? Had they already filled her order? She'd chosen material only two days ago.

"Hello?" It was Mr. Mizrachi. "There's a problem with the fabric you ordered. We don't have enough for three full floors. What I thought we could do is combine it with a different shade in a complementary color. With the two colors, there'll be enough. Actually, I think it will look even better than what we originally planned. How about coming over later today to see the material yourself? Things will move much faster if you come down here in person."

How about coming over? *How easy it sounds*, Sima thought, her head reeling. Her day, busy enough as it was, was steadily becoming unmanageable. First Tehilla and her stomachache, then the doctor's appointment, and now Mr. Mizrachi from Maale Adumim. But she had no choice. Choosing new curtain material for the nursing home was too important a job to entrust to anyone else. The color of the curtains in such places helped create the right ambiance. She trusted her taste, which had proved itself over and over again. In fact, she was responsible for most of the decor at Nachalas Avos. The wrong color or texture for the curtains was liable to ruin the serene atmosphere she'd worked so hard to create. She'd just have to go down herself.

The road from Jerusalem to Maale Adumim, she recalled, turned right before Ramot. If she left early enough, she might still manage to squeeze a visit to Ariel's and Danny's homes into her busy schedule. She hadn't been to see her grandchildren in ages, and this was a golden opportunity. The idea brought a smile to her lips, and she felt a surge of renewed energy.

19

ON HER WAY TO THE BNEI BRAK-JERUSALEM taxi stand, Sima passed a store selling imported children's clothes. She eyed the window display, debating whether to go inside. Buying quality clothing for her grandchildren was becoming something of an obsession, she realized. She loved to lavish pretty clothes and accessories on them, the kind their young parents couldn't afford — a warm pair of winter overalls, a name brand, of course, or a three-piece suit for the two-year-old. Sometimes it was an unusual sweater in the window that caught her eye, and once she'd bought a one-of-a-kind nightgown for Mali's three-year-old daughter.

Now, a plaid shirt with matching pants caught her fancy; it would be perfect for Chagi, Dassi's eldest. Perhaps she'd find a matching outfit for Duddy, his younger brother, too. Yes, she decided, she'd go in and ask. It was still fairly early, so she could spare the time to shop for the grandchildren. True, her pocketbook was overflowing with candies for them, but an outfit was still an outfit, a more substantial gift. She didn't want to show up empty-handed.

Inside, she let her eyes sweep over the shelves. If she was

going to buy something for Chagi and Duddy, she must find something for Daniel's Yossi. After all, she planned to stop by for a visit at their house, too.

Directly opposite her, hanging behind the saleswoman, was an adorable lightweight two-piece outfit in pale blue cotton. A crisp white collar added just the right touch. The saleswoman tried to show her another, newer garment that had just come in, something in a bright orange, but Sima preferred the classic pale blue to the more modern style.

"I like babies dressed in navy blue, white or pale blue," she told the saleswoman. "I know my taste is conservative, but children look so pure and angelic in those colors. For girls, of course, I prefer pink." She took out her credit card, paid for her purchases and left the shop.

■ ■ ■

Dassi received the phone call from her mother-in-law at four-thirty, when she was busy preparing sandwiches for the children before setting out for the park. "Hello, Dassi," Sima's voice had come over the line. "I'm here at the taxi stand on my way to Yerushalayim. I have some work-related errands to take care of, but I'd very much like to drop by to see you, too."

"Oh, that would be lovely," was Dassi's immediate reaction. She was truly delighted at the prospect of a visit from her mother-in-law.

"Until now I wasn't sure I'd really have the time," her mother-in-law went on, "but it seems I'll manage it after all. I have a meeting in Maale Adumim at seven. If the taxi leaves within the next few minutes as planned, I should be at your house at about five-thirty, and we'll have plenty of time together. Do me a favor, Dassi, would you? Can you give Riki a call and tell her I'll stop off there as well? Oh, I see the taxi filling up. I'd better run. See you!"

■ ■ ■

Riki left the neighborhood supermarket weighed down by two heavy shopping bags overflowing with groceries. She pushed them in the basket under Yossi's carriage and straightened up to glance at her son. He'd been fast asleep when she'd picked him up from the baby-sitter a few minutes ago. Now he was wide-awake, his large eyes staring in curiosity at the sky above. When he noticed his mother's face looking down at him, he broke out into a smile and raised his pudgy hands, begging her to pick him up.

Riki melted at the sight of him. Scooping him up in her arms, she whispered in his ear, "Oh, sweetie, you haven't seen your mommy in such a long time, isn't that right? You wanted your mommy, and she ran away! But don't worry. Now your mommy's here, and we'll be together for the whole afternoon!"

She pressed him close to her for another moment and suddenly, in a moment of reckless abandon, decided to forget about her original plans for the afternoon (including straightening up the house) and just spend the time sitting on a park bench with Yossi on her lap. She wanted to show him the children playing, the chirping birds, the green grass. She wanted to chat with a friend or acquaintance.

Why not? she thought to herself as she walked briskly in the direction of the nearby playground. *The work won't run away, neither will the dishes in the sink or the laundry waiting to be folded. Little Brachi isn't coming today, and it's too late to take a nap anyway. I might as well enjoy the afternoon in the park with my baby. He's entitled, after all, to spend some time with his mother, and I'm entitled to enjoy being a mother, too.*

Riki had been sitting on the park bench chatting with a neighbor for only ten minutes, bouncing Yossi on her knee, when she noticed her sister-in-law Dassi coming toward her with her two children. Dassi was all smiles.

"There you are!" she called out with a friendly wave. "I tried getting you at home and there was no answer. It's a good thing I decided to take the kids out to the park today."

Riki was still wondering why Dassi had been looking for her when Dassi explained. "Our mother-in-law called to say she's coming to visit us, and—"

"What do you mean, 'us'?" asked Riki in surprise.

"Us means you and me," Dassi said matter-of-factly. "She's got something to take care of in Maale Adumim, so she thought she'd stop by here on the way. She asked me to let you know, but you didn't answer the phone. I figured it wouldn't be the end of the world if she showed up without you knowing about it beforehand. But the kids wouldn't let me forget my promise to take them to the park, so I decided to come out for half an hour until she arrives. And then, surprise! I found you! Looks like it really was important that you get the message."

And how! Riki thought with a start. *If Dassi only knew what my house looked like right now, she wouldn't be grinning like that.* If Dassi hadn't told her about her mother-in-law's visit, she'd have sat in the park for another hour — and then she'd have had to invite her mother-in-law into the mess she hadn't gotten around to cleaning up. That was all she needed!

Her mother-in-law would never understand how it was that a young woman with only one child couldn't find the time to fold a load of laundry that had come out of the dryer a whole twenty-four hours ago. She certainly would not be able to comprehend how the same young woman could sit calmly on a park bench when she had a sink full of dirty breakfast dishes waiting at home.

It wasn't as if it happened every day. But on the day it did, her mother-in-law chose to come visit. She had to get home, and fast.

"It's a good thing you told me," Riki said to her sister-in-law as she stood up.

"Where are you running off to?" Dassi asked in surprise. "She won't be here for another half hour at least, and then she'll probably come up to me first. There's no need to rush."

"The house is empty," Riki stammered, quickly strapping Yossi into his stroller. "I have nothing to offer her."

"Don't be silly. From what I gathered, she's just stopping by for a short visit. Anyway, she'll be at my house first. I took some cake out of the freezer, so she won't be hungry by the time she gets to you."

That's Dassi for you, thought Riki. *She's always so calm. How come she never sees things my way? So what if she's Mrs. Perfect? Cakes always ready in the freezer, toys lined up on their shelves, dishes washed immediately after use. She never needs to run home to straighten things up because everything's always perfectly neat and clean to begin with. Can't she understand that things might be different for other people? Doesn't she realize that it's legitimate for someone — me, for instance — to feel slightly nervous when she's suddenly informed that an unexpected guest is about to arrive, especially when it's her shvigger? Why does she always put me on the spot? Why is she making things so hard for me with her innocent comments?*

Riki felt her nerves about to explode. She shifted from one foot to the other, listening to Dassi as though in a haze.

"So let's see your little Yossi," Dassi was saying warmly. "I haven't seen him in ages! What's new, Yossi?" The loving aunt was already bending over the stroller, unbuckling the strap and lifting out the smiling little boy.

■ ■ ■

The Bnei Brak-Jerusalem taxi service left Sima off on Strauss Street where she flagged down a taxi to Ramot. She felt pressed for time. Heavy traffic had held them up. Instead of arriving at her Dassi's house at five-thirty, as planned, she'd probably be at least a quarter of an hour late. Well, she'd still have enough time to enjoy playing with her grandchildren.

She gave the driver the address and settled herself comfortably in the back seat. She smiled, thinking of the warm welcome Chagi and Duddy were sure to give her. She was glad she'd bought the outfits. They were just perfect for those two. She was sure Dassi would be pleased. It was nice to see, time and time again, how similar their tastes were. The light fixture she'd purchased for the children's room as a gift for Chagi's birth had also hit the spot. "That's exactly the kind I wanted," Dassi had exclaimed with obvious pleasure. "How did you guess?"

In general, mused Sima as the taxi sped on, she had a much easier time with Dassi — not that she had anything against Riki, G-d forbid. Riki was definitely a smart girl with a good heart, but the fact remained that she and Dassi were on the same wavelength. She felt more secure with Dassi, as though she was on home turf. Dassi's way of thinking, her whole approach to life, suited Sima's own. They'd gotten along beautifully from the moment they'd met.

With Riki, unfortunately, things were different. She couldn't even be sure Riki would like the outfit she'd bought for Yossi. In fact, she was positive the style was different from what Riki usually bought. Riki's opinion on so many matters — how a home should look, what was more important and what was less so, what was pretty and what was not — was different from hers.

Actually, she often found herself at odds with Riki's opinion on various matters. But what could she do? She still wasn't sure whether the differences between them stemmed from the fact that they had very different personalities or from the fact that they had been brought up so differently. There was no arguing that Dassi's family was more like their own.

"Oh, no!" Sima clapped a hand to her mouth in dismay. A long line of cars stretched before them, slowed to a crawl by a broken traffic light. A policeman stood in the center of the road directing traffic. The driver muttered under his breath, while Sima uttered a quiet prayer that Hashem help her proceed quickly so that she'd still be able to visit her grandchildren, if only for a short while.

She wouldn't be so nervous if she had only one visit to make, but she wanted to make two stops. That was the price she had to pay for both sons living in the same neighborhood. There were, of course, advantages, but the need to squeeze in two visits every time she came to the neighborhood was a decided disadvantage. It wasn't easy, but she knew she had no choice in the matter.

At six-thirty, tired and distraught, Sima rang the bell at Dassi's house.

■ ■ ■

By seven forty-five, Riki was still waiting, her impatience mounting. She'd washed the dishes, folded the laundry, changed Yossi's clothes and even prepared cheese blintzes. Finally, she decided that perhaps the time had come to phone Dassi and find out just when her mother-in-law was due to arrive.

"Oh, I was just about to call you," Dassi said, sounding somewhat flustered, "but you beat me to it. Listen, Riki, she went to Maale Adumim about half an hour ago. No, she won't be coming to you. She asked me to apologize a thousand times over. She said she'd phone you herself as soon as she got a chance.

"What happened was that she got caught in traffic on the way over here, and she arrived at my house very late. You know how it is. She barely had time to drink a cup of coffee and spend a few minutes with the children. She was on edge all the time because she wanted to make it to your house. In the end, she saw it would be impossible. Her appointment was for seven, so she decided to skip the visit to you this time.

"She was really sorry, and she kept saying she'd made a terrible mistake, that she should have asked you to come over here instead of letting you wait at home. Anyway, it was past seven by the time she left, and she was on edge because she was late for her meeting. She asked me to call you immediately and explain what happened, but Chagi was so exhausted, I

TIGHTROPE ■ 147

wanted to put him to bed first."

"You mean she won't be coming?" Riki asked in disbelief. Had she heard right?

"No, she won't. That's what I've been trying to tell you for the past five minutes," her sister-in-law said. "Oh, and before I forget, she left a darling little outfit for Yossi at my house."

20

THIS TIME RIKI HAD A HARD TIME containing her anger, but contain it she did. It wasn't that she'd easily accepted her sister-in-law's explanation. As soon as her conversation with Dassi had ended, she found herself caught up in whirlwind of emotions. Deep inside, she'd known her mother-in-law wouldn't show up in the end. Call it a premonition or whatever. But how could she have just let her wait like that? The sight of the table set for company, the house all clean and organized, and Yossi lying contentedly in his crib only served to heighten her frustration.

Yossi looks so adorable right now, she thought, *so alert and happy. He isn't always like that.* In fact, he usually wasn't in a good mood at all when he saw his grandmother. Somehow, he was always tired or hungry or irritable when she saw him, and all the wonderful stories she heard about him on the phone seemed like the product of his doting parents' imagination.

This time, Riki had managed to put him down for a nap. For the past hour, while she'd straightened up the house and whipped up a batch of blintzes, her son had slept peacefully. Now that he was wide-awake and at his best, his grandmother wouldn't be coming to see him. She, Riki, would now have to entertain a well-rested baby who had no intention of going to sleep for quite some time, and she had piles of work to do.

These were the first thoughts that ran through Riki's mind, deepening her disappointment, which bordered on frustration. Her frustration, in turn, led to anger and then to feelings of condemnation.

If her mother-in-law knew her time was so short, why hadn't she given some warning that she might not be able to make it? Why hadn't she let her know earlier? And why was Dassi's house the obvious first stop? So what if Dassi was two years older than she was, and so what if Daniel was the younger of the two brothers? On their previous visit, Danny's parents had gone up to Dassi and Ariel first and come to their house only later. In Riki's opinion, they were two separate families, each of which deserved the same amount of attention. Danny was no less important than Ariel, so if their first visit had been to Ariel last time, and her mother-in-law saw her time was limited, she ought to have made her first visit to Danny's house this time. That way, at worst, Dassi would lose out, not her.

It was already eight o'clock. Yossi began showing signs of dissatisfaction. Riki hurried over to him, disturbed by the fact that she'd been so caught up in her thoughts that she hadn't even noticed it was past his mealtime. She hurried to the kitchen to prepare some baby cereal, suddenly realizing her husband was due to return home within the next few minutes.

At least he'll be treated to a festive meal, she thought, allowing herself a small smile. *He'll enjoy the cheese blintzes I prepared for his mother. When was the last time I found the time to prepare something special for our evening meals?* There. Every cloud had a silver lining. She shouldn't complain.

Something in her black mood suddenly gave way, and while she fed Yossi, she felt calm enough to consider her next step. Should she tell Daniel what had happened, and if so, how?

Somehow she didn't think it was a good idea to tell Daniel

about his mother's impolite behavior. If she were to tell him, she decided, she would have to be more careful and less spontaneous than usual about what she said. From previous incidents over the almost two years of their marriage, she'd come to learn that Daniel found it hard to hear complaints about his mother even when she was clearly in the wrong. During such conversations, they both got worked up, and it ended in Daniel becoming impatient or, worse, indifferent and misunderstanding her. This time, yes, this time she would go about it in an entirely different way.

How would her neighbor, Yehudis Weiss, react in such a situation? No sooner had the thought occurred to her than she dismissed it. Yehudis's mother-in-law would never have done such a thing to her, so what was the point of comparing? And she really did want to overcome her anger, to keep her peace and let things pass. She wanted to do so for her own sake, for the sake of her marriage. After all, she wouldn't want Daniel to point out her parents' faults.

Yossi finished eating and flashed her one of his adorable smiles. His rosy cheeks smelled of bubble bath. Riki hugged him to her, whispering, "Your bubby doesn't realize what she missed."

■ ■ ■

Mr. Yaakov Schiller's new caregiver stood next to the sink in the old man's room cutting strawberries into bite-size pieces. When he finished, he drew a container of sour cream from a plastic bag, poured its contents over the strawberries and sprinkled some sugar on top. He mixed everything carefully together and served the dish to Mr. Schiller, who sat wordlessly in the armchair before him.

"Here, I made something you like," the caregiver said kindly. "Remember when you told me your wife used to serve you strawberries and cream? Today, I passed the fruit and vegetable store, and I thought to myself, *I'll buy Mr. Schiller some strawberries and prepare them the way he likes.*"

Mr. Schiller took the bowl with trembling hands and smiled in gratitude.

"See?" said silver-haired Gavriel Vidal. "I think about you even at home. Go ahead and eat. They're delicious, and healthy too. You'll have a taste of home. Eat, Mr. Schiller. Would you like me to help you?"

Mr. Schiller shook his head. He preferred to manage whatever he could by himself. He couldn't abide the caregivers in the central dining room who tried to hurry up his mealtime. Sometimes an attendant would approach him and shove a spoon heaped with food into his mouth, not even taking the time to see if he was still chewing the previous bite. What was wrong with them? Didn't they have eyes in their heads? They were impatient, eager to get mealtime over with. They wanted to clear the dishes off the tables. He tried to protest, but it didn't always work. At least here, in his room, his caregiver was different. Mr. Vidal was a good man, kind and considerate.

Mr. Schiller sat and ate slowly, one spoonful after another. Sometimes the spoon shook slightly on the way to his mouth, and the sour cream dribbled onto his chin or clothes. That was when the devoted caregiver's presence was felt. Mr. Vidal would guide the spoon to his mouth with a steady hand and wipe the spills with a small handkerchief.

Mr. Schiller continued eating in peace. He felt a special calmness with the caregiver at his side. Gavriel knew how to check his pulse, and that was important to Mr. Schiller. Every so often, the old man would extend his hand and Gavriel would rest his finger on the proper spot and concentrate intently. "Your pulse is just right!" he'd announce, and Mr. Schiller would be calm again for another quarter of an hour.

The private attendant also knew how to wind the elastic bandage around his leg in a professional manner, unlike the nursing home attendants who did a hurried job and sometimes wound it too tight.

His daughter Naomi had done well to get him this caregiver.

At first, he hadn't wanted to hear of the idea. In his opinion, it was a waste of money. Enough went out of his bank account just to pay for the nursing home. But Naomi, devoted daughter that she was, had insisted.

"Papa, I'm traveling out of the country, and I just don't feel comfortable leaving you all alone in the nursing home. A private caregiver is something else. The one I'm sending you is a certified nurse. He'll know how to take your blood pressure, and I'm told he knows all about heart disease."

That's what his daughter had told him, and he'd agreed, especially because of his blood pressure. It calmed him down when Gavriel checked it constantly.

The bowl in Mr. Schiller's hands was emptied without him even being aware of it. His trembling hand moved the spoon to his bowl and up toward his mouth again and again mechanically.

Mr. Vidal stopped his hand. He gently withdrew the spoon and said, "There, there, Mr. Schiller, you see? It was so tasty you finished it without even noticing. I can bring you more strawberries tomorrow. Would you like that?"

Mr. Schiller did not respond. Gavriel rose, glanced at his watch and deliberated for a moment before saying, "I've got to go. Should I help you to bed first?"

Mr. Schiller nodded. If someone had to help him rise from his armchair and put him to bed, it might as well be kind Mr. Vidal. The old man liked his experienced hands and the manner in which he supported him under the arm, unlike the caregivers who helped him to bed each night with sharp, jabbing movements that often hurt.

Once Mr. Schiller was in bed, Mr. Vidal puttered round the room making sure everything was in order. He rinsed the bowl, straightened the tablecloth, then bent down and checked the old man's night table. "I see you're almost out of moisturizing lotion," he said to him. "The hand cream is almost finished, too. Would you like me to buy some more on my way here tomorrow?"

The elderly man hesitated before answering, then asked, slowly but deliberately, "Check to see exactly how much is still left."

Gavriel lifted the plastic see-through bottle filled halfway with lotion and showed it to Mr. Schiller.

The old man waved his hand dismissively. "No, there's plenty. I don't need more yet."

"That's a shame. Tomorrow I have some spare time. I can squeeze in some shopping." The caregiver hoped to change the old man's mind. He blinked nervously, and anyone more sharp-eyed than Mr. Schiller could have seen the displeasure on his face.

"No need. There's still enough," Mr. Schiller repeated, half-asleep.

"Whew! It's hot in here!" Gavriel rose from his place near the night table. "I don't think this heat is good for you, Mr. Schiller. I saw the stores are carrying little fans. You could hang one up right here across from your bed. They're not too powerful, but they do the job. Would you like me to buy you one?"

Mr. Schiller didn't respond. His caregiver's extra concern and steady stream of questions had begun to tire him. Now he just wanted to be left alone.

Gavriel Vidal, long experienced in caring for the elderly, knew when to call it quits. His usually kind eyes hardened, but Mr. Schiller did not notice.

Gavriel picked up the bowl to return to the kitchen, as he'd promised the director. It was important for him to gain her trust. After a moment's thought, he decided to take the sugar canister and refill it too.

"Okay, Mr. Schiller, I'm off," he called from the doorway to the drowsy old man. "Sleep well. I'll be in one more time just to return the sugar canister. It's empty, so I'm going to refill it in the kitchen. In the meantime, decide whether you'd like strawberries tomorrow. They don't cost much, and they're good for you. Think about it." He closed the door quietly behind him.

What a shame! I could have used some of the old man's cash in my pocket today, thought Gavriel in annoyance as he strode briskly through the corridor. *Go figure out these old guys' moods*, he thought angrily. *Sometimes they're as weak as a baby, and sometimes they're as stubborn as a mule.*

In the kitchen, he ran into the director. A bright smile replaced his dour expression. "I'm returning the bowl, as promised," he said cheerfully. "Mr. Schiller just finished eating, and he's in bed, almost asleep. I gave him a bath and a massage."

"Thanks so much for everything," Sima said warmly. She watched as Gavriel refilled the empty canister with sugar for old Mr. Schiller, wondering where Mrs. Stone had found so devoted a caregiver for her father.

21

GAVRIEL WENT HOME in a sour mood. Things were moving more slowly than he had hoped. In fact, they were not working out well at all with old man Schiller. On his way to the bus stop on Jabotinsky Street, he tried to reconstruct the chain of events leading to this sorry state of affairs.

When that woman — what was her name? Stone, yes, that was it — had called, she'd identified herself as the daughter of an old man she was about to leave for a considerable amount of time. She'd explained that she wanted to hire a private attendant to care for her father a few hours a day in the nursing home where he lived.

Gavriel had gathered that she was an only daughter who was ready to do anything to assuage a guilty conscience. He'd been under the impression that the minute he agreed to her request to take care of the old man, she'd feel free of her responsibility toward him and take care of whatever it was she wanted to do abroad. He'd assumed — mistakenly as it turned out — that her absence would allow him to do as he pleased.

Childless or lonely old men, he knew from experience, presented a wide range of opportunities for getting some quick cash. It was easy to lavish them with the loving devotion they didn't receive from their children, and it was just as easy to reap the rewards that usually followed. The possibilities were limited only by imagination and, of course, luck.

Well, good luck isn't going to play a major role in this case, Gavriel thought bitterly as he waited at the crowded bus stop. As soon as he'd begun taking care of the old man, it had become painfully clear that there were other children besides the daughter involved. True, he'd heard they didn't visit very often, but still, they hadn't abandoned their father completely.

Nor was the old man bitter toward them, like some of the old men Gavriel knew. Some felt betrayed by ungrateful children who wanted nothing to do with their aging father after all he had done for them. Mr. Schiller was, at the most, dejected and withdrawn, but certainly not angry. On the contrary, he turned to his faith, saying something about a person accepting G-d's decree with humility and looking at troubles as atonement for the sins of one's younger years.

Jews! Gavriel couldn't decide whether he loved them or hated them. One thing was certain — the minute he'd immigrated to this Jewish land, he'd had no luck at all. Actually, he'd made his first mistake back in Argentina, when he'd married Paulina, his Jewish wife.

At some point in their marriage, she'd begun talking about making aliya. She was worried about the anti-Semitic groups springing up everywhere. She told him that even though he wasn't Jewish, their children were, and they'd be in danger. He'd accepted her arguments and agreed that moving to a different country might be a good idea, especially after the country's economic setbacks — and his own mismanagement — devastated his business.

Together with his brother, he had started a private nursing home. A series of poorly thought-out decisions quickly led to failure. The original idea was based on his brother's qualifications as a licensed nurse who had worked in a geriatric institution for years. They were counting on that experience to bring them success in running a nursing home.

They were wrong. The skills were adequate for being a good nurse, but not for running a complex project. That took business and management know-how neither of the brothers possessed.

By the time Gavriel — Juan at the time (he'd left the name behind at the airport in his homeland) — realized his brother's performance was falling short of expectations, it was too late. He was already sunk too deep in the mire his brother had dragged him into. He lost a considerable amount of money and argued bitterly with his brother and the rest of his family. The nursing home closed down, and he was left with no source of income. The Jewish Agency offered fairly good terms for new immigrants, and the Law of Return promised a number of tempting benefits only a fool would turn down.

The smartest thing he'd done during his last days in Argentina was to steal his brother's nursing diploma, xerox it, and pay an expert forger for a new one bearing the Hebrew name Paulina had chosen for him. He assumed the name of her uncle, Gavriel, and used her maiden name of Vidal.

Gavriel had assumed the certificate would pave the way to a new profession in Israel. But things had not turned out as planned. True, the certificate had helped him get accepted into the agency that provided attendants for the elderly, but his salary was no higher than it would have been without one.

His desire for a fast buck drove him to embark on a new enterprise. Along with a partner, he opened a restaurant on one of the busy streets near Tel Aviv's central bus station. At first, things seemed promising, and his hopes had risen. After a few short months, though, he fought with his partner, and mutual distrust caused the venture to fail. He chalked it up to another stroke of bad luck.

Then he'd spotted the ad in the newspaper: "Wanted: qualified male nurse to care for elderly man." His eyes had lit up.

This was his chance. Why hadn't he thought of it until now? He could use his professional certificate to work privately.

He answered the ad, and for the first time since his move to Israel, he felt easy profit was within reach.

The weak old man he was hired to care for was wealthy — and terribly lonely. He had only one son who lived in Europe. The son spent a fortune on various caregivers and attendants but had practically no personal relationship or contact with his father. The grandchildren barely knew their grandfather, and he had almost no friends. It was the perfect setting in which to cultivate a sense of dependence on the devoted, professional, caregiver who seemed so familiar with medical matters. Gavriel had made it clear he was an expert on high blood pressure and heart disease. It wasn't long before the old man felt he couldn't possibly live without his wonderful nurse.

That was a great year for Juan-turned-Gavriel — the most profitable he'd ever had by far. It was indeed the Promised Land, he'd thought ecstatically. He won the old man over completely, earned his trust and got him thinking of him as an adopted son.

"I'm drowning in debt," he would tell the old man mournfully. "I once owned a nursing home myself, but it didn't work out, and all my assets were confiscated." On his way home through the crowded streets, he had smiled at the memory. The old man, worried about his devoted caretaker's welfare, had given him substantial amounts of cash.

"Go on, take it. I'm doing this because I know you really care about me," the old man would explain when his devoted attendant, looking overwhelmed with gratitude, seemed reluctant to accept his kind benefactor's gift.

The real fun began when the old man gave him his credit card and asked him to make various purchases and payments. *Those were the days*, he now sighed.

With a grin, he remembered the time he'd convinced the old man to renovate his home. The old man had put him in charge of everything, including negotiating prices with the workers. He'd haggled furiously over the cost of the work, extracting an almost laughably low fee. He then quoted a ridiculously high price to the old man, explaining that he'd hired the most professional crew in the city. The price, he'd explained seriously, was commensurate with the quality of the work the crew did. In fact, he'd continued, the original fee quoted was far higher, but he'd managed to bargain it down.

Naturally, the difference between real costs and what the old man paid went straight into his own pocket, enabling him to afford similar renovations in his own home. Paulina, good wife that she was, never questioned how her husband was suddenly able to afford it all. She innocently thanked G-d for sending her husband such a good job.

The bus pulled up at yet another bus stop, and more people piled on. There was a long line of people still clamoring to get on, and Gavriel hoped the driver would close the door in their faces and drive on. He hated long lines, and too many people were already standing in the bus. He found the long wait at every bus stop nerve-wracking. Back in Argentina, things were different. No long lines, for one. There were a lot of things in Israel he still hadn't made peace with.

Then, just when things were going his way, the old man had died on him. He was just about to set up a system for regular transferal of funds from the old man's account to his own. His unexpected death had put an end to Gavriel's grand plans.

And now this old man — what a waste of time he was turning out to be. He wouldn't even let Gavriel buy him strawberries! Did he suspect something? Was he more intelligent than he seemed? His children, although not overly devoted, were still in the picture, too.

Well, there was more than one way to get what he wanted. He decided to take advantage of small opportunities. A few shekels a day was better than nothing.

On Sunday, he'd bought soap for the old man, pocketing the

change. Two days later, he'd convinced him to buy expensive moisturizing lotion. He'd gained something on that too.

The bananas he'd bought yesterday and the strawberries he'd bought today were, ostensibly, gifts. The old man hadn't even thought of paying him back for them. He'd obviously swallowed the bait regarding his attendant's devotion.

Who knows? thought Gavriel. *Maybe his children will let him do as he pleases, or maybe I'll manage to win their trust as well.* Only time would tell.

22

IN THE AUDITORIUM ON THE TOP FLOOR of Ohr Rivka, three rows of twelve-year-old girls stood lined up in formation. They were tired and fidgety after two hours of rehearsing for their upcoming performance, and their teacher was far from pleased.

"You're not standing straight. You're slouching," she called out. "Girls, you must realize that time is running out, and we still have a lot of work ahead of us. We will go through the performance one last time today, and I expect you all to make the effort to get it right. And not just right," she added as an afterthought, "but perfect."

The girls wearily straightened their shoulders, and the rehearsal resumed.

Miri, the star of the performance, began reciting her lines. In keeping with the theme of pride in being a Jew, Miri began to recite a long, moving poem describing how each generation of *Klal Yisrael* is a link in a long chain. The verses stressed the importance of the bond between mother and daughter, emphasizing that link as the way in which the torch of sanctity is transmitted from one generation to the next.

As Miri read her lines, the uncomfortable knot in Riki's stomach tightened. The girl's delivery lacked impact. It sounded flat.

Riki herself had composed the poem late one night. Tears of emotion welled up in her eyes as she wrote the lines. Now disappointment gnawed at her, leaving a bitter taste in her mouth.

What had happened to Miri? All the teachers had told her there was no one who could read poetry the way Miri did, and, at first, it had seemed they were right. At the audition, Miri had recited a poem with great feeling and expression. She'd read fluently, and her clear voice had risen in all the right places. Naturally, there was room for improvement, but Riki had trusted the teachers implicitly.

During the first few rehearsals, Riki had been very impressed with Miri's aptitude, and her hopes soared. But when she tried to guide Miri, to teach her where and how to show emotion, to *feel* the depth behind the words, she had come up against a blank wall. For some reason, the talented student she'd pinned her hopes on found it hard to understand what was wanted of her. Her recital remained exactly as it had been during the first few rehearsals — clear and fluent, to be sure, but nothing more.

Now, when Riki and her students were tired beyond their limits, Miri's recital sounded worse than ever. The touching words came across weak and stilted. Riki felt frustration well up inside her. Now it was too late to give Miri's part to someone else, but why hadn't she done it before? Why had she relied on what the teachers had told her? She should have auditioned other girls before giving Miri the main part.

Only four days were left till the party. Everyone would be there — the principal, specially invited guests, parents, her own mother. She even wanted to invite her mother-in-law. She'd put her heart and soul into this performance, and Miri's poem was supposed to be the highlight of the evening, accompanied by a violin and special lighting effects. But it would all be hopeless if the recital itself was dry and stilted.

Almost worse was the girls' obvious lack of motivation, their mediocre performance during the past few rehearsals. What was going on?

"Girls!" Riki interrupted Miri. She stood up and took a deep breath before launching into her criticisms. "I'm asking you all one last time to please stand straight! And I don't want to hear any talking from the back row! I'm warning you all that any girl who does not take rehearsals seriously will not perform. Her part will be given to someone else even if it's only a day before the party. Anyone who is incapable of carrying out her part in a mature fashion doesn't deserve to have one!"

The girls straightened up. Miri stared at her teacher, wondering if she wanted her to continue where she had left off or start again from the beginning. The next lines were meant to begin with the words, "I see your face before me, Mother, your eyes filled with expectation. They watch me carry the torch, a true *bas Yisrael* forever."

Riki was still staring pointedly at two girls whispering in the back row when Goldy, impatient, decided to speed things up. Intending to get Miri started again, she began reciting the lines with the inflection her teacher always asked Gili to imitate:

"I see your FACE before ME, Mother," she recited with exaggerated emotion, "your eyes filled with ex-pec-TA-TION."

After a split second of surprised silence, the girls burst into peals of laughter, releasing their pent-up tension. The laughter continued, each wave bringing another in its wake. Goldy stood there, smiling in confused embarrassment. She hadn't meant to be funny. The words had slipped out of her mouth, just like that. But for the teacher, her outburst was the straw that broke the camel's back.

"You should be ashamed of yourself, Goldy," she scolded the blushing girl who was trying to disappear behind the girl in front of her. "Please tell me what exactly you find so amusing. We were talking about being mature and acting responsibly, and you just went and behaved in a childish way totally inappropriate for a girl your age. Please go down to the principal and tell her exactly what happened. Tell her you disturbed the rehearsal, and let her decide on a suitable punishment."

Goldy turned pale. She stood rooted to the spot, terrified.

"I didn't mean to disturb," she whispered.

"What you did was bad enough, even if you didn't mean to." Riki knew she wasn't being herself; her control was slipping. The day was almost over, and everything seemed to be falling apart. She felt she had to restore some order before the rehearsal ended. "Go down to the principal. Now!" she thundered at the quaking girl. "And I expect absolute silence and a serious attitude from the rest of you."

Her request was heeded immediately. Silence reigned. You could have heard a pin drop.

Miri continued with her recital, clear and fluent as always: "I see your face before me…"

On the way home, the heat did nothing to raise Riki's drooping spirits. As she passed the principal's office on her way out, she caught sight of Goldy's dejected profile. She felt a pang of remorse for having been so quick to punish the girl.

Was it fair to punish a sweet, well-behaved student so harshly for a one-time offense? Who said the girl had meant to disturb? Why hadn't she checked the facts before sending her down to the principal? Why had she allowed herself to lose control like that?

What if…what if Goldy Stein was nothing but the victim of Riki's own nerves and frustration? Had she vented all the stress she was feeling in anticipation of the party on the hapless girl's head?

Why was she so tense? Why were practice sessions turning into one long nightmare for both her and her students? Why was she such a nervous wreck, yelling and scolding all the time? She couldn't remember the last time she'd smiled at a student, and that wasn't like her at all. It wasn't so long ago that she herself had been a student who found it difficult to stand straight for three consecutive lessons, so why was it suddenly so hard for her to understand them?

There it is again. The sharp pain stabbed at her, its familiar ache settling somewhere under her heart. She stopped walking and took a few deep breaths.

She'd been having the pains for over a year. The doctor had explained that the attacks were stress related. Riki had laughed, certain she was joking, but the doctor's face had remained grave. "I mean it seriously," she'd told Riki. "These pains could signal a developing ulcer. You must curb your ambition, your drive for success."

Success. Was that it? Was that why she was so tense? Neither the warm, stuffy air, the burning rays of the sun, nor the noise of the heavy traffic on the street managed to blur the inescapable answer. Besides, she wasn't trying to hide from the truth.

Yes, she desperately wanted to succeed. Success was important to her. She wanted the party to be the greatest ever. Everyone would be there — the principal, the parents, her mother, her mother-in-law. It was essential they all see how wonderfully successful she was.

Why? The question came at her from all sides. She could even see it in yellow and red letters, pounding and flashing at her, demanding an answer. *Why*?

That was why she was pressuring her students. *And that is why, Riki, my girl,* she told herself, *you are not acting like your usual self. You're not the kind teacher you always wanted to be — the compassionate adult who sympathized and understood. Why is success so important to you? Why do you so desperately long for the approval of everyone around you?*

Suddenly, Riki's mind was filled with an altogether different image. *Yesterday — or was it two days ago? — you ran home in a fit of hysteria to straighten up the house for your mother-in-law's visit. What would have happened if you hadn't done it? What *do you think would have happened to you? What were you trying to hide, Riki? What was it you didn't want her to see? Are you afraid she'll find out that you aren't perfect?*

For some reason, Riki was now certain that her sister-in-law Dassi would never have run home like that, even if her house had been a mess. No, it wasn't the cake in the freezer that had lent Dassi her air of calm. It was something else, something she, Riki, didn't have.

The pain eased its grip, and Riki attempted to put things in perspective. *Let's say*, she thought to herself, *let's say the performance will be only ordinary. The poem won't have the impact I wanted it to. The girls won't be at their best.*

Standing on the sidewalk leading to her street, Riki felt it would be too terrible for her to bear. Something inside her broke down and wept.

23

THE INSTANT RIKI CLOSED THE DOOR behind her, she embarked on a whirlwind of activity. She relegated the despondent thoughts she'd been having to a far corner of her mind and concentrated on matters at hand. Yossi needed changing, and he was already making hungry noises. And, she noted, glancing at her watch, little Brachi was due to arrive any minute.

After she'd diapered, fed and played with Yossi, Riki laid him down in his crib. He seemed tired, and Riki assumed he'd fall asleep right away. That way she'd have more time for Brachi.

The last time the little girl had come, Riki had only managed to take care of her basic needs for the three hours she was with her. Today she wanted to give the child her full attention.

Ever since Brachi had entered her home and heart, Riki was constantly on the lookout for toys that might encourage the little girl's development. She'd designated a special place for all the toys and materials she'd collected, stashing them in a cardboard box wedged between the bed and the wall in the children's room.

Digging through the box in search of a toy to use, Riki suddenly realized what a fascinating and engrossing challenge caring for the child had become. She decided to open the new toy she'd bought the day before. In another month or two, the toy would be perfect for Yossi, but in the meantime, Brachi might enjoy it.

The toy had five doors that opened to release pop-up animals when the right movement was made. One door opened if you pressed a button; another, if you turned a handle. To add to the excitement, the animals made noises when they popped up. At this point, all Riki hoped for was that Brachi would grasp the connection between making the right movement and seeing the animal pop out. Riki was sure that learning about cause and effect would help the child's mental development.

She took out the toy along with the plastic soda bottle she'd decorated and filled with colored balls. When the bottle was rolled on the floor, Brachi avidly followed it with her eyes and start crawling after it.

Riki had come up with the idea at her pediatrician's office. The nurse there had all sorts of ideas for simple, inexpensive toys mothers could make themselves.

Yossi had crowed with excitement at the sight of the bottle and rocked on all fours in an effort to reach it, but it was Brachi who really benefited from the toy. Although she knew how to crawl, her movements were poorly coordinated, and she couldn't crawl far. But the last time she'd come, she'd crawled to the far end of the room in an effort to reach the bottle that kept rolling further away.

Riki was just laying out the musical mat she'd gotten as a gift for Yossi, when the familiar knock sounded at the door.

She opened the door to find Faigy holding Brachi in her thin arms. Both girls were relaxed and smiling. That first visit, when Faigy had stood pale and stammering in the doorway looking like she wished she could disappear, seemed like ages ago. Brachi's eyes lit up, and she gurgled excitedly and bounced up and down when she caught sight of Riki. Riki took the little girl in her arms while exchanging pleasantries with her sister.

"How are you, Faigy? How's your mother?"

Everything's fine, *baruch Hashem*. Guess what?" she grinned. "Yesterday, Brachi said, 'Bamba.'"

"Really?" Riki was incredulous.

"Uh-huh. She saw me eating Bamba, so she said, 'Bamba, Bamba' a few times. My mommy said it's all because of you."

Riki was thrilled. She sat down, sat Brachi securely in her lap, and asked her, "Did you really say 'Bamba'?"

"Bamba," repeated Brachi with a smile, and Riki gave her a hug.

"You've really earned some Bamba," she announced, rising to go to the kitchen. "You deserve it. You're a star pupil." Her thoughts suddenly returned to school, to rehearsals and to her students. *Is Brachi part of your student performance that must succeed at any price?* she asked herself.

She stopped short at the thought. Why did she care so much for the little girl? Why was she investing so much in her? Could her reasons be selfish ones?

Riki recalled her first conversation with Brachi's mother, after the little girl's first, unscheduled visit. The woman had apologized profusely. "I didn't know what arrangements had been made with you. I'm sorry about the misunderstanding," she'd said. She then proceeded to tell Riki a little about herself, her family and the little girl.

"You were like an angel from Heaven. I didn't know what to do," she had said. "You have no idea how important Brachi's development is to me. From the moment I learned I'd be laid up for a while, I was frantic with worry. You see," the mother had continued, "a regular child learns and develops even without constant outside stimulation. But with children like Brachi, it's as if the motor is outside their bodies and it's important to keep it running all the time. Without stimulation, effort and training, her development could be arrested, G-d forbid.

"I had to ask for help. I felt I owed it to Brachi." The mother's voice had taken on a defensive note. "I couldn't find anyone to replace the volunteer who left about a month earlier until Mrs. Perlstein called me about you. I apologize for acting as quickly as I did without first checking out the details of the arrangement. I guess I was so overjoyed they had found someone that I missed the part about it still being in the planning stages. I wasn't feeling well that day, and Brachi had been especially trying all afternoon. I wanted someone to be with her, to give her what I couldn't at the time. I can't burden her brothers and sisters too much either. After all, they're still children themselves.

"But obviously," she had chuckled, "things were meant to turn out this way. If I had waited, Brachi might never have come to you at all. You might have had second thoughts. The coordinator told me she was very impressed with the way you handled the situation and with what you did with Brachi in the short time she was with you. She couldn't stop raving about how you instinctively did all the right things. May what you do for Brachi bring you blessing and success."

And now she's saying "Bamba," thought Riki in amazement. During the last visit, Riki had repeated the word to her slowly and clearly, each time offering her a piece of the crunchy yellow snack. The results were amazing.

No! thought Riki, struck again by the frightening thought that had occurred to her earlier. This is something else. Here the challenge stems from something entirely different, more altruistic somehow. There is no school principal involved here, no audience at all. Aside from her mother and the coordinator, no one even knew about Brachi.

Here she didn't need any pats on the shoulder, not even from Brachi's mother. She was doing it all for the sweet little girl who was looking her directly in the eye and saying, "Bamba." Yes, she did it for the girl whose innocent eyes looked up into hers with an expression of pure love.

■ ■ ■

After Ma'ariv, as Daniel was about to leave shul, he was approached by Rabbi Levy, a distinguished neighbor. Rabbi Levy beckoned him to a corner, indicating that he wanted to speak with him privately for a few moments.

"I heard," he told Daniel in a serious tone of voice, "that you and your wife sometimes volunteer to help handicapped children, that you know a little about these things."

Daniel was taken aback. Since when had he been helping handicapped children, and what did he know about their needs? Did Riki's caring for one little girl turn them into experts on the subject? Before he managed to say anything, Rabbi Levy continued.

"I wanted to ask you if you might also be able to help a child with a learning disability. The child's father appealed to me for help, and I said I'd try. The boy is nine years old, and he's finding Gemara difficult. Do you think you could possibly take him on, that is, tutor him once or twice a week?"

Daniel finally found his tongue. "Forgive me," he said politely, "but I really don't know what gave you the idea I know anything about learning disabilities."

"Oh, I didn't mean to say I thought you had specific experience in this area. What's important here is the approach — a warm, understanding approach — and dedication. I heard you're the right person. I think it was Rabbi Perlstein, the principal of the Talmud Torah, who mentioned your name. His wife, I'm sure you know, is the coordinator of the *chessed* organization in our neighborhood. He suggested I ask you.

"There's no need to give me an answer right now," he went on, cutting off Daniel's attempts to interrupt. "Think about it and talk it over with your wife. Despite your objections, I trust Rabbi Perlstein's instincts regarding your approach to *chinuch*. I have the same impression myself."

Daniel walked home feeling excited and pleased. No one had ever asked him to study Gemara with a child. No one had ever told him he had the right approach to *chinuch* issues. And he'd never thought of his family as one that volunteered to help children with difficulties.

■ ■ ■

Late that evening, when Avraham Baum returned home from his job at the yeshiva, he noticed an envelope sticking out of the mailbox. *Why didn't Chaya see this?* he wondered, pulling it out.

It was an official envelope, bearing the triangular stamp of army mail. Avraham felt his heart skip a beat. He'd recently completed his yearly reserve duty, so what was this all about?

He carefully examined the envelope by the weak light of the single bulb illuminating the entrance to the building. The envelope was not addressed to him. The name in the see-through window was that of his son, Ephraim.

He quickly ripped open the flap and withdrew the official document. Yes, Ephraim Baum was summoned to appear at the draft board.

His worst fears were being realized.

24

AVRAHAM REREAD THE NEATLY TYPED LETTER from the army. Ephraim was being summoned to appear at the district draft office on August 31, three months from the day he received the notice. The summons was identical to the one every boy in Israel received on his seventeenth birthday, but for Avraham Baum it served as a poignant reminder of the crucial crossroads his son was facing. Would he finally settle down in a yeshiva, or would he choose to join the army?

Avraham was almost certain he knew what his son's choice would be. Lately, Ephraim had made no secret of his views on the matter, and they differed dramatically from those of his father. When Avraham had allowed Ephraim to switch from a yeshiva to the vocational school, which combined a half day of Torah study with job training, he'd done so in an effort to meet his son's special needs. Who knew better than he how hard it was for someone unequipped with the basic tools needed for intensive study to be seated next to a Gemara. True, his son Ephraim was more talented than he, and his Talmud Torah teachers had always claimed he had a good head on his shoulders. Avraham supposed that if his son had been blessed with a more placid nature, almost certainly he would have adapted well to his studies and achieved great things.

But it looked like Ephraim wasn't capable of making it in an ordinary yeshiva setting. Gemara study took more than just aptitude and intelligence. Ephraim had always found it hard to sit still and doubly hard to concentrate on reading anything, let alone a *blatt* Gemara, for more than a few minutes at a time. The world around him pulled him to it with far greater strength than did intellectual pursuits. He would rather take apart a car or climb a tree than read. The lure of modern technology grew with each passing year until, by the time he reached his teenage years, he was spending hours exploring it.

After his son's unsuccessful first year in yeshiva, Avraham decided that if he wanted his son to stay, at the very least, a good Jew, it might be better at that stage to find him a framework that fit his personality. In such a place, Avraham hoped, his son would develop his potential while continuing to absorb the values and principles that would keep him on the right track. He sincerely hoped that as Ephraim matured, he would settle down and reenter yeshiva.

Now, though, Avraham wondered if he had made the right decision. He regretted not discussing the decision with a rav before taking such a drastic step. Lately, his son's attitude seemed to be out of sync with his father's plans. During one short, candid conversation he'd initiated with his son, Avraham had suggested that Ephraim return to yeshiva for a year or two to strengthen himself spiritually before venturing out into the workplace. Ephraim had shrugged his shoulders and said, "Me and a yeshiva, Dad? You know we're not a good match."

"What makes you so sure?" Avraham had asked his son's receding back. Aside from an eloquent shrug of the boy's shoulders, no reply was forthcoming.

Now Avraham was worried. A face-to-face talk with his son could be put off no longer. There was no way out of it, even though Avraham knew he was not a man of words.

He sighed deeply. He'd tried to be a good father, and his disappointment was almost too much to bear. He desperately wanted Ephraim to build a good Jewish home, as he himself had done with G-d's help. True, he had also learned a trade, but those were different times. He'd grown up stronger than his son, infused with a sense of responsibility for his future. How could he explain that to Ephraim?

With a heavy heart, he folded the letter and buried it deep in a drawer.

■ ■ ■

That evening, Chaya Baum attended the wedding of a friend's daughter. She was sitting in the Bnei Brak wedding hall watching the lively, spirited dancing, when her eyes suddenly lit on a familiar face.

Why, it was Sima Abramson, her *machtenista*! What was she doing there? Sima was heading in her direction, looking this way and that, obviously hunting for the *ba'alas simcha*. She hadn't yet spotted her *machtenista,* Chaya Baum.

Chaya rose from her seat and made her way toward Sima. This was no easy feat, for the hall was packed with guests. Finally, she reached her, tapped her on the shoulder and smiled.

"Hello! *Mazel tov*! What are you doing here?" Sima asked.

"The *kalla's* mother is a good friend of mine. We go all the way back to high school, and we still keep in touch. What about you? What's your connection to this wedding?"

"We're relatives. The *chassan's* father is my husband's first cousin."

"That's nice. I know the *kalla* well, and let me tell you, the *chassan* must be something special if he's getting a wife like that."

"He really is a special boy."

The two *machtenistas* chatted as they walked to a table and sat down. Chaya poured them both a cold drink. Sima thanked her and sipped slowly from the glass as she settled back in her seat.

"Daniel and Riki came with the baby for a visit last week," she told Chaya. "She probably told you about it."

"Oh, of course," Chaya said. "They went to Bnei Brak to be *menachem avel* some relatives of yours, didn't they? She told me she left Yossi at your house. *Nu*, what do you have to say about him?" she asked with typical grandmotherly adoration.

"What's there to say?" Sima's voice was warm with affection at the thought of the little boy. "He gets cuter and cuter by the day. Has he grown since the last time I saw him!"

"Did you see how he's trying to sit up?" Chaya asked. "The truth is, Riki puts a lot of effort into encouraging his progress. You know, ever since that little girl began coming to her, she's been investing in the toys and things that help children develop. It looks like Yossi's benefiting from it too."

"What little girl?" asked Sima, leaning forward to make sure she was hearing right. The band was so loud. "Who are you talking about?"

Chaya was astonished. Could it be that Sima didn't know? "The little girl with Down syndrome that Riki takes care of twice a week. Don't…don't tell me you don't know anything about it!"

"That's exactly what I *am* telling you," Sima replied, composed as ever. A little too composed.

"Well, she obviously just didn't get around to telling you. But take it from me, that couple is something special!" Chaya's eyes sparkled with motherly pride. "Just think, on top of everything she's involved in at school, Riki volunteered to care for a child with Down syndrome twice a week. The mother recently had a baby after being on bed rest for a while, so Riki's help is extremely important. And she does this job like she does everything else, with all her heart and soul."

Chaya Baum was in her element. At last, here was her opportunity to tell Sima some nice things about Riki — all absolutely true, without any exaggeration — in a natural, uncontrived way.

"Riki sees it as a real challenge," she enthused. "She never cancels, not even on her busiest days. I'm sure you know that the bas mitzva party she's organizing is taking place in only a few days."

"The bas mitzva party she's organizing?" Sima echoed blankly.

"Yes. Of course, she's not the sole coordinator, but she's on the committee, and she has a major role in all the preparations. I think the party is scheduled for four days from now. I'm sure I'll see you there."

"Me? What makes you think so?" Sima shifted uncomfortably in her chair. She felt confused and uneasy, emotions she did not often encounter. "I did hear something about a bas mitzva party, but I didn't realize it was so important. I definitely did not realize it was in another four days! She didn't say anything when she was at our house."

"Well, I'm sure she will," Chaya said confidently. "She's so nervous and worked up about the whole thing, she probably just never found the time. But I'm sure she'll call you to invite you.

"Anyway, that's that," she concluded. "She doesn't take it easy. She's always doing something. She contributes so much to everyone and everything around her, and she manages to make sure no one loses out. Yossi seems happy and content. And Danny stands behind her, encouraging her every step of the way. I'm really impressed!"

Chaya's last words found their mark. Some of Sima's feelings of dismay melted away. Her Danny had a part in his wife's success, and her family seemed to at least appreciate it. Danny was and always had been a good boy with a golden heart, G-d bless him.

Sima rose abruptly. "I really only dropped in for a few minutes. I'm in a rush," she apologized to her *machtenista*. "If you see them, send warm regards. May we continue to merit much *nachas* from them."

She left the brightly lit hall and stepped into the dark night. Her heart felt heavy, weighed down by a feeling of distinct unease. The conversation she'd had with Chaya Baum had left a bitter taste in her mouth.

What exactly is bothering you? she asked herself as she walked along the street. *Chaya is her mother, and mothers are the first to know everything, aren't they? You know lots of things about Mali. If Mali were to volunteer to care for a child, she'd surely tell you about it first, wouldn't she?*

"Sure," whispered the trees, swaying in the light breeze. "Sure she would. But Mali would probably tell her mother-in-law too, and so would Dassi."

Where was Danny? Why hadn't he told her? Was she so far removed from them? Did she deserve such treatment? What about the party? She didn't know anything about that either.

Good! If that's the way they want it, that's the way it will be. If they don't want to tell me, I'm certainly not going to ask.

She turned the corner. She was surrounded on all sides by women walking home, probably also returning from various *simchas*. If she could only talk to one of them, share her problem with one of them, a woman her age, someone in the same situation who would understand.

But she didn't know any of them. Sima was alone, and so she buried the hurt and humiliation deep inside.

25

Two days after Chaya Baum and Sima Abramson met at the wedding, a day before the long-awaited party, Riki finally felt herself relax about the performance. After all, the girls knew their parts well by now, and Riki was sure that the magic of being on stage would bring out the very best in her students. The glare of the spotlights and the fact that their mothers' adoring eyes followed their every move would surely inspire them. Things would turn out as she had originally planned.

Now that her head had cleared somewhat, Riki turned her attention to other matters. The first thing on her list was to invite her mother-in-law to the party. She'd planned on inviting her long ago, but her doubts as to how the performance would turn out had made her hesitate.

"Hi! It's me, Riki."

"Hello, Riki. What's new?"

"*Baruch Hashem*, everything's okay. What's new with you?"

"*Baruch Hashem*, everything's fine here, too."

"Great! I'm actually calling to invite you to come to my students' bas mitzva celebration tomorrow."

"Oh, yes, I heard about it." Something in her mother-in-law's dry tone confused Riki for a moment. She'd expected a more enthusiastic reply.

"Well, it's going to start at six o'clock, and I'd really like you to come."

"Tomorrow, you say?" There was a brief pause. "Listen, Riki, I really appreciate the invitation, but I might have a problem. I have a dentist appointment for Tehilla about a tooth we should have seen to a while back. On top of that, I also have a meeting at the nursing home with the interior decorator. I'm not sure I can cancel it."

"Oh, but it will be such a shame if you can't come," Riki said uncertainly.

"Yes, but what can I do? I really would love to come. Too bad you didn't let me know earlier. That way I could have freed up my day."

Riki paused for a moment before responding, unsure of what to say. "It didn't occur to me that you might be tied up," she apologized. "I was so busy I just didn't think about it before. I don't want you to feel pressured. I wouldn't want you to go out of your way for me. If it's too hard, I'll understand. It won't be the end of the world. Of course, I'd be thrilled if you can come, but if you can't — I'll understand."

"We'll see." Did the voice sound tired or disinterested? "I'll try and arrange something. In any case, I hope everything goes well. Thanks for the invitation."

Riki was left with mixed emotions. On the one hand, she felt sorry her mother-in-law might not come. On the other, she was upset at herself for not having been more insistent. Why hadn't she explained to her mother-in-law how important her attendance at the performance was, and how happy she'd be if she came?

For a minute, she considered calling her mother-in-law right back, but something stopped her. If her mother-in-law had no qualms about telling her how hard it would be to come, how dare she, the daughter-in-law, demand that she make a supreme effort on her behalf? Especially...especially since her mother-in-law didn't seem to attach any special importance to the event. She had responded as if they were talking about a boring school function. If that was the case, what was the point in pressuring her?

Despite her mother-in-law's lukewarm reaction to the invitation, Riki still wanted her to attend and hoped with all her heart that things would, indeed, work out.

■ ■ ■

Sima was preoccupied after the phone call. So, the invitation had finally come. She wasn't sure how to relate to the whole matter.

The hurt feeling she'd felt at the wedding two days earlier had not yet completely dissipated. She was not at all sure that Riki really wanted her to come; she was probably just trying to be polite. Maybe the invitation had come as a result of Chaya Baum's prodding.

Sima puttered around the house, straightening up as she'd been doing before the phone call interrupted her. If not for the dentist's appointment and that meeting with the interior decorator regarding the new wing of the nursing home, she would not have hesitated to go. But it would take a lot of juggling and rescheduling for her to make it to the party. Was it worth it?

She replayed the conversation with her daughter-in-law. "Never mind! It's not the end of the world," her daughter-in-law had said. "Of course, I'll be really glad if you come, but if you can't — I'll understand."

Once again, Sima felt the by-now-familiar wave of hurt wash over her.

Why should I try so hard and go out of my way to cancel appointments if my daughter-in-law invites me solely to comply with the rules in some sort of "Handbook of Family Etiquette"? After all, I never noticed that my presence or opinion means much to her. She never tells me about anything important. She never so much as mentioned the child she cares for, and I heard practically nothing about the party until today. Why should I bother?

Sima began folding a small pile of laundry. Her hands moved of their own accord, folding item after item. Suddenly, she came across a small pair of green pants. She stared at the tiny article of clothing, wondering where it had come from.

Of course, she suddenly recalled. *These are the pants Yossi was wearing when he came to visit us last week. His mother changed him before the trip home, and she probably left the pants here by mistake.*

Yossi had been wearing a cute two-piece outfit that seemed new. She remembered it quite well. At the time, she'd asked Riki about the new outfit she'd bought for Yossi, the one she'd left at Dassi's house the day she'd traveled to Maale Adumim. She felt she had to ask because two weeks had passed since then, and Riki still hadn't said a word about it. It wasn't that she needed the thank-you but, still, when you buy someone a gift, it's only natural to want to know whether it was appreciated or not.

Riki had blushed at the question. It was clear she felt flustered, and Sima immediately regretted having asked.

"Oh, of course," her daughter-in-law had stammered. "Thanks a lot. I meant to call but I forgot."

How does one forget something like that? "Does it fit him?"

"Oh, yes, it's just fine," Riki had replied in a noncommittal tone, adding not another word.

Strange, mused Sima to herself as she continued folding laundry. Was that all she had to say about a gift purchased with much care and love, and an expensive gift at that? Dassi, for example, always thanked her over and over again and then made sure to bring the children over for a visit dressed in the clothes Sima had bought. Mali did the same. Not that she really expected it, but she appreciated the gesture. It demonstrated goodwill on their part and proved they appreciated her effort.

Riki's behavior, on the other hand, baffled her completely. She couldn't really explain it in words, but Riki made her feel as though everything she did was second-rate, not of primary importance. The things she did or bought didn't appeal to Riki's taste or at least were not appreciated. So why should she try so hard?

■ ■ ■

In his home on the outskirts of Petach Tikva, Gavriel Vidal was preoccupied with thoughts of his own. A strange thing had happened that day while he was caring for Mr. Schiller, and he wasn't quite sure what to make of it.

That morning, when he had entered the old man's room and greeted him warmly, Mr. Schiller had raised his eyes and looked at him sharply. Instead of returning Gavriel's greeting, he'd demanded, "Did you bring me the cookies I asked for?" Gavriel had no idea what he was talking about. He didn't recall him having asked for cookies.

"What cookies?" he'd asked.

"What cookies?" the old man repeated bitterly. Then, obviously impatient, he said, "At breakfast, I asked you to bring me some cookies, and you still haven't brought any. Why not?"

Gavriel was alarmed. "Mr. Schiller, please," he pleaded. "It's me. Me, Gavriel! Don't you recognize me? Look at me carefully. I'm not an employee of the nursing home. I wasn't here at breakfast at all. You must be mixing me up with someone else, Mr. Schiller. Look carefully."

Mr. Schiller stared at him in confusion for a moment before saying, "Oh, you're right. You say you're not the nursing home attendant. I'm sorry. I guess I got confused. My eyesight isn't getting any better. The attendant promised to bring me cookies at breakfast, and he still hasn't brought any."

Gavriel wasted no time. If cookies were what Mr. Schiller

wanted, cookies were what he would get. After all, what was he there for if not to provide the old man with all his needs?

Upon his return, Gavriel continued talking to the man under his care as though nothing out of the ordinary had happened. For a while, it seemed as though that really was the case. It happens that a person gets confused, especially an old person with weak eyesight. They discussed the weather and various health matters, and then, as Gavriel offered him a cup of tea he'd prepared to go with the cookies, Mr. Schiller said offhandedly, "Naomi's coming tomorrow."

"Naomi?" Gavriel was astonished. "Naomi, your daughter? Isn't she out of the country?"

"She's supposed to come," Mr. Schiller said stubbornly. "She always comes at ten. Yesterday, the day before — every day."

"That's impossible!" No one had told him anything about Mrs. Stone's return to Israel. Gavriel took a good look at the man under his care. Mr. Schiller returned his stare, and Gavriel noticed that his eyes seemed vacant. He recognized that look from somewhere back in Argentina. His father had had that same confused look. Toward the end of his life, he'd suffered from a form of dementia, a side effect of the rare blood disease with which he'd been stricken.

Could it be that the Jew is demented, and I don't even know it? Gavriel wondered. *Why didn't anyone tell me? Why didn't his daughter or the director mention it?*

Could it be, the thought flashed through his mind, *that they themselves are unaware of the true state of affairs? If this is the beginning phase, there's a reasonable chance they haven't yet noticed.*

From his experience with the elderly, Gavriel knew that moments of confusion were liable to occur without warning and then disappear as suddenly as they'd come, leaving the stricken person perfectly lucid. Perhaps he ought to let them know. There were some types of dementia that, if taken care of early enough, could be prevented. That much he knew.

Take it slow and easy, Juan! an inner voice warned. *Don't rush into things. Wait and see what happens.*

Now, after a refreshing afternoon nap, he tried to assess the situation. He was convinced the old man was showing signs of dementia. It might just work to his advantage.

Dementia. Here is the opportunity you were waiting for, Juan. Don't say anything yet. Who knows? Perhaps your salvation is at hand.

26

IT WAS EARLY EVENING, BETWEEN MINCHA and Ma'ariv. In the neighborhood shul, nine-year-old Motti sat beside a thin young man as the two studied a *blatt Gemara* together. The child looked up at his mentor and asked earnestly, "Do you think you can learn with me longer today?"

After much hesitation, Daniel had decided to accept Rabbi Levy's proposal to tutor the boy. He now looked at his young charge questioningly.

"What I mean is," the boy explained, "could you teach me some of the material we're going to be learning in cheder tomorrow? That way, I'll understand what the rebbe is saying."

"Did you participate in today's lesson?" Daniel asked.

"Yes, and I really knew it. The rebbe even said so in front of everyone. He said I was becoming a really good student. It's because of you, because you explained to me what we would be learning today. When the rebbe asked a question, I was the only one who knew the answer."

The child glowed as he spoke, and his radiant enthusiasm rubbed off on his young, novice teacher. Daniel felt a surge of joy and pleasure well up within him. He'd begun studying with Motti only two days before. Yesterday, after they'd finished reviewing the day's material, he'd noticed that Motti still seemed focused and attentive. *When the mind is alert and the heart is open and ready to accept,* he'd thought to himself, *that's the perfect opportunity to internalize knowledge.* On the spur of the moment, he'd decided to utilize the few minutes they had left to go ahead with new material. He hadn't expected such quick results, though.

"Okay!" he agreed happily to Motti's request. "If you're ready, so am I."

Despite the fact that the half hour Daniel had originally agreed to set aside for their study session was over, he continued teaching him.

As the two sat together discussing the material, Daniel became convinced that the child's only problem was his difficulty concentrating. Motti's questions and comments showed he was a bright child who had no problem grasping the material. The boy himself had said he found it hard to pay attention in class. It was much easier for him to concentrate, he'd explained, while studying one-on-one with Daniel, without the distraction of other students.

In a clear, illustrative manner, Daniel now tried to simplify and explain another few lines of the text. As soon as he saw the boy squirm impatiently in his seat, he closed the Gemara, signaling the end of the lesson.

"Okay, that's it for now," he told his student. "We learned a pretty big chunk of the next *sugya* you'll be learning in class. *Be'ezras Hashem,* when the rebbe teaches you this piece of Gemara tomorrow, you'll know what he's talking about. It's going to be a lot easier for you to pay attention, won't it?"

"I sure hope so." Motti smiled. "Even if the boy next to me rubs his eraser across his desk the whole time, I'll still pay attention."

In a very untypical gesture of affection, Daniel pinched the boy's cheek and then bid him good-bye.

After Ma'ariv, Daniel walked home feeling wonderfully pleased. He was still heady from the pleasure of his learning experience with Motti, and he was looking forward to sharing his conclusions about the child's abilities with his wife. With a start, he remembered that it was the night of the bas mitzva party her school was putting on. She was almost certainly not home yet, and Yossi was probably still at the neighbors'. He quickened his pace, his thoughts about himself and Motti giving way to feelings of curiosity about his wife's evening. Was the event successful? Would she return home in a good mood, like he was, pleased with the outcome of the difficult job she'd taken upon herself?

As he entered the building, someone flicked on the hallway light. It was Menachem Weiss, his neighbor, now coming down the stairs. His face glowed with a special light.

"I get a *mazel tov*," he told Daniel excitedly. "My wife just had a baby girl!"

"*Mazel tov, mazel tov*," Daniel wished him warmly, shaking his hand.

He then climbed the steps to his home.

■ ■ ■

Three blocks away, in the Ohr Rivka auditorium, thunderous applause echoed in appreciation of the bas mitzva performance. The girls had sung beautifully, their youthful voices rising in crescendo with the words of the theme song that both mothers and girls had come to know so well:

"I see your face before me, Mother, your eyes filled with expectation.

They watch me carry the torch, a true *bas Yisrael* forever,

Passing on the tradition, from generation to generation.

Yes, my dearest mother, for now until forever.

From generation to generation, generation to generation…"

When the principal rose to deliver her speech at the end of the evening, she thanked Mrs. Rivka Abramson for her tireless efforts in directing the choir, composing the songs and writing the theme song. Once again, the auditorium rocked with applause.

Riki felt the warm, appreciative glances from the direction of the mothers in the audience and could see the emotion in the damp eyes of those in the first row. She was looking, though, for one particular pair of eyes — the familiar, beloved eyes of her own mother, who had sat in the audience and watched her with an overflowing heart while whispering a fervent prayer for her daughter's success.

Riki made her way toward her, and the two embraced. There was no need for words.

"Are you her mother?" someone called out from the babble of voices swirling around them.

"That's her mother," the women whispered to each other admiringly.

Riki turned, aware that once again, she'd granted her mother great *nachas* and pleasure.

"*Ribbono shel Olam*," her lips moved soundlessly. "Grant me that I might give her pleasure over and over again. She deserves it." Deep inside, Riki felt that the words to the song she'd composed were in fact dedicated to her mother. It was her image that had appeared in her mind's eye when she'd composed them. The girls in the choir had presented her mother with them as a gift from her.

And yet…something was missing. Amidst the ocean of warm words and congratulatory hugs, she felt a void even the huge bouquet of roses she'd received from her students could not fill.

Her mother-in-law…

At first, Riki had saved her mother-in-law a seat in the front row, near her mother. After a while, though, both she and her mother gave up waiting and watching the entrance door. The empty seat was filled by another mother, but Riki's heart remained painfully empty.

Why hadn't she come?

The whole way home, after parting from her friends on the staff, her students, and her mother, Riki struggled with the two voices vying for attention within her.

Just forget it and be happy, one voice told her. *Thank Hashem that all went well, that the event was a hit, that the girls and the mothers, and, most of all, the principal, are pleased with your work. Isn't that what counts?*

Yes and no.

Apparently, the shower of approval and admiration she'd received from everyone that night could not make up for the lack of one particular person's confirmation that she'd done a good job — her mother-in-law. Maybe it was because she'd recently become aware that the most significant framework of one's life is that of one's family. *That's where your real life actually takes place,* she mused. *If you're not okay in that area, all other successes shrink in significance. That's the area you really need the approval of others.*

My mother already knows me, the voice continued. *For her, this was just an extra dose of nachas. My mother-in-law doesn't really know me very well yet. You might say she doesn't know the real me at all.*

Up until this point, her mother-in-law had never really had the chance to see her in the most flattering situations. Housekeeping, after all, was not the crown jewel of her talents.

Tonight, in school among her students, in a place where she merited applause and sincere appreciation, her mother-in-law had the best chance of feeling satisfied with her daughter-in-law. She could have seen her from a new, wholly different angle. So why hadn't Danny's mother made the most of the opportunity?

It's because such an opportunity is not important to her, argued the voice.

Without her even noticing it, Riki's disappointment gave

way to feelings of blame and accusation. *The things I'm good at mean nothing to her. I realized that from the minute she spoke so disparagingly about being a counselor. Maybe she disdains everything about me, even the hairstyles I choose. But why can't she respect me for the way I am? What about my feelings? I'm sure if Dassi invited her to a siddur party she organized, she'd go even if it meant canceling a dozen dentist appointments with Tehilla. But when it comes to me, well, I'm obviously worth less. Two weeks ago, when she came to Jerusalem, she went up to see Dassi first. Naturally. At the time, I tried to give her the benefit of the doubt by telling myself I was being overly sensitive. Well, here's proof positive that my feelings are entirely realistic, and I'm just not important to her.*

That time, she told herself, *I didn't breathe a word to Daniel of my disappointment. But I can't keep it all bottled up inside any longer! I want him to understand me once and for all. I want him to know I'm not imagining things. I think the time has come for him to talk to his mother openly about everything.*

27

DANIEL WAS ON THE PHONE with his mother. The night before, when he'd come home after Ma'ariv, Riki had told him about his mother's failure to show up at the school affair. She was close to tears, and Daniel saw the pain in her eyes. In a flash of sympathy, he decided he would try and speak to his mother.

Why not? He'd never done it before, but who said it was always best to remain silent? Perhaps it would be better if once and for all he let his mother know how Riki felt. Maybe she had no idea how her daughter-in-law's feelings had been hurt. If she knew, perhaps she could find a way to smooth things over.

"I'll speak to her," he assured his overwrought wife, who stared at him in surprise as he headed straight for the telephone.

It was only when his mother picked up the receiver at the other end of the line that he suddenly realized he hadn't prepared the words for so sensitive a conversation. He hadn't given any thought to what he would say, and his words came out awkward and stilted — and harsher than he had intended.

"You know, tonight was the bas mitzva party Riki organized."

"Yes," his mother said. "She told me about it. How was it?"

"Why didn't you come? She waited for you. She thought you'd come, and she's really hurt that you didn't."

Daniel waited for some sort of reaction, but his mother was silent. Her reticence confused him, and he struggled to find the right words to explain himself.

"Her mother was there, and even a close friend who lives in Telshe Stone came. Riki was embarrassed that her *shvigger*, of all people, didn't show up. She says she guesses you don't think she's important enough."

The silence on the other end of the line continued.

"Hello? Mother? Are you still there?"

"Yes, I hear you."

You hear, but you're not saying anything, thought Daniel. He felt he was sliding down a mountain at breakneck speed with nothing in sight to break his fall.

"What I'm trying to say is that I think an occasion like this calls for a special effort on your part. Riki worked so hard on the performance, and you know how sensitive she is. Maybe you could talk to her, tell her something to make her feel better."

His mother's response, the words pouring out in a torrent, knocked him off balance with its force. The words were calm and measured, but the quiver in her voice told Daniel the control was costing her considerable effort.

"I'm surprised at you, Daniel," she said. "I can't believe you've decided that it's up to *me* to soothe *Riki's* hurt feelings without first verifying why I didn't come. Perhaps I'm also hurt about something. Did that ever occur to you? That's not why I didn't come — I really did have a very difficult and busy day — but speaking as we are about hurt feelings, when do you think I first heard about this oh-so-important party? For some reason, no one bothered to let me know ahead of time.

"The friend who came in from Telshe Stone, and Riki's mother, too, surely heard all about the performance from the very beginning, but not me, Daniel, not me.

"And are you aware that I had to hear from Riki's mother that she's been caring for a little girl twice a week? Am I not important enough in your lives to hear it directly from you? Do I become part of your lives only when you can complain about hurt feelings? Don't *my* feelings deserve to be taken into consideration?"

At this point, his mother's voice sounded choked, and Daniel feared she was on the verge of tears. *No, Hashem, please!* He hadn't intended to hurt her. He really hadn't realized she felt this way.

"I buy you things, I try to help you — but even that is not remembered or appreciated. Why, it doesn't even merit a simple thank-you.

"I recently bought an outfit for Yossi. I spent time in the store selecting what I thought was just the right thing. I tried so hard to buy something especially beautiful and of good quality. Do you know that I didn't hear a single word about it until I brought the subject up with Riki?

"Look," she sighed, "you're her husband, and you need to understand her. That's your obligation. But your mother has a heart, too, don't forget. She's also only human, and I think you need to understand that."

Daniel began apologizing profusely, explaining that he hadn't meant to hurt her or to imply that she had done anything wrong. He thought she might be able to say a word or two to Riki and calm her down, because she didn't understand what had happened. It was a shame, he said, that she bore so much bitterness in her heart. Yes, he'd surely talk to Riki. He really had no idea how they'd never mentioned the child Riki was caring for. He himself had never thought it was something important enough to tell her about. She knew, after all, that he wasn't a big talker, and this was really Riki's project. As for the outfit, this was the first he'd heard about it. That is, he really didn't understand how it was Riki had never thanked her for it. It wasn't like her; he would ask her. "And please," he begged her, "don't take this conversation to heart." They appreciated everything she did for them. Who said they didn't?

He rambled on and on. Sima hurried to conclude the conversation. "Okay, fine, I won't take the matter to heart, and I understand perfectly."

The truth was, though, that Sima took the matter very, very much to heart, and the unintentional insult her beloved son had directed at her by accusing her of hurting his wife's feelings shook her up. Her son had never before dared to side openly with Riki.

Hours later found her still in emotional turmoil.

Daniel, no less upset than his mother, hung up the phone and told his wife about the conversation. He was less confident now; something inside him leaned toward sympathizing with his mother.

"Why didn't you thank her for the outfit she bought?" he asked quietly.

Riki sensed the accusation in the question. With no advance warning, she had turned from the accuser to the accused. She had lost her husband's empathy and understanding.

"What does that have to do with what happened tonight? So I forgot. So what? It happens to the best of us sometimes, doesn't it?" She herself didn't remember the reason for her forgetfulness. "I guess I was just too busy."

"That's no excuse!" exclaimed her husband. "She was also very busy tonight — that's why she didn't come — and see how hurt you are. You've got to remember to say thank you, no matter what. Negligence and forgetfulness can sometimes be as harmful as intentional insult."

Riki couldn't believe her ears. Daniel was berating her with harsh accusations. He had never spoken to her that way before. What was going on here? Was he siding with her or with his mother? Was he so easily swayed?

"So in the end, it's me who's wrong again, isn't it?" Her voice trembled. "I come home from school feeling hurt and disappointed. Once again, my mother-in-law has proven she doesn't care how I feel. I already know she's dissatisfied with me. Just once," she was now close to tears, "just once I wanted her to see that she has a daughter-in-law who's got some talent. Just once, I wanted her to feel proud of me. I wanted her to share my happiness, that's all. Is that so hard to understand?" Her voice cracked. "I guess it is. In the end, it's your mother who's the poor, misunderstood, wronged party. Just like always."

The following morning, Daniel felt disorientated and confused. He had trouble concentrating and couldn't learn properly.

He was still troubled by the bungled conversation he'd had with his wife the night before. He really did understand her, and he had intended to soothe her. Somehow, good intentions notwithstanding, he'd managed to aggravate the situation instead.

What could he do if he understood his mother as well? When he recalled how he'd hurt her, his heart contracted with pain and regret. He'd always tried not to hurt her, to give her as much *nachas* as possible. He never dreamed he'd be faced with a situation where fulfilling the mitzva of honoring one's parents would be so difficult and challenging.

What was he to do? Was he supposed to remain silent, indifferent to his wife's unhappiness?

Daniel had never been a big talker and had always avoided taking a stand on controversial issues. Now he felt he was being swept into the heart of events too critical for him to handle. His feeling of helplessness bothered him a lot and gave him no peace.

In his distress, Daniel suddenly decided on an unusual course of action, one that went against his very nature. He decided to speak to his *rosh kollel* and ask his advice on the matter.

■ ■ ■

Standing in a quiet corner alone with Rav Green, Daniel related the entire story in a hushed tone of voice. He discussed the complicated situation, explaining that he felt he was being forced into taking a leading role in a drama he wanted no part in. More, he wasn't at all certain what was expected of him in this no-win situation. He wanted to be a good, dedicated husband, supportive of his wife, but he wanted to be a good son to his mother as well. He felt torn between these two obligations. The problem, he said, was eating away at him, eroding the harmony in his home and upsetting his concentration in his Torah studies. What should he do?

Rav Green listened attentively to every word, keeping his warm, wise eyes fixed on Daniel's face the whole time. "It's a complicated situation," he said when Daniel finished, "but with Hashem's help, everything will turn out well. Interestingly enough, some couples encounter no problems at all on this front, and everything runs smoothly. Others have a more difficult time. Sometimes, the lack of communication stems from differences in personality or outlook, or one person doesn't find favor in the other's eyes. It can be any one of a dozen reasons. Even the Gemara states that friction between a mother-in-law and daughter-in-law can exist.

"But that doesn't mean there's no solution. There are some problems that only time can heal. In time, both parties mature and become wiser. They learn to see things in a different light. This situation calls for working on one's *middos*. Yes, it's hard work. You need lots of patience and faith that time will help heal all wounds and that eventually both sides will learn to accept each other for what they are.

"Sometimes, when matters get seriously out of hand, it makes sense to try and talk things over, the way you did. It's possible, though, that your good intentions amounted to nothing because of a poor choice of words or bad timing.

"Sometimes, it's a matter of phraseology. You could, for example, have said to your mother, 'You have no idea how important you are to Riki, how much your opinion means to her. She understood that you couldn't make it, but she was really disappointed and upset.' Your mother might have accepted the matter differently had you avoided the word 'hurt.' But let bygones be bygones, because there really are no hard-and-fast rules that apply equally to every situation.

"When communicating with people, it's important to try and gauge the other person's capacity and readiness to accept what it is we're saying. Timing is crucial. One must weigh the potential gain of speaking against the possible damage if one's words are misconstrued.

"You asked about your role in this matter, is that not so?" Harav Green's voice suddenly became brisk and practical. "You want to know *lema'ase*, what you are to do the next time something like this comes up. Let me tell you what I think." The *rosh kollel* began humming a Talmudic tune, stroking his beard as if still thinking the matter over. "It says in *Sefer Bereishis*, '*Al ken ya'azov ish es aviv ve'es imo, vedavak be'ishto* — a man shall leave his father and his mother and cleave to his wife.' The Torah, the master plan according to which the world was created, provides us with answers to every possible question, including situations like the one you now find yourself in.

"There's no doubt your main job right now is to see to the firm establishment of your own home, which is still in the early stages of construction, so to speak. It's up to you to bring back to your home a spirit of peace and tranquility, to cultivate *shalom bayis*. That doesn't mean you have to hurt your mother in any way. For the moment, let things be. Stop trying to mediate between your wife and your mother.

"Devote yourself wholeheartedly to your wife. Try to understand her feelings. Try to find the right words with which to soothe her ruffled feelings. Then, if you see she's receptive, you can discuss the value of remaining silent even in the face of insult. Give her *chizuk* that will help her act *lifnim meshuras hadin*. Encourage her to forgive and forget, even when she feels justifiably hurt. Tell her about '*Kol hama'avir al middosav ma'avirin lo kol psha'av*,' and explain that Heaven views a person in the way he views others: if he overlooks insults and slights, so too will Hashem overlook his own imperfections. Your encouragement in this area will pave the way for smooth relationships without blame or accusation. At a later stage, when your wife's distress eases, you might try to raise points in your mother's favor if you feel they will be well received.

"If you keep the lines of communication with your wife open, you will merit *hashra'as haShechina*. The Divine Presence will rest upon your home, and that will eventually pave the way for a healthy relationship between your wife and your mother."

28

JUAN PEREZ AKA GAVRIEL VIDAL walked slowly up and down the narrow side street in the outskirts of Tel Aviv three times before he finally spotted it. The half-hidden sign on the dilapidated building read "Attorney Rodriguez, Specialist in Real Estate and Property Law."

Rodriguez's name had come to his mind the night before as he lay in bed thinking through the details of a plan he'd originally dreamed up when caring for his first patient in Israel. Unfortunately, that old man had died before Juan could act on his plan.

Now that he was certain old Mr. Schiller was suffering from intermittent bouts of confusion, he might finally get a chance to carry out the plan he'd been forced to put off until now. First, though, he needed to verify the legal standing of a sick old man's signature on a document.

That's why he needed a lawyer.

He had racked his brains trying to come up with someone who either wouldn't suspect him or who wouldn't care. What he needed was someone willing to keep his eyes glued to the paperwork even if he was suspicious.

Rodriguez! That was it! The name had suddenly flashed through his mind.

Rodriguez, his old schoolmate, would certainly be more than glad to cooperate — in exchange for handsome remuneration, of course. Rodriguez had made aliya just a few years before Juan. Unlike Juan, he had done very well for himself in the professional career he'd begun while still in Argentina.

Juan walked up the worn steps to the second floor. At the door to the lawyer's office, he rang the bell and walked right in.

To his surprise, the interior of the office looked nothing like the outside. He took in the wall-to-wall carpet, the modern desks and cabinets, and the heavy floor-to-ceiling drapes. The formal atmosphere made him even more nervous. He pictured his boyhood friend as arrogant and aloof. He was no longer quite so sure about the working relationship they might develop.

The secretary paused in the middle of her computer work long enough to ask him what he wanted.

"I'm here to see Rodriguez," he said.

"Do you have an appointment with Mr. Rodriguez today?" she inquired crisply.

"No, but you can tell him Juan Perez is here. Tell him it's urgent. He knows me."

The secretary entered an inner office and returned after a brief delay. "Mr. Rodriguez will see you," she said.

Juan's meeting with Rodriguez was like that of two hunting dogs suspiciously sniffing one another. The attorney was far from naïve. He knew his unexpected visitor only too well. He was on guard, all senses alert, the moment Juan entered his office, even though he stretched his lips into a wide smile and greeted him warmly.

"Hello there, old friend! Come on in. What a pleasant surprise on an otherwise routine day. Would you like something to drink? Ramona!" he called to his secretary. "Can we have a cold drink? We have a most esteemed guest here today."

"So what brings you here, Juan?" he asked, getting right to the point. "How can I help you? I'm sure you didn't come all this way to reminisce, eh?"

Juan, who hadn't had a chance to open his mouth since he'd walked in, ignored the question. "Nice place you've got here. You're doing well, I gather. A real fancy first-class lawyer."

"Yup," his friend agreed, enjoying Juan's dazzled look. "Business is not bad, as you can see. Records, transfer of ownership, buying and selling apartments and lots more — it's a never-ending business. There are always customers."

As he spoke, Juan's eyes lit up. "Transfer of ownership — that's what I'm interested in. That's what I came to see you about."

"Hmmm," said the lawyer, leaning back in his leather swivel chair.

"I'm interested in transferring the ownership of an apartment that belongs to my wife's father. We'd like the apartment to be under both our names."

"Your wife's father?" Rodriguez raised his eyebrows in question. "I didn't know he was still alive."

"Oh, he's alive all right," Juan answered, with a nervous chuckle that alerted the finely tuned senses of his friend from Argentina.

The secretary came in carrying a tray bearing two glasses of cola.

Mr. Rodriguez waited until she closed the door behind her before asking, "He lives here in Israel?"

"Yes, in Ramat Gan," Juan answered smoothly. "But his apartment is empty. You see, he's in a nursing home, and his health is steadily deteriorating. We spoke with him — or rather, he spoke with us — about the matter. He feels it might be wise to transfer ownership of the apartment to us, perhaps through a will or some sort of declaration or affidavit. He doesn't know what will happen in the end, and he wants to be certain the apartment will belong to us afterward, to avoid problems."

"What kinds of problems is he afraid of?" the attorney asked in surprise.

"I don't know exactly. Isn't this the kind of thing that needs to be written down and certified?"

"It depends. Who else might claim ownership of the apartment?" Mr. Rodriguez asked. He wasn't about to let Juan avoid the question so easily.

"My wife's sister," Juan replied quickly.

"She has a sister?"

The conversation was turning into a battle of wits, like a game of tennis played by two pros.

"Yes. You don't know her. She lives in Jerusalem."

Rodriguez winked. "Okay. So what is it you want exactly?"

"I want to know how my father-in-law can sign a will without me having to drag him here. He's old and frail. I can't take him out of the nursing home. I'm also asking what's best for us. Perhaps we're better off if he gives us the apartment as a gift while he's alive, rather than bequeathing it to us in his will. Such a possibility does exist, doesn't it? I mean, the ownership could be transferred to us now. Am I right or wrong?"

"Both," came the reply. "If I understand you correctly, you're afraid your wife's sister won't agree to let you have the apartment. You want to take possession before she sees what's going on."

Without waiting for confirmation, he continued. "Good. You're right. According to the law, it's up to the claimant, not the defendant, to prove ownership of the contested property. In such a case, anyone wishing to make a claim against you would be required to present legal evidence that the property rightfully belonged to him. That's a matter of bureaucracy with complications that, from a legal standpoint, puts the claimant in a position inferior to your own."

Juan nodded. "That's what I thought."

"I'm not surprised you came up with the idea. It's just like you." Rodriguez chuckled as he thought back to their youth. "You always manage to make things work out to your benefit. Do you remember that time when you snuck out the answers to the math exam from the principal's office a day before the big test?"

Juan wasn't sure whether or not to smile. Was Rodriguez paying him a backhanded compliment, or was he implying something more sinister?

"We're talking business now," he said almost aggressively. "Why are you bringing up the past?"

"You're right. Sorry," Rodriguez said. "What you can do is ask this father-in-law of yours to sign in the nursing home in the presence of two witnesses who will then testify before me. That's legal. If you'd like, I can give you the necessary form to fill out."

The lawyer paused for a moment. "But you're still left with a serious problem," he said slowly. "If your wife's sister — or anyone else, for that matter — can claim that the old man was not in full possession of his senses at the time he signed, you've got a problem. You'll have to present a doctor's note affirming that the man was in full possession of his senses when he signed. Without that, you're liable to lose everything."

"A doctor's note," Juan repeated slowly, his mouth suddenly dry. He reached for his glass and took a drink. That would be no simple matter. What excuse could he possibly think of to ask for a doctor's note affirming Mr. Schiller's lucidity, and just who might the doctor be? Mr. Schiller had no reason to see any physician other than the regular Nachalas Avos doctor. Juan didn't realize that his expression had become drawn.

"Are you okay?" the lawyer asked, leaning forward.

"Uh, yes. I'm fine," Juan hurried to reply.

"Does the doctor's note pose a problem for you? Is this father-in-law of yours not 100 percent lucid?" His voice was tinged with concern when he asked the question, but immediately after, he lowered his voice and asked, "Come to think of it, I heard you've been working as a caretaker for elderly men lately, no?"

Juan sprang out of his trance with a start. His survival instinct mobilized him. No way was he about to let this man ruin his plans! His old friend, whom he had trusted, was turning out to be dangerous. He wasn't cooperating as well as Juan had thought he might.

He had received an answer to his questions, and he knew what he was going to do. "Yes," he said, rising to his feet. "I work for a nursing home. So what? Nice seeing you again, and thanks for the help. I'll get back to you if I need any more advice."

With that, he left.

Later, walking along the busy street, Juan fumed at Rodriguez. The nerve of him! Why did he have to bring up the stolen math test? Why all the insinuations that Juan was a sly, conniving sneak? Rodriguez, of course, had not said so outright, but the message came through loud and clear.

The visit was a waste of time except for one disturbing piece of information: the need for a doctor's note confirming the old man's mental soundness. How in the world would he get hold of something like that? The nursing home's doctor was a smart man and an honest one, too. Juan doubted he could pull the wool over his eyes.

Was he going to let the need for a doctor's note foil the whole plan? Since when did he allow such problems to get in his way?

What was it Rodriguez had said? "You always manage to make things work out to your benefit."

Wait a minute! Juan stopped short in the middle of the crowded sidewalk. Why hadn't he thought of it before? *Rodriguez,* he said to himself, *thanks for one great idea.*

Remember how you snuck out the answers from the principal's office? That was it! Documents could be surreptitiously taken from any office, not just the principal's!

He wouldn't have any problem obtaining a doctor's signature, not with the professional counterfeiters he knew. The certificate testifying that Juan Perez was a certified nurse was a fake, too. Yeah, he knew how to arrange it.

Success was within his reach. Juan almost laughed out loud.

29

A GROUP OF ELDERLY MEN SAT in a circle in the lobby of the Nachalas Avos nursing home, exercising under the supervision and guidance of Ben Gal, licensed physical therapist. Sima Abramson stood not far away, unobtrusively watching the group. She made it her business to observe, from time to time, all the activities the nursing home provided for its residents. That way, she could keep tabs on the level of professionalism, the content and the instructor's interaction with the residents. In addition, she liked to note to what extent the elderly people were benefiting from the activities.

At this moment, her attention was focused on Mr. Schiller, who sat in the circle along with the others. For some reason, he appeared rather withdrawn, somewhat detached from his surroundings. She noticed that he wasn't really participating in the activity. He seemed oblivious to the instructor's directions. The others were clenching and unclenching their fists according to the beat of background music, then thrusting their arms forward and back as instructed. Mr. Schiller, though, sat immobile until the instructor addressed him specifically and asked him to perform a particular exercise.

A red warning light flashed in the dedicated director's mind. *Something's happened to the poor man*, she thought in alarm. *I must check it out. On the other hand, he may be feeling down because his daughter is away.*

Sima sighed. During the past two days, since she'd spoken openly with Daniel, she found herself sighing all too often. The distress she'd felt then had never left her, and every little worrisome thing that happened troubled her twice as much as it ordinarily would have.

I ought to arrange a meeting for the family members of all the residents, the thought suddenly occurred to her. *We could call it a "Children's Evening," similar to the many "Parents' Evenings" our residents participated in for their children's sake. The evening would be dedicated to the discussion of how much a child's presence means to an elderly parent. (Child? Most of the residents' children were grandparents themselves.)*

Some people mistakenly think that if they hire a dedicated Filipino caregiver for their parents or register them in a good-quality nursing home that provides all sorts of wonderful services, they've done their part, fulfilled their obligation. After all, the elderly person is safe and lacks for nothing. Children often forget that their parents provided *them* with far more than their physical needs. If their parents hadn't showered them with love and affection, they would have missed out on an important childhood need. In the same way, even the best caregiver or the finest facility for the aged cannot take the place of one's children. Elderly parents need to feel warmth and love flowing from their children's hearts to their own.

Yes, Sima felt sure Naomi Stone's trip abroad had negatively affected her father.

She had no complaints about Naomi. She was a grown woman, a mother herself, and she certainly had the right to manage her affairs as she saw fit. When she was nearby, she did the best she could. But what about the rest of Mr. Schiller's family? They came, but only infrequently, and the visits were inevitably brief. They, like many others, depended on the nursing home to see to their parents' every need.

Sima strongly believed that there was no substitute for family. A father needs his children, and children know their parents better than anyone else. Often a visiting son or daughter alerted Sima's attention to small changes in a resident's behavior. This was the result of the natural bond, the bond of blood, between them. Sometimes, a child noted his parent's gaze seemed distant; sometimes it was an unusual physical mannerism that bothered a son or daughter.

Again, she sighed heavily. She was glad she had noticed the change in Mr. Schiller. She would speak to the family, and perhaps she really would arrange such an evening at some point. She would invite experts in the field to lecture on the subject. In the meantime, she'd speak to the doctor about Mr. Schiller. In fact, she would even ask Mr. Vidal, his caregiver, to take him to his regular family doctor. It was obvious Mr. Schiller trusted his caregiver implicitly and felt comfortable in his presence. That in itself was a good sign, and some consolation in the present circumstances.

Just then, Malka Weiss, the elderly Mrs. Weiss's daughter-in-law, entered the nursing home. Sima spotted her as she walked in, and her eyes lit up with joy. Here was a woman who served as living proof of the need for regular visits to a parent. It was an incontestable fact that ever since Malka began visiting more often, her elderly mother-in-law was a different person — less irritable and far happier. Even her appetite had improved.

Seeking to encourage this favorable change of behavior, Sima now walked toward the visitor with a smile. "I'm so grateful for what you're doing for your mother-in-law. I must tell you that since you began visiting more often, her appetite has improved and she seems happier."

For a brief instant, a startled look passed over Malka Weiss's face. She was taken aback by the director's comment, but quickly collected herself and returned a radiant smile.

"Thank you, Mrs. Abramson. I'm very pleased to hear that. I appreciate your telling me and encouraging me to continue. Quite frankly," she said, looking directly at Sima, "the decision to visit more often was a sudden one. It occurred to me on my birthday. There are moments, you know, when something just opens up inside you, and you see things in a different light."

She slowed her stride as she hitched her pocketbook over her shoulder to a more comfortable position, preparing for a longer conversation with the nursing home's director.

"Don't think it was laziness that kept me from visiting her this often until now. It was really because of the relationship that had developed between us over the years. It's hard to explain."

Actually, Malka wasn't sure why she was discussing this with the director in the first place. Was it her natural urge to apologize and defend herself? She didn't owe the woman any explanations or apologies. Still, she wanted her to understand.

"We had the kind of relationship where I felt I was totally unimportant to her. She was always talking about how much she missed her daughter, who lives abroad, and it was clear she preferred my husband's presence to mine. She never really made peace with the fact that her children had gotten married and left the nest. At least, that's how I see things today. From the first, I felt she didn't welcome me into the family, surely not as a daughter and barely as a daughter-in-law. Naturally, I reacted to her in a similar fashion, and our relationship never took off. That was the cause of my infrequent visits, which you noticed.

"Oh!" she suddenly exclaimed. "I do hope I'm not holding you up! You're at work, after all. You probably have important business to attend to, and here I am chattering away."

Sima assured her she wasn't disturbing at all. She found her conversation with Malka Weiss particularly interesting, and there was nothing pressing for her to do at the moment anyway.

"No, go right ahead. You're not disturbing me at all," she assured her. "Anyway, your mother-in-law is in the auditorium at a lecture. You know how much she enjoys these weekly lectures, so feel free to spend some time just chatting."

"Yes, she recently told me about the fascinating lectures you have here on the parasha. She really looks forward to them. It's nice that you're able to find the right people to deliver these lectures."

Sima accepted the compliment graciously. "It's not easy. Public speaking for the elderly requires a special approach and an understanding of their world." After a slight pause, she suggested, "As long as we're talking, why don't we make ourselves comfortable?" She indicated a table and chairs. "There's a nice quiet corner."

The two sat down in the comfortable lounge chairs that were partially screened off from the main lobby. Strangers to each other, they nonetheless felt a certain kinship. They were approximately the same age and dealing with the same issues in life. They intuitively felt certain they would understand one another.

"Anyway, what happened was," Malka continued where she'd left off, "I suddenly decided to change the rules of the game, plain and simple."

"The rules of the game? What do you mean?" asked Sima. "What game?"

"I'm talking about the relationship between me and my mother-in-law. I guess you could call it our 'familial dance.' Did you know I'm a social worker?"

"No, I didn't know," Sima said.

"It doesn't really matter, but maybe it explains why I sometimes use such terms. Anyway, my birthday was a lovely day, a beautiful gift lovingly granted by *Hakadosh baruch Hu*. Everyone went out of his way to make me happy, especially my two wonderful daughters-in-law, and I thought to myself, 'So what if your mother-in-law never accepted you as a daughter all these years? So what? Do you have to dance to her tune? Change the dance! It's as simple as that. You're a big girl. You're no longer the scared, insecure little girl you once were. Accept her as a mother, something you've never even tried to do before. And if it doesn't work, and you can't be a daughter, at least be a good daughter-in-law.'

"That's what I mean by 'changing the rules of the game,' or 'the steps of the dance.' It's hard, believe me," said Malka earnestly. "It's very hard to change the way you've been doing things for years. At first, my mother-in-law didn't know what had come over me. She was suspicious. It didn't take long, though, before she opened up to me. I believe a small seed of love was planted in her heart — and in mine. Today, she no longer asks when my husband will be coming to visit, she asks about me.

"I ask myself," Malka shook her head, "why I never tried to change things earlier, years ago!"

"It's like you said," Sima said thoughtfully. "You needed to grow and mature. A step like that requires true maturity." The admiration she felt came through clearly. "I don't think you had the courage to do something like that when you were younger. While we're on the subject," she said tentatively, "let me ask you a question. I'm concerned about a relationship with someone in my family that is — how shall I put it? — less than what it could be. Do you think the 'dance' you mention exists in every relationship?"

30

IT WAS QUIET IN THE NURSING HOME lobby; nothing disturbed the two women as they sat chatting comfortably with one other. For Sima, it was one of those rare times when she had nothing urgent to take care of. The male residents were still practicing physical therapy exercises under the supervision of the inimitable Ben Gal, and the women were in the auditorium listening to a lecture on the parasha, leaving her free to give her full attention to the intelligent, pleasant woman sitting opposite her.

"You're asking whether a 'familial dance,' as I put it, exists in every relationship," Malka repeated Sima's question. "Well," she paused momentarily to choose her words carefully, "I think this is true. Sometimes, it exists between a husband and wife or two friends or even just close relatives. Sometimes it's there between a parent and child. We move in a pattern of some sort without even being aware of it, which is why it's so hard to stop. It's a sort of behavioral style we unwittingly get dragged into.

"Take, for example, a child. Yes, a child, that's it!" Malka's voice rose in enthusiasm as she hit on what she thought was the perfect example. "Suppose a child begs for an ice cream cone.

His mother doesn't know whether or not to give in. He's already had one ice cream cone that day, and she thinks it's enough. The child continues whining. The mother's nerves are frayed from the incessant nagging, and she feels like an incompetent parent. She lashes out at the child with a barrage of complaints and insults, maybe even screaming furiously.

"The child bursts into tears, the picture of abject misery. He tells her that all his friends' mothers give their kids ice cream cones whenever they ask for one, and that he's the only one with such a mean mother. The mother feels guilty for having lost control and causing her child misery, so she tries to assuage her guilt by appeasing him. 'Come here, sweetie,' she says. 'You can buy an ice cream cone.' In a last-ditch effort to maintain some parental control, she adds, 'But just one. And only today. This is the last time I'm giving in!' But what's the difference? The kid got his way.

"That's the 'dance' — a steady pattern the child learns to recognize: first he whines, then his mother yells, then he cries and then she finally gives in."

"Well," Sima wondered, "what is the solution in a situation like that?"

"The solution is simply to become aware that there is a pattern that keeps repeating itself and to make a conscious effort to change it. The change can be made at the 'last stop,' where the child cries but the mother holds firm, or at one of the earlier points — say, for instance, where the child whines but the mother chooses not to lose control and yell. Either way, the child senses that something is different. The rules have changed, and his tactics are not working. He's thrown off balance. His crying and nagging are not working their usual magic. At that point, he too is forced to change. That's called 'changing the dance.'"

"So what you're saying is," Sima said slowly, trying to make sure she understood what Malka was getting at, "the mother needs to be more certain of her own position. She needs to ask herself whether the child is really suffering, or whether he is playing on her weakness."

"Exactly!" Malka cried triumphantly. "You've hit the nail on the head. A dance like that is a behavioral pattern we get swept into. To stop such a pattern, a person must access the mature part of his personality and ask himself, 'Wait a minute. What's going on here? What's happening to me? What do I want?'

"I want to tell you something," Malka said in the firm tone of one who has just reached a decision. "I want to share something very personal that just happened to me this morning. I haven't discussed this yet with anyone, but I'm just bursting to talk it over with someone. I'm sure I can count on you to keep it between us," she added in an undertone. "You don't know my daughter-in-law, and you're not a member of my family. There are some things it's better to talk about with strangers than with people close to you. That way, there's less of a chance of the conversation getting back to the subject of the story.

"It's a delicate subject. We're talking about my daughter-in-law, after all. I think my experience today is the perfect example of how to get out of an unfavorable dance you feel yourself getting dragged into."

Malka launched into her tale, unaware that there was in fact a good chance Sima might know her daughter-in-law, the subject of her story, very well. If not for the fact that Riki didn't talk to her own mother-in-law very often, Sima might have realized that the daughter-in-law Malka Weiss was talking about was Yehudis Weiss, Riki's neighbor. Riki herself never dreamed that Yehudis Weiss's grandmother was a resident at the nursing home her in-laws owned.

With neither of them the wiser, Malka told her story in the quiet lobby under the graceful green leaves of a weeping fig tree.

"Three days ago, my daughter-in-law gave birth to a baby girl," she related.

"How nice! *Mazel tov*," Sima interrupted with warm wishes.

"Thank you," replied Malka, continuing her story. "A few

days before she had the baby, my son, the proud father, called me. He told me they wouldn't be able to go to his mother-in-law's house after the baby was born, because she was caring for her own mother, a sick, elderly woman who needs constant care. They have a very small, cramped house, he explained, and the only spare room is now occupied by his wife's grandmother. He told me it had occurred to him that I might be able to take Chaim, their one-year-old, while Yehudis spent a few days in a postnatal convalescent home.

"What can I tell you?" Malka sighed. "It was hard for me to say yes. I work full-time outside the house. Taking care of a one-year-old under such circumstances is no easy feat. I told my son I would rather Yehudis come to our house along with both children. 'I'll cook and see she has everything she needs,' I explained, 'and in the afternoons I can help her with Chaim and the baby. Yehudis will only have the baby to watch in the mornings when I'm away. I think that's not a bad solution.'

"My son readily agreed, even adding that perhaps Chaim would stay home with him. He would go to his regular baby-sitter in the morning, and maybe he would find another baby-sitter for the afternoon. The main thing was, he stressed, that Yehudis have a comfortable place to rest. He thanked me warmly.

"*Nu,*" Malka raised her eyes to Sima in question. "What do you think happened in the end? I spent three days preparing for them. I got a room ready for the mother and the baby, and I even tried to arrange to take a day or two of vacation to be home with her. And then, this morning, just before I came here, my son called and said they'd changed their minds. My daughter-in-law's older sister had invited her to stay with her. She has a big house, and my daughter-in-law felt she'd be more comfortable there, my son said. She was worried it would be too hard for me to have her stay with me. After all, I go to work, while her sister is home all day."

The pain now evident in Malka's voice told Sima that the memory of the phone call still hurt her. "I really can't explain it, but I felt like I had been slapped in the face. I felt my breath catch. I couldn't talk. If my son had told me she wanted to go to a convalescent home, it would have been easier for me to accept. Those places provide a new mother with far more than an ordinary house run by a woman who works full-time outside the home. But why would she rather stay with her older sister in a house filled with children? I felt as if she were saying, 'If it's too hard for you to take care of my child, I don't need your favors! I have a sister who's willing to do that much for me.'

"Or even without bringing Chaim into the picture, to me her decision meant, 'I'll feel more comfortable with my sister than with you.' I meant so well. I tried so hard. I felt I didn't deserve such treatment. Do you understand what I mean?"

Oh, did Sima understand! She too would have been hurt if something like that happened to her. How easy it was for good intentions to be misconstrued.

"Things like that tend to happen," she murmured.

"True," nodded Malka. "My son heard my silence and didn't know what to make of it. I wanted to lash out at him and let him know how I felt or at least answer, 'Well, that's fine with me. Do as you see fit,' and then brusquely hang up without another word. I felt like acting as if I didn't care what they did or how she felt. Why should I offer to help? If there was any problem, they had a wonderful address to turn to — the darling older sister was there, wasn't she?

"I didn't even feel like going to visit her. All these bitter thoughts passed through my mind during those few moments of silence on the phone with my son. And then I heard his voice ask with trepidation, 'Ma? Is everything okay?'

"I suddenly thought to myself, *This is it! This is the dance*! If I allow myself to be drawn into it, things can become unpleasant. I'll feel insulted. I'll lash out and hurt them. I won't visit. And Yehudis, emotionally vulnerable after having a baby, won't understand what I'm making such a fuss about and will get doubly insulted. Her reaction toward me will reflect my feelings toward her, and we'll each get wrapped up and absorbed in our own hurt feelings.

"*No!* something within me cried out in protest. *It's up to you to stop this dance before it even starts, to nip it in the bud*, I told myself. I forced myself to think rationally. 'Listen,' I said to my son. 'I must admit I'm disappointed. I was really looking forward to having Yehudis come here. But if you've decided otherwise, I suppose you have your reasons.'

"'Yes,' he replied, the relief evident in his voice. 'Our main consideration is that her sister lives in the same city, so Chaim can stay with me and still see his mother every day.'"

Malka's smile was triumphant. "I can't begin to tell you how much better I felt. What he was saying made a lot of sense. It suddenly seemed so obvious. My wounded pride was restored, and I was no longer in danger of being swept up in childish thoughts and emotions that could have hurt us all."

"Is that what's called 'stopping the dance'?" Sima asked slowly.

"Exactly!" exclaimed Malka. "It's really very simple." Carefully weighing her words, she added, "You mentioned an unsuccessful relationship before. I don't know who or what you're talking about, and I don't want to pry, but I'm certain that if you look for it, you'll find some sort of pattern, some sort of a dance that you can stop."

Sima sighed. "Yes," she concurred. "I suppose that's so. I'll have to sit down and think about it." She still wasn't ready to discuss the matter openly with the woman sitting opposite her. She wasn't used to sharing her private feelings. However, she did trust her newfound friend enough to confide in her somewhat.

"In my case too it's my daughter-in-law I'm having trouble with," she whispered. "But it seems to me our relationship is more complicated than the one you described. Changing things won't be as simple as you make it sound. Besides, I don't think the other side, that is, the youngsters, are entirely free of blame, as they were in your case." She sighed again.

"Oh, I didn't say they're always right," Malka replied. "They make mistakes too. But for the sake of the quality of the relationship between us, it's up to us to at least try to be the more mature of the two sides. We must be the ones who change the pattern and stop the dance. We are better equipped to do so, Mrs. Abramson.

"Don't you remember?" she asked with passion. "When we first started talking, you yourself told me it took growth and maturity for me to change my relationship with my elderly mother-in-law. Our children are still so young."

Malka's voice grew soft and warm. "Picture them, young and inexperienced, busy with so many things, facing new challenges. Everything is new — new home, new spouse, new job, children.... Of course they make mistakes! At times, they are unintentionally abrasive. Sometimes they just don't know the right way to act. Sometimes they're unsure of how to approach a particular issue.

"But that's why we're here — to be the understanding party, the side that doesn't get carried away, the side that is mature enough to forgive, to put a stop to bad patterns that are forming. And you know what?" The social worker who was both a mother-in-law and daughter-in-law, as well as a newfound friend, smiled warmly at Sima. "It just occurred to me that the most important thing to remember is that even the smoothest relationships sometimes hit rough spots. But so what? The occasional pitfalls are an integral part of a warm, dynamic relationship between people."

31

DURING THE TWO DAYS SINCE her husband had spoken to her mother-in-law, Riki's pent-up feelings of disappointment and frustration gave way to an attitude of indifference. After that fateful conversation in which Daniel's mother had unburdened her heart to her son, Riki, too, had told her husband exactly what was on her mind — especially that she felt he was again taking his mother's side instead of his wife's. Then came a torrent of words in self-defense.

"So you want to know about the outfit she bought for Yossi, the one I didn't thank her for right away? Well, now I remember why I didn't call her to say thank you. I didn't like the color, and I thought it was very impractical for a weekday outfit, especially the white collar. I was debating whether or not it was okay to ask your mother if I could exchange it. I was afraid she might get insulted, so I postponed talking about it altogether. What could I do? Believe me, it wasn't because I didn't appreciate the gift or didn't care about her feelings that I didn't call right away to say thank you.

"I don't know if you remember how I got the outfit in the

first place. Your brother Ariel gave it to you in shul in a black plastic bag, and you brought it home along with your tefillin bag. It took me a few days to figure out where the outfit had come from.

"And why didn't I tell her about Brachi? I wasn't sure how she'd react, if she'd approve of the idea — so I just didn't tell her. Besides, I don't think you should do *chessed* to brag about it afterward. Do you?

"There was also a good reason for my not telling your mother about the bas mitzva party. I was under such pressure that I just didn't have time to let her know about it earlier. It's not my fault my mother happened to meet her two days before the party!

"I didn't want to make a big deal out of the performance. You know very well what your mother thinks of parties and counselors and extracurricular activities. I didn't want her to think I was giving the performance top priority in my life. I was afraid she would get the impression that it was taking up my whole day, that it was all I could think about.

"I also didn't want to tell her I was in charge of the entire event, the way my mother told her. But is that enough of a reason for her to decide not to attend? I don't think that's justified."

After the flood of words, Riki suddenly had nothing left to say. A moment of silence passed, and then another. Daniel stood silently at his *shtender* in the corner of the room, and Riki sat quietly on the sofa. Both were caught up in thoughts of their own.

Why? Why is this happening to me? Riki thought despairingly. *When it comes to my relationship with my mother-in-law, I feel I'm being sucked into a whirlpool with no chance of breaking away. Whatever I do or don't do is somehow no good. If I try to prove myself as a successful career woman, that's no good — she doesn't approve of women who invest too much effort outside of the home. If I lower my profile and try not to make a big deal out of a party I arrange, that also causes trouble. If I do things that go against her outlook on life, that surely displeases her, and if I try to avoid confrontation by not telling her about certain things I think she might disapprove of, that's also no good.*

No one appreciated or even noticed the fact that I didn't make a fuss when she visited only my sister-in-law. But when I got the outfit a few days later, sent over in a plastic bag with no identifying note, and didn't immediately call her up to say thank you, she got insulted!

She claims I don't appreciate the things she buys for us, that we rarely say thank you. When, except for that one time, did I ever fail to say thank you? I'm sure I always thanked her for every single gift, even the ones I didn't particularly like, the ones she bought without taking my taste into consideration.

And then, the one time it might be only fair to ask her outright if I could exchange a gift — which would let me really thank her and mean it — I get into even worse trouble.

What about my calling her every Friday just before Shabbos no matter how busy I am? Why doesn't anyone ever mention that? And how about all the times we go for Shabbos, even when I don't feel like it, just because I'm afraid she might be hurt if we reject her invitation? Whenever I'm there, I always try to give Tehilla extra attention, even if I'd rather spend the time doing something else. I listen to her and give her encouragement, because I get the impression she's having a hard time with her friends. But her mother never even notices, let alone appreciates it.

So that's it! I give up! Riki didn't even notice that she had actually thrown both hands up in the air. *It's obvious I'll never be able to please my mother-in-law. She just doesn't approve of me. I saw it at our very first meeting. Now Daniel, too, has gotten sucked into this whirlpool. He must be mad at me for putting him into such an uncomfortable situation.*

So what? I guess I'll just have to make peace with the fact that my mother-in-law and I don't get along. I don't care. From now on, I'm going to ignore the whole thing. I refuse to make any further effort to improve the situation. It no longer interests me. I'll be polite, of course. When she calls, I'll respond briefly and simply. If she wants to come visit, that's fine with me. If she doesn't, that's fine too. When it suits me, I'll go to them for Shabbos, and when it doesn't, I won't. I won't go out of my way at all. All I get is complaints anyway, so why bother? I'll go about my daily life as usual.

And another thing: I won't discuss the matter with Danny anymore. It's bad enough I don't get along with my mother-in-law. Do I have to let her ruin my relationship with my husband as well?

Having reached this decision, without sharing it with her husband, Riki ended her day.

■ ■ ■

When Daniel came home from *kollel* the following day, brimming with goodwill to discuss the matter with Riki in accordance with his *rosh kollel's* view of the situation, he couldn't quite find the opportunity to do so. It was as if his wife had completely forgotten yesterday's events. She displayed no interest whatsoever in discussing the situation.

He tried to broach the subject over their evening meal, but Riki's lack of response made it difficult to get anywhere. Finally, he gave up and told her about something else he'd been meaning to discuss with her since the previous night. He described his success with Motti, the boy he was tutoring. Today, like yesterday, the child had reported with obvious excitement how he had participated in class and how well he felt he was progressing. As if to confirm Motti's words, Daniel recounted, Rabbi Levy himself had approached him after davening to tell him that the principal reported that the child was showing marked improvement. He had asked Rabbi Levy to personally thank the young man who was working such a miracle.

Riki's heart soared upon hearing the news. She was not consciously aware of it, but she was surprised by her husband's success. She was glad others recognized his ability. Her husband's worth rose in her eyes.

Riki's enthusiastic reaction and open display of pride and

happiness at his success did wonders for Daniel. He continued speaking at length about his thoughts, his dreams and his ambitions. This was an unusual conversation for the couple, as Daniel was usually inhibited and rarely spoke about himself. Now that he was sharing some of his innermost thoughts, their discussion was richer, more interesting and intimate than ever before.

Later, the house was quiet once again. Daniel had gone to learn and Yossi was sleeping when the phone rang. It was Chaya Baum, Riki's mother. The night before, she had called just after Riki's emotional outburst. Of course, Chaya had just seen Riki at the bas mitzva party a few hours earlier, but she'd felt the urge to pick up the phone and tell her daughter yet again how impressed she was by the beautiful performance.

Riki hadn't been able to control herself. Quietly, so that Daniel wouldn't hear, she had told her mother about her husband's conversation with his mother. She repeated the discussion she'd had with her husband, and then, in a despairing tone, told her mother about her decision to ignore the whole thing.

Her mother had listened in silence, waiting until she had finished before commenting. "Be careful, Riki," she had said, concern evident in her voice. "When it comes to relationships between people, there's no such thing as a vacuum. Acting indifferent is also a statement of some sort. One teacher's silence, for example, often says far more than another teacher's rebuke. I'm not sure your decision to ignore it will produce the results you want. I think you'd better try and see things from your mother-in-law's point of view and behave accordingly."

"You too!" Riki had wailed before she could stop herself.

Chaya had inadvertently made the same mistake as her son-in-law. She didn't realize that when a person is upset, it's hard for him to accept logical explanations. What he needs is a listening ear and a shoulder to cry on; the rest will come later.

Now, a day later, Chaya decided to call and see how Riki was taking things, whether she'd calmed down. Just like Daniel, she was surprised to see that her daughter showed no interest in discussing the matter, acting as though it had never happened. Instead, Riki was telling her joyfully about Daniel, who was tutoring a boy. Amazingly, said Riki, her husband had found his way to the boy's heart within a few short days, and the principal had forwarded his thanks and congratulations.

Chaya was very moved, more by the pride and satisfaction in her daughter's voice than by the revelation of her son-in-law's latent talent. This was the perfect opportunity to offer her daughter the words of encouragement she'd long thought appropriate.

"You see?" she told her daughter. "I always knew Daniel was an example of 'still waters that run deep.' I was positive his fine qualities would rise to the surface. You'll see, Riki. Eventually his true personality will shine forth and blossom. *Hakadosh baruch Hu* knows what He's doing when He arranges a match, Riki. Daniel is worthy of you, and you of him."

Finally, the words she'd been longing to say for so long were out in the open. Chaya was sure they would be of much benefit to her daughter.

Later that evening, Chaya pondered what Riki had told her about Daniel's success with the boy he was tutoring. She thought about Riki's description of Daniel as caring and perceptive. Suddenly, an idea took hold in her mind and wouldn't let go. She made up her mind to talk it over with her husband or with Riki — or best of all, with Daniel himself.

They had their problems with Ephraim. True, he wasn't nine years old, like the boy Daniel was tutoring; he was a teenager. But he was running into difficulties, just like that other boy. He was confused, standing at the crossroads of his life, and they, his parents, had no idea how to go about helping him.

She would beg Daniel to try and learn with Ephraim. They

had been trying for a long time to find a young man who might take Daniel under his wing, hoping that such a relationship might benefit their son, but Ephraim had rejected them all. Was there a chance things would work out differently with Daniel? With Daniel, Ephraim wouldn't feel like a "special case," and Chaya knew he was very fond of his brother-in-law. If Daniel was displaying so much sensitivity and understanding toward a stranger's child, why shouldn't he try and help their Ephraim?

32

IT WAS A PLEASANT EVENING to be outside. The cool Jerusalem breeze brought welcome respite after the hot, dry spring day.

Ephraim strolled leisurely along the sidewalk flanking the wide boulevard. He liked the wide, spacious streets of the new neighborhood his sister and brother-in-law lived in. Not that he got to visit them often; he was too busy. Whenever he did come, though, he always enjoyed the wide expanse between the buildings on either side of the street. There was plenty of room for the inky night sky, the moon and the stars. Right now, the sky was filled with stars twinkling above the empty street. Mothers were busy inside their homes, settling their children for the night, while fathers were heading to shul. As for Ephraim, nothing urgent demanded his attention at this hour, leaving him free to walk until the last bus stop at the outskirts of Ramot.

The paper bag with roasted sunflower seeds he had bought on his way there crinkled in his pocket. The crowded bus that had brought him there hadn't exactly been the ideal place for relaxing; he had barely found room for his arms and legs.

Afterward had come the learning session with Daniel that had completely banished all thoughts of the tempting bag. Only now, on his way back into town, did he suddenly remember it again. Although the seeds had lost some of their original warmth, they were still fresh and tasty. Cracking the shells with his teeth and tossing them to the wind, Ephraim strolled alongside the broad streets feeling freer than he had in a long time.

So what? he thought, reflecting on the day's events. *So I did my father a favor and came here. It wasn't that bad, actually. Danny's a nice guy, harmless enough. We learned. What do I care? If this will make my parents feel better, I'm game. They're really good parents, just…just a little too demanding. Why are they so upset about my wanting to go out and work? What did Dad think when he sent me for vocational training?*

Ephraim suddenly felt a chill overtake him. *Hey, it's really getting cold*, he observed, shivering. His free hand automatically found its way into his pocket, and the shells began flying from his mouth at a faster pace. The peace he had felt at the outset of the walk was fast giving way to a vague feeling of impatience, irritation even. His thoughts shifted to the conversation he'd had with his father a week earlier.

"Dad," he had said, initiating the discussion at the end of a Shabbos he had spent at home, "I think I've had enough of studying. I want to start working already."

His father had looked stricken. "Why?" he managed to ask. "I mean, why now? You haven't gotten your diploma yet," he said, trying to buy time. "Wait until you finish."

"There's no point in waiting," Ephraim had said. "The courses there aren't for me. I'll never be an electrician. I want to start working and take a computer-programming course at the same time. It's a good profession. It pays well, and I think I'll like it."

His father had heaved a deep sigh. "I've been meaning to talk to you about the future," he began. "You got a draft notice a few days ago. If you start working, they'll draft you."

The news had an opposite affect on Ephraim from the one his father intended. Rather than being afraid, his eyes lit up as he asked with barely restrained excitement. "A draft notice? Why didn't you tell me?"

"I forgot," his father had replied unconvincingly. "Actually, I meant to discuss it with you today, but you brought the subject up before I got the chance."

"A draft notice doesn't scare me," Ephraim had shrugged. "I mean, I knew I would be drafted. I never thought anything else."

"I did."

"You did? What did you think?"

"Maybe I should have involved you in my plans," his father had said in a tired voice. "When I sent you to this school, I only meant it to be a temporary solution. I never completely gave up on your Gemara studies, Ephraim. To me, you're still a *yeshiva bachur.*"

"Dad, forget it!" Ephraim had raised his voice. "Those are hopeless dreams. I've told you that before, but you don't want to believe me. You saw how it was that year I spent in yeshiva. Isn't that why you decided to send me to this place? What's changed now?"

"Nothing's changed, Ephraim. I sent you there hoping you would eventually go back to a yeshiva for another year or two before you decided what you wanted to do with your life. After all, thirteen is not seventeen. I thought we'd buy time.

"Listen, Ephraim," his father had almost pleaded. "You can easily land a job later, especially with a diploma in your pocket. Don't act on impulse. Going out to work at this point in your life will mean no Torah and no livelihood either."

"Oh, don't worry. I'll make a living," Ephraim had hurried to reply. "Trust me. Let me give it a try." Ephraim had his strategy mapped out. "One of my friends told me his father wants to hire someone to help out. He owns a store in Bnei Brak that sells electrical appliances. He said he can even find me a place to stay."

"Absolutely not!" his father had declared vehemently.

At the sound, his mother rushed out of the kitchen. "What's going on here?"

"He won't do this to me," his father had shouted. The vein on the side of his neck bulged. "After all I did for him! What I went through — swallowing my pride to find a place with vocational training and knowing everyone was talking about it behind my back. Now that's not good enough for him either. No, now he wants to be a big shot and go out to work. What's the rush?" His father fumed while his mother hurriedly closed the windows.

Ephraim couldn't remember ever seeing his father so angry. The force of his reaction had stunned him — and made him mad. Even now, as he walked to the bus stop with the lights of the neighboring Arab village twinkling against the backdrop of darkness, Ephraim felt his heart pounding wildly. He had had no idea his father would object so strongly. He had thought his father had finally come to terms with the situation. Didn't he know his own son? Where did he ever get the idea that Ephraim might return to yeshiva? Didn't he realize he wasn't cut out for that?

What was his father afraid of, anyway? He knew Ephraim well enough to know he would never take the *kippa* off his head. His father could be sure it would never come to that. So what did he think? That Ephraim was totally irresponsible, that he would work for just anyone? Or did his father's protests stem from his embarrassment at having to face his friends in shul? Was it just that he was afraid of what everyone would say? If that's all it was, why should he, Ephraim, care?

After that talk, something happened that hadn't happened for a long time. It was like a wall went up between him and his father, a wall of silence. He wasn't sure who started it, but they stopped talking to each other.

He didn't go back to his vocational school. He didn't know

what his parents' plans for him were, but he just stayed home, spending most of his time locked in his room. The walk outside made him feel better. Maybe he would walk all the way to Geula.

The bag of sunflower seeds was now completely empty, and Ephraim suddenly found himself across the street from the last bus stop on the outskirts of the neighborhood. He sat down on the bench and waited.

Last night, as he lay on his bed listening to music, his mother had entered his room and asked to have a word with him.

"Ephraim, please listen to me," she said had quietly. "You've got to do something for your father. He's very tense about the situation. He can't sleep at night. I know things are difficult for you. You probably feel hurt. But he's your father, and he doesn't deserve this pain. He's tried very hard to be understanding throughout the years and to accommodate you even when it wasn't easy for him."

Ephraim had said nothing.

"No matter how much it bothers him what other people will say, everything he ever did for you was for your own good. So I'm asking you now to show him some appreciation. Show him that you care about him."

He had stared blankly at her, wondering what she was getting at.

"I spoke to Daniel," she had told him. "I asked him to learn something with you every evening, just until you decide what to do. It doesn't matter what, as long as you'll be studying Torah."

Ephraim had listened without committing himself.

"Do me a favor," she had continued pleading with him. "Show your father you're not on your way off the *derech*, G-d forbid. Show him that you're still the same Ephraim we always knew, that your Jewish soul is alive and well. I have no doubts on that count. I believe in you, but your father is worried. He needs to see some concrete proof.

"Learn something with Daniel every evening. It'll make your father feel better. It's a small thing to ask. Besides, I think you'll enjoy it too."

In the end, he had agreed, for her sake and for his father's as well. After all, he wasn't deliberately trying to make him worry, and he had nothing against a Torah-study session in the evening.

The *shiur* with Daniel had been fairly interesting. Daniel was an okay guy. He'd always said so.

■ ■ ■

That evening, when Daniel came home, his eyes were aglow with satisfaction. Riki was growing accustomed to seeing that special sparkle.

"You know," he said to his wife, "Ephraim really surprised me."

Riki lifted her head from her notebooks. "What do you mean?"

"He's got a really good head. Did you know that?"

"Sure," she replied, not at all surprised by her husband's discovery. "Didn't *you* know that?"

"No," came the honest reply. "I thought all his problems were because he was a weak student."

"If anything, it's the opposite," Riki said. "He has a phenomenal mind. That's what makes the whole situation so complicated, and that's why my parents are so heartbroken. If he had a learning disability, they would have come to terms with it by now. But with a head like his?"

"We decided to learn a *sugya* he had never studied before," Daniel related. "He came up with some terrific questions. He even managed to arrive at the same conclusion as some of the *mefarshim*."

"I'm not surprised." Riki was pleased her husband had taken note of her brother's ability. "His rebbes in elementary school also said that whenever he tuned in, he caught on immediately. The problem was that he rarely bothered to tune in. His interests lay in other directions. He always enjoyed technical stuff. He claims he's just not cut out for yeshiva learning."

"Ah, that's what *he* says," answered Daniel, his voice automatically assuming the tone he used in scholarly debate. "But I say that his claim is based on a mistaken view of himself and of learning in general. It's an erroneous outlook he probably formed as a result of some incident in his past. If you ask me, Ephraim has never in his life experienced real Torah study. What you said just proves it. He was tuned out and turned off. Usually when that happens, pressure is put on the boy to buckle down and learn. Ephraim probably never got the chance to learn without pressure, and so he never tasted the real sweetness of Torah. If I could only give him a taste of it when we learn together, I'm sure he'll change his mind."

"I'm not so sure about it. Not at this point," Riki said pessimistically. "He's pretty much made up his mind to go out to work."

"What's his big rush?"

"Oh, I don't think there's any particular ideology behind it," Riki replied. "I think he just wants to feel independent. He'd like some cash in his pocket. Nothing more than that."

"That's all?"

"That's what it seems like to me. I don't buy his theory about being an electrician. He's as good as anyone else in the computer course. He was always satisfied with the classes, but then, all of a sudden, he got this idea in his head. I wouldn't be surprised if it was a friend who planted it there."

Daniel sat quietly for a few moments, mulling over what his wife had said. Suddenly, his face lit up with excitement.

"If that's all there is to it," he said, "I think we might be able to get around your brother's stubbornness. We can work with him and against him at the same time."

Riki stared at him blankly. Her husband had lately begun revealing a lot of creativity in his approach to *chinuch*. "What do you mean?"

"I have an idea, but it's still very raw. I have to discuss it with my mother first. The actual execution of the plan depends on her."

"On your mother?"

"That's right."

Riki could not believe her ears. "How can your mother possibly help?"

33

Mr. Schiller arrived at the doctor's office in a special car provided by the nursing home. Although Dr. Geller, the doctor on staff, was available, Sima thought it would be a good idea if the elderly man's family physician examined him. A doctor who was thoroughly acquainted with his patient's medial history and who had examined him many times over a period of years would be better able to discern subtle changes in his condition. With Mr. Schiller's daughter still out of the country, Sima felt a special sense of responsibility for her charge's welfare.

Gavriel Vidal, Mr. Schiller's attendant, faithfully accompanied him to the examination. He gently wiped beads of perspiration from the old man's brow and adjusted his position in his wheelchair. It wasn't long before they were ushered into the doctor's office. The doctor, a robust bespectacled fellow, greeted them heartily.

"How are you today, Mr. Schiller?" he asked amiably.

Mr. Schiller mumbled something and tried to smile.

"Is everything all right?"

"Yes."

"That's good. So, tell me. What brings you here today?" He turned to the attendant. "Is there any specific problem?"

"Not that I know of," answered the devoted attendant. "Mrs. Abramson requested that you perform a standard checkup."

After a thorough routine examination, including an electrocardiogram, the doctor said, "Everything seems to be in order, aside from a slight rise in blood pressure. Are you tense about something?" he asked Mr. Schiller, his manner still jovial.

"Yes." The unexpected emphatic response surprised both the doctor and the caregiver.

"What are you anxious about?" the doctor asked. "Is something bothering you? Don't you like it there in the home?"

"It's fine."

"I see you even have a fine attendant who takes good care of you. So what's the problem? What's making you anxious? You can tell me."

Mr. Schiller was silent. What could he say? He himself couldn't pinpoint exactly what had triggered his unhappy emotional state. Nothing in his life was the way it used to be before his wife, Sheindel, passed away. Nothing was the same anymore these days. He felt so alone. There was no one to talk to. With Sheindel around, he always had a listening ear, and she, too, always had so much to discuss with him. Now there was no one. Oh, sure, there were plenty of caregivers. Some of them called him Yankele, as if he were some cute, mindless baby. Why, he was old enough to be their grandfather! Others called him Grandpa. Why Grandpa? Didn't he have a respectable name? His own grandchildren, who could rightfully call him Grandpa, never showed up to visit. No wonder he was treated that way. Who was interested in an old man anyway?

When Shula and Naftali, his children, came to visit, they sat silently on the sofa facing him, not knowing what to say. He could see Naftali's foot tapping nervously on the floor. After sitting a while in silence, he'd get up and walk around the room, checking to see if there were enough socks in the drawer and that the window opened and closed properly. Poor Naftali. He certainly cared about his father, but it never dawned on him to share his own personal life with him. It was as if his father had no part in these matters anymore.

From the moment Mr. Schiller entered this nursing home, he had known there was only one way out, and that doomed means of exit was drawing closer and closer with each passing day.

He couldn't even pray the way he wanted to anymore. While the new caregiver treated him with respect, calling him "Mr. Schiller" and checking his pulse quite professionally it seemed, he had no inkling of how to put on tefillin properly. Mr. Schiller wasn't going to tell that to the doctor; the doctor himself probably didn't know the first thing about putting on tefillin. Besides, why should he insult his caregiver? All he needed now was for him to get insulted and quit.

"Mr. Schiller, I asked you a question. Don't I get an answer?"

"Wh-what?" *What does the doctor want from me?*

"How do you like the food in the home?"

The food? It depended. Sometimes he didn't like it. Everything tasted bitter these days, but they pushed him to finish his plate anyway. "Eat, eat, it's healthy," they'd coax. "Come on, finish up." *Sheindel had never forced him to eat.*

"Does this happen often lately?" the physician asked the caregiver in concern.

"Does what happen?" Gavriel pretended not to understand the question.

"These long silences. I asked him a question, and he's staring at me without answering."

Gavriel shrugged, trying to mask his feelings of mounting alarm. *The old man had better not spoil my plans now!* he thought. *All I need is for him to drift off into one of his foggy moments right here in the doctor's office.* He restrained himself from pinching the old man's arm.

Mr. Schiller's mind wandered on. *What do they think I am — a child?* The therapists always wanted him to sit in a circle with the others and string beads, as if he were in kindergarten. Occupational therapy, indeed! They would ask him stupid questions like whether it rained in the summer or in the winter and how much was two plus eight. Shame on them! He had been one of the top accountants in the city, and they asked him questions like that. They thought all old people were slow. They wanted him to clap his hands and knead dough with all the old women. "It's good for your fingers," they'd say. Ridiculous! He had never kneaded dough in his life. Why should he start now?

He had always learned in the evenings — that's what he enjoyed best. However, the rabbi who came to lecture in the home gave one general lecture, each time about a different topic, and always so late in the evening that he was too tired to go downstairs to the synagogue. He wasn't able to daven properly, and he didn't learn properly — what excuse was he going to give the Heavenly Tribunal when his time came, that he was senile?

"Mr. Schiller, Mr. Schiller, you aren't answering me," the doctor prodded.

What was that? Was someone talking to him? Who was this person? Where was he anyway? Oh, it's the doctor. Uh-oh. He must have been confused again. What was happening to him lately? He hoped the doctor hadn't realized. If he had, they'd put him in the ward with the special care patients. That was one place he wanted to avoid at all costs.

"Does anything hurt you?"

"No. Thank G-d, everything's all right."

Now he would have to pay attention and answer quickly so that they wouldn't put him in that ward. "It's only my heart that aches, but as you must know, that's the way it is with elderly people. There's too much time to think about all kinds of things."

"You don't have to think so much, Mr. Schiller. Your general health is good." Then, to the caretaker, over Mr. Schiller's head, "His blood pressure is slightly elevated. It's important to keep tabs on it. I'm going to increase his medication. Make sure to tell the administration. It's very important. He looks a little down. I assume that's why the directors sent him to be examined."

Down? Something must be wrong. The elderly Mr. Schiller grew concerned. *They're not telling me everything.*

"Is something wrong with my heart?" he asked the doctor.

"Who said anything about heart trouble?" the doctor chuckled. "Everything's fine. Come, get up on the bed, and I'll check your heart."

Gavriel immediately offered his arm to help the old man to the far end of the room, where he helped him onto the examination table. When the doctor began examining the patient, Gavriel walked away, pulling the curtain behind him, ostensibly to give Mr. Schiller his privacy.

Finally, he was out of the doctor's sight. He would have to work quickly. He reached out and tore a blank medical form from the pad on the desk, fervently hoping the doctor hadn't picked up the slight rustling sound his action had produced. With the stethoscope plugging his ears, it was unlikely he had heard anything.

Gavriel picked up the doctor's stamp and pressed it to the document, which he then slid into his pocket. Later, he would give the paper to his friends, the professional forgers. They would fill in the blank form with the right words to help him realize his plans. He would need the doctor's signature as well, but that shouldn't present a problem. He would soon receive the prescription for Mr. Schiller's pills.

By the time the doctor finished his examination, he, too, was finished with what he had set out to do.

Back to your casual stance, Juan. Nothing out of the ordinary has taken place.

■ ■ ■

It was early afternoon when Shimon Abramson received a surprising phone call from his son Daniel.

"Hello, Dad. How are you?"

"Fine. Is anything wrong?" He was surprised to hear from his son in the middle of the day.

"Actually, there is something rather urgent. I'm not sure you're the one who deals with these matters, though. I tried calling Mother, but she didn't answer the phone. I'm looking for a job for my brother-in-law."

"Which brother-in-law?"

"Ephraim."

"Isn't he in yeshiva?"

"He's in a vocational school, but he's desperate to leave and go to work. He wants to earn money, but as you can well imagine, my in-laws aren't too pleased with the idea. I thought maybe we could find him some part-time work in the nursing home."

"What do you mean by part-time?"

"I thought maybe he could learn something with the men."

"Are you serious?"

"Yes. He's actually very bright. He's more than capable of preparing a *Chumash* or *Mishnayos shiur*."

"I don't think we need anything like that, Daniel. We already have someone who gives a shiur on the weekly Torah portion. We sometimes bring in speakers to address various *hashkafa* topics. More than that really isn't necessary."

"Dad." There was a slight pause, and then Daniel persisted in a determined tone that Mr. Abramson wasn't used to hearing in his son's voice. "It's very important to us. Perhaps you can work something out."

"I don't see the point. I wouldn't want him to pin his hopes on such a job. Besides, if the boy wants to go out to work, I doubt this type of arrangement will satisfy him."

"You may be right, but maybe you can still try."

"Why don't you speak to your mother? She's really the one who takes care of the *shiurim* and the activities. I'll try to connect you to her. She might be in the dining room."

"Mother?"

"Yes, Daniel. Is something the matter?" When Daniel called, it was usually in the evening.

"No, everything's okay. It's just that I'm on my lunch break, and I had time to call. I need your help."

"What is it?"

"I want to find a part-time job in the nursing home for my brother-in-law Ephraim.

"Why?"

"It's a long story. Riki and I think it would be good for him to work two or three times a week, and his school is close to Bnei Brak, so it wouldn't be a problem for him to get to the home."

"I see. But what could he do here?"

"He could deliver a *shiur* in the evening, maybe in *Mishnayos*."

"Are you talking about Ephraim?" For goodness sake! What was her son getting her into? Where was his common sense? Wasn't he aware of the tense relationship between Riki and herself? Was he looking to create more friction? Now she would have a real problem refusing. Why was he putting her in this position?

"Danny, I'm not sure I understand." She tried to keep her voice level. "I don't mean to offend you or Riki, but, as far as I know, your brother-in-law doesn't even learn in a regular yeshiva. Isn't he studying electronics or something? Does he know how to learn at all?"

"He has an excellent head," Daniel said calmly. "He's more than capable of preparing a basic *shiur* in *Mishnayos*, and I'm willing to make sure he puts a lot of effort into it. A challenge will spur him on, and I'm sure he'll do very well at it."

"*You* are willing, *you* are sure — what does his father say about this?"

"Well, this is my own idea," Daniel answered evasively. "It's my plan, and I'm trying to carry it out with your assistance."

Thanks a lot, thought Sima cynically, *but the nursing home isn't a rehabilitation center for rebellious adolescents.*

"It seems unrealistic, Daniel," she said, "and besides, there's no need for another shiur right now. We have a regular speaker each week for the parasha, and sometimes between Mincha and Ma'ariv there's a *shiur* on *Chumash* or *Mishnayos*."

"I didn't mean that he would give a speech or *shiur* exactly," Daniel said. "Don't you have some elderly resident who would be happy at the prospect of learning with a *chavrusa*?"

"One second, Daniel," she said, putting the call on hold as Gavriel Vidal entered the dining room with Mr. Schiller. Sima would have to call Claudia, another caregiver, to come take over so she would be free to talk to Mr. Vidal before he left. She wanted to hear about their visit to the doctor.

"Daniel, I can't continue talking right now. I'll think about what you suggested, and I'll get back to you later."

In his office on the ground floor, Shimon Abramson thought about the conversation with his son. It wasn't so much what Daniel had said that jolted him; it was the decisive, assertive note in Daniel's voice that had astonished him. He detected a new confidence and vigor in his son's voice. *This isn't the same hesitant young man I thought I knew,* he mused. *There is a definite change in Daniel — and it seems to be for the better.*

■ ■ ■

Gavriel left the nursing home that afternoon feeling happy and accomplished. He had two medical forms in his pocket. His plan was progressing more quickly and smoothly than he could have hoped. One form was blank except for the doctor's official stamp, while the other, a prescription for pills to regulate Mr. Schiller's blood pressure, bore the doctor's signature. He intended to make a copy of the prescription before he used it to purchase the pills. The copy would serve as a model for the letters needed to do the counterfeiting job.

The director had thanked him so warmly for his readiness to help her out with this small favor. He chuckled with pleasure at the irony of it all.

34

IT WAS LUNCHTIME AT THE NURSING HOME. Shoshana Coleman was a little late visiting her mother, Mrs. Blau. An appointment at the dentist had thrown her off-schedule that morning, leaving her with only half an hour to visit with her elderly mother and see that everything was as it should be.

Upon entering the dining room, she saw Claudia, the nursing attendant, serving the residents their cereal. Nadia, an aide, was moving efficiently between the residents, tying a large triangular napkin around each one's neck, bib fashion. Shoshana followed her movements as she deftly tied the makeshift bibs.

One man protested. "I don't need one."

"Yes, you do," she answered authoritatively and continued tying the bib.

He pulled away. "I said no!"

Nadia tensed. "Yaakov! Must you always make things so difficult?" she muttered in frustration.

Claudia, who had finished serving the oatmeal, came to

Nadia's aid. "You'll get dirty, Yaakov, and then you'll get upset. It's either that or wearing the bib, okay? You can't have it both ways."

"Yes I can. I know how to eat without getting dirty," responded Yaakov Schiller, his mustache twitching indignantly. "I'm eighty-three years old, you know."

"Please don't be so stubborn," Nadia pleaded impatiently. "Look around you. No one else is causing trouble."

Shoshana looked around her. Indeed, all the residents were sitting quietly and eating like good little children. No one else seemed bothered by the bib. Her own mother wouldn't dream of beginning her meal before the bib was tied around her neck. She was so accustomed to the nursing home routine, it seemed she almost couldn't function without it.

"Mother, your cereal's getting cold. Why don't you start eating in the meantime?" Shoshana would prod.

But her mother would remain insistent. "I don't have a bib yet. I need a bib."

How typical of Mother to act that way, thought Shoshana with a trace of bitterness. *She always had been a stickler for rules and regulations, and that was the major source of conflict between us.*

Shoshana had always been the somewhat sloppy daughter of a perfectionist mother. Her mother had tried so hard to fit her into a routine. It seemed to Shoshana that, despite all their conflicts and confrontations, the only habit Shoshana had committed herself to was her daily visit to her mother.

Now, looking at the old man the nurses called Yaakov sitting resignedly with the bib tightly fastened around his neck, she felt something inside her protest.

"I don't think that's right," she said to Claudia.

"What's not right?" asked Claudia, busy helping a woman with her food.

"What you did to that old man over there. If he doesn't want a bib, it's not nice to force one on him. He's a human being, you know, just like the rest of us, with the same feelings."

"What do you want? Would he be better off if he got himself dirty?"

"Yes, I think you ought to let him get dirty if that's what he wants. Would you want someone to force *you* to wear a bib against your will?"

"Now, Mrs. Coleman, you know that's not the same thing. When his shirt gets dirty, he gets very upset, and you're not the one who has to help him change his clothes."

"Aha! Well, why don't you come right out and say so?" Shoshana retorted, her tone triumphant. "Admit that his own benefit is not your sole concern!"

"What makes you say that?" Nadia said in an accusatory tone as she came over to stand behind Claudia. "Exactly what are we doing that's not for his benefit? He's just being stubborn. What's so terrible about eating with a bib? What did we do to him? You make it sound as if we tied his hands to a chair or refused to give him food. I think it's really unkind of you to speak that way, considering that you're here every day and see with your own eyes the dedicated care we offer your mother."

Nadia sounded hurt, and Shoshana realized that she might have overstepped her bounds.

"I have no complaints," she said soothingly. "You're all absolutely wonderful, and my mother is very pleased with the care she gets here. She wouldn't dream of eating without a bib. But that elderly gentleman seems to be a different story. You can tell it bothers him. Maybe you could be more considerate."

"Listen," Claudia said, her tone implying that she wanted to end the conversation as quickly as possible, "we're only the caregivers. We just follow orders. The director insists that everyone wear a bib at mealtime. Look, there she is now. She's coming into the dining room." She raised her voice somewhat so the director would hear what she was saying. "I think our nursing home can pride itself on the fact that our residents always look neat and clean, not neglected. That's what *I* think."

Sima, who had just finished speaking to Mr. Schiller's caregiver about the doctor's visit, overheard the tail end of the conversation between Claudia and Mrs. Coleman.

"What's going on?" she asked, making her way over. "Is there a problem?"

"She was complaining about the fact that we put bibs on the residents at mealtimes," said Claudia. "She thinks it bothers them and that we ought to be more considerate."

"Why do you put it that way?" Shoshana said indignantly. "Is that what I said?" She turned to face Sima directly. "What I said was that there is one gentleman over here — Yaakov, I believe his name is — who tugged at his bib and asked them not to make him wear it. He appears completely sane to me, and it looks like he knows what he wants. So I said I think his wishes ought to be respected, especially at his age. That's all!"

Sima looked at Mr. Schiller. He was sitting quietly in his seat and stirring his cereal, withdrawn as always, and completely unaware of the furor his protest had caused.

"You're right," she replied, trying to lighten the atmosphere. "We definitely believe in respecting our residents' feelings, and our devoted caregivers try very hard to treat everyone with respect, no matter what their age. After all, we wouldn't have opened a nursing home if we didn't respect the elderly."

Shoshana nodded, although the director's words did not really ease her indignation at the caregivers' treatment of Yaakov Schiller.

"At the same time, you must understand, Mrs. Coleman," Sima continued, "that this is not a private home. With all the goodwill on our part, there are certain rules that are vital to the efficient running of this home and are indeed for the benefit of the residents. A bib at mealtimes is a minor detail that shouldn't really bother anyone. The residents here all understand this and take it for granted. In fact, no one has ever complained about it before, and I don't think it justifies a fuss."

As far as Sima was concerned, the subject was closed. Mrs. Coleman, though, didn't seem to think so. The director's words had inadvertently hit a raw nerve.

"You have to understand," her mother used to tell her when she was a young girl, "that this is a house, not a warehouse for storing junk. You can't bring home every piece of junk you find on the streets." With those words, she would dispose of all the little scraps and trinkets Shoshana cherished as valuable treasures — little pebbles she had collected in the yard or wildflowers she had gathered in an empty yogurt container.

"No one else complains about going to sleep early in this house," her mother would say when Shoshana grew older and grumbled about her inflexible bedtime rules. "You're the only one who seems to have a problem with the rules. You're the only one who's unhappy. I don't think there's any reason to complain. It's healthy to go to bed early. Why, our neighbors all wish they would manage to enforce such early bedtimes."

Shoshana had found it very difficult to comply with those rules. She was by nature a night owl, the type of person who got the most done late at night.

Years later, when she wanted to develop her growing interest in art and painting, her mother had opposed that as well. "Tzila and Sarah and Leah and Ditza are all going to a sewing course. You're the only one with these ideas about painting. Why?" she asked, employing the by-then-familiar argument. "A good homemaker should know how to sew. Where are all those paintings going to get you? They're a waste of time and money, and just make a mess."

In the end, Shoshana had relented and registered for a sewing course, "like Tzila and Sarah and Leah and Ditza." To this day it still hurt her to think of all the years she had spent sewing dresses and hating every minute of it. Only now that her own children were married had she finally signed up for art classes. How she despised those words, "No one else ever complains about it," and "Why can everyone else manage to…" or "This is not a warehouse (or a hotel)." Whatever the exact words, the implication was always the same: There is no room here for you as an individual.

Shoshana felt a need to discuss this with the director. That resident Yaakov might be more of a free spirit, an independent soul, less of a conformist. So what if he was elderly? So much care must be taken not to place any human being into a rigid mold that could stifle his freedom to grow.

Shoshana wanted to say all this to the director, but the woman had already disappeared. Seeing that the discussion was over, she turned to her mother, who was still eating. "I'm leaving now. I'll see you tomorrow. Feel good in the meantime."

Her mother stared at her for a moment, a shadow falling across her face as she absorbed what Shoshana had said. "But you'll come tomorrow, won't you?" she asked worriedly.

"Of course I'll come. Don't I come every day?" her daughter reassured her as she left the dining hall.

On the ground floor, Shoshana deliberately passed the director's office so that she might check to see whether Mrs. Abramson was available for a short talk. Sima was sitting at her desk, sorting through her mail. When she caught sight of Blau's daughter (which is how she thought of her), she was surprised and a little annoyed. The flicker of exasperation on her face was not lost on Shoshana, who in turn lost some of her resolve and stammered, "Oh, if you're busy now, then never mind. It'll keep."

Although Sima did, in fact, have a tight schedule, her interest was piqued. It behooved her, as director, to listen to feedback from the residents' families. She usually gleaned important pieces of information from these talks, details that were pertinent to the care of the elderly residents.

"What is this all about?" She believed in getting right to the point.

"It's about the issue we discussed in the dining hall," Shoshana replied, advancing a few steps into the office.

Sima unconsciously sighed. Why had she encouraged Mrs. Coleman to continue the conversation?

"Look, I know you're probably thinking, *Why is this woman making such a fuss about something as minor as a bib?*" Shoshana plunged into stating her case. "It seems petty, doesn't it? Most people, including the elderly, don't see anything humiliating about wearing a bib. It's simply something that is there to help keep our clothes clean, so what's the big deal?

"Yet, out of a hundred people who see things that way, there might be one person who feels differently — in this case, his name is Yaakov. For him, wearing a bib is a degrading thing to do. Perhaps he associates it with little children sitting around a kindergarten table. If he also happens to be feeling anxious and afraid about his growing dependence, his decreased level of functioning and his emotional vulnerability, then the innocent bib turns into a huge threat to his existence. Don't you agree?"

Sima did not agree, not at all. She thought the woman in front of her was overreacting to a minor incident. She didn't bother replying, though. She just wanted to bring this unpleasant conversation to an end. In any case, she had every intention of continuing to conduct the affairs in her nursing home in the way she saw fit. This wasn't her first year at the job, and the home had earned an excellent reputation under her guidance.

"Look," continued Shoshana Coleman, as if she had read Mrs. Abramson's mind, "I know you've been running this home for years, and you're doing an exceptional job. It's not easy. The director of such a home must see things from an objective viewpoint, the way you do. Otherwise, you wouldn't be able to do your job properly. I know I'd never be able to do it. I'm too emotional — and you can't run a business on emotion.

"On the other hand, I once heard a speaker explain the words *"Keil Elyon gomel chasadim tovim"* as follows: Hashem's loftiness lies in the fact that although He has created Heaven and Earth and rules over the entire universe, He understands the individual needs of all His creations and treats them with kindness."

Shoshana stopped to catch her breath, and quickly continued before Sima could stop her. "Although there are thousands of people who happily walk the beaten path, we must be aware that there are some individuals with special needs. I was just such an individual," Shoshana said, getting carried away. "The one who didn't take the conventional path.

"Maybe that's why I'm taking this whole thing so seriously. My mother had preconceived notions of how life was meant to be, and she tried to make me fit the mold. What she saw as success was, in fact, very painful for me. To this day it hurts me to think of my dreams that were never realized and of the many misunderstandings between us.

"You know, I often considered bringing up these issues with my mother. Deep inside I still feel a tinge of resentment, and I wish I could get rid of it. If I were to discuss the matter with her, my mother might be able to explain her side of the story. Maybe talking about it would make me feel better. But I feel like I can't approach my mother. To me, she is still intimidating. If I ever remind her of something negative from the past, she sighs, 'That's life. That's the way it was meant to be.'"

If Shoshana had hoped for empathy and understanding from the director, she had achieved just the opposite. For some reason, Shoshana's monologue provoked Mrs. Abramson, and her original impatience with Mrs. Coleman turned into barely restrained anger.

"Mrs. Coleman, excuse me for interrupting you, but I also

have something to say about your sensitivity. This is not the first time in a casual conversation with me you've expressed resentment toward your elderly mother, and I must tell you that every time it annoys me anew. She's an elderly woman now. What do you want from her? How can a woman your age still be so obsessed with things that happened when you were a little girl? Don't you think the time has come to forgive and forget?

"You're a grown mother yourself," Sima continued. "Surely you know that parents make mistakes. She's your mother. I know her. She's a good woman who tries hard to do the right thing. You seem to relate to Yaakov Schiller so well — can't you put yourself in your own mother's place? Today she's dependent on you. She's not capable of giving you explanations, and if she were, she would surely tell you how difficult it was to raise a daughter so different from herself, a daughter she never really understood. She'd enlighten you on the hardships involved in raising a child like that and having everything you say or do interpreted the wrong way."

Shoshana was speechless. The director's response, so sharply critical, stabbed her to the core. She suddenly felt like a wayward child being disciplined by an adult. Yet although the director's attack made her feel ashamed and she was disappointed by its unexpected harshness, deep inside she realized that there was some truth to what she had said.

"Okay, thank you for your time," she mumbled, standing up to leave. "When I spoke of my own experience, I had no intention of denigrating my mother," she added as an afterthought. "I was just trying to prove my point that there are always unconventional people whose individuality is of the utmost importance to them. Sometimes, even when one has a justified goal, such as cleanliness for example, it is important to take note of these individual characteristics and be flexible. That's all.

"Yaakov Schiller may be a little different from the other residents. What may be acceptable to everyone else may not necessarily be good for him. Why should he be forced to suffer?"

Sima Abramson was once again left alone with her paperwork, but she found she couldn't settle down and concentrate. Perhaps she had been too harsh. She wasn't sure what had prompted her to tell Shoshana Coleman everything on her mind, but it wasn't the first time the woman had irked her with her "subtle comments," as she had referred to them.

Imagine! She can't even relate to her own mother, Sima thought, chuckling at Shoshana's revelation. Had Shoshana been her own daughter, oh boy. She didn't think she would get along with her either. She really was different, not at all like any of the other residents' relatives who limited their comments to what pertained to their loved ones.

Suddenly, a new thought nagged at her. Perhaps she herself was a little like the elderly Mrs. Blau, intolerant of those who didn't behave exactly as she did. No, she didn't think so. Sima mentally shrugged off the notion, much as she would brush away a bothersome fly. It was just that in this case she identified with Mrs. Coleman's elderly mother.

As far as Yaakov Schiller was concerned, she could definitely say that she understood him and cared for his personal needs. Hadn't she scheduled a doctor's appointment for him because he seemed depressed? It was true that he was somewhat different from the others. He never participated in the activities, as if he was above it all. Could it be that the general deterioration that she had noticed was only a result of depression? The doctor had reported that he hadn't pinpointed any specific medical problem. Perhaps Mr. Schiller was, indeed, simply depressed. Such things did happen, physical deterioration as a result of emotional depression. Could it be that Mrs. Coleman had a point?

The ringing of the telephone jolted her out of her reverie.

"Hello? Oh, Daniel, it's you. Yes, I know I promised to get back to you, and I didn't. A *chavrusa* for an elderly resident, you say? No, I didn't get to think about it yet. I'm sorry; maybe later. Daniel, please don't pressure me. I don't like this whole idea too much, you know. I told you already that we have Torah lectures here. Why would anyone need a study partner? Let me try to think a minute…

"Listen! I just had a brainstorm. It might just do him some good. He's a character. He doesn't usually go down to the shul or join any of our regular activities. Maybe a *chavrusa* would do him good. His name is Yaakov Schiller. You know what? It can't hurt to try."

35

EPHRAIM ENTERED THE THREE-STORY BUILDING with trepidation. He already regretted having agreed to his brother-in-law's proposal.

"My mother desperately needs someone to fill a slot in the nursing home," Daniel had informed him. At first, Ephraim had thought she was looking for a volunteer. Daniel had been quick to explain, though, that she meant someone who would be able to learn with the residents for a salary.

"Come on. Are you crazy?" Ephraim had retorted. "That's not the kind of job I'm looking for. You know me. I want to do more practical work."

"So what?" his brother-in-law had argued. "For now, take what you can get. This is a good opportunity for you to earn some money. What do you have to lose? Afterward, you can take things from there."

"About the money part, okay. But me? Teach? Come on, I barely know how to learn myself, and you want me to prepare lessons as if I were a rabbi or something. Forget it."

"Stop talking nonsense," Daniel had replied. "You know

how to learn perfectly well. The fact that you aren't too interested is another matter. To learn *mishnayos* with an elderly man you don't have to be a rabbi. It's enough to be an Ephraim Baum if you're ready to sit down and prepare the lesson."

The truth was that despite his surprise and hesitation, the offer had appealed to Ephraim. It sounded more realistic than the other offer, the one in the electrical appliance shop that his friend had told him about. Daniel had promised him that he would try to talk to his parents and discuss the possibility of adding more hours to the job, as, say, a handyman, to supplement his salary. "Who knows?" Daniel had urged. "Maybe you'll be able to get a permanent job in the nursing home if you prove yourself capable." Tempted by Daniel's words, Ephraim had agreed.

As he entered the lobby of the nursing home later that day, though, his confidence ebbed. The cluster of elderly residents seated in the lobby looked him over with curiosity.

"Have you come for Avigdor?" asked one old woman.

"No," Ephraim mumbled.

"I bet you he's Henya's grandson!" a man exclaimed. "You're Henya's grandson, aren't you?"

"Um, actually," Ephraim shifted uneasily, "I'm looking for the director, Mrs. Abramson."

"Oh, you're looking for Sima," came a chorus of voices.

"She's downstairs," answered one of the men.

"I just saw her leave," interrupted another voice.

"What are you talking about? She left in the morning!"

"Go on, go downstairs. She's in her office," suggested yet another.

"Who is he, her son?" someone wondered aloud.

"What son? That's not the way Sima's son looks. I know her son. He's a *yeshiva bachur* who wears a black hat and a white shirt."

The sounds of their animated conversation accompanied

Ephraim all the way down the steps. He had never dreamed that a group of elderly people could give him such stage fright. Perhaps he should have dressed more conservatively in honor of his new position.

The ground floor was empty and silent. All Ephraim saw was a row of closed doors. One door was slightly ajar, and Ephraim peeked inside. At the desk sat Sima Abramson, his sister's mother-in-law.

"Hi!" Ephraim tried to sound friendly.

Sima raised her head from her work. "Hello. Welcome to our nursing home," she said, returning his attempt to be pleasant. "You're Ephraim, if I'm not mistaken."

He nodded.

"How's your mother?" she asked, as politeness dictated.

"*Baruch Hashem*," he murmured.

She took in his appearance with a quick glance, noting that he was dressed rather casually for someone who was supposed to give a *shiur. He might have made an effort to look more yeshivish,* she thought. *That rumpled blue shirt doesn't quite lend him an air of credibility.* She sighed inwardly. *What can one expect from such a boy?* This was something she should have expected when she had acceded to Daniel's request.

"Have you ever been to our nursing home before?" she asked.

Pointless question, thought Ephraim. *Of course not!* Rather than respond, he merely shook his head.

Having run out of small talk, Sima got to the point. "So, are you interested in actually starting today, or do you want to get to know Mr. Schiller first?"

"Mr. Schiller?"

"Yes, he's the one you will be learning with. Daniel asked me if there was anyone else," she said as she stood up, "but at the moment there is only this opening. Maybe as time goes on we'll be able to arrange for more lessons."

Ephraim followed Mrs. Abramson out of the room and waited in the hall as she locked the door to her office. He replayed her words in his mind. The director sounded like she was doing him a favor giving him the job, but Daniel had said that she was desperate for someone who could take it on, not the other way around. What about the maintenance work he had mentioned? Ephraim followed her up the stairs in silence. They passed the same group of residents he had met earlier and turned into a long, narrow corridor.

Ephraim suddenly felt his confidence faltering. He was seized by the impulse to turn around and leave. It was too late to have second thoughts, though. The director stopped in front of one of the doors, knocked lightly and entered.

The curtains in the room were drawn, and the semidarkness made it difficult for him to see anything.

"Mr. Schiller?" Sima called out to whoever was in the room. She walked directly to the window and drew aside the curtains. "Are you in bed again? Why don't you go out and sit in the lobby for a while with everyone?"

"I don't have anything to do there," mumbled the form under the blanket.

Ephraim stood in the doorway, trying to follow the conversation. The elderly resident lay impassively in his bed, unaware of his presence.

"I brought you a guest," Sima announced cheerfully.

"A guest?" The voice from the bed perked up a little.

"Yes," repeated Sima, "a guest."

"Who? Naftali?" The elderly man lifted his head.

"No, not Naftali. I brought you a *bachur* who wants to learn with you. Do you want to learn some *mishnayos* together with him?"

"Learn?" Mr. Schiller didn't understand.

"Yes. Your daughter Naomi told me you enjoy learning and that you used to spend all day learning at home. Let me introduce you to Ephraim." She beckoned Ephraim to come inside. "You see, he's the guest I'm talking about. He came to learn with you. Come on up, Mr. Schiller. Ephraim will help you get organized. It's surely better to sit and learn than to lie in bed and let all kinds of depressing thoughts get to you.".

Mr. Schiller couldn't have agreed more emphatically. The thoughts churning in his mind were indeed depressing, to say the least. The worst part was that he couldn't confide in a soul.

Today he had committed an act of utter folly, something a mature person simply didn't do. He never should have given Gavriel his credit card. Gavriel had told him about a sale in a clothing store near his home where name brand men's shirts were being sold at discount prices.

"Your shirts are getting shabby," Gavriel had pointed out. "Look, this one has a bad coffee stain and that one looks like soup spilled on it. I don't understand. Don't your children care how you look? No one tells you anything. Why should they? I guess your appearance doesn't matter to them too much, as long as they're well dressed. But personally, I can't bear to see you looking this way. You are much too dear to me. These shabby shirts don't do you justice."

Gavriel had pulled out the entire pile of shirts from the closet and shown them to Mr. Schiller, one by one. Indeed, Mr. Schiller had agreed, they were badly stained and grayish from repeated washings. How was it he hadn't noticed until now? Sheindel would never have wanted him to be seen in such a state. What could he do, though, if Sheindel wasn't around to tend to his needs? Aside from Gavriel, there was no one in the world who really cared.

"You're also short on socks," the caregiver had continued. "I'm really surprised no one noticed. Do you have any money to give me to do some shopping? I think I'll need about three or four hundred shekels. It shouldn't cost more."

Mr. Schiller didn't have any cash on him. When Naomi was home, she withdrew money from his bank account and brought it to him whenever he needed it. Now that she was abroad, Naftali was supposed to take over. He had the ATM card, but he hadn't shown up yesterday as promised. Gavriel had tried to think of an alternative solution and suggested taking Mr. Schiller's credit card. He had been hesitant to entrust the card to the caregiver, which hurt Gavriel's feelings.

"What a shame," he had said. "I finally have the time today to do some shopping in the afternoon, and I'm afraid you'll miss the sale."

In the end, Mr. Schiller had handed him the card, but he felt uneasy about having done so. Of course, he knew Gavriel was trustworthy and that everything would be all right. But what would happen if Gavriel lost the card and someone found it? He'd been lying in bed and worrying about the incident since lunchtime. He didn't feel like sharing his anxiety with anyone, because he knew exactly what Naftali, the director or anyone else would say. "Who in their right mind gives a credit card to a stranger?" Perhaps they would even decide he wasn't responsible enough to run his own finances any longer, and they would appoint someone to do it for him. He dreaded the thought.

He certainly couldn't tell them about the loan he had given his caregiver a few days ago, either. He knew they would disapprove. "Papa, whatever possessed you to lend money to a stranger?" Naftali would ask. With all due respect to Naftali, Mr. Schiller thought ironically, he was closer to his caregiver than to his own son. Did Naftali care how he was dressed? Had he visited him lately at all? He was happy to be able to help Gavriel out. It was only this issue with the credit card that made him uneasy. After all, a credit card isn't something you lend out to other people.

"So you don't want to learn, Mr. Schiller?"

"Me? No, I *do* want to learn." Of course he wanted to learn. That was what he wanted to do most. But his head was preoccupied with his credit card. Perhaps he should discuss it with the director despite his reservations? Maybe she would reassure him that there was nothing to worry about. Perhaps she would even laugh at his overactive imagination.

"Okay, so let's get out of bed and freshen up. Ephraim, I'm leaving you here with Mr. Schiller. Help him get ready so you can sit down to learn together."

Sima left the room, leaving Ephraim, suspended between the roles of caregiver and learning partner, with the elderly Mr. Schiller. At the moment, both roles felt strange and unfamiliar to him. What was he actually supposed to do now with Mr. Schiller? One thing was certain, he silently vowed. The minute he got out of this place he was going to pick up the phone and give Daniel a talking to for getting him into this mess. This was going to be his first *and* his last time there. He could kick himself for having been so gullible. *Good for you. You deserve it, he chided himself, falling for flattery like that.*

Mr. Schiller stared at the boy shifting from foot to foot and didn't know what to say. He would gladly have told him to leave, but that wouldn't be nice. It wasn't the boy's fault that today his frame of mind wasn't conducive to learning. He found himself directing his frustration and anger at the administration. Why hadn't the director let him know in advance about this arrangement? Didn't they have any respect for elderly people? They thought they could just push him around — walk into his room in the middle of the day without asking and bring in a stranger and tell him to learn with him.

"Why don't you have a seat?" Mr. Schiller asked the *bachur*.

Ephraim sat down. "Can I help you with something?" he asked, finally having thought of something sensible to say.

"Yes. Would you be so kind as to find my glasses? It's a little hard for me to look for them without my glasses," Mr. Schiller asked, making a weak attempt at humor.

Ephraim stood up, sweeping his gaze around the room in search of the glasses.

"They should be there on the chair," Mr. Schiller said.

Ephraim quickly found the spectacles and handed them to the elderly man, who donned them and then stared at Ephraim as if seeing him for the first time.

"If you don't mind, can you bring me a glass of water?"

Ephraim dutifully filled a glass with water and brought it to Mr. Schiller. *What now?* The elderly resident seemed to have no intention of learning, and here he had spent a full hour preparing a lesson. Suddenly, though, Mr. Schiller sat up and asked, "So, what are we going to learn today?"

In the corridor outside the room, Sima lingered, anxious about what was going on inside. The whole situation seemed pitiful to her. The boy seemed to have no inkling of how to relate to the elderly resident. Once again, Sima had the feeling she was being dragged into a situation she had never intended to find herself in.

What have you gotten me into, Daniel?

36

"**ME'AYMOSAI — BEGINNING** at what hour is one allowed to recite the evening Shema?" Ephraim read the first mishna aloud, pronouncing every word slowly and clearly. "From the time the *kohanim* eat the *teruma*."

"It's best to start with *maseches Berachos*," Daniel had advised, and judging by Mr. Schiller's reaction, this was sound advice. When Ephraim had told him they would be learning this tractate together, Mr. Schiller had exclaimed with pleasure, "Ah, *maseches Berachos*! Excellent! Excellent!"

Ephraim stopped to explain the mishna. "The mishna is asking at what hour is one permitted to begin reciting *kerias Shema*. The answer is, from the time the *kohanim* come to eat the *teruma*. At what hour do the *kohanim* eat the *teruma*?"

He was about to answer the question himself, but quickly thought better of it and turned to his elderly *chavrusa*. "What hour does the mishna mean?"

Mr. Schiller remained silent. Ephraim repeated the question.

Shaking himself free of his reverie, Mr. Schiller answered,

"From the time the stars are out."

"Very good," Ephraim complimented him, pleased.

"Very good," Mr. Schiller mimicked, making light of Ephraim's praise. "What am I, a child in grade school? Do you know how many times I learned this *masechta* in my life? Maybe fifty times — and long before you were born." The elderly man proceeded to quote the Bartenura without even looking at the text. "Why doesn't the mishna say from the time that the stars are out? *Nu,* you answer me now. What does the Bartenura explain?"

Ephraim found himself switching roles and answering like an obedient pupil. "He explains that the mishna doesn't explicitly mention the time in order to teach us that the *kohanim* don't have to wait until morning to bring the *korbanos*. They could bring them as soon as the sun set."

"Good! Excellent!" Now it was Mr. Schiller's turn to award the praise. "You explained it very well," he beamed.

Ephraim felt surprisingly flattered by the compliment. He smiled with genuine pleasure, and enthusiastically read another few lines. He was about to explain them, when he realized, to his disappointment, that his elderly partner, who had been so actively involved only a few seconds before, suddenly seemed lost in a world of his own. His downcast eyes looked clouded, and Ephraim was unsure whether or not he was following. He decided to go ahead with his explanation nonetheless, hoping with all his heart that his partner was in fact listening.

Mr. Schiller's eyes were scanning the small print on the open Gemara, and his ears were absorbing the familiar chant. All at once he was back at the table in his living room at home. Sheindel was preparing shalosh seudos and he was learning with Naftali. What a treat, what pure unadulterated nachas. Just yesterday he had met Naftali's rosh yeshiva, who had wonderful reports of Naftali's progress. "Such an open mind," he had marveled, "and such diligence for a boy his age." Now Naftali was home for Shabbos, and they finally had a chance to learn together.

It was so long since they had last learned together like this. He hardly even needed to explain anything. Naftali grasped new concepts so well. When was the last time Naftali had spent a Shabbos home from yeshiva with his family? He would have to ask the rosh yeshiva to allow Naftali to come home more often so they could learn together. He could hear Naftali's voice intoning the words:

"Those who recite the evening kerias Shema while it is still light rely on the opinion of Rabbi Yehuda, who cites in another place 'until plag hamincha,' one and one-quarter hours before nightfall. Today, however, this practice is not accepted."

Naftali finished and added, "That's the way they used to do it outside Eretz Yisrael. Maybe living conditions were different then." What was he talking about?

Mr. Schiller chuckled to himself, leaving Ephraim to puzzle over what had suddenly amused the elderly man.

"Nonsense! What are you talking about?" Ephraim suddenly heard Mr. Schiller say. "Why do you say it is not accepted nowadays? Right here in this nursing home they daven Ma'ariv even before *plag hamincha*. They stretch Rabbi Yehuda's opinion quite far."

Ephraim didn't quite understand. "Why?" he asked innocently.

"Why?" Mr. Schiller echoed bitterly. "Because the staff is in a hurry to finish its work and go home. They give us supper while it is still light outside and put us to bed before sunset. The Arab caregivers who work the night shift want peace and quiet."

"Arabs?" Ephraim was shocked.

"Yes. They're quite kind, actually, but they want everyone to be asleep so that all will be quiet. When am I supposed to daven Ma'ariv, while it's still light outside? Sometimes I don't get to daven at all. Once I'm in bed, it's so hard to get up again." Mr. Schiller heaved a painful sigh and lapsed into silence.

Ephraim was momentarily at a loss for a fitting reply. His elderly partner was clearly following the lesson, yet it was obvious that his mind was far away. Should he close the *sefer* and let Mr. Schiller unburden himself to him? He felt a twinge of disappointment. It would be such a shame to stop now. There were several fine points in the Bartenura that he had toiled so long to prepare, and now he would have to keep them to himself.

Suddenly, in a flash of insight, Ephraim understood what the teachers must have felt like when his own daydreams had taken him far away from the classroom.

"So what does the Bartenura say after that, Naftali?" Ephraim heard the elderly man say again. Why did he keep calling him Naftali?

"The Bartenura notes that the whole night can be considered the time when people go to sleep; one may therefore recite *kerias Shema* until dawn."

"But here in the home the 'time when people go to sleep,' is only until the middle of the night. I go to sleep too early and wake up when it's still dark and not yet time to daven Shacharis. That's the second mishna, isn't it?" Mr. Schiller asked. "It says, 'When one can distinguish between pale blue and white.' In the middle of the night, one cannot distinguish between the two colors. So I toss and turn, waiting for morning until I doze off again. Then Gavriel comes to help me with my tefillin, but he never manages to get it right. If I may say so, he is a total ignoramus when it comes to these things. Have you ever met a Jew with a yarmulke and all, who doesn't know that you have to put on the *tefillin shel rosh* before the *tefillin shel yad*? He tells me it makes no difference, and I just don't have the energy to argue with him."

"Who is this person you're talking about?" Ephraim asked with interest.

"He's my caregiver. He comes every day. He's a nice enough person, but when it comes to tefillin, he's a complete ignoramus."

"Isn't there anyone else who can daven with you in the morning?"

"Who? Who should come? Naomi's not in the country, Sheindel can't come and you can't either."

TIGHTROPE | 267

"Me?" What did Mr. Schiller mean? "I learn in the morning."

"Yes, I know you learn, Naftali. We have to ask your *mashgiach* for permission for you to come in the morning just to help me with my tefillin."

Ephraim blushed in confusion. "I-I'm not Naftali, Mr. Schiller. Why do you keep calling me Naftali?"

"You're not Naftali?" A shocked expression spread over the old man's wrinkled face. "So who are you?"

Ephraim was stunned. All at once he understood that the elderly resident had been confusing him with someone else, an all too-common-phenomenon with elderly people, or at least with many of them.

"Who is Naftali?" he returned with a question.

"Naftali is my son. We learned these *mishnayos* many times together. I'm sorry — how could I have confused you with Naftali?"

"I'm just a boy who's come to learn with you. My name is Ephraim," Ephraim explained, pronouncing his name carefully.

"Ephraim," Mr. Schiller whispered intently, trying to register the new information.

Ephraim sensed his partner's embarrassment, and he was moved by a wave of intense compassion.

"Do you want to stop here for today?" he asked, trying to fill the uncomfortable silence.

"No. Why?" the elderly man surprised him. "I just want to request a small favor. Please give Gavriel a call and tell him I don't want him to buy the shirts for me. I won't be able to concentrate properly until I know that you've taken care of it."

Ephraim was at a loss again. He didn't know if this request was part of the old man's disorientation, or if the favor was a lucid request.

"Which shirts? Why was he going to buy you shirts?"

"It doesn't matter." Mr. Schiller was visibly agitated. "Just go call him and tell him not to buy them. Here's his phone number." He took a notepad out of his pocket and fumbled until he found the number. "Tell him that Yaakov Schiller said not to buy the shirts."

Ephraim was disconcerted. Somehow the tables had turned. The elderly man had taken over, and Ephraim found himself lamely following orders. So far nothing was working out as planned.

He found a pay phone at the end of the long corridor. He dialed the number and waited while the phone rang several times. Finally, a woman with a foreign accent answered.

"Hello?"

"Hello. Is Gavriel there?"

"No."

"When will he be in?"

"Late tonight."

"Can I leave a message?"

"Sure."

"I'm calling from the nursing home. Yaakov Schiller asked me to tell him not to buy the shirts."

"What shirts?"

"I have no idea. I only came to visit him. He asked me to tell Gavriel not to buy the shirts."

Ephraim hung up and returned to the room where Mr. Schiller anxiously awaited his return.

"*Nu*, did you tell him?"

"Yes, I delivered the message." Ephraim decided not to mention that he hadn't been able to relay the message directly to Gavriel. Why shouldn't the elderly man be at peace?

"Good," said Yaakov Schiller, relief flooding his face. "Now we can learn."

The two continued learning. This time Ephraim's elderly partner was more attentive. He participated enthusiastically, demonstrating his knowledge from time to time with astute comments, and Ephraim began to taste the sweet flavor of accomplishment.

Later, when a staff member knocked on the door to call Mr. Schiller for dinner, Ephraim was surprised to see that a full hour had elapsed.

■ ■ ■

In his home on Jabotinsky Street, sleep eluded Gavriel. Earlier, when he returned from taking care of various errands, his wife had given him the message from Mr. Schiller.

"What shirts was he talking about?" she asked.

"Oh, he asked me to get him some shirts," he answered nonchalantly, "and now he's changed his mind. These oldsters change their mind from one minute to the next. Well, he's too late. I bought them already." He deliberately omitted the rest of the story, the part about the credit card and all the other purchases he had made with it. He also refrained from mentioning the fact that he had copied down the credit card number for future use. There were quite a few items he hoped to acquire, courtesy of Mr. Schiller's bank account. Yes, it was better to keep such plans to oneself. His Jewish wife was much too law abiding for those types of things. Luckily for him she didn't ask him to attend synagogue services.

Now, though, the old man had gone back on his request, and that worried him. Who had he already managed to tell about the credit card? Who called and left the message? Maybe someone suspected him and had turned the old man against him.

Gavriel had a vague premonition that the ground under his feet was beginning to give way. His lips set in grim determination as he made plans to hurry with the execution of his scheme in regard to Mr. Schiller's savings.

■ ■ ■

It was midnight. Mr. Schiller slept peacefully in his bed at the nursing home. His sleep was untroubled tonight, his breathing more regular. After supper, he had asked the director if someone could take him downstairs to the shul to daven Ma'ariv. She had called the caregiver to accompany him downstairs and bring him back to his room when he was finished. This evening, he had finally gotten the chance to daven Ma'ariv at the designated time — a thought that filled him with pleasure. Before he returned to his room, he had met the director again and had taken the opportunity to thank her for sending that fine young man — what was his name again? oh, yes, Ephraim — to learn with him.

37

JUAN AWOKE AT DAWN TO DOUBLE-CHECK his plan. He was nothing if not thorough. The day would come, probably after the old man died, when his children would find out about their father's apartment being stolen from underneath their very noses. They would rise up in outraged protest and drag the matter to court. By then, time would be on his side, and they would find themselves in a very complicated position. The apartment would be legally his. Even the lawyer had said so. They would be required to present evidence attesting that the old man had not intended to do what he had done. It would be up to them to prove that the gift had been an elegant swindle.

Juan was glad he had already given the blank medical form to the forger. He had made sure to give him the wording of the doctor's confirmation that Yaakov Schiller was in full possession of his senses, just as he wanted it to appear on the note. This, he felt certain, would be the most convincing piece of evidence, solid proof the old man had given him the apartment in a gesture of gratitude and goodwill. He was certain it would hold up in court.

Juan withdrew from his pocket the form Rodriguez had so

graciously given him when he'd visited his office. The most important part of his plan was still ahead of him: he needed to obtain Mr. Schiller's signature on the bottom of the form. When it came to signatures, he always preferred an authentic one, if possible, to even the most professional forgery.

He had been mulling over the question of how to obtain the old man's signature for some time now, and had finally come up with an idea. He would begin by increasing the amount of time he spent with the old man. True, he had only been hired for the morning hours, but it would not hurt to give the impression that out of total devotion to his charge, he had begun staying until the afternoon. Sometimes, he decided, he would even show up during the evening just to make sure everything was okay. After all, he was becoming very attached to the dear old man, almost like a son. Aside from such devotion standing him in good stead during any legal battles, his constant presence would help him catch Mr. Schiller during one of his "foggy moments." Then he would get him to sign.

One thing Juan knew for sure — the old man would never willingly sign his apartment away. What made him so fiercely loyal to his children? It was hard to understand. Whenever Juan alluded to his children's disinterest in their father, Mr. Schiller's only response was to stare back at him in silence. During a rare moment when Mr. Schiller had once spoken about his family, his eyes had shone with boundless love for his children.

Juan was afraid of that love.

No doubt about it — despite his loneliness, despite his disappointment, Mr. Schiller would never willingly bequeath his apartment to anyone but his children. Juan saw no other option than to spend more time with him, patiently waiting for the right moment.

It was nine-thirty in the morning when Juan locked the door of his house behind him and set off for the nursing home. He stopped and felt for the *kippa* in his pocket. Good. It was there. The *kippa* was an invaluable tool of the trade, just like the carpenter's saw, the gardener's spade…or the burglar's gun.

Juan chuckled at the last comparison as he turned the corner, not knowing it might be the last laugh he would have that day.

■ ■ ■

Mr. Schiller was in an unusually good mood that morning. Even the other residents of the nursing home noticed.

"Yaakov, you look like a young man today," said Mr. Kramer, a nonagenarian still wonderfully young at heart.

"A young man I'll never be again," Mr. Schiller bantered. It did seem like an especially bright day, though, and he greeted his caretaker with a heartier welcome than usual. After a moment, his face clouded as he remembered something that had been troubling him. "I hope you didn't buy me those shirts."

"Oh!" exclaimed Gavriel, slapping himself on the forehead. In his rush to leave the house, he'd forgotten the clothes he'd bought. *It looks like we're changing places here*, he thought sarcastically. *I'm the one whose memory is going.*

"I — uh, I did buy them for you. What could I do?" he asked, spreading his hands in question. "I got your message too late. They're top quality, and the price was a bargain, but I forgot to bring them. I had so many errands to take care of."

What am I doing? he berated himself. *That's the wrong thing to say! You don't forget someone you're supposedly so devoted to. What made me say that? I could have found a better way to tell him I didn't have the shirts with me.*

Gavriel noticed that Mr. Schiller now looked disturbed. He wasn't sure what to make of the change in mood.

"What about my credit card?" asked Mr. Schiller. "Where is it?"

"You've got nothing to worry about," Gavriel chuckled, anxious to demonstrate his trustworthiness. "Your credit card is right here with me. What did you think, that I would keep it? G-d forbid. Of course I brought it! Here it is. Take it."

He withdrew his wallet with an elegant flourish and handed Mr. Schiller his credit card. He didn't need it anyway. He had all the information written down on a small piece of paper tucked inside his wallet.

Mr. Schiller's relief was obvious. The furrows in his forehead smoothed themselves out.

"Who was it that phoned me?" Gavriel asked as casually as possible.

"Ah," Mr. Schiller replied with renewed enthusiasm, "that was the nice young man who comes to study *mishnayos* with me. We learned *maseches Berachos*. It's been a long time since I studied Torah that way. Maybe you'd like to learn something with me too. It doesn't have to be *mishnayos*. We can learn *Chumash*. I'm sure you know some *Chumash*. I feel much better when I learn."

Gavriel's spirits plummeted in direct proportion to Mr. Schiller's upbeat mood. The old man, he noted, was unusually alert. A sinking feeling in the pit of his stomach told him a spell of confusion was not in the cards that day. He mumbled something about being tired and then said he thought a walk outside would be better than staying inside and studying. "It's good for the constitution," he said. "It's not a good idea to sit inside all the time."

Relax, he told himself. *You've got all the time in the world. If it won't be this morning, it'll be this afternoon. If not today, your chance will come tomorrow.*

Actually, he told himself, things were turning out well. He now had the perfect excuse to come back in the afternoon: the shirts.

38

SIMA WALKED AROUND THE DINING hall exchanging small talk with the residents. When she noticed Yaakov Schiller sitting quietly in his regular place in the corner, she searched for something to say to cheer him up.

"Mr. Schiller, don't forget. That young man Ephraim will be coming again today."

Yaakov Schiller lifted his face from his plate, his eyes sparkling with happiness at the mention of the name.

"He's coming again today?"

"That's right," Sima replied. "I'll be sending Claudia to wake you up at four so you can get organized before he comes," she added in her brisk, businesslike voice. "Okay?"

"Fine," replied Mr. Schiller.

Sima was pleased. She didn't want the elderly residents spending too much time in bed. Too much sleep during the afternoon hours inevitably led to insomnia at night. It wasn't healthy to spend time alone and brooding.

Daniel's plan wasn't turning out so badly. Aside from the

learning session with Daniel's brother-in-law, Mr. Schiller didn't take part in any of the activities offered by the home. Sima hadn't discussed the success of the arrangement with her son yet. In her opinion, it was too early to draw conclusions. She sincerely hoped that future sessions would be as positive as the first one. She knew from experience, though, that it wasn't always possible to predict success on the basis of a good start, and she didn't want to raise false hopes.

Sima didn't notice, though, that although she had been treading with extra caution where Daniel was concerned, she had been too impulsive with Mr. Schiller, raising his hopes and arousing his excitement and anticipation.

Mr. Schiller woke up at three-thirty and checked his watch, anxiously awaiting the young man who was supposed to come learn with him. When Claudia knocked on his door at four, he was sitting expectantly in his armchair. "*Nu*, isn't he here yet?" he asked impatiently.

At four-thirty, Mr. Schiller left his room to wait in the lobby. Five minutes later, when Ephraim still hadn't shown up, he began to shout agitatedly, "Mrs. Abramson, Mrs. Abramson! Where is Mrs. Abramson?"

"What do you want from Mrs. Abramson?" asked Georgette, the caregiver who happened to be passing by.

"I want Mrs. Abramson now!" Mr. Schiller banged his cane on the floor for emphasis. "She said the boy was supposed to come. Where is he?"

"Wait right here — and please stop shouting," Georgette commanded. "You're frightening everyone with all that noise. I'll get Mrs. Abramson right away to find out what happened to the boy."

Mr. Schiller's agitation caught Sima by surprise. "Why is he so worked up?" she asked Georgette. "The boy wasn't supposed to be here until five. Tell him I said to join Ben Gal's physiotherapy session until the young man comes."

Mr. Schiller refused to take part in the exercises. Passing a ball from one person to the next or throwing colorful sticks in the air were, to his way of thinking, activities more suited to little children than mature adults. He shook his head at the suggestion and stayed right where he was, sitting near the entrance, waiting.

When there was still no sign of Ephraim at ten minutes past five, Sima felt she had to take action. She began to have the uneasy feeling that Ephraim might not show up at all. How on earth would she placate the tense old man? The disappointment would be too great for him to bear, and she could surely forget about counting on his future cooperation in any constructive activity.

How could she have let this happen? Why had she mentioned the young man during lunchtime? True, she had wanted to lighten Mr. Schiller's mood, to perk him up and give him something to look forward to. But she should have remembered that Ephraim was an unstable young man who had been rejected by the yeshiva system after having been unable to function in accordance with its rules.

What had made her think that things would be different here, that he would feel some sense of responsibility toward her and the old man? It was inexcusable for him to behave this way. Mr. Schiller was eagerly awaiting him, and the disappointment would be a terrible blow. Where could Ephraim be?

Sima hurried to her office and quickly dialed Daniel's number. After a number of rings, Riki answered the phone.

Oh, no! That was all she needed. She had hoped Daniel would answer. She hadn't spoken to Riki in ages. That's the way it was. Riki hadn't called her since — when was it? — probably since that bas mitzva party. Yes, that was it. Since then, she hadn't phoned. They hadn't spoken at all since that day.

How long had it been? A week? Two? She hadn't made her regular *erev Shabbos* phone calls either. Sima had been very hurt, but she had decided to "stop the dance," to use Malka Weiss's metaphor. She had chosen not to make an issue over the missed phone calls. What was it Mrs. Weiss had said? "You be the smart one. Don't get swept into her dance. Start doing your own steps."

Yes, now she remembered. On Friday night, after Riki's *erev Shabbos* call had failed to come, she had taken the time to think things over. She had mentally reviewed the details of the conversation she'd had with Malka Weiss and tried to analyze her own reaction to her daughter-in-law's behavior. When, for instance, had she allowed herself to be pulled into Riki's dance, to borrow Malka's expression? She suddenly found herself reliving the Shabbos the young couple had spent at their home.

Riki had left the Shabbos table, offended, in the middle of the meal and had retired sulkily to her room, offering no explanation for her sullen behavior. Later in the afternoon, when Riki had come out for *shalosh seudos*, she had uttered not a word of explanation about what had transpired. In fact, she hadn't made any attempt at conversation at all. Sima had been so angered that she had felt her patience snap.

As she sat watching the Shabbos candles, Sima realized that it was then that she had unconsciously joined Riki's dance. *Okay, if you won't talk, then I won't either. If you act cold and indifferent, then so will I.* She had gone out to the porch with a book and become totally absorbed in her reading. After that, the dance had somehow continued of its own volition. Riki had taken offense at her mother-in-law's behavior and become even more withdrawn. Sima, in turn, had felt doubly hurt. Unfortunately, things had spiraled downward ever since, a rapid descent with no end in sight.

No. This time I'll be wiser, Sima thought to herself. Sometimes, it was good to discuss things with an experienced woman, someone discreet and perceptive, someone on the same wavelength as she was. She would make sure not to repeat her mistake. Riki hadn't called for almost two weeks? She hadn't wished her a *gut Shabbos*? She would overlook it. She would call Riki herself and bite back any critical remarks that might spring to mind. In other words, she would initiate a new dance.

That had been her decision. But why did Riki have to be the one to answer the phone just when she was so irritated? It was certainly not the ideal time for a chat that was supposed to herald a fresh start.

"Hello?" she heard her daughter-in-law say in a tired voice.

"Hello. It's me. I mean, your *shvigger*. How are you, Riki?"

"F-fine."

Fine! Not a single word of explanation did she offer as to why she hadn't called for two weeks. Her voice sounded remote and detached. It didn't matter, though, Sima reminded herself. She wasn't going to let herself be hurt by such things anymore.

"Riki, listen. I have to make it quick. I'm at work. There's been some kind of misunderstanding here regarding Ephraim. He was supposed to come today to learn with one of our residents. You surely know about this job that Daniel is trying to arrange for him. He was here yesterday. I didn't get to discuss it with Daniel yet." Sima's words came out in a jumble. "The old man is waiting desperately, and your brother hasn't shown up yet. I must reach him. Do you by any chance have a phone number where I can reach him?"

"Just a minute," came the slow, somewhat apathetic response. Sima heard the rustling of papers over the phone.

"I think this is it. It's the number for the pay phone in the dormitory. It's worth a try. Maybe you'll manage to catch someone."

"Thank you, Riki. I'll try."

"You're welcome. Okay, then. Good-bye."

Sima suddenly felt a rush of anger toward her daughter-in-law, who had treated her with such indifference, answering with a trite yes and no to a matter of such urgency, a problem that just so happened to have something to do with her, too. Obviously, that brother of hers couldn't be relied upon.

She was surprised her *mechutanim* had allowed things to go this far with Ephraim. She, in their place, would have hired tutors and professionals who could have helped the child right from the start. She would have tried anything to keep him in a yeshiva so he wouldn't have come to the point where people tried to set him up with jobs he was far too immature to hold down.

She had told her husband at the very beginning that this wasn't a regular, run-of-the-mill family. These things didn't happen in a family that functioned normally. In her family, at least, such a thing had never happened, and she didn't think it ever would. It was silly to spend time thinking about that now, though. There was nothing she could do at this point. They were her *mechutanim*, and that was that.

She had already emphatically told her husband that they would consider only a *bachur* from a top-notch family for Gila, who was next in line. This time, they would make thorough inquiries before they proceeded with anything, so they wouldn't have surprises on the evening of the engagement, the way they had with Riki's family.

Now, she had better get hold of that boy and put him in his place.

■ ■ ■

Riki wanted to go back to sleep, when she noticed the time on the clock in front of her. Was it five-fifteen already? Had Yossi really let her sleep that long? It was a good thing the telephone had rung to awaken her. Oh, well. It seemed Ephraim was making problems, and her mother-in-law was not pleased with the arrangement, just as she had predicted.

She had told Daniel it was a waste of energy to try and reform Ephraim. She had also told him she felt it wasn't a good idea to get his mother involved in Ephraim's problems. Daniel, though, had insisted. It was just lucky — for her and for everyone else — that she had a completely different attitude these days. She had decided that come what may, she no longer cared.

She had sensed the strong undertone of resentment and condemnation in her mother-in-law's voice, but these things failed to move her anymore.

How had she put it to Daniel? "Your mother will never approve of me no matter what I do. She has her preconceived notions about me, about us — about everyone. Since she'll never be satisfied with me, why should I bother to keep trying to please her?"

Riki felt a certain sense of freedom as she sat thinking about her mother-in-law's phone call. She felt her mother-in-law's words glide right over her without touching her. They didn't hurt anymore.

She was surprised to see how good she felt. It was so much easier this way.

39

EPHRAIM WOKE UP EVERY MORNING feeling depressed. All he wanted to do was roll over and go back to sleep forever. If the school's schedule hadn't forced him to get up, he might have done just that. As it was, the heavy feeling lingered all morning, until somehow, at around eleven o'clock, the cloud of melancholy began to lift and a lighter, more optimistic mood took its place.

This morning was no different. Last night, he had returned to his room in the dorm brimming with the wonderful feeling of fulfillment and self-confidence that comes from meeting a challenge. The satisfaction evaporated by dawn. The pale sky he saw through the window brought him back to a dreary reality, bursting the bubble of his self-delusion. How stupid it all seemed — the old man, the nursing home, the new job, all of it.

Why on earth should he, Ephraim Baum, become a *mishnayos* teacher? Why should he spend time every day diligently preparing a *shiur*? Why should he travel all the way to Bnei Brak to learn with an elderly man whose mind seemed to be going?

He suddenly doubted whether either he or the old man would benefit from the arrangement.

True, last night's study session held moments of satisfaction, but so what? That didn't mean anything. Now that he thought of it, no one had actually told him that he had done well, neither the old man nor the director, Riki's mother-in-law. He recalled seeing her standing near the entrance when he left, and she hadn't mentioned anything about having him come again.

Ephraim finally forced himself out of bed to face the new day, another empty day that promised only to be dull and mundane. He davened with no great measure of concentration, ate breakfast and began his morning studies. At noontime, one of his friends let him know that he had a phone call on the pay phone, but he chose to ignore the message. It was probably Daniel, anxious to hear how yesterday's session had gone, and he didn't feel like giving him a report at the moment. The entire project had lost its appeal.

After lunch break, Ephraim slogged away at his vocational courses, wondering how much longer he could carry on. Where was it all leading, anyway? Once again, he felt a pang of regret for having given in to his father's pressure so hastily. Why had he returned to this place?

At a quarter past five, his friend Rafi burst into the classroom, motioning for Ephraim to follow him out. "He has an urgent phone call," he explained to the perplexed instructor.

Ephraim left the room reluctantly. *It's Daniel*, he thought to himself. *Why is he on my back already?*

But Rafi quickly set him straight. "It's some lady calling. She introduced herself as the director of a nursing home. She sounded upset and asked me to call you to the phone immediately. Do you know who she is?"

Ephraim didn't reply. Feeling both surprised and mildly alarmed, he picked up the receiver. "Hello? Who is this please?"

"Hello. Is this Ephraim Baum?"

"Speaking."

"This is Sima Abramson, from the nursing home. Where are you?" Her tone was condemning, demanding an immediate response.

"I…we didn't set a definite time for the next session," he stammered. "I wasn't sure when to come."

"What do you mean, we didn't set a time? I thought it was understood that you were to come every day. You can't do something like this, especially not when elderly people are involved. Poor Mr. Schiller. He was so invigorated by the learning yesterday. He was all smiles this morning. He was in a wonderful mood — and now he's so disappointed. He's been waiting since three-thirty. How could you do such a thing?" The words came out fast, giving Ephraim no chance to compose himself. "Why didn't you come? What am I supposed to tell Mr. Schiller now?"

The learning invigorated Mr. Schiller. He's been waiting since three-thirty, and was smiling all morning because of me. Now he's disappointed. It couldn't be! All because of me? Was our shiur together so successful?

"I didn't think that's how it was," Ephraim murmured. In a firmer voice, he said, "Tell him I'll be there right away."

"What do you mean, right away? How long will it take you to get here?" the director asked.

Ephraim looked at his watch. It would take about twenty minutes to get there by bus. "I can be there in half an hour," he estimated. "Is it still worth it?"

"Of course it's still worth it, if only to restore his trust in you. We'll give him supper in the meantime, and afterward he'll be ready to learn with you."

■ ■ ■

Gavriel held the bag with the shirts in his hand as he waited at the bus stop on the main highway leading to Petach Tikva. He hoped the bus would not pull up to the bus stop before his good friend Pedro arrived with his companion.

He had met Pedro at the print shop that was going to help him with the forgery of the doctor's note. It had struck him then that Pedro was just the right man to testify on his behalf. He would sign an affidavit saying he, Pedro Gonzales, had seen old man Schiller sign the document. Pedro had agreed to his proposition — for a generous cut, of course.

This morning, among all the other things he'd had to see to, he had made up to meet with Pedro at the bus stop. He wanted Pedro and his friend to be familiar with the nursing home and, if possible, with Mr. Schiller himself. He wanted to be certain that Pedro and his anonymous friend (who Pedro had sworn was trustworthy) would be capable of standing up to cross-examination on the witness stand, if it came to that.

He stood impatiently at the bus stop. Why hadn't they shown up? They had made up to meet at five o'clock. It was five-thirty already, and there was still no sign of them.

Ten minutes later, Gavriel caught sight of Pedro and his companion walking toward the bus stop. *Just in time*, he thought, as he saw the bus approaching. Gavriel waved at them to hurry. Seconds later, when the bus opened its doors Gavriel ushered his two breathless companions on board.

"We'll talk when we're sitting down," he said to Pedro as they paid for their tickets. He looked for seats and found the perfect spot midway down the double-length bus: seats facing each other. Pedro and his friend settled onto one seat, with their backs to the driver. Gavriel faced forward, opposite them.

The bus was fairly empty at that time of day. In the seat behind Gavriel sat two children. In the seat in front of Pedro and his friend, a woman sat alone, looking out the window. In the seat across the aisle sat a lone *yeshiva bachur*, who Gavriel dismissed as insignificant. Reassured that they had their privacy, he leaned forward and motioned for his two companions to do the same.

Ephraim, the young man sitting across the aisle from Gavriel, was struck by the strange aura of conspiracy surrounding the three men. He noted the rapid exchange punctuated by emphatic gesticulations followed by the shocked expressions of the two passengers riding backwards. Something looked fishy.

Those guys must be criminals! He felt a surge of adrenaline course through his veins as he pictured himself the hero of an unfolding drama. He would trail the criminal to the scene of the crime, catch him in the act and turn him over to the police. Due to his commendable actions, he would be awarded a medal of honor with much pomp and ceremony, while swarms of reporters frenziedly fought to interview him.

Ephraim smiled as he realized how he had let his imagination run wild. The passengers across the aisle were probably ordinary citizens, innocent of any wrongdoing. It was only his rich imagination and tendency to fantasize that had turned them into suspicious characters. But so what? If he enjoyed imagining dramas like that — and he did — there was no harm in indulging in one, at least until it was time to get off the bus.

Ephraim pushed the button to get off at the next stop and realized his daydream was about to follow him into reality. The three suspicious characters also stood up and walked to the door. He let them go first and watched as they headed down the street in the same direction he was going. He followed at a slight distance. *If I'm playing detective, I might as well do it right*, he chuckled to himself.

The man in the middle of the threesome, the one with the silvery hair, was talking animatedly. The two men flanking him were listening intently. Ephraim was surprised to see them turn into the small street where the nursing home was located.

What was going on? Were they really plotting something, or was his imagination playing tricks on him again? The silver-haired man was pointing across the street to the entrance to the nursing home, using sweeping hand motions as he explained something to his friends. Ephraim quickened his pace, hoping to catch what he was saying. It was then he noticed that the three were speaking a foreign language. As he drew closer, they suddenly stopped talking. Ephraim turned his eyes from the threesome to look at whatever it was that had caught their attention.

A lone police car, its lights flashing, stood outside the nursing home entrance. What was going on? Was he about to become a witness to a real-life drama?

Ephraim shot a sidelong glance in the direction of the three suspicious characters in his melodrama, but to his utter shock they were gone.

While his head was turned, they had vanished into thin air.

40

EPHRAIM WALKED TOWARD THE PATROL CAR. The strange trio's sudden disappearance at the sight of policemen was too coincidental. Obviously, they were suspects in a crime and had slipped away moments before being apprehended. He would tell the law officers anything that might help them in their chase.

As he drew closer to the patrol car, though, he was forced to revise his original plan. The policemen were trying to break up a fight. Any connection between their arrival there at exactly that moment and the trio he suspected was purely coincidental.

"A quarrel between neighbors," someone told Ephraim. "It's not the first time the police were called in."

Ephraim was surprised and not a little disappointed. He felt ashamed at himself for having jumped to conclusions. Still, something didn't sit right about those men. Why would they run away when they saw the police unless they had something to hide?

Curiosity pulled him to linger with the crowd, but a look at his watch told him he'd better hurry. It was almost six o'clock, and his elderly partner was waiting to study with him.

Mrs. Abramson, who was standing at the nursing home entrance watching the scene outside, greeted Ephraim with a tense expression on her face.

"I hope Mr. Schiller hasn't despaired," she said, acknowledging his arrival with a nod.

Ephraim flinched at her comment. He suddenly realized he was afraid to face the elderly man.

How strange that a man in his eighties can be so intimidating, he thought. He had never been one to be easily intimidated, not even by teachers or other authority figures.

But it's not really fear I'm feeling now, he mused. *It's just that I'm afraid I've hurt his feelings*. Mr. Schiller was surely disappointed in him, and the sense of unease Ephraim now felt stemmed from the thought of meeting the elderly man face-to-face.

When he entered the room, Ephraim found Mr. Schiller slumped in his armchair, his head drooping onto his chest. His eyes were closed. For a moment, Ephraim was alarmed. Then he drew closer and heard the old man's steady, rhythmic breathing.

He stood there, unsure of what to do, overwhelmed by a sudden wave of regret. Why had he been so self-centered, thinking only of himself? Why hadn't he made sure to clarify exactly what Mr. Schiller expected of him? Why hadn't he asked Mrs. Abramson what the plans were?

He was standing there in the doorway fidgeting nervously when a caregiver suddenly brushed past him and entered the room.

"What's going on? Did he fall asleep? No, this is no good. Yaakov, wake up." The attendant shook Mr. Schiller's shoulder. "It's no good to sleep this way. You have a visitor. Are you his grandchild?" he asked Ephraim.

Mr. Schiller's eyes fluttered open. He shook himself awake, surveying his surroundings. He seemed utterly bewildered. His gaze rested on Ephraim, who saw the puzzlement in his eyes as the old man tried to place him.

Feeling awkward, Ephraim tried to help him. "It's me, Ephraim. I came to learn with you. Do you remember me?"

Mr. Schiller nodded, but Ephraim was not sure he had really recognized him. The elderly man didn't utter a single sound. He was subdued, allowing the night attendant to take over. He got up from the armchair and sat down near the table. Ephraim sat down near him, awash with regret, and opened the *Mishnayos* he had brought along with him.

"Do you want to learn, Mr. Schiller?" he asked in a loud, clear voice, underscored with gentleness.

Mr. Schiller nodded wordlessly again, and Ephraim, left with little choice, opened the *sefer* and began to read aloud.

"*Me'aymosai* — beginning at what hour is one allowed to recite the morning Shema?" He read the entire mishna in one breath and then began to explain. He couldn't figure out whether his elderly partner was listening or not. He found that the lack of feedback from his partner was affecting his own concentration. He shifted to the Bartenura, glanced at his partner and asked him, just to make sure, "Do you understand, Mr. Schiller?"

Mr. Schiller nodded weakly, leaving Ephraim to draw his own conclusions.

"Beis Shammai rules that…" He had already reached the third mishna. Without Mr. Schiller's participation, his explanations were very brief. At this rate, he reckoned, the lesson would be over very soon.

"Beis Shammai rules that Shema must be recited during the evening while in a prone position," Ephraim expanded upon the mishna, "and Beis Hillel is of the opinion that one may recite Shema in any position. The ruling is in favor of Beis Hillel. Rabbi Tarfon recounts that one night he recited Shema lying down in accordance with Beis Shammai's opinion. Later that night, he was attacked by robbers, and they said to him, 'You deserved to be killed, because you committed a sin by behaving in accordance with Beis Shammai's opinion.'"

TIGHTROPE | 291

"Just a minute. I don't understand something here."

Ephraim turned in surprise. Was that Mr. Schiller? He had intended to finish the session now, and here was Mr. Schiller, surprising him once more with his unexpected response.

"If one recited the Shema while lying down, it is considered as if he followed Beis Shammai, even though Beis Hillel rules that one may recite Shema in any position?"

Now this was a clever question that hadn't occurred to Ephraim. So Mr. Schiller had been paying attention all along. Ephraim quickly read the mishna again, trying to find a plausible answer.

"It could be," he hypothesized, "that Rabbi Tarfon recited Shema lying down with the intention of following Beis Shammai's opinion, and that's why he was judged so strictly. If, though, one recites Shema lying down, simply as a matter of convenience—" it had suddenly occurred to Ephraim why Mr. Schiller might be so concerned about this particular question "—then maybe it's not a problem," he continued. "How do you, for example, usually recite Shema?" he asked.

"I..." Mr. Schiller's voice trailed off to end in a sigh. "The truth is, lately it's happened more than once that I've recited the Shema while lying down. That's why I'm asking. I want to know what the halacha is in my case."

Ephraim had correctly gauged the reason for the elderly man's question. Wanting to help Mr. Schiller, he quickly reviewed the commentaries on the page. His eyes lit up as he hit upon the words of the Milechas Shlomo, who confirmed his own theory almost word for word. Excited, he cited the explanation for Mr. Schiller, who smiled in turn.

"Good! Good! It's interesting that I never noticed that particular commentary. It bothers me, the way I've been davening lately," he admitted to his youthful study partner.

Ephraim, feeling an enormous sense of satisfaction and fulfillment, encouraged him to go on.

"Why do you feel your davening isn't the way it should be?"

"That's just the way it is. You see that armchair there? I sit down there to daven, and suddenly I find myself drifting off. Gavriel shakes me awake, and before I know it, I'm dozing off again. Sometimes, I think to myself that maybe it would be better if I didn't daven at all. What value do such prayers have, anyway?"

A tremor swept through Ephraim. He wasn't sure what it was that affected him so. Perhaps it was the note of despair in the old man's voice.

"Why do you say that?" he protested. "A Jew is not allowed to talk that way. *Hakadosh baruch Hu* is your Father. He sees what an effort you make to daven every morning, even though it's so hard for you. Your davening is very precious to Him."

From where had those lofty words come? Where had he heard them? Yes, now he remembered. It was his *maggid shiur*. When was it he'd said that to him? A while ago. It was after he had made up his mind to leave yeshiva. It was a low point in his life, a time when he knew with stark clarity that he was second-rate, a failure compared to his friends.

One morning he had failed to show up for Shacharis. Rabbi Bronder had approached him afterward and had asked to speak with him. Ephraim had been expecting a harsh lecture, or at least a stern reprimand, but nothing of the sort had been forthcoming. Rabbi Bronder had just said, "I've noticed something very wonderful about you in the time I've come to know you. You always show up for davening on time. That's something many a fine scholar can't even boast of. I'm telling you this because I want you to know that Hashem sees your efforts, and to Him your davening is more precious than gold."

At the time, the words hadn't meant much. Getting up for Shacharis on time was second nature to him, part of the daily routine. He supposed it was a carryover from his childhood, one of those deeply ingrained habits that stick with you for life. His father had always gotten up early to daven. Summer or winter without fail, he would get up at exactly the same time before sunset. When Ephraim was old enough to go to shul with him, his father would wake him every morning during vacation, and they would walk together.

Those early morning walks were beautiful. In the clear early morning air, his father would talk to him, ask him how things were going in cheder and with friends. With his father's strong arm around his shoulders, Ephraim felt protected. Those warm moments left pleasant memories. No, it had never been hard for Ephraim to get up on time. Rabbi Bronder, though, called it an achievement. That had made him feel good, so good that he had decided then and there that come what may — whether he went to work or stayed in learning — he would never compromise on this issue. He would make sure to daven on time with a minyan three times a day, no matter what.

"I can't even speak properly anymore," Ephraim heard Mr. Schiller say. "My tongue works so slowly. Sometimes, it's hard to get the words out of my mouth. When you say Shema, as you surely know, you have to pronounce every word clearly. You're a *talmid chacham*, so you know what I'm talking about."

"*Talmid chacham*?" Ephraim felt like laughing, but the phrase, the wonderful phrase, had already found its mark. In his whole life, no one else had ever called him that.

"So I'm telling you," Ephraim said with all the conviction of a true *talmid chacham*, "that Hashem doesn't expect the impossible of us. What you can't do, you can't do. What counts are the sincere efforts you make to daven."

"Then what about you?" the elderly Mr. Schiller countered, departing from the topic of conversation. "You didn't come to help me put on my tefillin. If you're such a tzaddik, and you know everything, why didn't you come?"

"Me? You never asked me to."

"I certainly did," Mr. Schiller insisted, his tone that of one who had long since resigned himself to the fact that his requests usually went unheeded. "Maybe you didn't want to come, but I asked you."

"When?"

So the old man was confused, after all. What a shame.

"You're Ephraim, aren't you?" asked Mr. Schiller, sounding alert.

Ephraim was surprised. *So he does recognize me.* "Yes, I'm Ephraim."

"Yesterday I told you Gavriel doesn't know how to help me put on tefillin properly. I asked you if you'd be able to come."

He hadn't actually asked, but a little mistake like that could be overlooked in a person his age. Ephraim now clearly recalled the conversation. Mr. Schiller had confused him with Naftali, commenting sadly that it was a shame he couldn't come in the mornings. He had then suggested that they speak with Naftali's *mashgiach* about the matter.

"You know what?" said Ephraim, in a sudden flash of inspiration. "I'll speak with my *mashgiach*. If it's so important, then I'll come tomorrow to show the caregiver once and for all how to put on the tefillin properly, okay?"

"Excellent," Mr. Schiller nodded, obviously satisfied. Now that he had been reassured on the matter of the tefillin, and now that Ephraim knew with certainty that Mr. Schiller recognized him and understood what they were discussing, all the earlier hindrances disappeared and the learning really got off the ground.

Mr. Schiller asked some more pertinent questions about his davening, and Ephraim, whose confidence was bolstered by his ability to find the appropriate answers, searched for a pen and paper and carefully wrote down a few points that required further research on his part.

"At home, I'll try to think about what you asked me," he promised his elderly study partner. "I hope I'll be able to provide you with some clearer answers by tomorrow."

"Good, good," Mr. Schiller nodded. "I'll be patient. Just come."

■ ■ ■

It was close to midnight when Rabbi Karp, principal of the vocational school Ephraim attended, entered the study hall for a final check at the end of the day. He noticed that a far corner of the *beis medrash* was still lit, and a student was poring over a *sefer*.

At first, he couldn't identify the student in question, but when he cautiously inched his way closer, he noticed with surprise that it was none other than Ephraim Baum. Ephraim Baum was the last student he would have thought to meet in this setting, let alone at that hour.

Startled by the sounds behind him, Ephraim turned around. The principal quickly composed himself.

"Good evening, Ephraim," he smiled. "What are you doing here at this hour? You look like the classic *masmid*."

Ephraim laughed. "Not exactly." He pointed to the *sefer* on the table in front of him.

"*Maseches Berachos*?" The principal couldn't believe his eyes. "That's not what you're studying in class these days, is it?"

"No, it isn't, but I'm learning it on a personal basis." There was an almost apologetic note in Ephraim's voice. "That is, I am learning with an elderly man in the nursing home, for a salary. I promised to find him some answers to a few questions he raised. I thought it would take only a few minutes, but time has flown." He glanced at his watch as he spoke. "Wow! I didn't even notice that two whole hours have passed. I started with one question, and then I realized that the answer is comprised of various opinions and affects many more topics than I originally thought. It got a little complicated, and here I am, still sitting over it." Ephraim closed the *sefer*, anxious to end the conversation. As it was, he felt he had said too much. This whole encounter wasn't to his liking.

Why was the principal looking at him with such a stupefied expression on his face? What did he want from him? What had he done wrong now? He was sorry the principal had entered the study hall and disturbed him. He had been in the middle of a fascinating discovery that seemed to resolve a whole tangle of questions and contradictions. Oh well, he would have to continue the next day.

"Oh, Rabbi Karp, excuse me, please." Ephraim suddenly remembered that he was supposed to have asked Rabbi Karp for permission to come late to his morning classes on a one-time basis. The principal's coming into the study hall right then turned out to be a good thing after all. Ephraim had been so totally absorbed in the Gemara, everything else had slipped his mind.

41

THE FOLLOWING MORNING found Gavriel tense and jumpy. He was keyed up at the prospect of getting the old man to sign the deed of gift that would transfer his apartment to Gavriel's ownership.

His plan of the day before to acquaint the two would-be witnesses with the elderly resident had failed. He couldn't have foreseen that Pedro's friend, the third man who had been with them, would become alarmed at the sight of the police car and would drag the other two away with him. Afterward, Pedro had explained to him that his companion had already been mixed up in some shady deal and was known to the police — just his luck! He had told Pedro then and there to get rid of him as soon as possible. Someone who had gotten into trouble with the law was not the kind of witness he needed.

Despite yesterday's botched ending, he hoped to wrap things up today. He puttered about the room, tidying up, folding clothing and trying to give the room a pleasant, airy look. He wanted to put Mr. Schiller's mind at ease. Just in case he couldn't catch him during a moment of confusion, the way he had originally hoped, he would try to maneuver him into signing the deed under some other pretense, for which he had already formulated a plan.

He had recently come up with an idea that was ingeniously simple. He would tell Mr. Schiller about the new opportunities Holocaust survivors were being offered to file for reparations from Nazi Germany. In his pocket was the blank reparations form stapled carefully onto the document he really wanted Mr. Schiller to sign, in a manner that left the lower portion of the deed exposed so that it looked like a continuation of the first page.

He planned to tell Mr. Schiller that he would be happy to go down to the office that dealt with the reparations claims and file the request. All that was necessary, he would explain, was Mr. Schiller's signature. The elderly man would surely not notice that he was actually signing at the bottom of another form.

Gavriel was determined to carry out his plan that morning, no matter what. Just as soon as Mr. Schiller finished his prayers, he would find a way to introduce the topic of reparations.

As he reached for the tefillin bag, Gavriel had no inkling of what was about to happen to foil his plans.

Ephraim, too, had no idea of the dramatic events that were about to unfold. As he walked down the long, narrow hallway of the nursing home in the direction of Mr. Schiller's room, hoping to help him with his tefillin, everything seemed perfectly mundane. He was just mildly curious as to how his elderly partner would greet him that morning. Would he be happy to see him, or would he, perhaps, not recognize him at all?

He knocked on the door. To his surprise, he heard someone with a strong foreign accent call out, "One moment, please." He had little time to wonder about the stranger's identity, though. The door was flung open and a tall, silver-haired man stood facing him. "Yes? Can I help you?" he asked.

Ephraim's breath caught in his throat. He felt as if he had been flung into a real-life drama without being properly prepared. It was the man he had seen on the bus yesterday — the criminal! What was he doing here? Why was he in Mr. Schiller's room? How had he managed to get inside without anyone stopping him? Was he looking to steal something, or worse, to harm the elderly resident, G-d forbid?

Ephraim panicked. What if he had already hurt Mr. Schiller?

The torrent of fears and worries passed through Ephraim's mind at dizzying speed. His eyes sought out Mr. Schiller, half expecting to find him tied to his chair. To his surprise, the elderly man wasn't tied up at all. His hands were resting loosely on the chair's padded arms.

"Yes?" the man asked again, suspiciously. "Can I help you with something?"

"I-I came to see him," Ephraim stammered, pointing to Mr. Schiller. Thoroughly confused, he entered the room and went right over to Mr. Schiller.

"Hello, Mr. Schiller. I came about the tefillin. Do you need my help?"

"Yes, yes," Mr. Schiller said with obvious pleasure. "I'm glad you came. The gentleman here is Gavriel, my caregiver. Come, Gavriel. This is the *yeshiva bachur* I told you about. He studies *mishnayos* with me, and he really knows how to learn. I asked him to come today to show you the right way to put on tefillin. I'm glad you came," he repeated, looking at Ephraim with undisguised gratitude.

Ephraim was shocked. He felt as though the walls of the room were closing in on him. What was going on? Was this the caregiver Mr. Schiller had described as ignorant of all things Jewish, the one who didn't know the first thing about the laws of tefillin? What was the elderly man talking about? The man wasn't even Jewish!

Yesterday, when he spotted the silver-haired man and his two companions on the bus, he had taken them for foreign laborers, and suspicious ones at that. Now he found out this man was supposed to be helping Mr. Schiller daven!

Ephraim felt like his head was about to explode. He now noticed the yarmulke perched on the caregiver's head. Given its size, it was unlikely he would have missed seeing it the day before. Either he was out of his mind or someone was trying to pull the wool over Mr. Schiller's eyes.

"Okay," he heard the man say. "If you don't trust me enough to do it right, let him show me how. No problem."

Gavriel picked up the embroidered velvet bag and removed Mr. Schiller's tefillin. Both Ephraim and Mr. Schiller were too deeply engrossed in their own thoughts to notice the caregiver's expression as he struggled with the straps. They didn't see his lips tighten in anger or his eyes flash with suspicion.

No, this young man definitely did not fit in with Gavriel's plans. The boy seemed somewhat familiar, and there was a look in his eyes Gavriel did not like. A few days ago, when Paulina told him about the phone call she had received from Ephraim, he had intuitively sensed that the anonymous caller would bring trouble. How could he get rid of this intruder as quickly as possible?

Ephraim extended a trembling hand and took the bag. He removed the *tefillin shel yad* and took the elderly man's left arm in his hand. He noticed that the straps had been carelessly wound around the little black box. Obviously the tefillin had last been put away by someone unaware or unappreciative of their value.

"See?" said Mr. Schiller. "He always tells me it doesn't matter which one goes first."

"Of course it matters," Ephraim responded earnestly. "The halacha clearly states that the *tefillin shel yad* be donned before the *tefillin shel rosh*. It says so clearly in the Torah, doesn't it? *Vehaya l'os al yadecha uletotafos bein einecha* — isn't that so?" As he spoke, Ephraim carefully studied the caregiver's face. It bore a look devoid of comprehension.

"Here. You can wind them around his arm yourself," he said to Gavriel, handing him the tefillin. "I don't want to get in your way." His true purpose was to assess the degree of familiarity with which the caregiver performed this sacred task.

Gavriel took the straps and began to wind them around Mr. Schiller's arm. So far so good. He wound them once, twice, three times — six times altogether — and then he stopped. The elderly man did not even notice the mistake, but Ephraim spoke up immediately.

"One more turn," he instructed the caregiver, who pressed his lips together in irritation.

I must speak to the director, Ephraim thought as he closely monitored the caregiver's motions. *Does she know who this man is? Is she aware of the fact that he isn't religious at all?* He must tell her all this. *Why is he masquerading as a frum Jew? Anyone who wasn't completely straightforward and honest should not be trusted.*

Ephraim waited until Gavriel had finished binding the *tefillin shel rosh*. He then checked the placement of the *bayis* on Mr. Schiller's forehead and explained the significance of placing it in exactly the right spot. He examined the tefillin once more to see that everything else was done properly, and then reminded Gavriel about winding the *tefillin shel yad* around Mr. Schiller's arm seven times. He handed the old man his siddur, explained that he was in a rush, and left the room with a promise to return in the afternoon.

Sima was walking on the sidewalk leading to the entrance of Nachalas Avos when she spotted Malka Weiss, the perceptive social worker she had spoken to a few days earlier. The two reached the entrance to the main gate at the same time and wished each other a warm "good morning" like two old friends.

"How are you?" Sima asked.

"Fine, thanks. How are you?"

"*Baruch Hashem,* good. Are you here to visit your mother-in-law?"

They continued together along the cobblestone path bordered by rosebushes in full bloom.

"Yes," Malka said. "As I told you, I try to come at least twice a week. So far, I've been sticking to my commitment."

"That's really very kind of you," Sima said approvingly. "You know," she said after a moment of companionable silence, "I've noticed that coming to the right conclusions is no guarantee that the follow-through will be easy."

"What do you mean?"

By now, they had reached the entrance to the lobby. "I'm talking about the discussion we had last week," replied Sima. "I've given it a lot of thought and gained some insight, but there were a few more points I wanted to discuss with you."

Their conversation was suddenly interrupted.

"Uh, excuse me, Mrs. Abramson. I mean, good morning. Would it be possible to speak to you for a few minutes?"

It was Ephraim Baum, Riki's brother. "Yes?" Sima asked, her voice tinged with impatience. "Is it very urgent?"

He seemed to be debating her question. It wasn't especially urgent. It could probably wait until tomorrow. It was just that he was so anxious to get the load off his chest.

"It won't take long," he assured her.

Sima composed herself. Nursing home matters always took precedence over personal concerns. She just hoped he would be brief.

"Do you mind waiting a moment?" she asked Mrs. Weiss. "I won't be long."

Malka nodded pleasantly and sat down in a nearby armchair to wait.

"It's about Mr. Schiller's caregiver," Ephraim said, getting straight to the point. "Do you know who he is?"

"No," she replied. "I know he's an experienced caregiver who came to Mr. Schiller's daughter with excellent references. I've noticed that he does his job well and that he's very devoted to Mr. Schiller. Why do you ask?"

"Well, I think his background and identity should be investigated. Did you know, for instance, that he's not religious at all, and that he wears the yarmulke only while in the nursing home?"

Sima noticed that Ephraim sounded positively alarmed. "No, I wasn't aware that he wasn't religious, but that's not necessarily something to get all worked up about. It's not unusual for a caregiver to wear a yarmulke if he thinks it will reassure his patient. But how do you know he isn't religious?"

"I saw him on the bus coming here yesterday. He was with another two other men, and they looked suspicious. The three walked to the nursing home and stood outside it pointing and talking. When they saw a patrol car, they disappeared."

A smile of amusement twitched the corners of Sima's mouth as she listened to Ephraim's tale. *So, we've got ourselves an amateur detective*, she thought to herself. The dubious expression in her eyes, along with the remark that followed, weakened Ephraim's resolve.

"Listen to me, young man," she said in the confident tone of someone with years of experience behind him. "I, too, make sure to closely observe the caregiver's work and the way he attends to his charge, and it seems to me that he is doing a very good job and that he has Mr. Schiller's best interests at heart. Of course, I would be even happier if his yarmulke was genuine, and I admit that what you told me comes as a surprise. But as long as he respects Mr. Schiller and takes care not to offend his sensitivities or those of the nursing home, there is no real reason to find fault with him."

What about the fact that he goes to such lengths to hide his real identity? Is that normal? Ephraim wanted to ask, but didn't. *What about the fact that he doesn't know how to put on tefillin but doesn't admit it? Is that also the usual way caretakers act?*

"Mr. Schiller is pretty upset over the fact that Gavriel doesn't know how to help him put on his tefillin properly," he stammered at last. "That's why I came here this morning."

"Who told you he doesn't know how to put on tefillin properly?" Sima asked, sounding annoyed. Why was this boy standing here and arguing with her when he had promised he wouldn't take too much of her time? Where was Malka Weiss? She had been so happy to see her, and she had wanted to ask her a few more questions about the issue they had discussed. She wanted to find the magic formula to improve her relationship with her daughter-in-law, and just now, when the perfect opportunity had come along, Ephraim Baum had to show up and interrupt her with questions that were the nothing more than the product of an overactive imagination.

"Mr. Schiller himself told me he was very upset about his davening. Today I saw what he was talking about. The caregiver has no idea of how to put on tefillin," Sima heard Ephraim reply.

You, no doubt, know better, she thought sarcastically. *You entered this nursing home for the first time only two days ago, but you're already vying for the caregiver's position!*

"Well," she said, eager to be rid of the persistent young man, "I'll look into it. Now if you'll excuse me, I've only just arrived and I think this can wait until tomorrow."

Her desire to talk to Malka Weiss impaired her ability to hear the logic in Ephraim's arguments and to appreciate the well-articulated manner in which they had been presented.

"Okay," Ephraim replied, sounding defeated. "I'll be here later in the afternoon, if you want."

Sima shrugged and turned to look for the social worker, while Ephraim, embarrassed, confused and upset, left the nursing home.

42

"**I HOPE THAT WHAT I'M ABOUT** to say isn't *lashon hara*," Sima said to Malka Weiss, seated opposite her, "but I feel I must talk this over with someone who can help me find a solution."

Malka nodded in agreement. She refrained from telling the respectable director that she was accustomed to conducting discussions of this sort at least three or four times a week and that in her profession, such heart-to-heart talks were called consultations. She also neglected to mention that these sessions were usually booked by appointment two weeks in advance and were paid for in full. All she said was that in her opinion, discussions of this nature usually tended to be constructive and solution-oriented, so that they actually helped *prevent* the unpleasant situations that inevitably led to gossip and slander.

Malka's response came as a relief to Sima, who was uncomfortable with the idea that she was about to discuss her daughter-in-law with a relative stranger. She had no desire to air her dirty laundry in the open. To her credit, she had never done so before.

"That's what I think," Sima sighed. "After all, a buildup of negative emotions is probably just as serious an offense as *lashon hara*. We're not supposed to harbor hatred in our hearts. Not that I *hate* my daughter-in-law, G-d forbid, but from what I understand, we're supposed to find ways to rid ourselves of any hard feelings we might have toward others, and I must admit that there *are* hard feelings between us. I've been thinking about what you said last time. You told me to be the mature one, the wise one, the one who initiates change. Well, I decided to try and put your advice into action."

Malka had already visited her elderly mother-in-law. With clarity born of years of experience, she had sensed that her conversation with Mrs. Abramson would not be brief. While sitting in the lobby and waiting for the director to finish talking to the young man, she had made a conscious decision: helping the director was a worthwhile investment, and she would give her as much time as she needed. That's why she had suggested that she first go visit her mother-in-law before returning to the director's office, where they could talk undisturbed.

While waiting for Mrs. Weiss to return, Sima had tried to collect her thoughts. Not only were there so many questions she wanted to ask her newfound friend and confidante, but she knew this was an opportunity that might not repeat itself. She told her secretary that she wished to be left undisturbed for the coming hour, and pushed the busy button on her phone to block all calls.

Now the two were free for what Sima considered a friendly conversation and what Malka saw as a free consultation.

"It's been almost two weeks since that time I decided to speak my mind. Since then, she hasn't phoned," Sima began.

"What made you decide to be so open?" Malka asked.

"Oh, it was a bas mitzva party that she coordinated. I didn't attend, and she was insulted. Why can't she understand that sometimes people just can't make it to a particular event? I was under a lot of pressure here at the nursing home at the time.

Anyway, my son phoned me up and implied that I ought to apologize to her.

"That's when I felt I'd had it. *What about all the apologies she owes me?* I thought. Was she Miss Perfect, an angel who never stepped on anyone's toes, intentionally or otherwise? I found myself composing a mental list of all the different times I could have played the insulted one. There were the times I bought things for the couple and never received any acknowledgment, instances of hurtful behavior at the table, times I wasn't treated with the respect I deserve. These are all things that ordinarily I'd never make a big deal about, but when he suggested that I owed *her* an apology, it made me see red.

"But that's not the point." Sima now looked directly at Malka. "You told me to be careful not to get caught up in her way of acting, to try and identify the dance. So I said to myself, 'Okay. Let's say that sometimes you get carried away and start acting unfriendly whenever she does. Let's change that. From now on, you'll act friendly even when she isn't.' I decided I wouldn't wait for her to call me. I'd call her and be the one to start a pleasant conversation.

"But things didn't work out the way I planned. I had to call my son about something urgent, and *she* answered the phone. I was very tense at the time. One of our elderly residents was waiting anxiously for a young man who hadn't shown up, and I was trying to track the boy down. It wasn't the right time for the friendly, heart-to-heart talk I'd planned. We had a conversation, but she sounded so cold and distant that all my good intentions went right down the drain."

"Why?" Malka probed.

Sima had no problem giving an answer. "For one, because she hasn't phoned since then. All right, so you don't call for two weeks. Then your mother-in-law calls and you are, for argument's sake, in the middle of taking a nap, so you can't respond like a mensch. Fine, I can accept that. But then why don't you pick up the phone later and apologize or offer some explanation? Tell me I caught you at a bad moment, that you were busy or sleeping or whatever. But to say nothing? How patient and forbearing do I have to be? Why am I always the one who has to try and give in to her?"

"Don't tell me you're giving up so fast," chuckled Malka. "You wanted to make a change in the relationship, and you've certainly earned my respect for the courage you displayed in trying to pinpoint your mistakes — and for your decision to do something about it.

"First of all, though, we must realize that no real change actually took place on your part because, as you mentioned, you never did get around to having that friendly conversation with your daughter-in-law. Besides, Mrs. Abramson, for real change to take place, a great deal of patience and perseverance is needed. We mothers see that all the time. How many times do we resolve to change our parenting techniques, to speak to our children in a more gentle tone of voice, for instance, or to ignore certain behavior and offer more praise and less criticism?

"Even if we are 100 percent successful in changing our own behavior — a rare accomplishment and certainly not one done overnight — often, despite our best efforts, the child's behavior seems to stay the same. Or, sometimes, the child reverts back to his old behavior after a brief change for the better. That's when we often feel like giving up. What we fail to realize is that the child may just be testing us to see how serious we are about changing the way we act toward him.

"Perseverance is the key. After you analyze the situation and arrive at the correct conclusions, stick to your goals — even if the other side doesn't seem to be cooperating."

"So you think I should continue along the same lines," Sima asked thoughtfully, "being the one to call, asking how everyone's feeling, acting pleasant and friendly no matter what the response?"

"Definitely. Don't fall into the trap she is unintentionally setting," Malka said decisively. "For some reason, she seems to have chosen to adopt an attitude of indifference. Since I've never spoken with her, I have no idea why she might have done so. What's important right now is that *you* make sure not to reflect her attitude back. If you do, it could lead to a complete breakdown of communication between you.

"By the way, have you ever tried to talk about what happened or what might be bothering her? Did you ever ask her why she stopped calling you?"

"No," Sima answered slowly. "No, I must admit I did not. I'm not really good at that sort of thing. Also, I'm afraid of what her answer might be. Who knows what she'll throw at me? Talking about it together might do worlds of good, but I don't think I'm up to it. I think I'd prefer to just go on being nice to her and leave it at that."

"That's fine," said the social worker approvingly. "It's a valid option, and one that makes sense to you. Let me ask you something else. What about compliments? Do you compliment your daughter-in-law often enough?"

"Compliments?" Sima repeated the word as if hearing it for the first time. "What do you mean?"

"Compliments, plain and simple." Malka smiled. "You know — expressions of appreciation or admiration for things she does. Kind words. Do you give her any?"

Feeling acutely uncomfortable, Sima found she had a hard time answering the question so unexpectedly thrown at her. *Compliments. When was the last time she had complimented Riki?*

"Uh...I think so. That is, every so often. I'll usually let her know if I like what she's wearing or something like that. What sort of things should I be complimenting her on?"

"You can compliment her on anything you feel she does well, whether it's a character strength or something she said or did. What do you admire about her? Is there anything you admire about her?"

Once again, Sima found she had difficulty answering. "Yes.

Definitely." She spoke slowly, organizing her thoughts as she spoke.

"Like what, for instance?" Malka prodded.

"Uh, she's…she's a very good mother." Sima was surprised by her own response. It was only now, when she was pressed for an answer about Riki's strong points, that it occurred to her that her daughter-in-law was an excellent parent. "She devotes a lot of time to her baby, even though she's very busy. He's always well cared for and happy."

"Did you ever tell her that?" Malka asked.

"Well…not really. I mean, I'm aware of it, but it never occurred to me to tell her. Do you know what I mean? I'm not the type of person who goes around handing out compliments for every little thing. Besides, I'm sure she knows I approve of the way she takes care of the baby."

"Don't be so sure," Malka cautioned. "Even if she does know it, your saying so will emphasize your approval of her. Compliments are worth their weight in gold. Often, we admire things we see in those closest to us yet we never tell them. 'What for?' we think. 'He or she surely knows how I feel.'

"But people are not mind readers. A person — and this holds true especially for children — might even mistakenly think he's not loved or appreciated just because no one ever bothers telling him he is. Every single one of us is like that. You've got to spell these things out loud and clear. Don't be stingy about giving compliments, especially when it comes to your daughter-in-law."

"She's also very talented. They often put her in charge of large-scale projects." Sima was warming up to the subject. "She has a lot of strong points."

Malka thought she detected a note of pride in the director's voice.

"It's hard to believe," Sima continued, "but aside from teaching and directing all those plays and performances she's always putting on, she finds time to get involved in *chessed* projects. She's taking care of a little girl with Down syndrome two afternoons a week. Isn't that incredible? I'd never be able to make that kind of a commitment."

"Do you approve?" Malka asked.

"Well, the truth is, if they had asked me, I would have told her not to do it," Sima said frankly. "Even though I'm only her mother-in-law, I am worried about her overworking herself. Since they didn't ask me, I can only say that I feel more admiration than disapproval."

"Did you tell her that?"

"Did I tell her what?"

"That you admire her for doing something so selfless?"

"Uh...no, now that you mention it, I don't think I ever said a word. You see, the truth is, they never even told me about the whole thing. I found out in a rather roundabout way, from my daughter-in-law's mother. You can imagine why a compliment was the last thing I felt like giving her. I was hurt and insulted that they never told me about it. To this day, I have no idea why they tried to hide it from me. What were they so afraid of?"

"What, indeed?" The question flew out of Malka's mouth before she could stop it, but she had no wish to retract it. Although it was, perhaps, too direct and too sharp, sometimes such thought-provoking questions were exactly what brought about change.

"What, indeed?" echoed Sima. "Believe me, I've asked myself that question more times than I can count. It's just one long, continuous puzzle. I think I'm acting nice and friendly, and then all of a sudden, out of the blue, she turns into a sourpuss, and I have no idea what I might have said or done to offend her. Her reactions are totally unpredictable. I never know what it is I might have said to cause her offense. One day I think we've got a really good relationship, and the next day — thunderous silence.

"That's how it's been right from the start. The evening before the *vort*, we went shopping together for a watch, and we enjoyed each other's company. We spoke about so many different things, and we really got along well. Everything seemed just fine. Suddenly, at the *vort* the following evening, she was cold and withdrawn. I didn't know what to think then, and I don't know what to think now. Whose fault is it, hers or mine? I sometimes wonder whether it really is possible to do anything to change it."

"Of course it is!" Malka's reassurance carried the enthusiasm she sincerely felt. "You've made terrific progress already. You've not only analyzed the situation, but you've expressed a desire to do something about it — even if it means that you are the one to change first. Believe me, if you stick to your decision not to get dragged into mirroring her reactions, to act maturely, to see the good in her and tell her what you see, she too will eventually change.

"From what you've told me so far," the social worker said thoughtfully, "I get the impression you're inadvertently hitting a sore spot. That's the only explanation I can think of for the behavior you describe."

"Like what?" It was a novel thought for Sima.

"I don't know. It's probably something that has nothing to do with you, but whenever you say or do certain things, you unintentionally hurt her and cause her to withdraw."

"I'm not sure I know what you're getting at."

"Let's say, for instance, that a mother-in-law says to her daughter-in-law, 'I think the baby is cold. He needs a sweater' — something simple like that. Or, 'He looks hot,' or 'He must be thirsty.' These are normal comments anyone could make and they carry no hidden meaning. If, though, the young mother thinks her mother-in-law doesn't really trust her mothering skills — and especially if she grew up doubting her own competency in this area, for whatever reasons — she could very easily misinterpret even the most well-intended comment the wrong way. On the other hand, a different young mother, equally inexperienced but without her insecurities, wouldn't give those remarks a second thought."

"I see what you're getting at." It now seemed obvious to Sima. "You're saying that there must be something about what I say or the way I say it that upsets her — even though I don't mean to."

"Exactly. You're stepping on a sore spot."

"But how can I be expected to know what her sore spots are? I'm not a mind reader!"

"You don't have to be a mind reader," Malka laughed. "All you have to do is pay attention. Watch to see when she gets upset. Even if you can't figure out what set her off, remind yourself that her reaction has nothing to do with you and everything to do with her sore spot. Once you realize that, you'll find it much easier to forgive her. That plus plenty of compliments will help smooth the relationship."

Malka stood up, and Sima rose to accompany her to the door. What a relief! Finally, she had some insight into what was going on. The program of acting reasonably pleasant with her daughter-in-law, no matter what her response, and complimenting her good points sounded manageable.

Sima felt something akin to compassion for Riki, young and inexperienced as she was.

43

GAVRIEL SAT IN **MR. SCHILLER'S ROOM**, never taking his eyes off the sleepy old man. He was feeling disgruntled and depressed at the way things were, or weren't, working out.

He hadn't planned on the young man's involvement. He was infuriated over the story with the tefillin, and the boy's comments had him worried. His carefully laid plans were liable to be foiled.

Soon, the two hours he was alone with the old man would be up. After that, other staff members were liable to come in and disturb his plans. The doctor might come in, or the physical therapist, or Georgette might come to take Mr. Schiller down for lunch. The old man had driven him crazy with those straps of his, but now that they were finally wrapped securely around his arm, he had curled up in his chair and dozed off.

Gavriel was growing steadily more impatient. He rose from his seat, approached Mr. Schiller and tapped him on the cheek to wake him up. Mr. Schiller opened his eyes, blinked in confusion and nodded off again.

Gavriel walked to the window. Looking out at the busy street below, he suddenly recalled the forged doctor's note Pedro had given him yesterday. Where had he put it? He quickly checked his pockets. From his right pocket, he pulled out the form requesting reparations for Holocaust survivors. No, that wasn't what he was looking for. He stuffed the form back in his pocket and checked his other pocket. Yes, there it was. It looked like an ordinary form, signed by Dr. Geller, Mr. Schiller's physician. It was a perfect duplicate of the original.

Gavriel held the form up to the window so that he could examine it more closely by the light of the sun. He wanted to check it for flaws.

No, it was absolutely perfect. A smile of satisfaction spread over his face. They had done a nice job at the printer's. He would have to remember to tell them. Everything was there, black on white, in the doctor's writing.

To whom it may concern: I hereby confirm that Mr. Yaakov Schiller, eighty-three years of age, visited my office on June 6, 2001 for a thorough examination. I found that —

"Shmelke! Is that you?"

Gavriel whirled around. The old man was sitting in his chair, his eyes wide open and staring directly at him.

"Shmelke? Is that you?" he repeated.

"Shmelke?" echoed Gavriel. "Shmelke? Who's Shmelke? I'm Gavriel. Don't you recognize me, Mr. Schiller?"

Mr. Schiller's moment of confusion was over as quickly as it had come. His face took on the by-now-familiar look of apologetic embarrassment that Gavriel had come to know so well.

"*Oy vey*. I must have gotten confused. Of course you aren't Shmelke. How could I have forgotten? Shmelke is long gone."

"Who's Shmelke?" Gavriel asked. He sat down at the old man's side, curious about the name he had never heard the old man mention before.

"Shmelke was my brother," Mr. Schiller replied in a weak voice. "He left Vienna before it all began and made his way to

Eretz Yisrael, while we…we stayed behind to suffer under the Nazis, *yimach shemam*."

The Nazis! Gavriel felt a shiver of excitement run down his spine. His luck was finally changing. He'd been looking for a way to start a conversation about reparations and now it'd fallen right into his lap! He'd have to play his cards right.

"You must have suffered a lot, didn't you?" He walked closer to Mr. Schiller, distractedly tossing the piece of paper in his hand on the nightstand. His face assumed a mask of compassion.

"Suffered?" echoed Mr. Schiller incredulously. "Suffering doesn't nearly come close to describing what we endured. It was Gehinnom, not suffering." He closed his eyes for a moment, and Gavriel felt his blood pressure rising. *Not now, Mr. Schiller. Don't you dare fall asleep on me now of all times!*

"Which camps were you in?" he quickly asked to keep the conversation going. "Were you at Auschwitz?"

He'd heard of Auschwitz from Paulina. He wasn't that interested in the Holocaust the Jews loved to talk about all the time, but one of Paulina's aunts had died in Auschwitz. Now, thanks to the little bit he knew, he was able to conduct a decent conversation on the subject without sounding like a complete ignoramus.

"I was at Auschwitz and Dachau too. Afterward, I ended up in Landsberg. My parents were there too, and my brothers and sisters. Everyone was there…and everyone was murdered."

"Did you get reparations?" *Finally! Now we're getting somewhere!* Gavriel was keyed up and reached nervously into his pocket to make sure the reparations application form was still there.

"Reparations!" Mr. Schiller spat out the word. "What good are reparations? Yes, I got some money, not much. What difference does it make? Can money ever make up for the pain and suffering?"

"No, of course not." Gavriel played along with the old man's views, readily agreeing to keep the conversation flowing. "But at least it can make life easier. If you can afford a nice, air-conditioned room and the best doctors, life is a lot more pleasant."

"Shmelke had brains and luck," said Mr. Schiller, as if he hadn't heard the caretaker at all. "He made his way to Eretz Yisrael before it all began, and that's how he was spared. He wanted me to come too, but I didn't want to leave my parents. I was the oldest son, and I was already helping out in the store. Then the murderers came and destroyed everything. They put us in cattle cars and they—"

"You know what?" Gavriel interjected, trying to steer the conversation back on the desired course. "Just yesterday I heard that it's still possible to get reparations from the Germans. Even people who already got some money are eligible to get more. There's another elderly man I work for who asked me to bring him the forms to fill out. Look, I'll show you."

Gavriel withdrew the papers from his pocket, flipped through them and pulled out the one he needed. The rest he stuffed back into his pocket. "See this?" he said, waving the paper in Mr. Schiller's face. "All you have to do is fill out your name and a few other details, sign the form and send it in to the lawyer's office. I'll be happy to drop it off for you myself, if you want," he offered solicitously.

"The other man I work for, Mr., uh, Levy, asked me to take care of it for him. If you want, I can do the same for you. In fact, you can sign this form, and I'll pick up another one for him."

But Mr. Schiller wasn't interested in the form. *The cattle cars… Shmelke… Mama and Papa…* The memories came flooding back. He had the caretaker at his side, listening and taking an interest. Why shouldn't he unburden his heart? He hadn't spoken to anyone about his wartime experiences for a long time.

"Do you have any idea what a cattle car is like?" he asked his attendant. "It's a boxcar without windows. There's no air. You can't breathe. Hundreds of people crammed together like…like cattle. The worst was the thirst. All we wanted was a drop of water, even one drop, but they gave us nothing.

"The children were crying. 'Mama! Mama!' they screamed. All I could think of was my own mother, such a sweet, gentle woman, and so small and vulnerable. I searched for her with my eyes. I couldn't move. I called out 'Mama! Mama!' too, just like the little children, and then I heard her answer from the other end of the car. '*Ich bin du. Kum helf mir. Kum, Yakova'le,*' she called."

Yaakov Schiller began to sob. "I couldn't get to her, I couldn't help her — how could I? To this day, I remember her voice, calling '*Kum, Yaakova'le.*'" Tears streamed down his wrinkled face as he shook with quiet sobs. He hadn't cried like that in years, not for his mother, not for himself and not for the terrible memories.

Gavriel felt ready to explode. Only two minutes ago, he'd been sure his luck had changed for the better, and now this! His plans were being thwarted at the last minute, just like always. No! He wouldn't allow it.

"That's just what I was saying," he said loudly. "You've suffered enough." He stared into Yaakov Schiller's pain-filled eyes. "Enough!" he almost shouted. "Now you need to receive reparations. This form is meant for you. Just sign here, and I'll go to the office and drop it off. You'll get a lot of money. They're giving to everyone now — those who already got some money and those who still didn't. You've got to take whatever you can from those villains."

Mr. Schiller felt a pen being stuffed between his fingers, a piece of paper rustling in his face and heavy breathing at his neck. Someone was pressing on his shoulders and it hurt. Suddenly, he noticed that his arm was still wrapped in his tefillin straps, and he recalled that he was still in the middle of davening.

"Wait a minute. I've got to finish my prayers," he said, flustered and distressed. "What's the hurry? Soon."

Gavriel was on the verge of losing his carefully maintained

control. He wanted to shake the old man violently. *Why? Why soon? What was so complicated about signing your name on a piece of paper? Why did the old man insist on standing in his way all the time?*

He glared at his charge with barely suppressed anger. *The tallis, the tefillin — it was all their fault. No wonder everyone hated the Jews! Stubborn mules, that's what they were, all of them!*

How he wished he could rip those black straps off the old man's head and arm. *Enough! Enough of those endless prayers, of the gibberish he uttered in that whiny, annoying tune. A fine time the Jew had found to mourn his dead parents, a fine time indeed.*

Mr. Schiller raised his head to look for his caregiver. He felt a sudden tightness in his chest, and he was hot. He wanted to ask him to please open the window. His eyes suddenly met Gavriel's, and he flinched. Those eyes burned with hatred. They threatened him with their terrifying glare. *No! It couldn't be!* He recognized that look. It was the look he had seen in the eyes of the men who had locked them up in the cattle cars and led them to their deaths.

"Wh-what is it?" Gavriel asked, flustered by the intensity of the old man's stare.

"The window. Please open the window."

Gavriel regained control. He couldn't pressure the old man like that. He would have to slow down. He hoped he hadn't blown his chance, that the old man hadn't sensed his excitement and grown suspicious.

He made a conscious effort to soften his features, and asked in a kindly voice, "Open the window? Of course. Why didn't you ask me before? Would you like to drink something?"

Mr. Schiller breathed a sigh of relief. He must have experienced another one of those lapses he'd been suffering from lately. Sometimes, past and present mingled in his confused brain. It was only Gavriel, his kind and dedicated caregiver, and everything was okay.

Someone knocked at the door. Gavriel was back in his usual position, calm as always, the form in his hand the only evidence of the drama played out in the room moments earlier. Claudia opened the door and greeted the two of them with a cheery "good morning."

Gavriel responded politely as he hurried to stuff the reparations form into his pocket.

"The physical therapist has arrived," Claudia said. "He's waiting for Mr. Schiller. Can you please take him downstairs?"

"Of course." Gavriel smiled. He'd expected an interruption of this sort. His chances for today were over. He would have to try again tomorrow.

He wheeled Mr. Schiller to the physical therapy room.

The small piece of paper on the nightstand remained where it was, forgotten.

44

EPHRAIM ENTERED MR. SCHILLER'S ROOM at five o'clock sharp. He had taken great pains to be punctual this time. He had no desire to face the stern director's disapproval again. Also, he had begun to develop a strong emotional attachment to his elderly study partner.

The old man had been on his mind all day. He couldn't shake the feeling that Mr. Schiller was not absolutely safe in the hands of that hypocritical caregiver of his, no matter what Mrs. Abramson said. Something was amiss, and Ephraim was concerned.

Several times that morning Ephraim had caught himself thinking about what he was learning, which was a new and most unusual experience for him. He turned the mishna he'd prepared over and over in his mind, mentally reviewing all the *chiddushim* he'd come across while preparing the material. To his amazement, he discovered he was looking forward to his study session with Mr. Schiller.

When he entered the room, Mr. Schiller was sitting in his armchair in the same position Ephraim had found him in the day before, his head lolling and his eyes tightly closed. This time Ephraim knew better than to panic, but was distressed by what he saw all the same. *He's too sleepy*, Ephraim said to himself. *Could there be any reason for his lethargy other than old age? Is anyone checking this out?*

Maybe I should tell the director, he mused, instantly recoiling at the thought. He still felt humiliated at the way she'd brushed off his suspicions earlier that morning. She'd surely do the same this time, too, and condescendingly reassure him that there was an experienced, professional staff on hand to take care of such things. He could already picture her explaining to him that drowsiness was common in the elderly.

Despite his youth and relative inexperience, Ephraim knew better. A year or two before his grandfather had passed away, Ephraim's father had returned home from the hospital one evening very disturbed. He told the family that his father hadn't recognized him and had suddenly begun talking nonsense. What made it especially frightening was the suddenness of the change in personality.

Ephraim's grandmother, his mother's mother, was visiting them at the time. She had encouraged his father to see that the senior Mr. Baum received a thorough exam. As a volunteer at a geriatric hospital, she had firsthand knowledge of such matters. An exceptionally wise woman, Ephraim remembered her telling his father not to let the matter pass. "A lot of things that people consider a normal part of the aging process are actually symptoms of a problem that is often treatable."

She'd gone on to tell stories of how people who suddenly turned incoherent were found to have suffered a mild stroke or a fall that went unnoticed. "Rapid physical deterioration, mental confusion, lethargy — these things have to be checked out," she'd told them. "Sometimes the problem is caused by a chemical imbalance in the blood or even interactions between two different medications. Insist that they look into it!"

Fortunately, Mr. Baum had heeded his mother-in-law's

advice, and the doctors discovered their patient was suffering from an infection that had gone undetected. Once they started antibiotics, the elderly man had gotten back to himself almost overnight.

Mr. Schiller is also sleepy and unfocused at times, Ephraim thought, *even though usually he's as coherent as anyone. Who's to say this is a normal state of affairs? Maybe it's worth checking out.*

He tapped Mr. Schiller on the shoulder, fervently hoping the elderly man would recognize him immediately. He hated seeing him in a confused state of mind. Unlike many people older and wiser than he, Ephraim had seen the real person inside Mr. Schiller's shriveled body, and it was for this person his heart ached. It hurt him to see the elderly man in such a wretched state.

To his relief, Mr. Schiller sprang awake at his touch and recognized him immediately. "Oh, you're here already?" he asked, obviously pleased. "What time is it?" He looked up at the wall clock hanging opposite him but discovered he wasn't wearing his glasses.

"I need my glasses," he said. "Do you see them anywhere? I can't seem to find them."

Ephraim scanned the room, looking for the errant glasses. The nightstand was cluttered with various objects — a bottle of water and some plastic cups, a small vase with several flowers, an alarm clock, a siddur, various papers — but no glasses. His gaze swept over the bed and the rug beside it. *Ah! There they were, at the foot of the nightstand.* As he bent down to pick them up, he noticed a small piece of paper lying beneath them. He picked that up as well, taking it for a prescription Mr. Schiller had accidentally dropped. He was about to hand it to him to ask whether it was important when the scrawled writing suddenly took on shape and meaning, forming a statement that stopped him cold.

"I hereby confirm that Mr. Yaakov Schiller, eighty-three years of age, visited my office on June 6, 2001 for a thorough examination. I found that he is of sound mind and completely aware of his surroundings. He was in full possession of his senses, suffering from no symptoms of dementia. Sincerely, Dr. Geller."

But that's not true! was Ephraim's first thought upon reading the doctor's words. *It's a lie! Whoever wrote these words obviously has no idea what he's talking about.* He knew for certain that Mr. Schiller was suffering from some sort of dementia, and that its symptoms showed up at close intervals. True, most of the time the elderly man was in full possession of his senses and was well aware of his surroundings, but at times he seemed to drift off into a different world. Such a condition, Ephraim thought, ought to arouse the suspicions of any doctor worth his salt.

Why had the doctor written such a statement and for whom? Perhaps this was an old document? He glanced at the date. No, it was issued only one week earlier. Should he ask Mr. Schiller what this was all about? No, the contents of the letter were rather sensitive, even somewhat humiliating.

His last resort was to discuss the matter with the director. Unwittingly, Ephraim sighed. He'd have to show her the paper and tell her what was going on. Why would the doctor write that Mr. Schiller suffered no symptoms of dementia when it was obvious he did? Maybe the doctor wasn't unaware of Mr. Schiller's lapses. If he wasn't, the sooner he was told, the better.

"*Nu*, did you find my glasses?" Mr. Schiller's voice jolted Ephraim back to the present. He realized he was still holding the glasses in his hand, and that Mr. Schiller was looking at him expectantly.

He hesitated. Maybe he should ignore the piece of paper. Why get involved in things that were none of his business?

He cared too much for the elderly man to do that. Besides, it was a mystery, and the thought of solving it appealed to his sense of adventure.

"Here they are, Mr. Schiller," he said. "Listen, I've got to leave to take care of something in the office. I'll be back in a minute. Would you like to drink something in the meantime? Here's the *mishnayos*. Perhaps you ought to familiarize yourself with the mishna before we begin. If you remember, we finished *mishna gimmel*, and we're about to begin *mishna dalet*."

He poured Mr. Schiller a cup of juice and opened the *mishnayos* to the right page. Somewhat reluctantly, his elderly study partner agreed to his suggestions. Perching his glasses on his nose, he began to read the text as Ephraim quickly left the room.

Sima was in the middle of an absorbing conversation when she saw Ephraim waiting at her door. She signaled him to wait.

The matchmaker on the other end of the line had come up with an interesting proposal this time. In fact, she had suggested a match Sima had secretly been hoping for, for a long time.

The boy was a genius, of course, as was only fitting for her talented daughter Gila. He studied in Pe'er Yisrael, a yeshiva for outstanding learners. Most important of all, he came from a distinguished family of lofty lineage. The father, in addition to being the owner of a large number of successful factories, was a noted public activist. His wife managed a charity organization that provided aid for the needy. In short, everything was so perfect that Mrs. Abramson's breath had caught in her throat when the matchmaker first mentioned the name, hardly daring to believe she'd heard right. She'd always told her husband Gila deserved the cream of the crop. In her heart of hearts, she'd believed that was precisely what she would get, and now she saw her intuition being proven right.

Riki's brother was still lingering at the door. Thank G-d the family she'd be investigating now had no such brother in the background. *Hashem doesn't strike twice*, she thought. *Not that Daniel's shidduch was a blow, G-d forbid.* She felt ashamed of herself for harboring such an unkind thought. But the truth was, she'd had to compromise when it came to Daniel. Now Hashem was making it up to her.

"Listen," she told the matchmaker, "we're definitely interested. Naturally, we'll need some time to find out more about the boy and his family. We'll be in touch."

Still in a state of emotional excitement, Sima hung up the phone. She found it hard to come back to earth. The last thing she felt like doing was freeing her time and attention to talk with Riki's brother, who was waiting impatiently outside her office.

45

"**Excuse me,**" **Ephraim began** apologetically. "I'm sorry to disturb you, Mrs. Abramson, but I think this is something you'd want to know about. It's pretty important."

Sima reluctantly tore herself away from dreams of Gila's glowing future to let Ephraim's words sink in. At the sight of the boy's earnest demeanor, she quickly returned to reality.

"Yes. Of course. Sorry to keep you waiting," she said perfunctorily. "What seems to be the problem?"

Ephraim showed her the medical form. She read it in silence, skimming the text quickly: *"I hereby confirm that Mr. Yaakov Schiller... visited my office...sound mind...completely aware...in full possession of his senses... no symptoms of dementia. Sincerely, Dr. Geller."*

"Well, what's wrong?" She raised her eyes in question, not sure what the young man was driving at. Ephraim, for his part, couldn't understand why she was being so obtuse.

"Don't you think the doctor ought to be told that Mr. Schiller *is* suffering from some form of dementia, that there are times when he's not in full possession of his senses? It seems to me his doctor ought to know about it so he can find out what's causing it. When I came today, Mr. Schiller was asleep in his chair, just like he was yesterday. He seems sleepy all the time."

Ephraim felt like biting his tongue. This wasn't what he'd planned to say at all. He had intended to call the director's attention to the document. Something about it struck him as suspicious. Why would anyone go to the trouble of preparing a carefully worded document testifying to something so untrue? That's what he had come to discuss, not Mr. Schiller's condition. Somehow, he was finding it hard to explain himself.

Sima was still not clear exactly what Ephraim was talking about. She glanced at the document once again, this time with more concentration and attention.

"Wait a minute," she said, looking up, confusion written all over her face as the meaning of what she was reading began to crystallize. "Who did you say wrote this?"

"It's signed by Dr. Geller," Ephraim said, pointing to the signature.

"How did you get hold of it?"

"I found it on the rug in Mr. Schiller's room a few minutes ago. I didn't want to ask him what it was. I figured it was better to come and show you." He gained confidence from her silence and continued. "Why would a doctor write a note saying that his elderly patient suffers no symptoms of dementia if he does? And if the doctor doesn't know about it, shouldn't he be told? It's important. When my grandfather, may he rest in peace, acted the same way, they found out he had an infection. Once that was cleared up, he went back to being himself."

Ephraim stopped suddenly, embarrassed by his babbling. Why would Mrs. Abramson be interested in his grandfather?

"Acted what way?"

"What do you mean?" Now it was Ephraim's turn to be confused. "Don't you know that Mr. Schiller sometimes gets mixed up? Sometimes he doesn't even recognize me. He sort of drifts off into the past."

"The past?" Sima echoed mindlessly.

"Yes, the past. Two days ago, he mistook me for his son Naftali, who is still learning in yeshiva. He told me he wanted to speak to my — that is his son's — *mashgiach*."

"He doesn't have any children still learning in yeshiva," Sima remarked. "This Naftali you mentioned is at least forty years old. Still, I don't think that's reason for concern. It's fairly normal at his age."

How did I know that was what she'd say?

"It's normal for elderly people to confuse names," Sima went on, oblivious to Ephraim's chagrin. "They forget. We're used to it here. It's nothing to worry about."

Ephraim's concern for Mr. Schiller overrode his interest in the doctor's note. He was upset by the director's attitude.

"I know that," he said tightly, controlling his mounting irritation. "But he's also very drowsy. My grandfather was like that, too, and—"

"What do you mean by drowsy?" the director interrupted him. The boy's words, or perhaps his obvious agitation, had finally lit a red warning light in her head.

"When I come at five o'clock in the afternoon, he's always sound asleep. He's sitting in his chair with his head drooping down. Even when we study together, he'll suddenly get sleepy. He himself told me that he falls asleep during davening in the morning. It really bothers him."

Sima mulled over what she had just heard. *The boy may just have a point.* She had never noticed that Mr. Schiller was suffering from any of the symptoms he'd mentioned. She didn't like to admit it, even to herself, but she hadn't heard about them from anyone on the staff. How could that be?

"His caregiver is with him when he davens," she now said firmly, in an attempt to dispel the impression Ephraim was creating, "and he never mentioned that Mr. Schiller was unusually drowsy."

"Maybe that just proves that the caregiver can't be trusted," Ephraim retorted. "Why don't you see for yourself? I'm telling you something's wrong. Mr. Schiller's too sleepy. Besides, he sometimes forgets who I am or where he is. If it was *my* grandfather," he added, "I know my parents would check it out right away."

Sima sighed. "Mr. Schiller's children are not at all like your parents. If all sons and daughters would be just a little bit more involved in the lives of their elderly parents the way you say your parents are, plenty of things would be different. Nothing does an elderly person as much good as the presence of his children. Even the most caring attendants are no substitute for a family member. Something like drowsiness is difficult for a staff member to detect. Our staff members deal with so many elderly residents that it's hard for them to pay much attention to each one as an individual. Usually changes in personality and behavior are reported by family members."

Sima's tone was somewhat apologetic, but Ephraim didn't notice. He sensed, though, that she was open to hearing what he was saying, though she hadn't said so outright.

"Still," she continued, "I still find it hard to believe that no one else has called my attention to the fact that Mr. Schiller is confused. We have noticed a general decline in his mood and in his ability to function, but nothing more. That's why we sent him to be examined by his family doctor. There's not much else we can do."

Sima was speaking more to herself than to the youth standing at her desk. If Ephraim was right, this was a case of serious neglect. Who was responsible? She? The family? The doctor?

"Perhaps that's because it always happens at specific times," ventured Ephraim, the idea having just occurred to him. "My grandmother said such lapses of memory are often the result of an unfavorable combination of medications. When does he usually take his medication?"

"At eight in the morning," said Mrs. Abramson quietly, "and at four in the afternoon." She stared at Ephraim as though she was suddenly seeing him for the first time. *Ribbono shel Olam! How did I not think of this myself? Medication! I must check the combination of his medicines. If I'm not mistaken, he recently began taking a new pill. I should have made the connection between that and his sudden decline. This brother of Riki's is obviously brighter than I thought.*

"That must be it," she heard Ephraim say, his tone triumphant. "I arrive an hour after he takes his pills. And in the morning, it happens during davening — Mr. Schiller himself told me so. The caregiver must have his reasons for neglecting to mention the matter to you."

The caregiver. *It was he who had taken the old man to see the doctor. Was he really unaware that Mr. Schiller was suffering from the symptoms Ephraim had described? She ought to ask him directly, the doctor, too. Why had he written such a statement? Who had asked him to?*

A dozen question marks began whirling together in a confused jumble inside her head. She felt the need to sit down by herself in a quiet place and sort out her thoughts.

She thanked Ephraim for his devotion to Mr. Schiller and sent him on his way. Two things were clear to her as she watched his figure recede down the hallway: one, he really and truly cared about the elderly man, and two, there was much more to him than met the eye.

When Ephraim returned to the room, Mr. Schiller was still drowsy. He jumped at Ephraim's touch and then smiled in relief as recognition washed over his face.

"Oh, it's you. For a minute I thought you were Gavriel. Come, have a seat."

A spark glittered in Ephraim's eyes. "Are you glad it isn't Gavriel?" he asked.

"Yes," replied Mr. Schiller. "I feel more *heimish* with you. We sit and learn together. All he does is talk and talk and push me into signing things."

"Signing things? Like what?"

"All sorts of things."

"Did you sign any of them?"

"No. Actually…I'm not sure. I don't remember. I don't think so. I wanted to finish davening. Reparations, shmeparations — what good will reparations do me? It's just a big legal mess, and nothing ever comes out of it all anyway. I know all about it, but boy, was he mad."

"Who was mad?"

"Gavriel, who else? I've never seen him that angry. But then I thought it must have been my imagination."

"What was your imagination?" Ephraim sensed that the old man was about to stop talking, but he refused to let up.

"The livid expression on his face," explained Mr. Schiller slowly. "I raised my eyes to his, and I saw the face of a *rasha*. He had a look of evil. I was terrified. I thought he wanted to kill me. Then, a second later, when I looked again, he was his old self, polite, asking me if I wanted something to drink. That's when I realized it must have been my imagination.

"I've been getting confused a lot lately," the elderly man said, smiling sheepishly. "I sort of see things that aren't really there. You know, sometimes I think you're Gavriel or that Gavriel is someone else. What can I do? But now I'm glad it's you. He's okay, but I've had enough of him this morning."

■ ■ ■

Sima sat at her desk, trying to put it all together. She'd phoned Naftali Schiller and asked him to come down to the nursing home for a meeting. She planned to tell him that now that his sister Naomi was abroad, it was his duty to come here more often and keep an eye on his father. True, the nursing home was supposed to deal with its residents' health issues, but in cases where there was a specific problem, she didn't want to shoulder the full responsibility. She wanted to update him on the situation and hear what he had to say. Who knew? Perhaps his father had similar symptoms in the past. After all, she didn't know everything about him.

After hanging up the phone with Naftali Schiller, Sima had tried to reach Mr. Vidal and hear what he had to say about the symptoms Ephraim had described. Was he, in fact, drowsy during his prayers? And if so, why hadn't the caretaker told her?

Mr. Vidal wasn't home, though, and Sima hesitated to leave a complicated message with his wife. Instead, she merely requested that he call the director at Nachalas Avos as soon as he got home regarding a medical document found in Mr. Schiller's room.

The next thing she wanted to do was phone Dr. Geller himself and ask him why he had written such a statement. His response would surely shed some light on the matter. In addition, she wanted to update him on the facts she had just become aware of and ask his advice on the best way to deal with the problem.

The truth is, she mused, *the boy is right. Often, when we conducted tests because we were concerned about mental changes in a patient, we discovered physical factors that were easily treated. Even an early diagnosis of Alzheimer's can allow for treatment that slows the rapid deterioration caused by the disease.*

It was interesting that a youngster such as Ephraim displayed such awareness and understanding of the elderly. Not many mature adults, even professionals in the field, could boast of the same. She discovered she was truly impressed by Ephraim Baum. As she flipped through the Rolodex on her desk for the doctor's number, the phone rang, startling her.

It was her son Daniel. He excused himself for disturbing her, explaining that he was looking for Ephraim, who had phoned him earlier in the day and left a message with Riki asking that he call back. He had called the dormitory, but the boy who answered said Ephraim had already left.

"By the way, how's the study partnership going? Better? Abba told me he was late yesterday. Was he more responsible today?"

"More responsible? He's extremely responsible!" exclaimed Sima, her voice filled with admiration. "I must admit that I erred in my initial judgment of him. The boy is far more serious and responsible than I originally thought."

Sima was about to launch into a description of her conversation with Ephraim when it occurred to her that it would be nice to share some warm and appreciative thoughts with her daughter-in-law.

"Compliments," as the social worker had told her earlier that day, "are worth their weight in gold." Now she had a perfect topic of conversation for a friendly chat with her daughter-in-law.

"You know what?" she said to her son. "This is something I have to tell directly to Riki. I know how happy she'll be to hear good things about her brother. She can pass them on to her parents."

Surprised, Daniel called Riki to the phone. "It's my mother," he whispered, handing her the receiver before she could balk.

"Hello?"

"Hi, Riki." Her mother-in-law's voice sounded warm and friendly. "I told Danny that I just had to speak to you directly.

"About what?"

"About your brother Ephraim. Riki, I must admit, I didn't know him until now. Today I discovered how special he is. First of all, he captured the old man's heart right from the beginning, and let me tell you, elderly people, like children, are very difficult to fool. They sense who really has their best interests at heart, who respects them and is truly concerned for their welfare.

"In addition, he obviously has some knowledge of the functional or even medical aspect. Today he brought to my attention something that might have otherwise remained undetected. He thinks the old man he learns with is too drowsy and confused, and he came to tell me he thinks the matter should be checked out. If it indeed turns out that something is wrong, your brother will have prevented irreparable damage. Do you see? What impressed me was that, aside from being so responsible, he has a certain sensitivity that most youths his age don't have."

By now Riki was listening attentively to her mother-in-law's words, and she found herself responding in a pleasant tone of voice. "My father was very devoted to our grandfather," she said, "and he involved us kids a lot in the care. I suppose that's where Ephraim developed this sensitivity you're describing, as well as the medical knowledge. As for his discovery," she chuckled, "he always was curious by nature."

The two continued chatting for a few minutes. Sima, though, was pressed for time, and Riki really didn't have much to say other than "Thanks for the compliment," and, "Yes, I'll be sure to tell my parents what you said about Ephraim."

Sima hung up, finally free to phone the doctor. His response was both puzzling and distressing. "I'm sorry, Mrs. Abramson," he had said, "but I never wrote any such note. Might there be another Dr. Geller who examined the elderly man? No? Well, then, the only explanation I can think of is that someone forged my signature to make it seem I wrote something I never did."

46

WHY ON EARTH WOULD ANYONE want to forge Dr. Geller's signature? The question pounded relentlessly at Sima's tired mind. Why — and to whom — might the stability of Mr. Schiller's mental state be important enough to risk forging a doctor's signature?

One thing was certain. Something underhanded was taking place right under her nose. Maybe it had something to do with the family. Maybe Mr. Schiller's children could shed some light on the matter.

She desperately wanted to discuss the issue with her husband, but he was due home very late that evening, possibly after midnight. That meant she would also have to save the news about the proposal for Gila until the wee hours of the morning, and here she was, just itching to get some information. She had a hunch the investigation into the *shidduch* would be brief.

Sighing in frustration, she stood up, gathered the papers scattered across her desk and put them in her briefcase. With a last look at the office to see that all was in place, she turned to go. The nursing home would run smoothly without her for the rest of the day. She, though, knew she wouldn't be able to sit at her desk a minute longer. There was too much to think about. Back home, in her spacious, elegant kitchen, with the homey sounds of percolating coffee and omelets sizzling in the frying pan for supper, she'd relax. In the island of domestic routine, the muddle in her head might just straighten itself out.

Ephraim spotted the director on his way out to the bus stop. He wasn't sure of his next move. Several ideas presented themselves for consideration, but none promised sure success.

Was he seeing intrigue where there was none just to satisfy his desire for adventure? What Mr. Schiller said about the caregiver's threatening look and his attempts to get him to sign some document seemed straight out of a mystery. All the pieces of the puzzle fit neatly in place: The caregiver was a scoundrel who was trying to con his elderly patient into signing a will that would bequeath the old man's wealth to him alone.

He'd recently read a similar story in a newspaper. The children of an elderly woman were suing their mother's caregiver, accusing her of emotionally dominating the elderly woman as she grew weak and ill. Their mother's will left all her worldly possessions to the caregiver, completely cutting out her own children. Could the same thing be happening here with Mr. Schiller? Or was he just letting his imagination run wild and making people fit into parts he wanted them to play? After all, he had no real evidence.

There was the director right now, locking the door to her office. She'd be gone in a minute. Should he tell her about his suspicions? What would she think of him? She'd probably dismiss him as nothing more than a kid with his head full of fantasies. He nodded a polite good-bye as he passed her, and she responded absently.

Thinking of the certificate reminded him of the old lady from the story in the paper. On the witness stand, the caregiver had brought a document signed by a doctor as evidence. "Family Fights Will," one headline had screamed. "Lawyer: 'Deceased

Sane When She Signed,'" blared another.

Wait a minute — that's it! Now it made sense. The note was going to be used as proof. Now he was sure his theory was right.

Having arrived at this decision, Ephraim pushed aside all his previous doubts and approached Mrs. Abramson.

"Did you find out why the caregiver didn't report Mr. Schiller's periods of confusion?" he asked uncertainly.

"No, I wasn't able to reach him," Sima replied, taking up the conversation where they had left it.

"If you ask me, he's out to get something." Ephraim now spoke with confidence. "Mr. Schiller told me he tried to make him sign a document applying for reparations. Did you know that? Did anyone grant him the authority to ask Mr. Schiller to sign anything?"

"What?" Sima thought she hadn't heard right.

Did she know anything about it? No, she didn't. The boy was out of bounds. She'd given him some credit for his responsible attitude today, and already he was taking charge, asking her questions like that! He ought to be put in his place before he grew too cocky. This wasn't the first time he had tried to besmirch Mr. Vidal's reputation. Naturally, she would continue trying to reach the caregiver that very evening, from home. She had to get to the bottom of this and find out just who was out to get something. Was it Mr. Vidal? Or was it the boy himself?

■ ■ ■

Riki was having a good day. First she'd had that surprisingly pleasant conversation with her mother-in-law, and she'd hung up feeling warm and happy inside. And then came the surprise with Yossi. An hour after she'd hung up the phone, she suddenly heard strange sounds coming from the direction of Yossi's playpen. She turned around to see what he was up to and found him holding onto the sides of the playpen with all his might. Grunting and straining with effort, he pulled himself onto his knees, and then he was standing!

Riki cried out in excitement. Yossi, who realized he had mastered an accomplishment of note, looked at his mother with his big blue eyes and squealed in delight. By now Riki was doubled over with laughter. Yossi wobbled on his chubby legs, his hands holding fast to the bars of the playpen. Suddenly he lost his grip and plopped down, his squeals of joy giving way to sobs of disappointment and frustration.

Riki hurried over, extending a pair of motherly arms to her distraught son. She hugged him fiercely to her.

"Sweetie! You're Mommy's little genius, did you know that? You're a big boy!"

She danced around the room with him, ecstatic at her son's impressive accomplishment. Finally, out of breath, she sat down on a chair, Yossi still in her lap. In her mind's eye, she was already planning how she would tell everyone the good news. Her husband, her parents, her in-laws — how thrilled they would all be!

Cuddling Yossi, she noticed how big he'd become. When had she last taken him to the pediatrician's? She couldn't remember for certain, but it was some time ago. At least a month had passed since she'd last weighed him.

"You've grown," she whispered into Yossi's ear. He was already wriggling out of her grasp, trying to get to the vase in the center of the table. She laughed. "It won't be long before we can't hold you anymore, you little troublemaker! Before I know it, you'll be off to cheder." In her mind's eye, she saw him standing at the door with a knapsack on his shoulders, handing her a note from the rebbe.

"And then you'll grow even bigger." She was getting carried away now, her thoughts jumping ahead to distant times. "Like your father!" She hugged him close, savoring the moment. She wouldn't always be able to hold him this way. After all, everyone grew up. That was life. Even his daddy had once been a little boy. She'd never really tried to imagine her husband as a baby. Sure, she'd seen pictures, but they'd always seemed like photographs of someone far removed from her. In her eyes, her husband's life had begun in his teenage years. She couldn't imagine him any different from the way she knew him today: tall, somewhat ungainly and very serious.

But he had once been a baby. She recalled the photographs her in-laws had shown her during their engagement period, suddenly seeing them in a new light. He'd been a singularly charming child, not all that different from Yossi. He, too, had sat in his mother's lap, and she'd loved him fiercely and kept track of his development, glowing with joy as he mastered each new stage. Perhaps she'd even cried out in excitement, as Riki had just done.

And that woman is my mother-in-law.

Riki had trouble imagining Sima Abramson in the role of a young mother, but that's doubtless what she had been. Perhaps she'd also laughingly called her son a troublemaker.

She held Yossi at arm's length, trying to see him from a new angle. "So what does that mean, exactly? Are you going to grow up just like your father? Will some seminary girl come and snatch you away? Will everything she says and does declare to one and all that your time with me as the center of your world is over?" Riki was surprised at the pang she felt. The threat was tangible. She was really afraid of that unknown young girl, whoever she might be.

"Sometimes she'll complain and tell you all about how terrible I am — that I have no taste, that I stick my nose into things that are none of my business. And you, Yossi, maybe you'll even believe her sometimes. Maybe you'll just wave your hand in dismissal, like your father does sometimes when he's trying to calm me, and say, 'Forgive her. She means well.'"

As if he understood her pain, Yossi snuggled close to his mother and placed a hand on her shoulder. Riki felt tears sting her eyes. Perhaps it was her mother-in-law's kind words that made Riki see her in a new light, or maybe it was the magic touch of her son's silken curls brushing her cheek, but Riki suddenly felt a wave of sympathy for the woman who had mothered her husband.

"My darling little Yossi," she whispered, "just grow up strong and healthy and be a *talmid chacham*. And may you have a good wife who will appreciate and respect you. The main thing is that she realize how wonderful you are. She'd better not be catty. That would hurt me terribly, sweetie."

And Hashem, please, I beg of You, please don't pay me back for my behavior with a daughter-in-law like myself. Let Yossi's wife like me. Make her understand how precious he is to me. And please, if it is at all possible, help me learn to like my own mother-in-law... or at least get rid of the grudge I hold against her.

47

IT WAS NOT THE MOST CONVENIENT time for Naftali Schiller to visit his father. He had an important meeting scheduled, but the director at Nachalas Avos had called and asked him to come. Her tone of voice had left no room for argument. He'd canceled his meeting and driven over.

Naftali paced up and down in his father's room with the same sense of restlessness that always characterized his visits to the nursing home. He invariably felt at a loss for words, unable to think of anything appropriate to say. He had already asked his father how he was feeling, whether he had eaten and how he had slept. His father's mumbled one-word answers did not make for prolonged conversation, and Naftali was not verbose enough to make small talk on his own.

When he had run out of things to say, he stood up to check that his father's possessions were in order, as he did every time he came to visit. He made sure there were clean socks in the closet and cookies (his wife had sent a batch last time he'd come for a visit) in the cookie jar. His glance took in the coffee table in search of mail that might need his attention. Most of the time, his father's mail consisted of routine bank statements and occasional updates from the Social Security office or the health fund he belonged to.

There was an envelope under the porcelain vase, Naftali noted. Reaching for it, he saw that it was a bill from the credit card company. A quick glance at his watch confirmed that today was indeed the date upon which the credit card company generally sent reports to its clients.

As soon as he saw the bill, Naftali realized something was wrong. There were too many rows of numbers in the "Charges" column, something most unusual for his father. What could his elderly father have possibly purchased at the Ayalon Mall two days ago? What had he paid 580 shekels for in a clothing store?

"Papa," Naftali asked hesitantly, "did you buy anything new lately?"

"New?" his father repeated, pausing for a moment to think. "Why do you ask?"

"Your credit card bill shows you spent a pretty big amount two days ago."

"Ah, the credit card." The words seemed to remind him of something. "Yes, now I remember. I bought some new shirts."

"That must be the purchase from the clothing store."

"My caregiver, Gavriel, bought them for me," Mr. Schiller said.

"How many shirts did he buy?"

"Four or five. They're over there, in the closet. You can take a look."

Naftali went over to the closet, where he found five new shirts neatly folded on one of the shelves. The label, he noted, was that of a cheap brand. They could not possibly have cost 580 shekels.

"What else did your caregiver buy for you?" he asked his father.

"What else?" The elderly man wrinkled his brow in concentration. "Some cookies, I think," he said. "Maybe a chocolate bar once or twice."

"With the credit card?" The question was almost a shout.

"With cash," his father said, offended. "What made you think he paid with the credit card? I gave him money for the cookies. I gave him the credit card just for the shirts."

"You gave him your credit card?"

"Yes," the elderly Mr. Schiller replied defensively. "I didn't have money left. You didn't bring me any. I didn't have a cent in my pocket."

"Papa," Naftali said carefully, "I left you lots of money the last time I came to visit. How did it go so fast? What did you buy with the money I gave you?"

"What did *I* buy?" his father asked sarcastically. "Since when can I buy things for myself? *He* bought."

"Who?"

"Gavriel, my caregiver. He bought me soap. He bought me hand cream. Once he bought me some strawberries."

"Is that all? Is that why there's no money left?"

Mr. Schiller was silent. He realized how absurd he sounded, and he understood his son's mistrust. It really did sound ridiculous that such a sum of money had been frittered away on some cookies and strawberries. He decided not to tell his son about the money he had loaned Gavriel. Naftali was sure to get upset and angry, and rightly so. But what could he do? Gavriel had promised to pay him back. He had told him he owed a lot of money and said he was afraid he'd be evicted from his home. Besides, he was such a nice man, always buying him whatever he needed. He kept an eye on his blood pressure, too. If Gavriel got upset and left him, who would check his pulse every morning? Naftali would never understand.

■ ■ ■

By the time Naftali Schiller left her office, Sima felt on the verge of collapse. Where was her husband? Why had he chosen this day of all days to be out of town? Late last night, he had called her from Beersheba, where he'd been on business, to tell her he had a meeting the following morning in a nearby city. He thought it made sense to spend the night at a local hotel and return home in the evening, if that was okay with her.

Sima had agreed, of course, but by this morning, she felt she'd had it. She never dreamed things had gone so far or would move so fast. She hadn't anticipated that she would need her husband's help and advice so badly.

When she had looked up and saw the young Mr. Schiller standing in the doorway of her office, she was surprised to see that he looked somewhat angry. Somehow their roles had been switched. She thought she would be the one to say her piece and ask the questions (after all, she was the one who had asked him to come), but he began interrogating her, firing one question after another at her in rapid succession.

"Where does my father's caregiver live? When is he due to arrive? Do you know if my father had any unusual expenses in the past month?"

He spread the credit card statement on her desk, pointing to the long list of numbers with a trembling finger. "Look, here's a bill for two thousand shekels from items bought two days ago at the Ayalon Mall. My father doesn't recall buying anything that expensive. Do you know anything about it? Could it be that you purchased a new accessory for his room or something else we don't know about?"

"Do you think the nursing home management would spend such a sum without telling anyone about it?" Sima looked offended.

Naftali apologized, but that didn't change the situation. On the contrary, Sima's confirmation that it was not the nursing home that had run up such a big bill only complicated matters.

346 ▌Tightrope

"My father told me he gave the credit card to his caregiver, who offered to buy him some shirts. I think you've all given this caregiver a little too much leeway," Naftali complained.

"Excuse me, but we weren't the ones who hired him, if I recall correctly," Sima pointed out. She refused to be burdened with full responsibility for the matter.

"But you are the ones who are here all the time. You're the ones who are supposed to keep an eye on everything that goes on here, aren't you?"

Her heart rapidly plummeting, Sima remained silent. Naftali's accusatory tone caused her to suffer pangs of guilt. *It looks like that boy, Ephraim, was right all the time. Vidal is a professional swindler.*

Why hadn't she listened to the boy? She couldn't think of anything to say to save face now.

"Perhaps we should wait for the caregiver to arrive, and we'll take the matter up with him?" she said finally.

"When is he supposed to arrive?" inquired Naftali.

She glanced at her watch and felt faint. It was already ten-thirty. Mr. Vidal usually showed up at nine o'clock sharp.

"He should be here any minute," she said in a weak voice. She felt her self-confidence ebbing by the minute.

Naftali turned to leave the room. "I'll wait for him in my father's room," he said. "I think you'd best not tell him anything. I'd prefer to catch him off guard. I want to see his reaction when I ask him some very interesting questions. I don't want him to have time to prepare his response."

Alone in her office, Sima felt her world crashing down around her.

With trembling fingers, she called Mr. Vidal's home. No one answered. She should have guessed that would be the case. If the man was a swindler, he wouldn't be showing his face here anymore. She had given him ample warning when she left the message with his wife about a strange note found in the old man's room. Obviously, there was some connection.

Ephraim had told her about Gavriel's attempts to get the old man to sign something. Why had she been so thickheaded? Why hadn't she realized what was going on under her very nose? Was she really so naive?

She was well aware, after all, that there had been cases where acquaintances of elderly people had tricked them into signing documents bequeathing all their property to the interested party. Last year, two members of a certain family had attempted to take their mother out of the nursing home, claiming the place was not good for her and saying they wanted to care for her in their own homes. She had sensed something amiss and insisted on placing a few phone calls before releasing the woman. In the end, she learned that not all the siblings were in agreement with the move and that the two had only their own self-interests at heart. The rest of the family had been grateful for Sima's intuition and common sense.

So what was happening to her now? She berated herself over and over again, unable to believe she had gotten herself into such a mess. If she was too dense to notice what was going on, why hadn't she at least listened when Ephraim had painted such a clear picture of the problem? Had she discredited him because he was so young and inexperienced? Or had she perhaps been predisposed to treat anything he told her with skepticism?

What should she do now? It seemed the swindler had indeed managed to steal a considerable amount of money from the trusting old man. If that was all, Sima felt she could handle the situation, but what about the signature the caregiver might have finagled from the old man?

Sima felt hysteria rising, an altogether unfamiliar feeling. Calm and levelheaded by nature, she usually kept her composure even in tense situations. This time, though, she felt her control slipping. Her hands were clammy, and her stomach was tied in knots.

Where was Ephraim? She had to verify an important detail imme-

diately, while Naftali Schiller sat in his father's room, waiting for Gavriel. What exactly did he know about that form Gavriel had asked Mr. Schiller to sign?

"*Ribbono shel Olam,*" she whispered, "please, anything but that." If the swindler had managed to get Mr. Schiller's signature, this was surely the end — of her, of the nursing home, of their family's good name.

Mr. Schiller's family could not be expected to keep this quiet. They would spread the story in order to warn others to be on guard. People would lose trust in the nursing home. How could anyone send an elderly parent to a home where the management couldn't provide minimal security from swindling caregivers?

Where was that boy's telephone number?

There it was — a pay phone number. She quickly stabbed at the buttons on her phone, willing it to connect. As if to spite her, she received a busy signal. She thrust the receiver onto the phone base with a loud click.

Why did this have to happen now, of all times? Now, when Gila was looking for a *shidduch*, when a good name meant everything.

What would the family of the boy suggested for Gila think when they heard the story of the swindler at Nachalas Avos? Would they still consider making a *shidduch* with them? No one would remember the dedicated care the management had provided for its elderly residents for so many years. All everyone would talk about was the one instance where a swindler had slipped through their fingers. The story would fly from person to person, gathering details along the way.

Sima's fears grew out of all proportion until she was no longer thinking logically. Who would ever want to be a *mechutan* with such irresponsible people — with people who had suffered such a serious financial crisis? The family whose son they were interested in would surely refuse to even consider such a proposal.

Sima closed her eyes in pain as she contemplated forfeiting

the boy that had been suggested, the yeshiva's pride and joy. Why did Gila have to suffer this? If she, Sima, was so irresponsible, why did her dear daughter have to suffer? Gila was still as wonderful as always, wasn't she? Did her daughter have to suffer for her parents' sins?

Have I been too greedy? she thought in anguish. *If I want a good chassan for my daughter, is that asking too much?*

Why isn't someone answering my ring? Why didn't I listen to my daughter-in-law's brother, who had the brains to see what I did not? I didn't give him enough credit. Oh! Someone finally picked up the phone.

"Hello? Can you please call Ephraim Baum to the phone? Please tell him I'm calling from Nachalas Avos. It's extremely urgent! I'm staying on the line."

Sima felt a wave of relief wash over her when she finally heard his voice. She hoped he would be able to shed some light on the matter and that everything would fall into place, putting an end to her problems.

"I have one very important question," she said, getting straight to the point. "Did Mr. Schiller actually sign anything, or did Gavriel's attempts come to nothing?"

"That's exactly what I tried to find out," Ephraim replied worriedly, "but I couldn't get a definite answer. Mr. Schiller wasn't sure if he had signed or not. Like I told you, he drifts in and out. He knows it, too, so he doesn't trust his memory."

The tension rose within her once again. She felt as though she was choking. What should she do?

"I-I just don't know what to do," she heard herself telling Ephraim. "His son is here, waiting for the caregiver, who I feel sure won't be showing his face here anymore. I thought of phoning the police, but if his efforts to make the Mr. Schiller sign were unsuccessful, there might be no point in dragging the police into this."

"It can't hurt," said Ephraim, "and it might help."

"On the other hand," Sima continued, "if he did trick Mr. Schiller into signing something, the most important thing to do is to inform the family. I shudder to think of the consequences of such a signature on a will or something like that in the hands of a swindler."

Is this really Mrs. Abramson talking? wondered Ephraim. *What happened to the supremely confident nursing home director? Why does she sound so afraid and desperate?*

"I understand that this is a very unpleasant situation," he said slowly and thoughtfully, "but I think that if the police find him fast enough, no money will be lost. If you ask me, you should tell the family what's going on no matter what the consequences may be.

"My parents always say, 'No one ever loses out from doing the right thing,'" he continued, his youthful voice ringing confidently over the phone. "What's the worst that could happen? Even in the worst-case scenario, the family will appreciate that you were open and honest with them. People understand that such a thing can happen."

"Really? You think so?" Sima asked in relief. She was clutching at Ephraim's words as a drowning man clings to a raft. To think she had once thought it not fitting for such a boy to walk the halls of so honorable an institution as Nachalas Avos!

48

SEVEN-YEAR-OLD TEHILLA ABRAMSON opened the front door with the key she wore on a chain around her neck. *That's it!* she thought, slamming the door behind her. *I'm not going to that stupid day camp anymore. Just because they're in seventh grade, Adina and Shira think they're so big and so smart no one can tell them anything. All they do the whole time is tell everyone to sit down and fold their arms. Besides, it was hot there, and the fan didn't help at all, and Devori kept insulting her. I'm calling my mommy,* she thought petulantly.

It was the first day of summer vacation. The day camp arranged by the school Tehilla attended wouldn't be starting for another week. Sima had hoped that the one run by Adina and Shira, two neighborhood girls, would occupy Tehilla until then. Obviously, though, things weren't working out very well, and Tehilla's phone call couldn't have come at a worse time. Sima was sitting in her office trying to come up with the best way to break the unpleasant news to Naftali Schiller, still waiting in his father's room, that Mr. Vidal was in fact a conniving swindler.

"Tehilla, sweetie," she said impatiently, "call back later, okay? I have some very urgent business to take care of."

"But, Mommy — I'm *bored*!"

"There's ice cream in the freezer. Take some, and then you can color in the new coloring book I bought you."

"But, Mommy, I finished the whole book already," she whined.

"Tehilla, please! Don't start with that now. Go back to day camp just for today, and we'll see what to do about it tomorrow."

"But, Mommy, Devori calls me names."

"So ignore Devori and play with the other girls."

"I don' wanna."

"Tehilla!" Sima's voice was strained. "I have no time now. Go back to day camp immediately, and tomorrow, as I said, we'll think of another plan. All the other girls on the block go to that day camp. You're the only one who's making trouble. That's enough now. Gila will be home at noon. She'll make you lunch and maybe she'll take you to the beach later in the afternoon."

Sima hung up without giving Tehilla a chance to protest. Gila, she sighed. *Instead of being home now to help out, she's at school helping arrange some sort of a bazaar.* Sima disapproved of what seemed to her like the million and one activities that stole her daughter away from home. It was vacation, after all, wasn't it? She needed Gila so badly these days. She hoped she would at least take Tehilla to the beach. She really didn't know what she would do with her otherwise. Why was Tehilla so spoiled? Why were all the other girls willing to stay in day camp until four o'clock while only her daughter insisted on going home?

"And then there's that big shot Esti who bosses everyone around. She teases me and makes fun of everything I do and…"

Tehilla realized with a start she was talking to thin air. Her mother had hung up on her! Frustrated and angry, she continued her diatribe even though no one was listening. "I don't like her! She's got freckles and a big mouth! I'm not going back."

Sima had a flash of inspiration. She could ask Dassi to have Tehilla over for a few days, just to help her get through this week until the real day camp began. Dassi would be glad to help, and although Chagi and Duddy were younger than Tehilla, they could still play together and enjoy one another's company. She knew Dassi often took her children out on interesting trips. Sima thought there was a good chance her idea could work out.

Not wanting to waste another minute, Sima immediately called home. Tehilla must have been waiting near the phone, because she answered immediately.

"Tehilla, listen. I thought of a good idea for you. How would you like to go to Dassi for a few days? You can stay there until Shabbos. I think you'll have a wonderful time!"

A moment of silence ensued as Tehilla thought over the idea. After brief deliberation came a surprising answer. "I'd rather go to Riki."

"Riki?" Sima was surprised. The idea had never even occurred to her. Because of the sensitive nature of their relationship, she was afraid of making additional mistakes, and she felt uncomfortable asking Riki for a favor. She felt far more comfortable asking Dassi.

"But Riki has only Yossi at home. What will you do there the whole day? You'll be bored."

"No, I won't. Chagi and Duddy fight with me all the time, and Dassi gets upset. Riki has stickers and all sorts of things for kids to do, and lots of times she talks to me."

■ ■ ■

Riki could barely hide her surprise when she heard her mother-in-law's voice on the phone. What was going on? First they ignored each other for two weeks, and now they were having one conversation after another.

Her mother-in-law sounded less relaxed than she had the last time they'd spoken, reminding Riki of the underlying tension that generally characterized their conversations. Riki felt her facial muscles tighten of their own accord.

"Riki, I'd like to ask you for a favor that I hope won't prove too difficult for you. The truth is that I intended to ask Dassi, but, surprisingly enough, Tehilla wanted only you."

Riki had no idea what her mother-in-law was driving at. "What's it all about?" she asked hesitantly.

"Oh, I'm sorry. I'm so mixed up today that I'm having a hard time explaining myself. I'm stuck in a really tough situation here at the nursing home. Don't ask. Anyway, Tehilla's day camp starts next Monday, and I don't have an arrangement for her until then. For some reason, she's not happy in the day camp run by the girls in our neighborhood. I suggested that she go to Dassi for a few days, but as I already told you, she doesn't like that idea either. She wants to go to you. Do you think you can have her over for a few days?"

"Of course, with pleasure!" Riki responded. "She can play with Yossi and Brachi — that's the little girl who comes here. I think she'll enjoy helping me take care of both children."

"Are you sure you can handle it?" Sima still felt doubtful. Was she doing the right thing?

"Definitely. No problem."

"All right, then. We'll find a way to get her to you. Maybe Gila will bring her in the afternoon. Thanks a lot, Riki. I'll talk to Dassi, too, just in case. That way, if you find it too hard, you can send her over there for a day or at least for a few hours."

"It won't be too hard. Why should it be?"

Sima hung up, the click of the receiver music to her ears. *Look at that! Riki was happy to help out.* She'd had no idea Tehilla was so fond of Riki. A smile of relief spread over her face. At least one thing was successfully taken care of that morning.

■ ■ ■

In her home in Jerusalem, Riki did not share Sima's sense of pleasure. After her initial response, warm and sincere as it

TIGHTROPE ▌355

was, Riki felt her spirits drop. At first, she couldn't figure out what had made her mood sink so rapidly, but it wasn't long before she was able to put her finger on what it was her mother-in-law had said that irked her so.

Dassi! Yes, what was that all about? What exactly was her mother-in-law implying by telling her that she had initially planned on sending Tehilla to Dassi, but that "surprisingly enough" Tehilla wanted to come to her? What was so surprising? Didn't she realize what a backhanded compliment that was?

She didn't think her mother-in-law had purposely intended to insult her. She didn't think she was being cruel. Paradoxically, it was her mother-in-law's good intentions that bothered her. Even when she was trying to be kind, her mother-in-law just couldn't hide her true feelings about who she felt closer to, who she trusted more, who was her first choice and who was a last resort.

Why did my mother-in-law have to tell me, over and over again, that she really preferred to send Tehilla to Dassi, that I got chosen by default? Why did she first think of Dassi and not me? And why did she have to tell me that?

Riki felt the spark of warmth and understanding she had felt toward her mother-in-law as she'd cuddled her son in her arms the previous evening flicker and die out. The familiar feelings of bitterness, pushed to the side for a brief time, welled up within her once again.

That's the problem with my mother-in-law, she thought. *Even when I want to be nice, she somehow manages to slap me in the face with her insensitivity, telling me, "You're not really part of us."*

Just yesterday I asked Hashem to grant me a daughter-in-law who would like me even though my behavior toward my own mother-in-law is far from perfect. But now I feel certain that I'm not the one to blame for our strained relationship. After all, didn't I want to be a good daughter-in-law? Don't I make an effort to please her? She just doesn't want to accept me. It's as clear as day. As I once told my mother,

"She's always saying 'in our family,' as if everything that they do is 100 percent fine, whereas what we do is wrong or no good." She probably doesn't think we're good enough for her, and the whole shidduch was just a last resort.

Being a good daughter-in-law is dependent upon having a good mother-in-law. G-d willing, I will accept my daughter-in-law with open arms, like a daughter, and that's why she'll love me in return.

For a moment, Riki tried to imagine her future daughter-in-law, and she once again felt a stab of apprehension. Well, of course, you had to daven to Hashem for a good daughter-in-law. She should be kind, pleasant and above all, appreciate other people's efforts on her behalf and not be bent on interpreting everything as meaning that someone is out to get her.

If I get a daughter-in-law who disapproves of everything I do, or who behaves foolishly, well, that would definitely make things difficult, so of course you have to daven for a girl with good middos. But let's take someone like myself — not perfect, of course, but trying to work on herself. Shouldn't such a daughter-in-law be warmly welcomed?

Too bad I can't talk this over with anyone. Yehudis Weiss, my neighbor, for example. I'd love to hear her opinion on the subject. What does a successful relationship depend on — the mother-in-law or the daughter-in-law? Am I to blame? Would Yehudis be the good daughter-in-law she is even if her mother-in-law was someone like…Sima Abramson? I'd love to know.

49

THE YOUNGER MR. SCHILLER felt too drained to share the day's events with his wife. By the time he finally returned home in the early evening, he was so tired, all he wanted was some peace and quiet.

Seated comfortably in his armchair in the air-conditioned room, he sipped at the cold juice his wife had poured. He closed his eyes, hoping to relax, but the day's events persisted in flashing before his eyes. He couldn't believe all that had happened to him in one day.

Was it only this morning that the director at Nachalas Avos, looking pale and drawn, had informed him of the possibility that his father's caregiver had persuaded the elderly man to sign a document of some sort, a will, perhaps, or a deed of gift?

He recalled the shock he had felt, the dumbfounded disbelief. He had wanted to scream, scold, accuse, interrogate...but what he had done instead was ask the director for the use of her phone.

He called Esther, his sister in Jerusalem, briefly outlined what had happened and asked her to come immediately. He sensed that, more than anything else, he needed his family nearby. After all, the problem affected all of them.

As he hung up the receiver, the door to Mrs. Abramson's office swung open to admit a teenage boy who was panting and perspiring. "I had to come," he said. "I couldn't concentrate anyway."

Mrs. Abramson had introduced the boy as Ephraim Baum. It seemed obvious she felt relieved by his presence. At first, he couldn't understand what the boy had to with anything, but it soon became clear. The boy's resourcefulness was amazing.

"This is Naftali Schiller, Yaakov Schiller's son," Mrs. Abramson had said, addressing Ephraim. "His father told him today that he gave his credit card to Mr. Vidal on several occasions. The credit card bill indicates that considerable sums of money were billed to Mr. Schiller's account. We're wondering what would be the best thing to do now."

"Sitting here and thinking about it is not the solution," he had wanted to shout in anger, but the boy beat him to it.

"Well, first of all," Ephraim had announced, puzzled it hadn't occurred to the two adults in the room, "you've got to cancel the credit card."

Naftali remembered feeling surprised at the boy's common sense. Of course. His first step must be to notify the credit card company. It was so obvious. Why hadn't he thought of it himself? Sure, his father now had the card back, but so many purchases were by phone nowadays that it would present no problem to an experienced swindler to take advantage of the opportunity.

While he began looking for the phone number, the boy had continued talking. "We have to act fast," he had said. "The police won't be in a hurry to act until you bring them concrete evidence of a crime, and we don't have any proof yet, just our suspicions. By the time the police decide to interrogate the caretaker, he'll have disappeared with the money and the will. I suggest we all go down and surprise him at his house. Do you have his address, Mrs. Abramson?"

Mrs. Abramson, like Naftali himself, had seemed astounded by the audacity of what the boy was suggesting. Wordlessly, she flipped through her Rolodex and pointed to the desired address. The three set out together.

Now, sitting in his armchair at home, Naftali couldn't for the life of him understand how he had allowed a young boy to lead him on such a dangerous chase. They knew absolutely nothing about the caregiver's background. Now that they had discovered he was a swindler, there was no way they could guess if he was dangerous or even violent. Looking back, Naftali felt certain that were it not for the shock he had received at Mrs. Abramson's announcement, he would never have gone ahead with Ephraim's plan. Most likely, he would have gone to the police for help, or at the very least, taken people with him to confront the man, in case of trouble.

It turned out well that he had let the boy lead him like a child. As they say, G-d watches over fools.

As the threesome walked up the congested, factory-lined street leading to the industrial area of the city, they suddenly spotted Mr. Vidal coming toward them. He had just left a building, and in his hand he held a large suitcase, as though he was off on a long trip. His face registered fleeting surprise as he noticed them, but he controlled his emotions perfectly and greeted them with a smile.

"What's going on, Mrs. Abramson? Don't tell me you've come all the way here to find me. I'm so sorry I didn't let you know I wouldn't be coming today. I suddenly got an absolutely awful toothache, and I had no choice but to see a dentist. If Paulina had been home, I would have asked her to call and let you know I wouldn't be coming today, but she was at work."

"Can we have a few words with you?" asked the director, her face a tight mask. She pretended she hadn't heard a word he said.

"Uh...is it urgent?" he asked in feigned innocence. "I'm in a pretty big rush. My cousin's getting married tonight, and the wedding's way up north, in the Galilee. I've got to catch the bus."

"Yes, it is urgent. Please give us your attention for a moment."

"We've already canceled the credit card," came Ephraim's voice, surprising them all. Gavriel wheeled around to face him.

"I want you to understand that we know everything," Ephraim continued, aware that he was dropping one bombshell after another. "We've discovered the purchases you made with the credit card, your forgery of the doctor's signature and the signature you forced out of Yaakov Schiller."

"What? What signature?" Gavriel did not so much as blink, but his face had grown cold and hard, the smile now a distant memory.

"You asked him to sign a document that would help get him reparations, or something like that," Ephraim said. "The old man himself told me about it."

"The old man told you, did he? Ha, ha, ha!" It was an unpleasant laugh. "Do you mean to say you actually believe everything the old man says? He tells lots of stories. He often mixes up stories about events that happened fifty years ago with things that took place five minutes ago. Why would I ask him to sign such a form? I'm insulted."

"Mr. Vidal," Sima spoke in a tough voice, "if you knew that he was confusing past events with the present, why didn't you tell me? As an experienced caregiver, don't you know that any strange behavior ought to be reported, for the sake of the patient's health?"

"Why should I report such behavior? It never occurred to me that you didn't know about it."

"We trusted you. We sent you to the doctor with him," Sima said.

"That's right!" Ephraim interrupted. "Mr. Schiller was very drowsy lately. Why didn't you comment on that? Are you a caregiver, or aren't you?" Then, to the director, "I had the feeling he was lying all along. He never cared a thing about Mr. Schiller."

The veins in Mr. Vidal's neck bulged, and his eyes flashed fire. Naftali was afraid of what might develop, and he wanted desperately to tell the boy to back off. Outright threats and insults weren't going to get them anywhere.

"If you'll excuse me," Mr. Vidal roared in anger, "I have a bus to catch!" He tried to push Ephraim out of the way.

"Juan? What's going on there?" came a frightened voice from behind them. A stream of words in a foreign language followed. They turned around to see a woman standing on the opposite side of the street. She began walking quickly toward them, waving her hands and shouting, "What is this all about, Juan?"

Who was Juan? Who was the woman talking to? Naftali didn't understand what was going on, and it was clear the others were just as confused. Why was the woman so excited?

It all became clear when Gavriel opened his mouth to respond. "Paulina," he began, continuing with rapid-fire Spanish.

"Paulina, are you Gavriel's wife?" Sima asked, the first to come to her senses.

"Yes, I'm Juan's wife. That's his Spanish name." She turned to face her husband once more, pointing to the suitcase and asking him something.

Naftali was certain she was asking him why he was holding a suitcase. Unlike her husband's contrived expression of nonchalance, Paulina looked painfully confused. Naftali decided to enlighten her. "He says he's going to a wedding," he volunteered.

"A wedding? Whose wedding?" Almost immediately, Paulina realized she'd made a mistake. Her husband's enraged face and the words he spat out made that perfectly clear. Naftali, pretending he hadn't noticed a thing, responded, "In the Galilee. Didn't he tell you about it?"

Again, the two exchanged words, their tones angry and accusing. Finally, Paulina turned to Mrs. Abramson and asked, "Are you the director?"

Sima nodded.

"Juan, why here?" she asked her husband in Hebrew, her tone pleading. "Let's go inside and talk this over in a civilized manner."

"We can finish out here. I'm in a hurry." His tone was curt and angry. It was clear he was losing control. Naftali realized it was up to him to seize the moment.

Now, at home in his comfortable chair, Naftali was certain Hashem had granted him the strength and ability to say what had to be said.

"Yes, Mr. Vidal, or Juan, if you prefer — we'd like to finish off right here. You have two choices: you can return the money now, or the police will be brought into the picture."

"Police? Why police?" asked Paulina, her voice rising in hysteria. She stood at her husband's side like a supporting angel. A window in an adjacent building opened, then another and another. Someone asked Vidal something in Spanish.

"Please, come inside," Paulina begged. The director hesitated. She was afraid of walking into a trap. A glance at the distraught Paulina convinced her there was nothing to be afraid of. The woman was obviously not faking it. "Not here, outside," she was pleading. "Let's work everything out inside."

The disastrous mess inside the house caused Paulina to cry out in surprise. Clothes were strewn on the beds and chairs, and a dirty coffee mug and the remains of a sandwich graced the table, along with various papers. The room looked as though someone had been in a hurry to leave.

Paulina removed the clothes from the chairs and motioned

them to sit. Vidal began speaking to his wife in their native tongue, trying to explain something.

"He says," she turned to her guests, "that it was only a loan. He would never take money without permission, G-d forbid."

Naftali didn't know whether she really believed her husband or was just trying to get him off the hook. Truth be told, he didn't care. A loan? Very well, so long as Vidal returned the money they would leave in peace.

"I would never steal from a sick old man," Gavriel said in a softer voice. "He's a good man, Mr. Schiller, and he lent me money sometimes."

"That's imposs—" began Ephraim, but Naftali stepped firmly on his foot, signaling him to be quiet. After all, he was only a boy, and his recklessness could have ruined everything at that sensitive moment.

"If you don't approve, I won't do it anymore."

Before Naftali could stop him, Ephraim cut in, "Fine, but what about the money you already took?"

"How much did he take?" asked Paulina in faltering Hebrew. Naftali responded with the amounts he knew of. "He'll return everything," she said confidently.

Gavriel glowered furiously, but she stared back defiantly. It was not difficult to guess what his ominous look meant, but Paulina held her ground.

"Pay them now!" she told him in Hebrew. "I have the money I've been saving up for David's college. You know where it is."

Juan left the room, the bravado gone from his stance. He returned with a handful of crisp bills and counted them out one by one into Naftali's hand. The atmosphere was tense.

"Would you like something to eat?" Naftali's wife stood in the doorway, her face concerned. "You haven't eaten since the morning."

Naftali snapped out of his reverie, returning to reality with a thud. "No, thanks, I'm not hungry now. Perhaps a little later."

After Gavriel had given him the money, they had spoken about the signature. The caregiver was wounded to the core by the accusation. He vehemently denied the charges, and Paulina was firm in her support of her husband. The tension mounted steadily until Ephraim, once again, saved the situation.

"Okay," he said. "Fine. Why don't we ask Mr. Vidal to sign a statement right here and now, in our presence, saying that he never asked Mr. Schiller to sign anything and that he has no document in his possession that would transfer any of the elderly gentleman's property to his possession. If he signs such a statement in the presence of two witnesses, I believe it will be legally valid."

What a brilliant idea! And so simple, too. Why hadn't he or Mrs. Abramson thought of it?

They all agreed, and the caretaker gritted his teeth and signed the statement.

The three rose to leave. As they stood in the doorway, with Paulina politely saying good-bye, Gavriel turned to Naftali and said, "Do you really think your father would ever sign a document bequeathing me anything that's coming to you?" His tone was bitter. "If that is the case, you really don't know your father!"

His eyes glittered as he spoke, and for the first time that afternoon, it was clear his words were honest and sincere, straight from the heart. "Your father loves you! I'd say he loves you more than you love him. I don't know why. You sure don't deserve it. But that's the way it is. Your father's not the kind of person who would sign something like that, no matter how confused he was. He never said one unkind word about any of his children. He loves you too much, much too much if you ask me."

Juan wheeled around and slammed the door behind him. His words lingered in the hallway like a resounding slap in the face.

The day's events continued playing through Naftali's mind, and he began to mull over issues he had never really thought much about before.

They met in Mrs. Abramson's office — Mrs. Abramson, Naftali, and his sister Esther, who had made the trip from Jerusalem.

Somehow, Esther had managed to make it to the nursing home within two hours of receiving his message. Somehow, she was suddenly able to postpone all her many affairs at work and at home. Papa had become top priority.

At first, Esther had been insistent about taking legal action against the caretaker, but the director had then told them about the symptoms of dementia their father was displaying. She explained that he occasionally lapsed into brief periods of confusion and uncertainty. It was only now that Naftali understood Mr. Vidal's puzzling comment about the lack of credibility of his father's statements.

Sima explained that this condition could conceivably present a problem if they filed a lawsuit. A skilled lawyer would try to prove that Mr. Schiller had willingly loaned Mr. Vidal money but that his failing memory made him forget having done so. He would cast doubt on the old man's testimony regarding Mr. Vidal's efforts to make him sign a document.

The strange note bearing the forged signature of Dr. Geller was indeed evidence against Mr. Vidal, but it would not incriminate him in a court of law. Who could say for certain that it was Mr. Vidal who had forged the signature, and not someone else?

Esther saw the sense in Mrs. Abramson's words, and she and her brother decided to be grateful for what they had managed to recover. They offered heartfelt thanks to the One Above Who had guided the events to their benefit, particularly Paulina's appearance at just the right moment.

They had fleetingly considered blaming the management of the nursing home for having allowed such a thing to happen, but they both knew they had no grounds for complaint. After all, the one who had discovered what was happening was none other than the young man hired by the devoted director to relieve their father's loneliness.

"His bouts of confusion," she told them, "might be an expression of deep loneliness. Of course, they might also be the symptom of a medical problem that needs to be checked, or even a combination of both."

Naftali and Esther realized that if anyone was to blame, they were no less guilty than the director. What was it the swindler had said? *Your father loves you — but you don't deserve it.* They had been too absorbed in their own private affairs. They hadn't shown enough interest in their father's daily life, preferring to leave his care in the hands of others.

This was the result. Even today, Naftali recalled with a pang of shame, he had gone to the nursing home that day only because the director had asked him to come. Fortunately, he had noticed the credit card statement and questioned the charges. Otherwise, who knew how much damage might have been done?

He didn't feel up to telling his wife about all these disturbing thoughts yet. They were far too painful. He could only mull them over in his own mind. She, for her part, wished he would come out of the shell he had withdrawn into. Perhaps then he would finally tell her what was going on.

Early that morning, the director told him that following Ephraim's discovery, they reduced the dosage of one of his father's medications, and there seemed to be a marked improvement in his condition. Indeed, throughout the day, Naftali had seen no sign of the confusion the director had described. How embarrassing that a young man from outside the family was the one to call their attention to their father's problem. What had his sister Naomi asked of him before going abroad? Just that he drop in for a brief visit twice a week to see that everything was okay. Was that too much to ask of a son? He hadn't done even that. There was always some pressing reason he couldn't make it, something more important than a visit to his father.

Now he knew the truth. He hadn't put off the visits because he was too busy. After talking it over with his sister Esther, he realized it was something else entirely that made him — and her — avoid visiting their father. It was Papa himself. He had changed over the past few years. He wasn't the same father they remembered from their childhood. He had been growing steadily more withdrawn, until a vast chasm gaped between him and his children.

Once, perhaps as recently as two years ago, Papa had been a smiling, friendly person, a pleasant conversationalist. For some inexplicable reason, he had grown increasingly taciturn, waiting for his children to carry the conversation. Had the change in him come about as a result of their mother's passing, Naftali wondered? He couldn't say for sure. He couldn't put a finger on the exact time the change had come about, for it had been gradual, and therefore unnoticed at first.

It reached the point where he had nothing to say to his father. Visits became tedious, even depressing. Esther said she had felt that way too. Only Naomi had maintained close contact. He'd thought that was because of the special relationship the two had always enjoyed, but now he thought it might have something to do with the fact that Naomi was more selfless and giving than the others, including himself. Were all eldest children like that? Or was that just her nature?

Esther had returned home to her family, and Naftali had decided to stay on at the nursing home and spend some more time with his father.

After lunch, Papa had fallen into a deep sleep, and Naftali

had dozed off in a chair near the bed. At four o'clock, a nurse tapped on the door and entered to give his father his medication. Papa had awakened groggily and had seemed greatly surprised to discover that Naftali was still in his room. Naftali wasn't certain whether his father was pleased or not.

"You're still here?" he asked. He then swallowed his pills in silence, asked for his glasses, and sat quietly. The nurse left the room, and Naftali was left wondering what to say. He wasn't sure whether it was wise to tell his father the full story about the swindling caregiver. What was the point? As he was deliberating, he heard another knock on the door, and a moment later Ephraim appeared in the doorway.

"Can I come in?" he asked hesitantly. Naftali nodded, and the young man entered the room, striding eagerly toward the old man. He warmly clasped his hand, saying, "I came early today." To Naftali, he said, "It didn't pay to go back to the dorm. I knew I'd be back in the afternoon to learn with him, so I stayed in the neighborhood.

"How are you, Mr. Schiller?" he asked, turning his attention back to the elderly man. "Are you up to learning with me today?"

Naftali noticed with amazement bordering on incredulity that his father had come out of his shell to nod enthusiastically and smile. A light seemed to go on in his usually lifeless eyes.

Naftali hurried to pour his father a cup of water, help him sit up and freshen his face. Ephraim opened the *sefer* lying on the table to the right page. He then sat down opposite the elderly man and began reading the mishna in a strong, clear voice.

From his seat across the room, Naftali paid close attention to the boy's explanations. There was a certain beauty to the way he dealt with the subject matter, building up theories one step at a time until they culminated in a logical conclusion. He also noticed that the young man maintained eye contact with his father the entire time, taking in his every move. This was unusual for a young person. Most adolescents, Naftali knew, were very self-absorbed. He was especially surprised that this boy, whom he had considered somewhat rash and reckless (judging by his behavior outside Mr. Vidal's house), was in fact proving to be exceedingly patient.

He watched as the boy repeated his explanations over and over again, somehow managing to convey the impression that the numerous repetitions were an ordinary part of his own learning technique rather than specially designed for his partner's slow pace.

As the minutes ticked by, Naftali watched as his father became increasingly alert and active. He was surprised to discover that his father's ability to learn was as fresh as ever. The elderly Mr. Schiller paid close attention to what Ephraim was saying, asked pertinent questions and suggested explanations of his own. Throughout the session, he looked at Ephraim with an expression of absolute trust.

Naftali felt a stab of envy at the rapport between the two. Once, long ago, he had studied that way with his father. He remembered seeing that same sparkle in his father's eyes and feeling the warmth flow between them. He thought those things had died out, that he had lost them forever, but the young man, apparently, had managed to rekindle the flame.

What was it about the boy that brought out such a positive reaction from his father? Naftali couldn't put his finger on it. Maybe it was his remarkable patience, or perhaps his respectful manner.

"What yeshiva are you in?" Naftali asked, suddenly curious.

Ephraim raised his eyes, clearly disturbed at the interruption. "Uh, it's not that far from here."

"What do you mean? What yeshiva is there around here?" He wondered which notable yeshiva was fortunate enough to have this *bachur* as its student — a serious, scholarly boy who was infused with a special something rarely found.

Ephraim named the institution that combined technical studies with a half-day learning program. He kept his face buried in his Gemara, which made his voice sound muffled and distant.

"You mean you're not in a yeshiva?" Naftali found it impossible to conceal his surprise. "You? I would never have believed it. You sound like a real *lamdan*!"

Naftali now understood what it was that had piqued his interest. The boy was indeed a *lamdan*, but he wasn't an ordinary *yeshiva bachur*. What a shame. What a waste.

Naftali wasn't what you would call a *ben Torah* in the accepted sense of the word. He was a businessman. But he valued Torah and those who studied it, and he knew a fine scholar when he saw one. This boy had the gentle graces of a real Torah scholar.

"What a shame," he murmured, voicing his thoughts. He sighed.

Ephraim stared at him for a moment, saying nothing. The elderly Mr. Schiller turned to Naftali and said, "He'll be a *rosh yeshiva* yet. He's a wonderful teacher."

Now, in the evening, Naftali contemplated the day's events. He thought about the interesting young man, about the way he learned with his father, about the new Papa he had seen — and the idea just leapt into his head. Yes! It was clear the boy had ignited the long-dormant love for Torah study in his father's heart, bringing him to life once again. He, too, could learn with Papa. No longer would they sit, side by side, together yet far apart. Learning together — that was the solution! He would study Torah with his father, and that would bring joy and life to their time together. The bond they once shared would be renewed.

TEHILLA STOOD IN THE KITCHEN doorway chattering away. Riki listened attentively as she washed the dishes.

"So when I brought the new Magic Markers to school, Esti said in front of everyone, 'Boy, is she spoiled! She can't even walk to school on her own two feet. Her father has to drive the little princess every day in his car.' That's what she said. Then everyone laughed at me.

"So what if my father drives me to school?" she asked plaintively. "Is that a crime?" Tehilla paused, waiting for her adored sister-in-law's response, which was not long in coming.

"No, it's not a crime," Riki said, turning to look at Tehilla. "If your father wants to drive you, why shouldn't he?"

"That's what I say! But it makes Esti real mad. She gets mad at lots of things I do. Today Devori called me a snob. She forgot all about the ice cream I gave her last Shabbos, and I know why. It's all because of Esti. Whatever Esti says, Devori does."

"Do you often give Devori nosh?"

"Uh-huh."

"Why?"

"Because I want her to be my friend. Sometimes I promise her candy — Shlomit too — but they always forget I gave them stuff and end up calling me names."

"That can be pretty annoying," Riki empathized as she set down the final dish. "Maybe you shouldn't promise them anything at all."

"I can't," Tehilla wailed. "They won't ever play with me!"

"Says who?" Riki dried her hands and gave Tehilla her full attention. "How do you know they won't play with you unless you promise them something? Did you ever try it?"

"No. I'm afraid. I know they won't play with me if I don't give them things."

"Why not?"

"I don't know." Tehilla shrugged. "That's just how it is."

"But why? Aren't you one of the good kids?"

"Yeah."

"And aren't you smart?"

"I guess so, but…"

"But what?" Riki persisted.

"They say I'm spoiled."

"Are you?"

"*I* don't think so."

"So why do they say you are?"

Tehilla thought a full two seconds before answering. "They say I cry over every little thing."

"Do you?"

"Lots of times, like when I bring something new to show everyone, they tease me, so sure I cry. Who wouldn't?"

"Hmmm." Riki felt she was starting to get the picture. "Do you like to show everyone what you get?"

Tehilla nodded. "Uh-huh. But so what?"

"Maybe they think you're showing off," Riki suggested.

Tehilla didn't say anything.

"Let me tell you what happened when I was your age," Riki said.

Tehilla was all ears.

"There was one girl in my class who came to school every day wearing something new. Everything matched, right down to her ponytail holders. Her father also drove her to school, just like you. And do you know what, Tehilla? I was jealous of her, really jealous. *My* father didn't have a car, and *my* clothes were plain and ordinary. I knew I wasn't supposed to be jealous, but I was. I was sure she was the luckiest girl in the world. Once, when everyone was crowding around her desk to see her fancy new pencil case, I felt so jealous that I made fun of her right in front of everyone. I don't know what I said, but I remember it made everyone laugh."

"What did she do?" Tehilla asked.

"She put her head on her desk and cried."

"I would too."

"What I couldn't understand," Riki said, "was why a girl who was so lucky and had everything she wanted would cry just because of something I said."

Right then, the doorbell rang. Riki asked Tehilla to wait a minute while she went to see who it was.

"That's not fair," Tehilla grumbled to Riki's receding back. "Why did the doorbell have to ring right now?"

In the doorway stood Yehudis Weiss, Riki's neighbor, holding her baby. "Hi! I came to say hello. Did I catch you at a busy moment?"

"It's okay." Riki wasn't going to deny her favorite neighbor a full welcome. "Tehilla and I were just discussing some very important issues." She smiled meaningfully in Tehilla's direction.

"Oh! I didn't know she was here," Yehudis said in surprise. "I see the two of you are good friends."

"Yes, we are," Riki said. Then, in an undertone, she added, "She likes to talk to me."

"Am I disturbing?"

"No, we can finish our conversation later. She's here for a few days, and she hardly goes down to play. Mostly she helps me take care of Yossi, and whenever she gets a chance she tells me what's going on in her life."

"Sounds like she needs a listening ear."

"Could be," Riki said, heading for the dining room with her friend. "My mother-in-law is a very busy woman. I'm not sure how much time they get to spend together."

"Tehilla's the youngest, isn't she?" Yehudis asked.

Riki nodded. "Let me tell her I have a guest and that we'll finish talking later. I'll let her color for a while. On second thought, she can fold the laundry. She likes that."

When Riki returned to the dining room, Yehudis said, "It's interesting what you said about Tehilla. We were just talking about it last Shabbos at my mother-in-law's house. She does counseling, and she recently organized a discussion group for mothers on the subject of intergenerational communication.

"She says that sometimes even mothers of older children feel the need to attend a parenting class. Raising a child in a family where most of the siblings are grown or even married is entirely different from doing it in a family of small children. She says that a child growing up in a home where everyone else is grown-up can feel neglected despite the fact that life is, in many ways, very easy for him. This happens because no one really talks to him. The adults may hear him out because they don't have a choice, but they don't really listen or value his opinion."

"That's sounds exactly what it's like for my sister-in-law." Riki felt Yehudis's description hit home. "People pretty much give in to her to keep her happy. I've heard that when children get what they want by throwing a temper tantrum, they find it hard to get along outside the home, where other people are less likely to give in to them. What do you think?"

"Absolutely. A child like that is going to lack basic social skills."

Riki refrained from telling Yehudis the content of her conversation with Tehilla, and only said, "I'm glad you stopped by. I think what you just told me will come in handy." She smiled. "I didn't know your mother-in-law is a therapist."

"She's not exactly a therapist," Yehudis corrected her. "She's a social worker, but people ask her advice about all kinds of things. She's a very smart woman."

That gave Riki an idea. "Let me ask you a question," she said. "Do you think your mother-in-law would be willing to give me some of her time? There's something I'd like to discuss with her."

"You would?"

"Yes." Riki got past her embarrassment by saying, "Don't worry, it's not about *shalom bayis*." She laughed. "I've got a few questions she just might be able to answer."

"Why not?" Yehudis said. "You don't have to tell me what it's about. I was surprised, but come to think of it, I ask her for her advice too. I can't promise she'll have the time, but I'll ask. She's supposed to come over to me sometime this week. I'll tell her I have a great neighbor who's heard all about her. I'm sure she'll be happy to meet you."

They continued chatting over a cup of coffee until Yehudis left. Soon after, Yossi woke up, and Riki fed him and played with him for a while. Then Daniel came home, and they all ate supper together, enjoying the warm family time.

After supper, Riki was once again busy with Yossi, bathing him and putting him to bed. Tehilla went to sleep too, and Daniel left to learn. Only then did Riki remember, with a pang of conscience, about her unfinished conversation with Tehilla. What a shame! Perhaps tomorrow she would find a way to bring up the subject again and try to help Tehilla see things from a different perspective.

She felt sorry for Tehilla. It must be terrible to be rejected by your friends and teased all the time. That kind of thing can leave a scar that lasts a lifetime.

It dawned on her that she too was carrying some sort of childhood scar. She wasn't sure what it was or where it came from, but she sometimes felt insecure — not the way Tehilla did, but in a different way. Why, for example, did she care so much what her mother-in-law thought of her? Why did she feel so hurt by everything she said? Even if she didn't openly express her pain, she cried inside and felt depressed for days.

The girl she had told Tehilla about, the one whose father always drove her to school, was named Naama. Riki remembered how envious she had been of even her name. The girl was one of those sweet, pretty girls whose fancy clothes made her look like a little doll. Riki was sure her classmate led the charmed life of a princess, free from the problems and hardships ordinary mortals faced. Why not? Her father was rich, she lived in a big house, and, most of all, everyone wanted to be her friend.

How strange to look back on it! It was even stranger to see that Tehilla, externally so much like the girl Riki had envied, really felt scared and vulnerable inside. She wondered if Naama had felt that way. Then there was Esti, who Tehilla described as powerful and full of self-confidence. The way she acted reminded Riki of how she herself had treated Naama. Could it be that her friends had thought she was strong and filled with self-confidence?

Most likely, Esti saw Tehilla as the strong one. Tehilla Abramson had everything a girl could seemingly want — the latest Magic Markers, gorgeous clothes and a father who drove her to school in his car every day.

What a strange world, mused Riki. *Who is really weak and who is really strong?*

Apparently, strength and weakness were inner qualities that didn't depend on external conditions. Strength was something a person either had or didn't have.

Riki knew one thing for sure. She didn't have it, and she never had. The question was why?

She had been asking herself that question for a long time. It was like an unsolved riddle waiting for her to solve it. Every so often, it would surface with a vengeance. Like when she had organized the end-of-year party. She realized she was pushing the girls too much, but she didn't know why. The question had tormented her. Why was success so important to her? She had always tried hard — too hard, she thought in retrospect — to succeed. She used to study frantically to get good grades, as if she had to prove herself to someone, to receive confirmation that she was okay. Was it because good grades made her father and mother so happy? She had always felt she was giving her parents real *nachas* when she got good grades.

Riki recalled the time she had come home from school with first prize in a school Torah competition. Her mother had been standing on the sidewalk talking to Mrs. Levenstein, their upstairs neighbor and her mother's close friend. She remembered proudly telling her mother about the prize and then turing to go in the house. As she walked away, she overheard her mother say to Mrs. Levenstein, "Mark my words, that girl will go far, *be'ezras Hashem*. You see? Even a home like ours can produce outstanding children. Sometimes, the brightest stars are born to people like us."

Riki hadn't understood what her mother meant by "a home like ours" or "people like us." Now, as an adult, she realized her mother must have been referring to the single-parent home she herself had grown up in. At the time, the only message Riki got was that their home was somehow different from everyone else's. For some reason she didn't know about, their home was not as good as everyone else's, but she, Riki, could make her mother feel happy and proud by succeeding in school. Her success helped her mother prove they were just as good as anyone else.

Could that be it? Riki wondered. Could that be the reason she was always trying so hard to prove herself? Could that be why, no matter how much success came her way, she still felt so insecure?

It just might be, she realized. Maybe that was why she had felt so insecure around Naama or anyone else who came from a wealthy or prominent family. That must be why she had pushed herself and others to put on the most spectacular performance the school had ever seen. Now she realized the significance of the theme song she had written: "I see your face before me, Mother, your eyes filled with expectation.…" Though she hadn't known it at the time, those words had been with her all her life. When she wrote the song, they had welled up from deep within her and spilled out onto the paper.

That was why she had known, even before her engagement, that she would have to compromise when it came to finding a *shidduch*. And that was why she cared so deeply about her mother-in-law's opinion, why it was so important for her to prove that she was okay and that her family was just as good as anyone else's.

She remembered how her father would tell her mother, when he thought she wasn't listening, that now everyone would see that even the daughter of a simple workingman like him could turn out to be a fine girl, that she had no less *yiras Shamayim* than the daughter of the greatest Torah scholar in the city. How she desperately wanted her mother-in-law to know that it was true!

But her mother-in-law didn't think so at all. She was always saying in that haughty tone of voice, "In our family, we do this," and, "By us, we do that." It was as clear as day that she didn't approve of Riki as her daughter-in-law. Dassi, on the other hand, was wonderful. Dassi's father, Riki noted bitterly, was an esteemed *rosh yeshiva*.

How she longed for her mother-in-law's approval. But what could she do if it wasn't forthcoming?

THE GROUP OF WOMEN GATHERED in one of the classrooms of the local elementary school. They pulled the chairs into a semicircle, leaving the place of honor for Malka Weiss, leader of the group.

One of those present had started the group, and news of its formation had swiftly passed through the neighborhood from one woman to another. A friend had told a friend, who told a neighbor, who told a cousin and so on, until they had a reasonable amount of participants to begin.

They all had one thing in common: They were experienced mothers juggling a number of roles — as mothers of small children, daughters of elderly parents and caregivers of grandparents. Standing at the crossroads of life, they often felt it was a struggle to cope with it all.

At the first meeting, the women had agreed that everything discussed would be confidential. By now, the fifth meeting, a sense of mutual trust and respect had developed between the participants, and they shared their thoughts and feelings freely with one another.

Pessie, who had recently married off her eldest daughter,

spoke about the difficulty of separation. Her daughter had been her right hand for years, but even more important, she'd been a friend. Her absence was keenly felt. Sometimes, Pessie said, she felt like dropping in on her to visit or calling her daughter for a long talk or asking her to stay just a while longer when she came over. She knew she ought to be glad that her daughter was happily married, but still…

The other mothers empathized. They told her not to worry about feeling that way and said the feeling would mellow with time.

Rachel told them that before the wedding, her daughter used to consult with her on every important issue in her life. Now, *baruch Hashem*, her daughter held her husband in great esteem. Now he was the one who had the final say on everything that mattered. She knew this was the way things should be, but she sometimes wondered whether it might be okay every once in a while to interfere and offer her opinion. She so badly wanted everything to go well for the young couple. If her experience could help them, why deprive them of it?

Malka had not planned on dealing with that particular subject at this meeting, but she preferred to go with the flow rather than stick to a preset agenda. She spoke about the difficulty of separation, and the sincere desire of mothers to share their advice with their married children, a desire stemming from love and an unselfish desire to give.

"However," she warned, "it is important to remember that at this point, the strongest expression of love for our children is our ability to give them room to become independent. It is written, 'A man shall leave his father and mother and become one with his wife,' and the message is directed at us, as parents, as well. Our mission as mothers of married children is to stand back and allow the couple to cement their relationship, even if it sometimes seems our own relationship with our child will suffer as a result.

"Speaking from experience," Malka said with a smile, "I

know it's a lot easier said than done. It's not always easy to watch your children run their home differently than you might like or raise their children in a way you disapprove of. But theirs is a different home, and we must keep that in mind. It's a new home, and it's up to us to give those building it our respect, our trust and a sense of security. That's the strongest form of parental support we can offer.

"Most of all, don't worry." Several women chuckled knowingly. "Our married children have no intention of abandoning us. They're just trying to build their own nests the way they have always dreamed of. They want to test their own wings, even at the risk of occasional failure. If we offer our support in the right areas and express our faith in their ability, they'll be willing to listen to us when it really counts.

"And remember — we occupy a special place in their hearts. They will *always* see us, their parents, as an integral part of their family's development."

"I'd like to add," a woman named Batya spoke up, "that the experience teaches us to appreciate our own parents' restraint. We don't have to be afraid of separation. If we are aware it exists and accept it, our children eventually begin turning to us for advice again.

"There are so many things about my own parents that I'm only now beginning to understand," she went on. "Like the things I asked for as a child that my parents refused. Now that I'm a parent, I have a better understanding of the decisions parents face, as well as their all-too-human limitations."

Heads nodded around the circle of intent listeners.

"How many of us have promised ourselves that we would *never* get angry with our children the way our mothers sometimes did? How many of us said there would *never* be any tension in our homes, that we'd never raise our voices? Then, suddenly, you're a parent yourself, and you find yourself falling short of your expectations. Only then does it occur to you that maybe your own mother also tried hard not to yell or get angry, but that she wasn't always successful. Maybe she too was upset with herself for failing in certain areas."

"That's very true," a woman named Rivka seconded. "Hashem sees to it that we discover these things sooner or later and that we gain understanding in hindsight. I think there are some things that only time can work its magic on. That's the way life is."

"It's the same between mothers-in-law and daughters-in-law," Yael spoke up. "There are so many things about my mother-in-law I've only recently begun to understand and appreciate. For instance, whenever I had a new baby, she always took care of the other children. I pretty much took it for granted. After all, who should watch them if not her? Now that I look back on it, I'm not sure I always thanked her the way I should have. Sometimes I even got mad at her for spoiling them too much by giving them candy whenever they asked.

"Today, when I take in my daughter-in-law's children when there's a new addition to the family, I feel the full brunt of the responsibility, and I ask myself, How did she do this so many times without saying a word about how hard it is? Why didn't I tell her how much I appreciated it?"

"I know what you mean," Batya agreed. "I think we're at a stage where we can see things in a broader perspective. When I was young, I didn't help that much when I went to my mother-in-law's house for Shabbos or *Yom Tov*. Besides being busy taking care of the children, I felt strange about interfering in another woman's housekeeping.

"My mother-in-law took it all in stride, as if my behavior was perfectly normal. Now that I host my own daughters and daughters-in-law, I see how much I appreciate their help. Looking back, I think it would have been in place for me to help out more. My mother-in-law had girls in the house who took care of everything, and at the time, that seemed perfectly okay to me."

"That's why I say that time works its own magic," repeated

"In short, let's just say we're a very average family. From my in-laws' point of view, my family might be considered a bitter pill to swallow." Riki chuckled nervously as she realized she was repeating the same cliché over and over.

"Every since that day, that has always been my feeling. I've been married to her son for two years now, I'm the mother of her grandchild, but she still has not been able to make peace with the fact that I'm her daughter-in-law."

"What makes you say that? How do you see it?"

"Oh, I see it all the time. When I try really hard to act nice, she doesn't seem to notice. I never hear her express any appreciation or admiration."

"In what way do you 'try hard to act nice'?"

Mrs. Weiss's question was seemingly straightforward, but to her surprise, Riki found she had trouble finding an answer.

"How do I try? Oh, I used to try and phone her every *erev Shabbos*. I...uh, well, what do you mean? I try to respect her as much as I can. For example, she wanted to send her youngest daughter away for a few days, and I offered to have her stay with me. If she invites us for Shabbos, I always go, even though I don't always feel like going. She, on the other hand, doesn't bother showing up at events that are important to me. I directed a big performance earlier this year, and she wasn't interested in attending. The things that matter to me mean nothing to her."

"What about you, Riki?" Malka asked quietly. "Do you take an interest in the things that are important to her?"

Once again, Riki floundered for an answer. "Things that are important to my mother-in-law?"

"Yes."

"Like what?"

"Well, that's for you to say."

"What is important to her?" Riki wondered aloud. "I guess home decorating, interior design, things like that. I know she cares a lot about how my house looks. My taste is different from hers, though. I like plainer things. That's a problem, too. She always buys me things that suit her taste, as if she's trying to force me into a lifestyle I don't like. It's the same with clothes for Yossi. She buys things *she* likes."

"Do you ever try to adapt yourself somewhat to her taste?"

"I don't see why I should."

"You're right. You don't have to give up your sense of style. But you might try, sometimes, to compromise somewhat in order to placate your mother-in-law in areas you know are very important to her."

"The truth is, I think I might be too sensitive and self-centered to start paying attention to things that are important to my mother-in-law," Riki admitted. "That's why I wanted to talk to you so much. I think I get too easily hurt and insulted. When she bought Yossi a crib, I couldn't bring myself to thank her, because I was mortified by the way she kept saying, 'Everyone in our family buys at So-and-so's' — as if I had no parents, as if no one in my family ever bought a crib! Why doesn't she just trust me and ask me what I like?"

Malka realized Riki's words reminded her of part of a conversation she had once had with Sima Abramson. *Her reactions are totally unpredictable. I never know what it is I might have said to make her withdraw. One day I think we've got a really good relationship, and the next day, thunderous silence.*

It was during that conversation that it had occurred to her that Mrs. Abramson's daughter-in-law might have an inferiority complex. She'd been convinced the young woman's reaction was the result of her mother-in-law's unintentionally touching on a sore spot. How right she had been!

Riki's description of her family made it clear she was burdened by a number of complex emotions. Chances were, Malka thought, this was Riki's sore spot.

Malka had been fortunate enough to experience an abundance of *siyatta diShemaya* since she'd begun working in her chosen field, advising people in all sorts of difficult situations. Every time something like this happened, she felt a surge of elation and gratitude for the spark of understanding and intuition Hashem had granted her so she might help others work things out.

"And when I reached that conclusion," Riki continued, "I asked myself, Who is at fault here, me or my mother-in-law? If I had a different mother-in-law, one who was kinder, warmer, more accepting, would I be a better daughter-in-law? Like I said, I have all the will in the world. So what exactly is going wrong?"

Malka thought for a moment before responding. She admired the brave young woman. Not many people would stop to ask themselves such questions and actively seek out answers. That was exactly what she'd meant last night when she had thought about the potentially beautiful years lost to needless dissension between mothers-in-law and their daughters-in-law. She believed it was possible to overcome such difficulties. Perhaps this young woman would serve as evidence that this was true, if Hashem would only put the right words in her mouth. Malka viewed this conversation as a challenge, and she weighed her every word carefully before she began.

"Of course," she said slowly, "in an ideal world, a mother-in-law and daughter-in-law would be similar in many ways and take an instant liking to one another. As we both know, though, that isn't always the case. We have the power to change things, though, and it makes no difference really who is at fault. Usually both sides play a part in building the relationship. I call such a relationship a 'dance.' As soon as one side changes the steps, the whole dance changes.

"Let us take, for example, the case you described. You say your mother-in-law acts aloof and is unwilling to accept you as you are. You may or may not be right. It doesn't really matter. What's important now is that you feel that way. The feeling you harbor that she perceives your family to be less worthy than her own makes the issue particularly sensitive. Your family's perceived inferiority is painful to you. Whenever she does or says anything that can be viewed as an expression of her belief that your family is inferior, it's as if she's stepping on your toes and you scream in protest.

"We all have corns on our toes, Riki, even those of us older and stronger than you. But not everyone steps on them, and most people are not even aware of their existence."

Riki wrinkled her brow in concentration, trying to understand.

"When you went shopping with your mother-in-law and she said what she did, she unwittingly stepped on your toes. Ever since then, you've been more sensitive. Since that episode, you've been preoccupied with the issue of your family's standing. Whenever your mother-in-law later said or did anything that could have been interpreted as looking down on them, you were on the offensive, which served only to further aggravate the situation."

"Okay, but is it my fault that my corns hurt?" Riki asked defensively. "I think my mother-in-law ought to be extra careful not to offend me, and then everything would be all right."

"True. If your mother-in-law would avoid this sensitive topic, you would certainly get along better. Because, like I said, if either side in a relationship changes the steps to the dance the entire relationship changes. But the fact that you are sitting here and not her means that we should be thinking of ways for *you* to mend matters."

"So you agree that I'm no more at fault than she is?" Riki pressed.

"I agree with you that if your mother-in-law would originally have welcomed you with open arms, expressing no reservations and giving you no reason to feel she felt superior, you would have been a better daughter-in-law. After all, you have a pleasant nature and the will to work on a positive relationship.

"On the other hand, we can't ignore the fact that if you had no sensitivities about your family's standing she could have been a far better mother-in-law. Despite her original reservations, she would have gotten to know you and appreciate your qualities with time and slowly come to love you."

"So you're saying I didn't really allow her to see me at my best," Riki said quietly.

Riki was silent for a few moments, her face thoughtful as she mulled over what she had heard. "So how can I protect myself from feeling hurt without our relationship suffering?" she finally asked.

"I suggest that you leave that alone for now," replied Malka. "Perhaps the hurt will eventually heal on its own. Right now, the best way to neutralize its sensitivity is to change the way you react. The next time your mother-in-law buys you something you don't really like, you will think, *She doesn't trust me*. But you'll identify the source of your pain and tell yourself, *That's my corn screaming out in pain. I'm going to ignore it for the moment. The gift isn't all that bad. My mother-in-law wants my house to look nice. I'll just be pleased and thank her warmly, even if I'd never have chosen this myself.*

"The following day, you'll call her and tell her how touched you are by her thoughtfulness. You can even add that it's just the kind of thing you were looking for.

"At first, your mother-in-law will be confused. This is not the dance she's used to. She now sees she has a wonderful daughter-in-law who wants to make her feel good. Buds of fondness begin to blossom. Who cares about your family background? What difference does it make what your father does or who your grandfather was? There's a new person here she wants to get to know.

"On a different occasion, she might say something that will feel like she's stomping on your toes. Again, you'll identify the reason for the pain and say, *I'll ignore it.* You won't break down. You won't get mad. You won't be thunderously silent. You'll react rationally, and eventually you'll see that she really meant nothing at all. And even if she did mean to be hurtful, she'll change her mind.

"Slowly, a more positive relationship will develop. Your reactions will put your mother-in-law at ease. You'll begin to trust one another. Pleasant experiences will begin taking the place of unpleasant ones. Your sensitivity will begin to fade.

"Then," Malka smiled encouragingly, "you'll find you have the strength to ignore insults and deal with them as they should be dealt with. Most important of all, you'll find you have it in you to forgive."

53

ON HIS WAY FROM THE DINING ROOM to his room in the dorm, Ephraim stopped at the pay phone. At this hour he could still catch Daniel before he left for kollel.

Last night, sitting in the library preparing the *mishnayos* to study with Mr. Schiller, he'd reached the conclusion that the material was too complicated for a novice like him to manage on his own. He realized he was missing some basic concepts integral to understanding a *sugya* like the one he was tackling. He felt he needed the guidance of an experienced scholar. Daniel was the only person Ephraim could think of who might be able to help him. The few study sessions they had shared had left him feeling good.

He dialed the number, and it was Daniel who answered the phone. Daniel listened carefully to his brother-in-law's request.

"Do you see what I mean?" Ephraim asked. "I'm not sure I have a solid understanding of the material. I've noticed that sometimes, when I study a dispute between the *Tannaim*, I understand the issue using my common sense, but who says that's right? There are also halachos relevant to the issue that I know I haven't really mastered. I don't know what to do. This job is turning out to be more complicated than I originally thought. Do you think it would help if I continued studying with you?"

Daniel thought it would definitely be a good idea. At first, they would set up a session or two that would encompass a number of *mishnayos*. Then they could just take it from there. The only question was where. He was in Jerusalem and Ephraim was in the Tel Aviv area.

"It sounds fine. There's only the matter of where and when can we get together."

"I could drop by your place one evening this week," Ephraim offered.

For some reason, Daniel wasn't taken with the idea. He didn't want it to be a casual arrangement; he wanted a commitment.

"Listen," he said as an idea suddenly came to mind. "I've got to be in Bnei Brak this week for a friend's wedding. I'll come early, and we can meet someplace."

"Where?"

"How about in a yeshiva somewhere. Let's say at Ponovezh. Its *beis medrash* is the best place I can think of for *chavrusa* study. We'll see what we accomplish in one session, and then we'll decide where to go from there."

Ephraim agreed. It didn't really make much difference to him where they studied as long as Daniel would help him with the project he had taken upon himself and had come to enjoy so much.

In Jerusalem, Daniel could barely contain his excitement. The conversation he'd just had with his brother-in-law filled him with a sense of satisfaction and joy. Ephraim was taking a serious interest in the material he was studying. It seemed as though he was being drawn into the world of Gemara just as

Daniel had hoped. Was it too early to rejoice? Maybe, but he could certainly hope for the best.

Riki was spreading a rug on the floor. "Is Brachi coming today?" he asked. He knew Riki usually put down the rug in anticipation of the little girl's visits.

"Yes," said Riki. "And so is your mother. She's coming to pick up Tehilla and take her home."

"Oh, I completely forgot about that."

"You may have forgotten," Riki said with a smile, "but I didn't. I have no idea how I'm going to manage this morning. I've got loads to do, and I don't know if your mother will stay for lunch or not."

"Why don't you ask her?" Daniel suggested. "Or do you want me to?"

"No, forget it," Riki replied. "I don't feel comfortable asking. I don't want her to think it's such a big deal for me to have her for a meal. I'll prepare an entrée just in case, and maybe I'll make a fruit salad, too. I hope Tehilla will agree to watch the children so that I'll be able to cook in peace."

Daniel was concerned. He glanced quickly around him, sorry he had forgotten about his mother's visit. He could have gotten up earlier and washed the dishes at least. The table was littered with bits of paper his sister had been cutting yesterday. He felt as though he was abandoning his wife to deal with everything on her own.

"You could have canceled Brachi's visit for today," he said.

"No, I couldn't," replied Riki, sighing. "Her mother asked me more than a week ago to have her this morning. Besides, she's been making a lot of progress lately. Did I tell you that last week she grabbed hold of a chair and stood up all by herself, just like Yossi?"

She had told him. Of course she had. Daniel remembered. Riki had been as excited as if Brachi were her own child.

"Her mother says it's all because of my input. She can't stop thanking me. That's why I wouldn't feel right about skipping a visit. What can I do?"

Daniel shrugged. How could he argue with such noble sentiment? He wished her good luck and promised to return at noon to greet his mother.

Riki was left alone to prepare for the rest of the day. She had a clear plan of what she would do and when, which helped restore her calm somewhat.

Tehilla would watch Yossi and Brachi with the help of Esther, the neighbors' daughter. Riki was happy she'd thought of introducing the two girls to each other. They had been playing together for the past three days, and they seemed to be getting along very well. In the meantime, she would be in the kitchen making lunch. She hoped to work with Brachi while the food was cooking. At eleven o'clock, after the little girl went home, she would put Yossi to sleep and straighten up the kitchen and living room while Tehilla took care of the children's room. Hopefully, she would be ready for her mother-in-law when she arrived.

Riki's plan seemed to be pretty much on target except for a few unexpected developments. Esther brought along Ruchie and Shaindy, her two little sisters, because her mother said that otherwise she couldn't go to play with Tehilla. At that point, Riki couldn't very well tell Esther to go home, especially since she knew Tehilla would be far less motivated to watch the little ones without the company of a friend. Instead of four children, the cramped living room now held six. And instead of just playing some board games, they decided to play "day camp," with crayons and paste — the works, even a midday snack.

All this still did not unnerve Riki completely. According to the plan, Brachi would be gone at eleven. Yossi was showing signs of fatigue, which meant she could count on him going to sleep as planned. She could still reasonably expect to have time to get the house together.

While the children were playing, Riki washed the dishes,

cleared the counters and wiped the kitchen cabinets. She made an entrée and cooked rice as a side dish. She had just finished blending fruit for Yossi when Brachi's sisters arrived to fetch her. She kissed the little girl warmly and went to feed her son.

Casting a worried glance at the messy living room, she asked Tehilla and her friends to pick up the crayons and papers. She suddenly remembered that she hadn't yet packed Tehilla's things. *Maybe I should have skipped Brachi's visit, like Daniel said,* she thought. *Maybe if I had told her mother about my difficult day, she would have made other arrangements.*

"Your mother will be here soon," Riki said to Tehilla with more of an edge in her voice than she intended. "Could you please go to your room and collect your stuff? Put it all in one pile, okay?"

Tehilla dutifully obeyed. She left the arts and crafts on the table and went to the bedroom, the three other children trailing behind her.

As she debated whether to send them home, Riki heard bloodcurdling screams coming from outside. At first, they sounded muffled and distant. Then they drew closer, frightening in their intensity and hysteria. She heard doors opening, one after another, and then slamming shut. A babble of voices rose outside her door. Amid the noise, Riki identified the familiar voice of her neighbor Yehudis Weiss. It was she who was shrieking hysterically, "Help!"

Riki sprang to her feet. She ran to the children's room and almost threw Yossi into Tehilla's arms. "Watch him until I get back. Someone's in trouble," she yelled in Tehilla's direction, running to the door. She yanked on the knob and flew down the stairs.

54

"**Help! Call an ambulance!**" The cries for help were clearer now. Riki heard her neighbor Mrs. Lefkowitz shouting, "Quick! Call an ambulance! He's not breathing!"

Suddenly, she found herself next to Yehudis, who was shouting in a terror-stricken voice, "Riki, help me! He's not breathing! Moishy's stopped breathing!"

Without stopping to think, Riki grabbed the unconscious child from his mother's arms.

"What happened?" she asked as she ran inside Yehudis's apartment with the baby. "How did he stop breathing?"

"I don't know," Yehudis sobbed. "He was sitting babbling in his high chair when he suddenly went blue in the face. I grabbed him out of the chair, and he went all limp! Riki, do something. Why isn't the ambulance here yet?"

Riki's thoughts raced frantically. Was there anything they could do now, before the ambulance arrived?

"Yehudis, calm down. He'll be okay. He'll come to any minute now." What was it she had learned at the first-aid course she'd taken in high school? Oh, maybe something was stuck in his throat, choking him!

Riki forced herself to focus; she had to think clearly now. She recalled learning the Heimlich maneuver at the course. Without missing a beat she sat Moishy on her lap facing away from her and used the fingers of both hands to press into his upper abdomen with a quick upward thrust. She remembered the instructor telling them it was important to be gentle about it and that if it didn't work the first time, it should be repeated.

For a moment nothing happened. Then the baby made a choking sound followed by two strong coughs. An olive pit shot out of his mouth, and he began to cry.

Little Moishy continued crying, while Riki, shocked by the life-and-death trauma she had just gone through, sat motionless. When the paramedics arrived, they found her still sitting there, clutching the child fiercely to her. It was only when a pair of strong arms took the child from her that she finally realized it was all over. As the doctor checked Moishy, he muttered, "Good! You did just the right thing. Well done."

Yehudis, still white as a ghost, looked directly into Riki's eyes and whispered, "You saved my baby, Riki. I'll never forget it, as long as I live."

"Hashem saved him for you, Yehudis," Riki said, her voice barely above a whisper.

When she got back to her apartment, Tehilla and her friend Esther crowded around her, anxious to hear what had happened. Riki wanted nothing more than to be left alone for a few minutes, but the girls were obviously frightened by the emergency and needed to have everything explained to them.

Riki answered the flood of questions. She suddenly realized that her mouth was dry and her heart was pounding wildly. She barely managed to drag herself to the couch and ask Tehilla for a cup of water.

Yossi was crawling on the floor, his clothes sporting multicolored stains and his little hands black.

"Tehilla, did you pack your things yet?" Riki asked. Tehilla shook her head.

"I didn't get to it. I was busy watching Yossi and making sure he didn't get into trouble. My mommy called. She said she's already at the central bus station, and she'll soon be here."

"What?" Riki sat bolt upright. "She's already at the central bus station? Why didn't you tell me right away?"

Tehilla was taken aback by the force of Riki's reaction. She couldn't understand what her sister-in-law was getting all worked up about.

"What's the big deal? She only phoned a couple of minutes ago."

"Okay, never mind." Riki sank back on the couch cushion again, feeling defeated. A sinking feeling took over as she surveyed the room. The house was a mess, no two ways about it. Papers and crayons littered the table, and toys were strewn all over the room. Maybe that wasn't the end of the world, but Yossi's bottle dripping all over the floor was really inexcusable. She didn't even want to think about the kitchen, where the breakfast dishes were still sitting on the table.

How had she let this happen to her? She had no idea where to begin. What would her mother-in-law think? Should she start telling her the whole story about Moishy?

Riki knew she had to get up and give the place a once-over even if she only had five minutes. That would at least give her enough time to straighten up the hall so that her mother-in-law wouldn't get the shock of her life as soon as she set foot in the apartment. Despite her good intentions, though, her legs refused to obey.

I don't care! a small inner voice said defiantly. *I don't have the energy to put on an act anymore. I don't owe anyone any explanations. How long do I have to kill myself to try and please my mother-in-law? This is who I am, take it or leave it. Some days I manage to get to everything and my house sparkles, and other days, like today, it's a mess.*

I want to be a good wife and mother, but I think it's important to leave time for living. I'm the type of person who drops everything when I hear beautiful music. When someone needs a listening ear, I stop what I'm doing and listen, even at the expense of everything else. When Tehilla poured her heart out about how lonely she is, I listened and then went out to the park to find her some friends. That's who I am, and I'm tired of trying to prove myself to my mother-in-law.

Riki sat on the couch feeling physically drained but in some ways stronger than ever. This time, she knew that her indifference to the way her home looked stemmed not from weakness or despair, but from the knowledge that she was going to be the person she wanted to be. She felt calm.

How long had it been since she'd handed her mother the first-prize certificate she'd received in school, knowing that her mother was as pleased as could be that she had managed to raise such wonderful children? How many years had passed since then? How many incidents had taken place since then to prove that she was fine just the way she was? Why did she still feel the constant need to prove herself and justify everything she did, over and over again?

Today she was a different Riki, that was for sure. She was a married woman who was raising a child and working to support her husband while he continued learning. She was no longer an insecure little girl. She was a confident young woman who now reached out to give to others. She took care of a little girl with special needs, and she opened her home to Tehilla during vacation, even if that home wasn't the most immaculate.

From her position on the couch, she called out to Yossi, "Come here, sweetie. Come sit on Mommy's lap."

"Tehilla, please go to the kitchen and take out a tray with glasses. There's a cake in the freezer. Please take it out so that it will defrost by the time your mother gets here."

That was really what she needed to focus on, the things her

mother-in-law would appreciate after her long ride. A neat house was really for her own ego. Malka Weiss had asked her what she did to try and please her mother-in-law, and she hadn't known how to answer the question. Now she realized that a lot of the things she did ostensibly to please her mother-in-law were really to bolster her own self-image.

I have to greet her warmly. I'll let Yossi charm her, and I'll offer her a piece of cake and a cold drink.

"Tehilla, I think I hear someone knocking. Can you get it?"

At the very last minute, before the door opened, Riki thought that perhaps she ought to explain that the place was a mess because of the emergency. Why should her mother-in-law torment herself needlessly by the thought that her daughter-in-law was a hopeless housewife?

Sima was having a good day. The bus ride to the taxi station was quick, and the taxi sped off to Jerusalem almost at once. She sat next to the window. A pleasant breeze and the rich sound of classical music filled the car.

She arrived at Daniel and Riki's at eleven-thirty. She planned to spend an hour visiting her son and daughter-in-law before setting off for home with Tehilla. She hoped to be back by early afternoon.

She climbed the stairs quickly, eager to see Tehilla, Riki and her grandchild. On the second floor, she almost bumped into a woman she didn't recognize who asked, "Are you Riki Abramson's mother?"

"No," smiled Sima. "I'm her mother-in-law."

"Oh. I'm one of Riki's neighbors. You don't know me, but I've seen you here once or twice, and I assumed you were Riki's mother. I want you to know you've got a really special daughter-in-law."

"Thanks," replied Sima. This wasn't the first time she'd been told she had a special daughter-in-law. In fact, sometimes she wished Riki were more ordinary.

"I'm not saying it just to be polite," Mrs. Lefkowitz continued. "She's amazingly resourceful for someone so young. Had you arrived here a mere quarter of an hour ago, you would have walked right into the drama. A neighbors' baby was choking, and Riki saved his life." Mrs. Lefkowitz paused dramatically. "I'm still all shaken up. I was just on my way up to your daughter-in-law to see how she's doing."

"What happened?" Sima asked in alarm. "Whose baby was choking?"

"It wasn't Riki's baby. It was a neighbor's child, and he's fine now. The neighbors were all hysterical, but Riki was so calm and knew just what to do."

Sima finally understood the import of what Mrs. Lefkowitz was saying. "How did she handle it?"

"I'm not sure what it was she did. But one thing is certain: she kept her wits about her. What can I tell you, Mrs. Abramson? Your daughter-in-law is exceptional."

Sima didn't even hear Mrs. Lefkowitz's final words as she hurried up the stairs to Riki's apartment. She felt a warm glow of pride. She hadn't known about this part of Riki's personality, but actually, she found she wasn't surprised. After all, Riki was Ephraim's sister, and he had also displayed a great deal of resourcefulness. Perhaps it was something in their genes. She was suddenly filled with a strong desire to see her daughter-in-law in person, as if something in her outward appearance or personality had dramatically changed as a result of what had just happened.

She knocked on the door and immediately heard the familiar sound of Tehilla's footsteps hurrying to open it. "Mommy!" Tehilla cried, throwing herself into her mother's arms. Hand in hand, they walked inside.

Sima glanced around, looking for Riki, but she wasn't anywhere in sight. Instead, she saw the messy room, the papers strewn all over and the toys scattered in all directions. This was not the way the house usually looked when she came to visit. Three little girls stood over to the side, staring at her in silent wonder. Sima held back a cry of surprise and instead asked, "Where's Riki?"

Before she could finish her question, she spotted her daughter-in-law getting up slowly from the couch, holding Yossi in her arms.

55

AS SOON AS HE SAW HIS GRANDMOTHER, Yossi crowed in delight and waved his chubby hands in glee. "You know your bubby, don't you?" Riki said with a smile, the warmth in her tone diffusing the tension of Sima's entry. "You're saying hi to her, aren't you?"

"Of course he knows me!" Sima exclaimed, flushed with pleasure at her grandson's effusive welcome. She planted a kiss on his cheek and ruffled his hair.

"Come in, have a seat. Do you see what's going on here?" She waved her hand in the general direction of the dining room. "I planned on straightening up before you came, but I just didn't get to it. The morning didn't exactly go as planned."

Sima was startled by her daughter-in-law's straightforward approach. Riki had never been so open with her before. The truth is, she had been surprised, even slightly annoyed to be honest, by the mess, but Riki's matter-of-fact explanation took the wind out of her sails. All she felt now was sympathy and fondness for the young woman who was being so refreshingly honest with her. She waved her hand in dismissal. "It's nothing.

Don't worry about it. The main thing is that everyone is healthy. I heard about the drama you had this morning. They told me you saved that baby's life."

"Who told you that?" Riki was surprised — and relieved. Now when she told her mother-in-law about what happened, it wouldn't sound like she was using it as an excuse for the mess.

"I met one of your neighbors on the way up. She said you had the presence of mind to do the right thing in what was a frightening emergency."

"It was," Riki said, with a catch in her throat. The memory of the ordeal was still fresh in her mind. "You can't imagine what was going on here. I was scared stiff. People were shouting hysterically. I ran down to my neighbor Yehudis's apartment. When I got there, no one was doing anything. I grabbed the baby from her arms, not really knowing what I was going to do. Whatever it was, I figured I would be in a better position to think clearly than she was."

"How did you know what to do?" The note of respect and admiration in her mother-in-law's voice was not lost on Riki.

"My little sister once choked on a piece of Lego," Riki said, "and I remembered that my grandmother had performed the Heimlich maneuver in order to get the piece out."

"Did your grandmother work as a nurse or hold a medical position of any sort?" Sima recalled that Ephraim had also mentioned something about his grandmother. He said it was she who had taught him to watch and pay attention to sudden behavioral changes in elderly people. That was how he had noticed Mr. Schiller's problem.

"No, she never worked in any medical field," chuckled Riki. "She's just a wise woman who's been through a lot. She has lots of life experience."

"I guess that's the way it is when one has to bring up a family on one's own. You have to be resourceful."

Riki tensed. *Why did she have to say that? My grandmother is a wise woman, period. What difference does it make whether or not she*

TIGHTROPE | 409

was alone? Why does she have to drag that up?

Riki wasn't sure if her mother-in-law was trying to insinuate anything or not.

Stop it! a small voice inside her whispered. *This is one of your sore spots screaming in protest. Don't you know your mother-in-law by now? She has no idea this will upset you. She doesn't always think about the possible ramifications of what she says. Just go on with the conversation, and don't let it get to you.*

"Tehilla, would you please pour a cold drink for your mother?" Riki's voice quivered slightly. "There's some cake, too. If you bring it in, I'll slice it."

Sima noticed her daughter-in-law's sudden tension. "Are you feeling okay?" she asked in concern.

"Oh, I feel fine," Riki quickly replied. Yossi once again waved his dirty little hands in his grandmother's face, and she responded by tickling him under his chin.

"I left Yossi with Tehilla," Riki said, suddenly aware that despite her decision not to apologize about the state the house was in, she was in fact doing just that. *Or is there a difference between explaining and apologizing?* she mused. "He crawled around all over the place and had a great time. I didn't get to cleaning him up since then. When I got back upstairs, I suddenly felt drained, too exhausted to lift a finger. Oh, here's the cake. Tehilla, do you mind bringing some napkins, too?

"Tehilla was wonderful. She helped me so much with Yossi. She even played day camp with him."

Sima looked at the papers, scissors, glue and crayons strewn across the table, understanding dawning in her eyes. "I assume this is where she held her day camp?"

"Uh-huh," Tehilla said before Riki could respond. "This is my friend Esther. We've been making a day camp for her baby brother and Yossi every day. Today her sisters came too."

Sima turned to survey Esther and her sisters with more attention than she had given them before. They were still standing shyly at the side of the room, taking in the company silently.

"Are you Tehilla's friend?" Sima asked Esther.

Esther nodded, and Tehilla gave a grin. "That's Shaindy and that's Ruchie. Mommy, can I stay here at Riki's house more?" she asked suddenly, to Sima's surprise.

"You want to stay here?" She was amazed. "But your school's day camp starts tomorrow."

"I don't want to go," Tehilla said petulantly, shrugging her shoulders for emphasis. "It's a lot more fun here!"

"I'm sure it is," Sima replied with a wry smile and a meaningful glance at the messy table. "I'm not so sure Riki thinks it's that much fun. What makes you think she'll agree to let you stay? She doesn't have to entertain you all summer, you know."

Riki gave a tired smile. "Me? I'd love it. Tehilla helps me with my shopping, she watches Yossi and—"

"And she also makes a huge mess," Sima ended with a chuckle. "It's really nice of you, Riki, to agree to have Tehilla stay on, but I don't think I'll allow it. She's registered at the school's day camp, and it has a full program of activities and trips planned. There's no reason she shouldn't go."

Tehilla continued to whine and protest, but Sima was adamant.

A huge yawn Riki didn't manage to stifle gave away the extent of her exhaustion, and Sima's motherly instincts were aroused.

"Let me have Yossi," she said, reaching out to take him. "You go rest. You must be exhausted after what you went through this morning. After a traumatic experience like that, I wouldn't be surprised if you felt it for days. We'll watch Yossi until you get up."

"No, it's okay," Riki protested. "I'm not that tired, and Yossi's just about ready for his nap anyway."

"Good. If he seems tired, we'll put him to sleep. Really, Riki, go lie down for an hour."

Her mother-in-law rose with the air of brisk efficiency that so characterized her. "Tehilla will show me where his diapers are. Meanwhile, we'll pack her things, and her friends will help her organize the day camp equipment." She smiled. "We've got a lot to do until you wake up. Besides, you're so tired you're falling off your feet."

Riki felt uncomfortable. She was surprised by her mother-in-law's unexpected offer, but she wasn't sure what to make of it. She gratefully mumbled her thanks and retired to her bedroom.

Sima remained in the living room with the children. She diapered her darling grandchild, washed his face and hands, and changed him into a clean outfit. When was the last time she'd had the opportunity to care for him like that? Even Tehilla was amazed at the sight of her dignified mother bending over little Yossi and singing a nursery rhyme in a babyish voice.

Sima put Yossi to bed and went into the dining room to help the girls clean up. Tehilla began rolling up the rug spread out on the floor.

"Tehilla, what are you doing? Why are you rolling up the rug? Just shake it out and put it back."

"But Riki only takes out this rug when Brachi comes," Tehilla explained, "and she already went home."

"Brachi? Who's that?" Sima couldn't place the name for a moment.

"She's the little girl Riki takes care of, the one that doesn't walk yet."

"Oh. Yes, now I remember," Sima recalled what she had heard about Brachi. "Do you mean to tell me she was here today too?" she asked in disbelief. Her daughter's nod confirmed that this was indeed the case.

Sima moved on to the kitchen. A few dirty dishes were in the *fleishig* sink. The remains of someone's breakfast were still on the table, and the open blender still bore traces of the pureed fruit Riki had prepared for Yossi.

She takes too much on herself, Sima thought. She spotted a glass bowl filled with a fresh fruit salad, apparently prepared in her honor. On the stove stood a pot of fluffy white rice, still warm, and a frying pan of sautéed vegetables.

Sima suddenly realized how much effort her daughter-in-law had put into making her visit pleasant. She felt a surge of maternal emotion well up within her, like what she felt whenever she visited Mali, her own daughter.

For the first time, she saw her daughter-in-law in a different light. She was no longer on the other side of no-man's-land, waiting to be drawn into Sima's camp. She was just a young woman, not much older than her own daughter Gila, and she wasn't all that self-confident. She had made an effort to welcome her mother-in-law properly this morning, but, through no fault of her own, things just hadn't worked out. She was just setting out on the path of life, trying to live life as she understood it. Sometimes she made mistakes, but she was generally successful in her endeavors.

Sima glanced at Tehilla, who, along with her new friends, was busy picking up bits of paper from the floor. She silently thanked Hashem that her child was happy here, and that Riki had effected a positive change in Tehilla. *Daniel, too, has changed*, the thought suddenly flashed through her mind. His intervention in Ephraim's problem was proof of that. He was no longer the same shy, hesitant *bachur* he had once been. Her husband had even mentioned the change.

So what exactly did she want? That Riki be a carbon copy of her? That she do everything the way her mother-in-law thought appropriate? What for?

Actually, Riki was better at some things than she was. She, for example, would never have allowed such a mess in the dining room just to suit the whims of a seven-year-old. Nor would she have taken a child like Brachi under her wing. Riki did, though, because such things were important to her, because she was different from her.

That was the point. She was different from her. Could it be

Sima Abramson, had a hard time accepting people who ͨerent from her?

ͤima had the uneasy feeling that this might be the case.

What was it that Mrs. Coleman, the elderly Mrs. Blau's daughter, had once told her? "I was different from my mother and my brother and sister. My mother fit a certain mold, and she wanted to force me into the same mold, but I was different."

Obviously, she too fit a certain mold. And Daniel... He had always been different from her other children. She had always wished she could change him to be more like Ariel, who was so outgoing and popular, but she had never succeeded. Was it possible that her efforts had done more harm than good?

Now the same thing was happening with his wife. She had a distinct picture of the way she wanted her daughter-in-law to behave. She wanted her to keep a cleaner house, and she wished Riki didn't dedicate so much time and effort to other projects. She wanted her manners and taste to be more refined; she wanted her to think and speak more like she herself did. But it wasn't working, because Riki was different.

She was struck by the absurdity of trying to force someone to fit a preconceived mold. What she would have to do instead was learn to accept people as they were, with all their varied personalities and behaviors. She would have to accept her daughter-in-law the way she was, the things she liked and approved of along with those she didn't. It was a package deal. And there was a lot of good to appreciate, she had to admit.

Today, Riki's levelheaded behavior had saved a baby's life. That was something plenty of other daughters-in-law would not be able to do. Sima felt a surge of real motherly pride well up within her. *Riki's sense of calm control is undoubtedly a component of her unique personality.* This time, the word *unique* was definitely complimentary.

Despite her mother-in-law's best intentions, Riki had trouble falling asleep. She was too tightly wound up.

Too many events had taken place that morning, and they flashed through her mind as though she were watching them on a screen.

She relived the pressure she had felt early in the morning in anticipation of her mother-in-law's visit. In her mind's eye, she heard Yehudis's cries and saw the baby's blue face.

Through the closed bedroom door, she heard her mother-in-law's footsteps as she walked through the apartment, caring for Yossi and doing the dishes. This was the first time her mother-in-law was acting the role of a concerned parent. It gave her a warm, pleasant feeling, but at the same time, made her uneasy. She found herself rehashing the initial moments of her mother-in-law's visit — the startled look in her eyes, her own discomfort at seeing her mother-in-law's shock, and then her brief explanation. She had never dreamed she'd be able to utter those words, but she had: "I planned on straightening up before you came, but I just didn't get to it. The morning didn't exactly go as planned."

Riki replayed the scene several times. Saying what she really thought and felt was new for her. She had always preferred to remain silent and keep things to herself. She had always thought it would be impossible for her to admit outright that she hadn't done something she knew she really should have. Today she had done it.

If only I can continue this way, she prayed in her heart. She had no doubt that part of the barrier between Daniel's mother and herself had crumbled the moment she uttered those words. From that point on, the tension had almost magically melted away and the conversation had flowed in a pleasant stream.

The experience itself amazed her. Even more amazing was that it had been so easy.

56

EPHRAIM LEFT THE DORMITORY BUILDING and walked toward the bus stop. He glanced at his watch. It was six-thirty on the dot, and he had arranged to meet his brother-in-law at the entrance of Ponovezh at seven. He should make it right on time. He was in good spirits. All was right with the world.

As he approached the yeshiva, the familiar voice of his friend Asher assailed him from behind. "Hey, Ephraim! Wait up!" Asher panted as he trotted closer. "What's going on? Why did you run off? I looked for you in your room, and Shmuel told me you just left."

"What's the matter?" Ephraim was impatient. He was in a hurry.

"My father just called. He says he has to know now what you decided."

"About what?" Ephraim had no idea what Asher was talking about.

"What do you mean, about what? What's with you? Don't you remember you told me you were looking for a job?"

Of course. How could I have forgotten?

He had asked Asher to put in a good word for him when he heard there was an opening for an assistant in his father's electronics store. In the meantime, though, he'd found a job at the nursing home. He'd be getting his first paycheck the next day. He hadn't mentioned the job to Asher. He'd been so busy he'd forgotten.

"Oh, yeah. So what about it?"

"My father said you could start working on a trial basis for three months. He wants you to start right away. There's someone else who's interested in the job, so you've got to make up your mind fast."

Asher waited expectantly for some positive reaction from Ephraim. After all, he'd really put himself out to help him. He was disappointed.

"When does he want me to start?" Ephraim said noncommittally.

"Right away, like tomorrow morning. But don't panic," he continued, the look of surprise on Ephraim's face startling him. "Next week's fine, too."

Ephraim was in a quandary. Taking a job meant leaving his technical program, which is what he had wanted to do until quite recently. Now, when leaving was a real option, he wasn't so sure anymore. He now saw the whole issue in a different light. The idea of leaving seemed reckless and even immature.

"I've got to think it over," he told his friend, uncomfortably tracing circles in the sand with his shoe.

"Hey! I thought you already thought the whole thing through a long time ago," Asher said. "I pestered my father for nothing. Here I go and convince him to hire you, telling him he shouldn't worry, he'll never regret it, and now you say you need to think it over. What's going on?"

What was going on? Ephraim couldn't say for certain. He knew only one thing: The sense of restlessness that had been plaguing him had almost entirely disappeared. It had been replaced with a sense of — something else. He wasn't sure what.

"What can I tell you?" he mumbled apologetically. "When I asked you, I was sure about it. Things changed."

"Suit yourself. My father wants an answer, that's all. He has someone else lined up. But remember — it's a great job plus there's plenty of opportunities for promotion. Let me know if you change your mind."

■ ■ ■

Malka Weiss sat talking with her elderly mother-in-law in the lobby of the Nachalas Avos nursing home. Ever since she had decided to come more often, the older woman was decidedly more cheerful. At least, that's what the director, Mrs. Abramson, had said.

The elderly Mrs. Weiss no longer spent her whole day grumbling and complaining. Her sarcastic comments were now hardly heard, and the bitter expression on her face had softened. Malka herself felt her mother-in-law had grown warmer and more considerate toward her. It was as if the cold, impenetrable armor she had worn for so many years had cracked. Deep in her heart, Malka was glad.

As they chatted about all sorts of trivialities, the conversation drifted to the subject of family. Mrs. Weiss's oldest granddaughter was getting married at the end of the winter. She had begged her grandmother to come to Antwerp for the wedding.

"We've always been close," Mrs. Weiss said. "'Please come,' she begged me the last time we talked. 'Don't worry — we'll take good care of you. You'll have your own place to stay.' She wants me to stay for a long time, maybe even a month. But how can I?"

"Why not?" asked her daughter-in-law. "I think you'll enjoy yourself. It's good to have a change of scene. You'll get to spend time with the family there."

"At my age, it's hard to give up my routine. I'm comfortable here. I have my doctor, too."

"There are good doctors in Belgium, too," Malka chuckled. "I think you should accept the offer. You'll have a wonderful time."

"You think so?" asked the elderly woman, still hesitant.

"I'm sure so." A pleasant evening breeze rustled the curtains behind them, bringing with it the scent of jasmine from the courtyard.

Mrs. Weiss shivered slightly. "What I would really like," she said slowly, gazing into the distance, "is to finally have our whole family together on the same side of the ocean. That's what I would really love. If only everyone would come to the wedding — Aryeh, Menachem — the whole family together."

"The whole family together." She didn't include me in the list. After thirty years of marriage to Menachem, I'm still not considered family.

The absurdity of the situation hit Malka, bringing with it at the same time an old familiar ache. She had thought the wound was healed, but obviously she had been wrong.

She had long lamented the fact that her mother-in-law didn't think of her as a daughter or even an integral part of the family. At some point in her marriage, she had realized that this came from her mother-in-law's difficulty in separating from her son and accepting the fact that he had left the nest.

Malka had once heard a noted speaker's theory on the issue. The lecturer had said that this phenomenon was especially common among Holocaust survivors whose children represented all their hopes and dreams — all their security. When these children married, the parents had a hard time. Some dealt with the transition well; others did not. Malka had accepted the theory without checking the source. It helped her overlook the phenomenon and pretend it didn't exist. In fact, she had used her own personal experience with her mother-in-law as an example of how not to behave to a daughter-in-law.

That was why she was so surprised by the pain she now felt. *Could it be that some wounds never heal? What about the self-improvement I'm always talking about? Only yesterday, I assured the young Abramson woman that if she would only try to ignore her sensitivities and work on herself, she would grow stronger and learn to forgive. Where is my own forgiveness? How is it that time has not healed me?*

Malka felt the same pain she had felt in the early stages of her marriage. It was as if the wound had reopened.

I visit you almost every day. I try so hard! I care for you. I want to love you. Yet you still aren't ready to accept me. Malka felt a wave of anger and bitterness rising up in her throat. She couldn't believe this was happening to her. She scraped her chair back, as if in protest. For a moment, she considered getting up and leaving, but she pushed the thought aside, aware that it was an immature thing to do. She had long ago outgrown such impulses.

She glanced at her mother-in-law, who still wore the same dreamy expression on her face, oblivious to the emotional turmoil she had aroused in her daughter-in-law. She was in a trance, wistfully reminiscing about bygone days, of the family togetherness that had once existed.

The time has come, she chided herself, *for me to learn to make peace with what I cannot change.* Perhaps this was what she should have emphasized when speaking to her daughter-in-law's young neighbor and to the women who came to her workshops.

When all is said and done, each individual has his own personality. That's what she should have said, and that's what she would say. *It's not always possible to change people's attitudes or outlook on life, even if that's what we would like. Let us concentrate our efforts on ensuring that we are behaving the way we should. In most cases, our own positive behavior affects the other side and causes change there as well, but even if it doesn't, it's not the end of the world. Our own personal development, the tense atmosphere we prevented, the pleasant relationships we learned to create as a result of our experience — that's what really counts.*

Malka suddenly realized that she was no longer angry, no longer bitter. True, she had discovered that some wounds never completely heal, but she also knew that time and self-control did wonders for one's spiritual and emotional health, giving strength to overlook the pain — exactly as she had told Riki.

"So, what do you think?" her mother-in-law asked. "Do you think Aryeh and Menachem would agree to come with me?"

Malka gazed at her mother-in-law's face for a few seconds, deliberating over her response. She suddenly felt she had gone beyond the stage where she would let such petty trivialities get to her. She was fond of her mother-in-law, faults and all, and she had long ago learned to change the steps of the dance.

"What about me?" she asked, smiling warmly. "Don't you want me to go with you to Belgium, too?"

The elderly woman stared at her daughter-in-law in surprise. She hadn't expected such a response to her question, and it was obvious she was taken aback, even confused. Did she want her daughter-in-law to come? She honestly hadn't given the possibility any thought. Did she want her there? Well…yes, of course she did. It would be wonderful if Malka came. In fact, she'd feel even more secure that way. Menachem didn't always know what to do when she felt short of breath. Strange, it hadn't even occurred to her that Malka might be able to attend the wedding.

Malka sat on the edge of her chair, waiting expectantly for her mother-in-law's answer. Their eyes locked. In a flash of understanding, the elderly mother-in-law realized that she had hurt Malka's feelings.

"Of course I want you to come. But I know you're so busy with your lectures that I didn't think you'd be able to take time off. What do you say about it?" she asked, clasping Malka's hand in her own. "You know you're like a daughter to me."

ALL THE WAY TO THE YESHIVA where he had made up to meet with Daniel, Ephraim was lost in thought. The job offer was both tempting and confusing. How could it be that he had once wanted a job so badly, but now that it was finally offered to him on a golden platter, it was no longer so appealing? He was unwilling, hesitant, or maybe even indifferent.

How long ago was it that he had thought a job would be the answer to his problems? It wasn't that long ago at all…perhaps two, three, four weeks ago? He had argued bitterly with his father, certain his world was coming to an end. He had felt he could not go on in an educational framework of any sort. He'd been frustrated, unable to make peace with himself.

Now, though, feelings of that sort were no longer troubling him. Could it be that the job with Mr. Schiller had something to do with his change of attitude? Since he had begun learning with the old man, he was filled with a sense of satisfaction and accomplishment. It was an undeniable fact that life was not as boring as it had once been, and the desire to abandon everything and flee the framework he was in had all but disappeared.

And yet…the offer was an offer. It sounded good. The opportunity to earn some serious money was definitely appealing.

What should he do? Perhaps he ought to talk to Daniel.

Daniel stood waiting for him at the entrance to the yeshiva, and the two entered the study hall together.

Ephraim was stunned by the scene that unfolded before his eyes as he entered the room. In a huge study hall with endlessly high ceilings, hundreds of *bochrim* sat swaying over open Gemaras, learning, arguing and explaining. Their total absorption in *limud Torah* was obvious to any observer.

The yeshiva atmosphere was not new to Ephraim, but the level of intensity emanating from the *beis medrash* was a surprise for him nonetheless, perhaps because he wasn't prepared for it. Before he'd entered the yeshiva building, his mind had been preoccupied with affairs that belonged to a different planet entirely: *Should I accept the job or should I not? The army or electronics? Electronics or computers?* Torah study had never been a topic of central importance for him; he had never understood how it could be the essence of one's life, the way it was for these *bochrim* at the yeshiva.

Standing at the entrance to the yeshiva's *beis medrash* now, Ephraim suddenly understood the place Torah occupied in the hearts of the hundreds of *bochrim* here, boys of his own age. The animated hand motions combined with the cacophony of voices to create the atmosphere of a roaring ocean. Ephraim felt as though he had landed on a different planet, and he was very moved.

The two found an empty spot in the corner of the study hall and sat down to learn. They opened the *masechta* to the right place and began reviewing the *mishnayos*. Ephraim presented his questions and doubts. He had known he would enjoy studying with an experienced *lamdan* like Daniel, and he was pleased to see he was right. All the obstacles that had troubled him while studying alone disappeared under the tutelage of his brother-in-law, and he was able to get right to the heart and soul of the *sugya*.

Daniel explained and clarified complex topics with the expertise of a professional teacher. His insights were deep and penetrating, and he displayed a comprehensive understanding of the material.

Surprisingly enough, Ephraim kept the pace. The subject and Daniel's explanations interested him greatly, and for the first time, he found himself willingly listening to a Gemara *shiur* and trying to understand. This was the first time Ephraim merited to study Torah in this unique manner, and he was swept up by the fervor of his surroundings. It was only when Daniel suddenly stopped short and said he had to leave for a few moments to make an important phone call that Ephraim raised his eyes from the text and took a break to look around him. He no longer felt stunned by the noise. On the contrary, it felt wonderful to be so close to all this, to actually be a part of it. He felt he would easily be able to blend into this world of enthusiastic Torah study.

He had never before considered himself in the category of *bnei Torah*. Even when his father had enrolled him in the yeshiva at the end of eighth grade, he had known he wouldn't last long. It had never been a concrete decision, however. Today, he knew that his attitude stemmed from his own negative opinion of himself. He had convinced himself that he didn't belong. Now, though, he was no longer so sure of it.

Someone was tapping him on the shoulder. Ephraim turned around, trying to identify the *bachur* who was looking at him with a glint of curiosity in his eyes.

"Hello! What are you doing here?"

Ephraim couldn't place the *bachur*.

"Don't you recognize me?" the *bachur* asked with a smile.

Ephraim squinted slightly, wrinkling his forehead and trying to recall the name behind the face.

"I'm Shechter," the *bachur* said. "Reuvi Shechter. Remember?"

Reuvi Shechter! Of course he remembered. Reuvi Shechter from cheder. They'd been together in sixth, seventh and eighth grades. How the boy had changed! Reuvi had been the top student in the class, beloved by all his rebbes and teachers. He was an absolute angel who never so much as looked up from his *sefer* in the middle of class. Reuvi Shechter had sat next to the door, and every time Ephraim was kicked out of class, he'd had to pass right next to Mr. Perfect Student, whose superior, self-righteous attitude had made him sick to his stomach.

A shadow clouded Ephraim's face. The pure and lofty thoughts and emotions that had welled up within him a moment ago disappeared in a flash. The memories that rose up in his mind dulled their brightness.

"Yeah, I remember. Sure I remember," he replied, his mouth turned up into a light smile. He recalled the time he had been unable to answer the rebbe's question, and Reuvi had enthusiastically raised his hand to show that he, of course, knew the answer. He remembered how the *melamed* had showered Reuvi with praise for his brilliant explanation, and a feeling of bitterness welled up inside him.

"What's new? What are you doing here?" Reuvi asked.

"Exactly what you see," replied Ephraim, tensing up. "Sitting and learning."

"But you don't really belong here, do you?" Reuvi continued in all innocence, unaware he was hitting a sore spot.

"Uh, no…not exactly." Ephraim lowered his gaze. *Who says I don't belong? Who decides who belongs and who doesn't?*

"What's the story? What yeshiva did you go to?"

Reuvi's question made Ephraim squirm in his seat. *What a snob! Maybe it was Reuvi and people like him who were to blame for the fact that he was not in a yeshiva. He was one of those people who always made sure to remind me that I didn't "belong" in a yeshiva framework. Why doesn't he just leave me alone?*

Reuvi continued chatting away, somewhat surprised at his former classmate's cold reception. "Someone told me you left the yeshiva world quite some time ago, and now I find you sitting here. Well, life is full of surprises. I sure never expected to run into you here."

"No? Where did you expect to find me?"

Reuvi was thrown off balance. "Uh…I don't know…," he stammered.

Outside the classroom? Wandering the halls? Ephraim felt like asking. He was very bitter. Something deep inside him rebelled against his friend's questions, against his past reputation, against the stigma that had attached itself to his name. *Yeshivos were only for the best of the best, weren't they? And who if not Reuvi knew exactly who was the best and who wasn't? Just wait, my friend. I'll show you who's the best!*

"So, you didn't expect to find me here." His smile was laden with irony. "Surprise, surprise. Here I am."

■ ■ ■

It was late. Daniel was on his way home, and Riki paced the house restlessly, finding it difficult to concentrate on anything at all.

A short while ago, her mother-in-law had phoned with exciting news. Gila had returned from her date, and both sides had given a positive answer. The couple had spoken with both sets of parents via the telephone, and the *vort* was to be held the following evening. Riki had asked her mother-in-law whether she might share the good news with her mother.

"Of course. What's the question?" Daniel's mother had replied. "We don't want to publicize the matter yet, but your mother is family, and I personally respect and value her friendship immensely. I have no doubt that she and your father know how to keep a secret, and I know they will be true partners in our happiness." Her mother-in-law's words had been music to her ears, and Riki's joy at the impending event had increased tenfold.

Riki's mother had been surprised by the intensity of her daughter's emotional involvement in the *shidduch*. She hadn't known Riki felt so close to her sister-in-law. In fact, Riki herself was surprised by the trust and admiration Gila had displayed toward her. Last night, she had called to talk with her, and they were on the phone for almost two hours. Gila had openly discussed her doubts and hesitations, asking for Riki's advice.

"He's really nice. He's very smart — a powerhouse learner they say — and he seems knowledgeable in all areas," Gila had said, "but he talks so much! He told me all about himself, his yeshiva, his friends. What's that supposed to mean? Is it something to worry about?"

"Why? What's wrong with that?" Riki asked, finding it difficult to understand what was troubling Gila. She remembered how she had wished that Daniel would open up more instead of being so quiet.

"I'm not sure he cares enough about other people," Gila said. "How can I be sure he knows how to listen?"

Riki was thoughtful. "I don't think it's either one or the other," she said. "A talkative person can still be a *ba'al middos* and a good listener."

"Riki," continued Gila, "what I want most of all is someone honest. Someone like Daniel. Daniel is the antithesis of a show-off. Whatever he does, he does because it's right, not to impress other people. Everything he does is straightforward and true. He's very special."

Riki had listened in silence. It was true; Daniel was truly special. Deep inside, she had always known that, but Gila's enthusiastic declaration made her more aware of her own feelings. Today, for example, Daniel had gone to meet with Ephraim. He had traveled all the way to Bnei Brak just to help her brother. Riki knew he would have done that for anyone — not just her brother — because he felt it was important to help a fellow Jew find his way to the path of truth. Daniel was a truthful man, and he did what had to be done without stopping to make all sorts of considerations. In fact, Riki thought that was what had helped him find his way to Ephraim's heart. He had truly believed that her brother was capable of studying Torah, and Ephraim had sensed his brother-in-law's trust. Her father couldn't believe it. He was afraid to be happy, but he was full of admiration for Daniel. As for her mother, she was overjoyed, no doubt about it.

So how was it that she had thought she was "settling" when she had gotten engaged to him? How many deliberations she had had then! She'd been ashamed to share her thoughts at the time, but her sister-in-law was now openly discussing her doubts about a personality trait she, Riki, personally found appealing. No one was perfect. Everyone had his or her fair share of doubts and deliberations before agreeing to a *shidduch*. It was only her own sore spots that made her think she was the only one with doubts. She had agreed to the *shidduch* because that was what was meant to be, because Daniel's good qualities overshadowed any disadvantages. That was the truth.

"Keep asking," Riki advised her sister-in-law. "Something like that is easy to find out. It could be he was so talkative because he was nervous, or maybe he just thought it was up to him to make sure conversation flowed. Don't jump to conclusions. Go out with him again. Give him another chance."

Gila had agreed, and Riki had been tense the whole day. When she finally heard about Gila's decision to go ahead with the *shidduch*, a cry of joy had burst from her lips.

The *vort* was called for the next day, and then they'd get ready for the engagement party. In her mind's eye, she was already planning the cake she wanted to bake in her sister-in-law's honor. She'd gotten a delicious recipe from one of her friends. She planned to cut the cake into the shape of a house and surround it with a field of green candies and marzipans. The house of her sister-in-law's dreams, which would, G-d-willing, materialize into reality.

Riki walked to the window facing the bus stop. Had the bus

arrived yet? Was that her husband she saw, walking slowly down the street?

She turned back to the room and surveyed the overcrowded bookshelf, the painting on the wall, and the table, covered with a lace tablecloth and decorated with a vase containing a pretty flower arrangement.

I wish all this for Gila, she thought warmly. *I wish her a house as beautiful and wonderful as the one in which I'm building my own dreams.*

SIMA STOOD AT THE KITCHEN COUNTER, preparing her famous mousse. An engagement party for the extended family and friends of both the *chassan* and *kalla* was planned for the following night. The Abramsons had hired a caterer, but Sima had decided to prepare some of her own specialty cakes, as well as a spectacular dessert.

Gila, the *kalla*, was not home. She had made up to meet her future mother-in-law at a jewelry shop to choose a watch.

Riki was in a nearby bedroom, trying to put Yossi to sleep in the crib that had once belonged to his father, Daniel. Riki was off from work the following day, so she had decided to come to Bnei Brak that night to run some errands and help out in whatever way she could.

Ever since her mother-in-law's last visit to her home — when Riki had decided to spend less time defending herself and more time paying attention to the things that were truly important to her mother-in-law — Riki felt far more relaxed and at ease in her company than ever before. It was as if energy that had previously been wasted on self-defense was now freed up to be channeled to elsewhere. It was just as Malka Weiss had said: "When people are busy defending themselves, they tend to withdraw."

Riki heard the front door open and then close. She heard Gila mutter a brief "hello," and then quick footsteps drew close to the room she was in.

"Gila?" she heard her mother-in-law call from the kitchen. "Is that you?"

Riki glanced over her shoulder in time to see Gila pass her room and continue on in the direction of the bedroom she shared with Tehilla. "Gila!" came her mother-in-law's voice. "Are you back?"

Gila mumbled something unintelligible, and Sima's hurried footsteps sounded in the hall. She tapped on the closed bedroom door, opened it a crack and stuck her head inside. "Gila? Are you back? What happened?"

"Nothing. I just want to put the bags down. Why should anything happen? Why do you look so worried?"

Riki abandoned her position at the baby's crib. Yossi was already half-asleep. She stepped out into the hall, following the conversation between her mother-in-law and her sister-in-law with great curiosity.

"You look flushed," Sima said with concern. "Are you sure nothing happened?"

"Absolutely nothing."

"Come into the kitchen and tell me how it went. I've been waiting to hear. Did you choose a watch?"

"Yes, I picked something out. She'll bring it with her tomorrow. It's pretty. It's hard for me to describe it. I'll come into the kitchen in another few minutes, okay? I'm tired from all the walking we did. I'll come in soon."

The weariness Gila was displaying was not at all like her, especially on such a special night, when she ought to be feeling in particularly high spirits. Her strange behavior aroused the concern of both Riki and Sima. The two exchanged a glance of puzzlement, then wordlessly made their way to the kitchen, where Sima took her place by the mixer again.

"Something's happened. I'm sure of it," she said. Riki nodded in agreement. Just then, Gila appeared in the doorway, her too-rosy cheeks evidence of inner turmoil.

Attempting to sound casual, she asked, "Did you order the rolls yet?"

Sima laughed. "Of course I did. Did you think I'd wait until the last minute?"

"Who did you order from?"

"Flour Delights. Why?"

"Uh..." Gila's flushed face suddenly turned white. "Moshe's mother asked me to tell you that their family does not eat from that bakery. She said she knows she has no right to tell you what to do, but she wanted you to know that most of their guests won't eat if the rolls are from Flour Delights."

"What do you mean they won't eat?" Sima protested. "That bakery's been in business for years. It's got a reputation for strict kashrus supervision, and everyone buys there. What's wrong with it?"

"I don't know exactly. I think she said someone discovered they weren't sifting the flour properly. Their machinery is already old or something like that. Anyway, she said she felt obligated to let you know in advance."

Sima was silent. The words she would have liked to say stuck in her throat. She felt an intense pressure building up inside her. She took a glass out of the kitchen cabinet and filled it with water from the bottle on the counter.

"Will you have a problem canceling the order?" Gila asked, the tension evident in her voice.

Her mother shook her head. No, she didn't think she'd have trouble canceling the order if she phoned right away. But what a slap in the face! What was she supposed to understand from such a request? That the level of kashrus in her home did not meet the exacting standards of her new *mechutanim*? What was wrong with the Flour Delights bakery, which was frequented by everyone in her neighborhood, including many noted Torah scholars and rabbanim?

"There's something else too," Gila added. She took a deep breath before continuing. "I have a feeling you won't like this very much, Mommy, so please don't get upset. She thought Moshe had already told me about this, and she was surprised to hear I knew nothing about it. She asked if Hershel, Moshe's older brother, could come into the kitchen to take *ma'aser* from all the fruits and vegetables before the meal starts. That's the way they do it, she said."

"What?" Sima couldn't believe her ears. "She wants to send her son in to *ma'aser* everything? What do you mean? We *ma'aser* everything ourselves, and everything is in order with our standards of kashrus! Don't they trust us? I mean, if they don't trust us that far, why did they make a *shidduch* with us? I don't understand. Yes, the *mechutan* is a very distinguished man and a public figure as well, but between you and me, he's not that much higher on the social scale than your father, who owns and runs a nursing home. What is the meaning of this show of snobbery?"

"It's not snobbery," said Gila, unsuccessfully attempting to assuage her mother's outrage. "She explained that this is just the way they do things in their family. It has nothing to do with how much they trust the other people involved.

"She also said that if it had been just their own immediate family, she wouldn't make a fuss, because they really don't want to make a show of being more *machmir* than anyone else. But it's all the father's brothers, and all his uncles…you knew that, didn't you? It's a very important family. You told me so yourself, and you were happy about it, weren't you?

"Well, they're *makpid* to always take *ma'aser* by themselves from all their food, and they all trust Hershel. That's the way they do it. She says Hershel went in to take ma'aser by their first *mechutanim* as well."

"That's the way they do it, that's the way they do it," said Sima, mimicking her daughter. "The very sound of those words annoys me. Stop it." She tried, in vain, to control her rising anger. Her daughter's attempts to mollify her only added fuel to the fire.

Yes, they were a distinguished family and of course she was glad. She truly did want an esteemed family this time, as her Gila indeed deserved. They had davened for something truly special, and that was obviously what they had received. But maybe it was too special, way over their head. She didn't like it one bit.

"Mommy, please don't take it so hard. What difference does it make? So what if Hershel comes in to take *ma'aser*? Let him do whatever he wants, and that's it."

"Oh, Gila, please. There are some things I understand a little bit better than you. I have no objections to Hershel coming in and taking *ma'aser*, and I certainly won't stand in his way. But it's their attitude that gets me, the emphasis they place on 'how we do things' and on 'the way it is by us.' Where's their tact? Is this principle of theirs so important to them that it's worth ruining the atmosphere of the *tena'im*? Don't you think I'm right, Riki?" Sima asked, suddenly turning to her daughter-in-law, who had been sitting quietly on the side, listening to the conversation.

Riki did not respond. She stared at her mother-in-law, her gaze both thoughtful and troubled.

An uncomfortable silence filled the room.

"Is something wrong, Riki?" her mother-in-law asked. "Are you feeling alright?"

"I'm okay," replied Riki in a monotone. "I'm just thinking about the situation…" She opened her mouth as if to speak, then closed it again. Finally, after a few moments of hesitation, she began speaking in slow, measured tones. "It really is very difficult to hear such implications from the other side, but I don't think they necessarily mean it that way. She — Gila's future mother-in-law, that is — has been placed in a situation where she has no choice but to tell you about their *chumros*. It might also be the tension that's always present in the beginning. I didn't like hearing the words 'by us' either. It hurts, especially in the beginning, when the two sides don't really know each other very well. As time went on, though, I told myself it was probably just part of the initial tension. I'm sure you didn't mean everything I thought the words 'by us' implied."

"By us," she said? Initial feelings of tension? When was that? What "beginning" was Riki talking about? Sima was lost in thought.

■ ■ ■

The *tena'im* was held the following evening. Everything went smoothly. The *chassan* and *kalla* were ecstatic. The food was properly tithed by Hershel, and the rolls were delivered by Levy's Bakery.

Sima was calm but tired after spending a sleepless night tossing and turning.

After the conversation she'd had with Riki in the kitchen, she hadn't been able to fall asleep. She'd gotten over the issue regarding her *mechutanim*, even finding justification for their behavior. After all, what else could they have done? What choice did they have? The *chassan's* mother had even phoned to excuse herself and explain, over and over again, that no insult was intended.

It was Riki's comment that caused her so much anguish. She didn't want to ask Riki directly for an explanation, as she was fearful of what might develop. As she lay in bed later that night, though, the "beginning" that Riki had been talking about suddenly floated up in her mind. She recalled how they had rode together on the bus on the day before the engagement. She had been eager to make it clear to Riki what kind of family she was

TIGHTROPE | 435

about to join. "In our family," she had told her new daughter-in-law, "we don't get swept up by the latest fashion trends. My mother-in-law is a very distinguished woman, and so are all the uncles. I think you ought to wear your hear in a ponytail, because 'by us,' like I said, we are all distinguished people who approve of a quiet, refined look."

How would a *kalla* feel after hearing such declarations? How on earth could she have done something like that? How would Gila, for example, feel if such a thing happened to her, and how would she herself feel?

A lot worse than she had felt upon hearing about her *mechutanim's* desire to have their son *ma'aser* the food at the engagement party.

But Riki was right. It was the tension that was always present in the beginning. She had seen Riki dressed somewhat flamboyantly at the *vort*, and she'd been alarmed. At the time, Shimon had told her, "What are you so tense about? Some things take time. Don't do anything that might have a long-term effect. What's really important in the long run is a good relationship with your daughter-in-law." What was the metaphor he had used? "It's better to lose the battle and win the war." But she hadn't wanted to waste time. She had felt it would be better to make matters clear from the very start, to avoid problems in the future. As a result, she had very quickly found herself on a narrow, obstacle-ridden path with no end in sight.

Standing in the middle of the hall, Sima graciously greeted her guests. Out of the corner of her eye, she followed the goings-on, making sure everything was proceeding smoothly. Her daughter-in-law Riki had been standing at her side since the beginning of the affair, greeting everyone with her warm smile and making certain every guest found a place to sit. She was dressed beautifully, in such good taste.

What had she been so afraid of? Why hadn't she listened to Shimon? It was true — some things happened on their own if you gave them the time. When you're loving and welcoming, it's only natural for the other party to respond in kind. Instead, she had made her daughter-in-law feel...what? Unwelcome? Had her daughter-in-law realized she'd had doubts about the shidduch, about the family? Was that what Riki had sensed when she had stressed the "by us" in every other sentence she had uttered?

The poor thing! Sima was not at all certain she hadn't repeated that phrase on a host of other occasions. What was it Malka Weiss had said? "Try to pay attention and notice what word or phrase causes her to withdraw." Ribbono shel Olam, You opened my eyes yesterday. You sent me a new machtenista to put me in my place. I thank You deeply for having granted me the opportunity to get to the root of the problem.

Sima felt that a loving Hand was guiding her gently on to the right path. The One Above had witnessed her troubled situation, and was helping her onto the right path.

There was Riki's mother, standing at the entrance to the hall. How she admired that wonderful woman. If only Riki knew that! She had long ago seen the beauty of her simple, unassuming manner. And Ephraim, where was he? She hoped he had come too. It was important to her that he be present at their *simcha*. She owed a lot to that boy. Sima hurried to the entrance to greet Chaya Baum and introduce her to the new *machtenista*.

On the men's side, preparations were underway for the reading of the *tena'im*. Sima took her place at her daughter's side, surrounded by relatives and friends. A moment passed, and the decorative plate shattered to bits, accompanied by the sound of emotional cries of "*Mazel tov!*" Everything seemed fuzzy and unclear, except for the surge of joy welling up in her heart. She hugged her daughter fiercely, wishing her all the joy in the world. If only she could promise her a life free of hardship and pain —

The crowd pressed forward to wish her *mazel tov*. Her daughter Mali, her daughter-in-law Dassi — Sima glanced around, searching for Riki. Here she was, hesitantly making her way toward her. Why was she so hesitant? Why was she always last? Sima drew her toward her with a warm hug. "Riki, I've been looking for you," she whispered.

"Me, too," murmured Riki. As her mother-in-law held her close, feeling that her ability to welcome and accept had tangibly expanded, her heart did, too.

59

LIFE WENT ON AT ITS USUAL hurried pace. Summer passed, and the emotionally laden *Yamim Nora'im*, too, were but distant memories.

Chaya Baum, wrapped in a thin sweater and carrying a large handbag, locked the door to her home and stepped out onto the street.

Outside, a fall breeze blew gently, and the early morning air was still chilly and damp. Chaya tugged the sweater closer to her and hurried to the bus stop. She practically danced the whole way there, a song of thanksgiving in her heart. That morning, she'd become the proud grandmother of a new grandchild.

Daniel and Riki had a new baby boy. Daniel had phoned with the exhilarating news only a quarter of an hour ago, and Chaya had reacted with both surprise and delight.

They hadn't wanted to wake her in the wee hours of the morning when they had left for the hospital, thinking to spare her the gut-wrenching hours of tension as she waited to hear some news.

Chaya wasn't sure she appreciated their efforts. Had they

asked her, she probably would have told them that she preferred to be a part of the nerve-wracking anticipation that preceded such events. After all, she was Riki's mother, in both good times and bad, in both easy times and difficult ones as well. Besides, Chaya thought to herself, a mother's prayers, along with the pounding of her concerned heart, were powerful tools indeed up Above. But they hadn't asked her, so that was that. She could barely contain her joy and gratitude to Hashem for the blessings He had showered upon her.

Her daughter was happy with her husband, really and truly happy. This she knew as only a mother can.

True, there had been some difficulties at first. She had sensed it. Some she had gleaned from half-sentences uttered by Riki that left her feeling anxious and worried. Now she knew that a young couple just setting out in life can be compared to a newborn baby who waves his arms and legs in all directions, eventually tries to stand, falls, and then picks himself up and tries again. Such a couple needs nothing more than support and other people's confidence in their ability to grow stronger and manage on their own. Today, Daniel and Riki stood steadily on their feet, devoted parents to Yossi…and a new baby, too. When Yossi was born, they had summoned her in middle of the night to accompany them to the hospital. This time, they had preferred to go alone. At first, she had felt rejected, but she now had the good sense to be genuinely happy.

There would surely be other challenges ahead. After all, is there anyone whose road through life is completely smooth? Is there anyone whose life is without struggle?

G-d willing, she would be there for them whenever they needed her.

They're wonderful, those two, she thought. They took the best from both sides. She had nothing to worry about anymore. They were emotionally strong, and they had the tools they needed to cope with whatever life threw at them. They were hard workers who weren't afraid to face challenges head on, and they had their own, personal *siyatta diShemaya*. There was no longer any reason to project her fears onto them. It made no difference what kind of home she had come from, whether her life had been easy or hard. What was meant to emerge had emerged! Every one of us, Chaya knew, is granted his own opportunity to erect his own strong and solid edifice.

Daniel had integrated so beautifully into their family; he was so caring and involved. It was he who had been Hashem's messenger to help them with Ephraim.

Ephraim. How the time had flown. Soon Ephraim would need to build his own home. He too had inner strength, thank G-d.

The bus pulled up, and Chaya wondered why the numbers on the front seemed blurred.

■ ■ ■

In the twilight chill, on the path to the cemetery lined by thistles and colorful wildflowers, a group of people accompanied Yaakov Schiller to his final resting place.

They were few in number. Naftali Schiller, with his wife and children. Naomi Stone and her family. Esther, the daughter who was an accountant in Jerusalem. A few neighbors who still remembered the old man who used to live in their apartment building were there too, along with a handful of friends and acquaintances. Shimon Abramson and a small group of representatives from the nursing-home staff had come as well.

Sima Abramson walked behind them, somewhat apart. On the side of the path was another woman who felt she belonged here — Shoshana Coleman, the daughter of the elderly Mrs. Blau. She had been visiting her mother at the nursing home when she heard the news of the old man's passing, and she had felt a sudden urge to accompany him on his last journey.

They walked together, but apart, each lost in his own thoughts.

Shoshana thought about her wheelchair-bound mother at

Nachalas Avos. Time was passing quickly, and her mother wasn't getting any younger. She was glad she had spoken to the director that time. She had never even gotten around to telling Mrs. Abramson how much that conversation had helped her. At the time, she had bared her heart to Mrs. Abramson, revealing the scars she bore from the way her mother had raised her. The director had looked at her sternly and said, "But you're no longer there, Mrs. Coleman. Today, you're a mother and a successful woman. How much time has passed since you were a child? I'm sure you're aware that all mothers sometimes make mistakes, and that some children are particularly hard to deal with."

Yes, she knew she had never been an easy child. Her mother, too, had been the victim of a variety of influential factors: personality traits, education and the various circumstances of her life. The barriers between them had melted, and it felt good. Who knew how much time she had left to perform the mitzva of honoring her parent? And her mother needed her so badly these days.

Standing next to the bier, Naftali Schiller recalled the good times he'd had with his father. Shabbos, singing around the table — and the spark of pleasure in his father's eyes when he, Naftali, returned home from yeshiva. He remembered how his mother would serve him a bowl of steaming hot *cholent* and the cakes she had baked especially for him. Was he as good a father to his children as his father had been to him? During the past few weeks, his father had returned to himself, thank G-d. They had sat over the Gemara and learned together, just as they used to. It was all because of that *bachur*, Ephraim.

Naftali wept silently, his throat choked. Tears filled his eyes. A tissue. He'd forgotten to bring tissues. A father is a father, even at age eighty-five. It was so hard to say good-bye to one's father. At least they had sat and learned together. Papa had smiled often during his final days. That special spark of pleasure had returned to his eyes.

At the end of the small procession, Sima Abramson looked at

the flowers blossoming all around her and thought of her new grandchild born earlier in the day. It's interesting, she thought. This morning in Jerusalem, a new little person began his journey on the path of life, while here another person ends his. She knew this wasn't the end, of course — just the transition to a different world. Whatever Mr. Schiller had accomplished in this world, everything he had learned, would help him up there, in the higher, better world to which he had been summoned.

Out of the corner of her eye, she noticed Shoshana Coleman walking alongside her. *Oh! I didn't know she was here. It's nice of her to come. She didn't have to. That's the positive side of her involvement in everything. I used to get upset when she interfered in everything, but obviously, even seemingly annoying character traits have their redeeming aspects.*

The path grew narrow. A stone blocked her way, and Sima pushed it aside with her foot. For a moment, her thoughts turned to the mother of her newborn grandchild. She hadn't had a chance to visit her at the hospital, or even talk to her on the phone. She hoped Riki wouldn't be hurt, that she wouldn't interpret it as lack of interest on her mother-in-law's part. She didn't have the strength to deal with such sensitivity. Hashem was her witness that on a day like today, she wouldn't have managed to visit Mali, her own daughter, either. She would explain — and Riki would understand. Something in their relationship had changed. Riki wasn't as suspicious as she had been. She no longer made an issue over trivialities. Tomorrow, G-d willing, she would go and visit her. She'd bring flowers. She really did want to see her. Something within her had opened up to Riki. Actually, something within her had opened up to life in general. Was it because of Riki?

Maybe this was real life. It wasn't just about picking the wildflowers alongside the path or enjoying the view or pushing aside a stone that bothered you. It wasn't just about meeting interesting people who fed your ego or about getting ahead and accumulating wealth.

Real life was where you met yourself face-to-face on a narrow path, and there was no place to go but forward.

How panic-stricken she had been that evening coming home from Daniel's *vort*. "Can't we back out of it?" she had asked her husband. "It's too late for that," he had replied.

The Master of the universe had arranged for Riki to become part of her life so that she would be forced to ask herself certain questions. As a result, she had grown, emerging richer for the experience and better equipped for the rest of her journey.

And to Riki, He had given her! Sima smiled at the thought. Riki too had surely learned her own invaluable lessons from the relationship.

No one is perfect. Each of us is struggling to complete his own unique mission on earth, to fulfill his own obligations and face his own challenges. *What's interesting,* though, Sima mused, *is that the narrowest spots, where it looks like there's no way through, the ones we want so desperately to avoid, often lead to the broad avenues we seek. Trapped between rock-solid walls on either side, with no room to turn around but only to move forward, we sometimes find the way blocked. When we find a way, using inner strengths we never knew we had, to get past the obstacle, something in the very essence of our soul expands.*

Sima felt she had just gotten through one of those narrow straits and was now standing on the other side, taking her first deep breaths of clear mountain air. The view was breathtaking.

The group of mourners arrived at the grave site. Naftali Schiller recited Kaddish for his father as the last rays of the sun faded.

As they were making their way out of the cemetery, a figure ran breathlessly forward. At first, no one knew who it was, but as the man drew closer, they realized it was Ephraim.

"I didn't hear about his passing until now," he said apologetically. "I was sitting and learning when suddenly Daniel called. Is it all over? What a shame! I didn't get a chance to say good-bye. I'm going up to the *kever*," he announced, making a sudden decision. "I'll recite a few chapters of *Tehillim*."

Sima watched as he ran ahead. *There goes a bachur I once considered a disgrace to my family*, she thought. There he was now, dressed in a white shirt and black pants, like a real *ben Torah*, his tzitzis flying in the wind as he ran.

The autumn leaves swirled gracefully around Ephraim as he stood alone, facing the freshly turned earth that now housed a man who had come to be his friend. His heart was pounding wildly. He wanted to pray but could not. He wanted to weep, but the tears would not come.

All was silent. Ephraim stood there, numb with pain.

Suddenly the words came. They had all gone, and he could speak freely with no one but Hashem and his beloved friend to hear him.

"Dear Reb Yaakov," he began, addressing the modest marker stuck into the mound of earth and seeing before him his beloved friend's face straining to hear every word. "You know, I've been sitting and learning in a yeshiva for a whole month. I suddenly realized that's where I belong. I know I can do it. I'm not looking for a job, and I've left the vocational institution. I still have a long way to go, but I love it. I'm enjoying every minute."

Ephraim was suddenly struck by a strange thought. He had never even told the elderly Mr. Schiller, or anyone else, for that matter, about the small news item he'd come across in the daily paper. The article had reported the capture and arrest of a ring of credit card swindlers in the Tel Aviv area. Juan Perez's name had appeared on the list of those arrested. He had intended to tell Mr. Schiller about it, but somehow, he'd forgotten. He had been so engrossed in his studies that everything else faded into the background.

"My mother and father credit Daniel with my return to yeshiva," he continued. "Daniel thinks it was Reuvi Shechter who made me mad enough to want to prove I really belonged there. But I know, my dear friend, that it was you who are responsible for my return to the yeshiva — and for my love of Torah.

"When I came to see you the first time, Mr. Schiller, I saw an ordinary man whose zest for living was gone. The only thing that could ignite a spark of true joy in him was the inner knowledge that as long as he studied Torah his life was full of meaning. When I saw that, I knew there would be no escape — I would return to Torah study. It is impossible to run away from a truth so powerful. You, with your white beard and bent back, were at the end of the road. You impressed upon me that life goes by too fast for us to notice its passage. There may be plenty of missed opportunities along the way, but there is also a final destination. Although right now I'm still young, I knew that when I reached the end, I didn't want to look back and feel like I'd missed the boat. So I went back to yeshiva, Mr. Schiller, and the credit is all yours.

"I loved you, Reb Yaakov. May your burning love for Torah serve as a brilliant light to surround and envelop you on High."

The heavy clouds suddenly dispersed, and the glittering stars shone down, illuminating the way for Ephraim.